SATURDAY & THE WITCH WOMAN

Published by WordCrafts Press
Cody, Wyoming 82414
www.wordcrafts.net

SATURDAY

&

THE WITCH WOMAN

a novel of remembrance

Thomas Oliver Ott

WordCrafts

ILLUSTRATIONS

ACKNOWLEDGMENTS

My journey to discover Saturday's story benefited from outriders who kept me on my writer's trail: My Aunt Nadine Boykin who introduced me to Saturday's story over sixty years ago; Dr. Duvon Corbitt who guided my interests in Caribbean history; Dr. Roland Duncan who encouraged me to specialize in Haitian history; and Mary Donna, my wife, who handed me a pen and pad during a flight to Seattle, and told me to start writing Saturday's story.

There is assemblage of others who read and commented on my manuscript: Victoria Ott, Elizabeth Luckey, Rebecca Forsman, Beaumont Shelton, Elisa Tunno, Carl and Judy Schuler, Crystal Broughan, Katherine Gunter, Paula Slusher, Chuck and Michelle Hyde, Theresa Guzman Stokes, Mimi Kraemer, and Faye Hortenstein. Thanks also to David Olive of Olive Photography.

I especially want to recognize Sue Nazworth of the University of North Alabama who kept books on interlibrary loan headed my way; Gin Phillips, an accomplished novelist, who made constructive comments about my manuscript; Tim Stevenson who added his beautiful illustrations to my work; and my wife whose computer skills proved essential to my determination to re-discover the nearly forgotten story of Saturday's life. It is to her that I dedicate this book.

AUTHOR'S NOTE

In the following pages, I expressed Saturday's life through a series of letters which he wrote to his foster white children over a forty-year period, beginning in 1804. Although fictitious, the eleven letters (epistles) accurately describe the history and social landscape of Saturday's time, and are loaded with facts about his life. These letters I carefully crafted, using my skills as a historian. By sewing bits and pieces of Saturday's life together, I have produced a story that I believe the reader will find exciting.

Saturday's letters tell the true version of his life, not just what plantation masters and their families wanted and even required hearing. His writing style was eloquent, as revealed in scribed evidence in the author's possession. Despite being a slave, Saturday not only had the gift of literacy, but was widely read and spoke seven languages: Two were African (Ewe and Yoruba), two Afro-American (Haitian Creole and Lowcountry Gullah), and three European (English, French, and Spanish).

As Saturday unfolded his life's story, he recognized the danger of releasing it before his death, even to his "boys" who are my ancestors. Thus, not until Saturday's death in 1850 did Philip, the older of his two children and stationmaster of a small town depot, begin reading Saturday's letters that he had hidden in his office. His stage for the readings was the depot kitchen; his audience was his wife and Wahl, an old slave cook. As the letters began revealing Saturday's life, the cook and Philip entered into and became important players in Saturday's story.

While Saturday's explosive and often tragic life events sprang from his letters in the depot kitchen, other equally powerful events occurred in the little town of Branchville, setting for the story. Locals hung on every word of those advocating South Carolina's secession from the Union. Local militias mustered and small towns like Branchville bragged on their readiness to face a federal invasion. Those taken in by fire-eating rhetoric especially looked to Robert Barnwell Rhett and his views favoring secession. South Carolina had begun its ten-year surge to the Civil War.

The Depot
Branchville, South Carolina
Built in 1833

MAIN CHARACTERS

Aunt Caroline: Plantation "mama" at Bréda Plantation
Bayon de Libertat: Plantation manager at Bréda. Toussaint's friend
Bull: The navigator on *La Marie*
Comte de Noé: Manager of properties owned by Comte de Bréda
Catherine Chartrand of Mille Fleurs Plantation: Saturday's owner
Canga: Maroon leader who protected Saturday and Jean-Pierre
François Leclerc: Evil captain of *La Marie*
Gaspard Ardisson: Maréchaussée officer and Canga's antagonist
Guillaume Delribal: Hated plantation manager at Bréda
Juan de Flores: Captain of Guamacaro District in Matanzas, Cuba
Jean-Pierre Bréda: Toussaint's son; Saturday's surrogate brother
John and Philip Chartrand: Children of Catherine & John Chartrand
Louise Julienne Chartrand: John's wife
Susan Elizabeth Chartrand: Wife of Philip Chartrand
Toussaint Bréda: Saturday's surrogate father; leader of the Haitian Revolution
Uncle Philip Chartrand: Catherine Chartrand's advisor and lover
Veronica Chaillot: Catherine's strong-minded mother
Denmark Vesey: Mastermind behind a Charleston free Negro and slave conspiracy
Wahl: Slave cook at the Branchville, South Carolina, railroad depot
Yaya: Maroon leader and close friend of Jean-Pierre Bréda
Zèbre: Childhood friend of Saturday

Philip Chartrand
(1785 to 1857)
Branchville, South Carolina

The Obituary

A little boy awakened to a gentle morning breeze drifting across his bed. He felt happy as he surveyed his room. Every toy a child could want was there: Lead soldiers in French Bourbon colors and a wooden horse were his favorites. His parents must be wealthy. He must be privileged.

Walking across his floor, he came to the room's only window: a large wooden jalousie. Through its slats, he spied a huge live oak and a royal palm side-by-side at the roof's edge.

"Must be friends," thought the imaginative child.

But try as he might, he couldn't open the sash, making him feel confined and lonely.

Seeking to exit his room to the floor below, the boy picked the first of three doors. He opened it, and cheerful music floating up from a ballroom greeted him. He barely stepped down the hall gallery before finding that missing stairs prevented his descent to his parents and their guests. Disappointed, he returned to his room and picked the second door. It opened into a darkened hallway filled with mournful voices. He quickly shut the door and opened the third. Its hall looked bright and peaceful, almost cheery. But as the child stepped forward, a huge ball of flame drafted toward him at incredible speed. He jumped back, as a woman's face emerged from the fiery mass. Her beautiful auburn hair floated between tongues of flame, accenting her gentle face. She extended her arms for an embrace, but the little boy pulled back in horror. Did she beseech her rescue, or did she want to pull him into the fire? Fear

1

gripped him. He raced to the jalousie, intending to kick out its louvers and escape down one of those trees near his window. But fate blocked his retreat. Both the live oak and the palm were missing. Only a waterfall of blood cascaded over the eaves. He felt trapped.

The grinding sound of a freight wagon stirred Stationmaster Philip Chartrand from his fitful sleep, as the early train would soon arrive. Sweat drenched him, not because of Branchville's heavy humidity, but because of his disquieting dream. He didn't know its meaning, but it began years ago just after he and his brother had escaped history's greatest slave rebellion. Now it had returned. He had even considered seeking advice from a conjurer, Lowcountry descendant of an African witch doctor. Supposedly, a conjurer was born with a caul (membrane) over his head, permitting him to see the "other side." He further had the power to drive away evil spirits. But Philip had little faith in these wizards of the woods and thought such stuff nonsense. He did, however, recognize that his aged mind, like an old house, had many hidden closets unbeknownst to its owner.

Stumbling across the planked depot deck, Stationmaster Chartrand began his duties on a Carolina Lowcountry morning, just the cure for a nightmare. At the platform's edge, he stopped to admire the early sunrise. Heat from the previous day had dissipated, a dewy freshness covered the earth, ground fog began its skyward lift, birds took flight, and even old hounds usually hiding under the depot came out and stretched in homage to Nature's daily miracle. To the sixty-five-year-old stationmaster, it seemed almost like a birthing event. He knew that his time was short, and wondered how much of it remained? Now in old age, Philip still had an impressive six-foot physique and a young man's energy. He had grown a mustache to offset what he considered a plain face, but others, women especially, found his dark complexion and penetrating brown eyes alluring.

Sometimes, as old people do, Philip used day's starting moments to track the course of his life. There had been failures, mostly

2

financial; a few were personal like the deaths of his mother and his first wife. Most of all, he stopped now and then to remember an old slave named Saturday who had rescued him and his brother from a blood bath and set them on pathways to a better life. But here he was. He relished his job and adored his wife.

By his own estimates, he considered himself a winner, as he gently leaned against an iron-wheeled baggage cart. Like a man lighting a cigar after a winning poker hand, he swelled with pride, as he was both stationmaster and owner of the depot's restaurant, The Branch Eating House. But now his self-reflections gave way to his duty. He waited for "The Carolina," pride of the South Carolina Railroad, which ran from Charleston to Columbia at the average speed of thirty-five miles per hour. No American railroad had a faster train in this modern year of 1850.

Philip loved railroading and followed the construction of South Carolina's and arguably the nation's earliest railroad that ran through Branchville, America's first rail junction. In 1831 he witnessed the operation of "The Best Friend of Charleston," the road's initial engine; when it exploded, he rejoiced that workers assembled from the wreckage "The Phoenix," the road's second locomotive. By 1850 the "American Locomotive" replaced these earlier beasts of the iron rails.

One of these newer types approached in the distance puffing, chugging, trailing smoke, sounding a mournful whistle, and pulling a caravan of enclosed wooden coaches. It was "The Carolina" up from Charleston and on time. As the train slowed to a stop, Philip stepped toward the baggage car, zigzagging to avoid jets of escaping steam. But just as he made the gauntlet, the baggage car door slid open, and a steam-shrouded figure flipped a mail bag near Philip's feet. He picked up the Charleston mail and dragged it into the station.

Inside the depot waiting room, he stepped around the ticket counter and started pigeonholing letters into a mail rack. This was his favorite duty because a mysterious sender might spark local gossip. But a shrill whistle blast, marking "The Carolina's" departure for Columbia, brought Philip's mind back to filing the Branchville mail. He pulled a stack of letters from the mail bag, sending each along its way with the speed and skill of a card dealer. Now and then, he paused briefly if a letter caught his eye, like the cutely decorated envelope from Cousin Lou Adams in Charleston to her spinster cousin in Branchville. Off he went again, dealing letters with lightening quickness, when suddenly he stopped to grasp a letter addressed to him. How strange!

Philip rarely received mail, and this came from his brother, John Chartrand in Cuba. John was everything he was not: He was a wealthy plantation owner, Uncle Philip's favorite nephew, and married to one of Charleston's more beautiful women. In the consideration of their extended family, John was the better of the two brothers. This made Philip whisper a comment under his breath: "I know how Joseph's brothers in the Old Testament must have felt. What does he want? He never writes to me without a purpose." A terrible thought then crossed his mind that a family member had died. His trembling hands pulled the letter from its envelope.

Someone had died! Saturday who raised him; Saturday his dearest friend and mentor; Saturday was dead. The news buckled Philip's knees, while dread compelled him to put down his brother's letter. But he read on anyway.

Ariadne Plantation
Matanzas,
May 29, 1850

Dear Brother:

I have sad news. Saturday died. The Angel of Mercy took him after the long journey of his life. He did not suffer.

I am aware of our disagreements, but we both have a common bond in our love for Saturday. He raised us. He loved us. He was a father to us. It fills me with regret that you missed out on

Saturday's last years. During that time he seemed to wither as old people do, but he neither lost the joy in his soul nor his love for us. Your name was often on his lips. There can be no doubt but that he felt your spiritual presence to his very last day.

Most plantation owners along the Canímar River in Matanzas Province attended his funeral. Even James Innerarity and his Cuban "wife" were there from La Heloise Plantation. All these masters had endeavored to hold their own slaves to the standard of Saturday's loyalty to the Chartrands.

You remember Saturday's devotion to Catholicism and of my promise to arrange his full burial rites anywhere he desired, even at the Church of San Carlos in the city of Matanzas. He chose, however, the Church of San Cipriano in Limonar Parish as his final resting place. Limonar was dear to his heart, as it had become an important site for newly freed slaves. He served as an unofficial town elder, and counseled those who would listen about the joys and responsibilities of freedom.

There are two curiosities related to Saturday's preparation for burial that I must mention. Servants found a small folded parchment in his left shirt pocket too worn to be legible, and when they removed his shirt, they discovered a voodoo amulet on a tarnished chain around his neck. The charm represented Ogun, one of voodoo's more anti-white and violent spirits. It was to him that slaves who attacked our plantation in Saint-Domingue raised their cane knives and machetes in salute. This surprised me and other planters at Saturday's funeral because we believed that he had accommodated himself completely to masters and white men. What could this irony mean, Philip?

Give my best to your family.
Your Devoted Brother,
John

When Philip finished John's letter, he stared out a depot window at the track running past the Branchville Station to Hamburg on the Savannah River. He wasn't watching for a train. Only his mind's eye saw something. It happened sixty years ago. He was a child again. Old memories flooded his head: flames licking up a stair-case, men with knives, his mother's screams, a black savior's helping hands, and terror at every step. A woman's touch brought Philip back to what he had just read.

"What's wrong?" she asked. It was Susan Elizabeth who ten years earlier moved to Branchville to assist Philip's management of the depot restaurant and to help him raise his four children after the death of his wife Lavinia. Business partner and nanny soon became lover; eventually lover became wife.

In late bloom of early womanhood, Susan Elizabeth brought order to Philip's life. Her angular facial features and straight black hair suggested an Indian ancestor, since early white traders often took Native American wives. A mysterious air, animal magnetism, flirtatious charm, and quick wit gave charge to looks otherwise ordinary. Her left cheek bore a tiny scar that she had received as a skinny-dipping teenager escaping the depot water tank and Lavinia's scolding. The scar, she frequently teased, began her friendship with the Chartrands.

Susan Elizabeth attracted men, and kept Philip's customers coming back, especially single men who hoped that she might pick one of them over him. But she never did. She loved this older of the two Chartrand brothers. Sympathy and pity, however, were not her better character traits, especially concerning Saturday, whom she knew only through conversations with Philip.

She hugged Philip, kissed him, clutched John's letter, and said "I'm so sorry, Sweetheart. Saturday was a fine man." But then she casually tossed the letter on a side table, and left the room.

"You never read the first word. Damn you!" Philip whispered under his breath. "So who around here cares anything about Saturday?"

Then he remembered Wahl. She had been Uncle Philip's slave in Saint-Domingue and had fled with him in 1791 to Cuba to escape the Great Slave Rebellion. There she served Uncle Philip as his plantation cook in Matanzas Province until he later gave her to his favorite nephew, John Chartrand. After years of serving the Chartrand family, she bought her freedom and moved to Limonar, joining other former slaves. In 1844, she participated in the Escalera Conspiracy in Matanzas Province which Spanish authorities brutally suppressed. Trouble, however, only began for the shaken province as Captain-General O'Donnell, Spain's top colonial official in Cuba, directed arrests and tortures of thousands of suspects. He especially targeted free blacks, putting Wahl and Limonar under his suspicions. At any moment, Spanish soldiers might have occupied Limonar, arrested Wahl, and burned the village.

Time grew short for cook and hamlet, when John begged Philip to escort Wahl to Branchville where she would direct his depot kitchen. He reached Matanzas Province in 1844 to bring her to South Carolina. John and Saturday then told Philip of a collection of letters which Saturday had written describing his life. They warned that these missives only be read after Saturday's death, and must be smuggled out of Cuba before O'Donnell discovered them and used them as evidence for more arrests. So Philip arrived at his brother's plantation, collected the female fugitive, and hid the mysterious letters in the false bottom of a steamer trunk. With John's escort and local reputation, Philip got past Spanish authorities without a search, claimed Wahl as his slave from Charleston, and boarded a ship at Matanzas bound for South Carolina.

But Philip feared that Wahl, now in her seventies, might hate him. Brother John once described her as a black Aphrodite who distracted him from her fine meals. Her tight body, flashing eyes, and pearl white teeth margined with inviting ruby lips infused passion into any husband and jealousy into any wife. Aging had worn this once beautiful woman almost back into the lump of clay from which The Almighty had fashioned her. Withered skin and dimples turned to furrows now defined her face. Her eyes no

7

longer flashed, and most of her once pearl-like teeth were missing.

Wahl, however, was a proud woman. She walked with a measured arrogance as if she had just won some battle, but her once vivacious personality had become sullen. When Philip met her to bring her to Branchville, she only responded with a penetrating stare. She was sizing him up which worried Philip even more. All the way to South Carolina, she uttered few words to him. Her "Yes, Massah" made up most of them, but she could express a whole conversation by the way she intoned those two words. Philip thought that she might be angry because she would be classified as his slave for her to enter South Carolina. He had anticipated her response, promising that she was slave in name only. Did she appreciate his rescue of her from Captain-General O'Donnell, or did she plan to kill him while he slept? Now five years later, Wahl's behavior had mellowed toward Philip, but down deep, he knew that she still resented him.

Despite wondering about Wahl, Philip determined that she should be his audience when he read Saturday's secret letters. She had known Saturday both in Saint-Domingue and in Cuba, and understood him better than anyone in Branchville besides himself. He also resented Susan Elizabeth's indifference to the matter. By excluding her from the readings, he was "getting even."

Now with a plan, Philip walked down the wall aisle of the common room housing his serving area. He took pride in his restaurant's heart pine floors, whitewashed horizontal wall planking, stamped tin ceiling, and ten large wooden tables which could each seat twelve customers at a time. When Philip reached the room's only fireplace, he paused to look through a window. This sash like the others contained four panes of glass, each measuring two by four feet. The New England Glass Company produced these wavy wonders by blowing hot glass into a mold that left slight ripples when it cooled. These state-of-the-art windows were the depot-restaurant's greatest point of luxury and a source of local pride.

The sash also afforded Philip a view of a huge oak tree, known to residents as The Branch Oak. For nearly two hundred years, it stood where the Cherokee Indian Trail split north and west. The northern path led to Orangeburg and Columbia, while the western one led to Hamburg, on the Savannah River. Indian and white traders once used the old oak as a gathering point to drive cattle and deliver wares to the Charleston market. Now the South Carolina Railroad's right-of-way followed these trails. The western branch plus its stem ran all the way to Charleston, some 120 miles. Originally early settlers near the oak called their wilderness community "The Branch." Later the railroad in a fit of sophistication changed the name to "Branchville."

Secretly, Philip enjoyed a little game involving the oak and the image distortions of the glass windows. Looking through the uneven glass, he could make The Branch Oak appear to shimmer, like breeze-rippled spring water. His amusement lasted but a moment, as he entered the depot waiting room.

Four long wooden passenger benches, a roll-top clerk's desk by a ticket window, a pot-bellied stove, and spittoons centered on tobacco juice stains were the only adornments in this otherwise bare room. Philip rushed past a dozing traveler, the room's only occupant, and to another doorway leading into his office. Upon entering, he softly closed the door, went to a desk next to a windowless wall, gripped and pulled on it with all his might until it finally separated from the wall, lifted a false panel on the back, and brought out the parcel of Saturday's letters. So many times he wanted to read those secret writings, but never did. Now the moment arrived to open them. Philip felt excited and sad all at once, like receiving a gift from a dead friend's hand. He took the first letter, while returning the others to their hiding place.

Philip's last customer left the depot restaurant by mid-evening. Quickly Philip stepped through its backdoor, and arrived at Wahl's detached kitchen. Turning its doorknob, he sensed that he was entering into the portal of Saturday's life story.

The First Letter

When Philip stepped into the depot kitchen, pleasant food aromas lingered after a busy day at the restaurant. Wahl had cleaned the iron cooking pots and skillets, washed the cedar paddle for stirring ingredients, stacked firewood by her stove, and dampened the fire in her hearth. Wahl might be angry, but she was also efficient.

Afraid of the old woman's reaction, Philip searched for something clever to say, but only blurted out, "Wahl, I have sad news about your friend Saturday. He died and is buried in the San Cipriano Church Cemetery at Limonar."

Wahl looked up, unmoved, like a person who is not only used to death and destruction but expects them. Philip felt the urge to embrace her, but their icy relationship prevented it, making him wonder if he picked the right listener.

"Wahl, I have a letter from Saturday that you need to hear," Philip quickly announced, hoping to get beyond her sullen behavior before she could raise a defense.

Her "Yes, Massah!" with its usual sarcastic tones let him know that his ploy had failed. He then became forceful, told her to sit down, and produced Saturday's letter. But Wahl stood defiantly, turned her back to Philip, and continued her chores. Philip ignored her, and began reading Saturday's letter anyway.

15 Elliott Street, Southside
Charleston
March 14, 1805

10

Dear Philip and John,

Life really begins with memories that become passengers in our minds over time. I remember Mother's gentle touch, the fires associated with community gatherings, my father standing like a giant in the armor of a Lucumí warrior, and the spear point that sliced open the side of Mother's hut. And even though time has draped a veil over most of my childhood, I recall well the Dahoman raiders that began my life's story.

Who were these Dahoman intruders who herded hundreds of Lucumís along jungle trails to Abomey, their capital? What I am about to tell you is information that Aradas and Lucumís told me as part of their adult experiences. After all, I was only seven years old when invaders kidnapped me.

In the early eighteenth century, the Empire of Dahomey occupied much of the Slave Coast. They fought and conquered the Aradas and Whydah with its important port. These victories gave Dahomey a route to the sea and guaranteed its dominance over the slave trading nations of West Africa. Retribution followed triumph, as Dahomey sought revenge against the Lucumís and other allies of their archenemy, the Aradas. This suited the kings of Dahomey who sought victims for their slave trade with Europeans, not new territory and subjects. Their vicious raids depopulated the West African interior, as vast numbers of slaves exited their homeland through Dahomey's ports and its captured port of Whydah.

The king of Dahomey gripped the trade with an iron fist, giving priority to his acquisition of firearms. Even European slave traders dared not provoke the king who confined them to coastal outposts, forcing them to deal on his terms. While the king's agents brokered contracts with white traders, the newly inducted victims into slavery were confined in compounds called *barracoons*. Those unfit for the trade faced sacrifice in Dahoman blood lust ceremonies.

These were the demons that dragged the Lucumís, Mother, and me from our burning village to Abomey. I can almost recall my terror, while staying close to Mother and pretending to be brave.

My missing father taught me the ways of the warrior and to be proud of my name: "Kwambe Ansong" (Born on Saturday, Seventh Born Child).

When Mother and I arrived in Abomey with the Lucumí captives, we discovered a strange world. Our guards guided us past the Twelve Palaces of the Dahoman Kings, each with long rows of human skulls decorating royal walls. These Dahoman war trophies they had gained by decapitating their enemies and boiling their skulls leaving only bone. On one wall, I saw thousands of Arada skulls polished by time, reflecting a radiant African sunlight. Seeing my fear, one Dahoman escort delighted in scaring me. He pointed to unoccupied ledges and laughed, saying that they were reserved for Lucumí skulls, and mine would be first.

Winding our way through Abomey's streets took my mind off our taunting guards. Abomey teemed with merchants, shoppers, warriors, and even white people whom I saw for the first time in my life. These were the greater white slave traders in Abomey, there to pay tribute to Bossa Ahadi (1732-72), the Dahoman king.

At last, we reached a large compound called "Azali." Here our captors interrogated us, and culled priests and priestesses from our midst to add to their king's magical powers. Craftsmen and others with special skills joined this group for the more mundane court needs of Bossa Ahadi. Our examiners assigned the rest of us for sale to white traders residing in Whydah.

Years later, I reflected upon King Bossa Ahadi, the Dahoman ruler who made Mother and me slaves to white men. What he did to us, however, dimmed in comparison to what he did to others. Upon assuming the throne of Dahomey in 1732, he had any subject bearing the name "Bossa" executed to avoid claimants to his crown. When he died in 1772, he was entombed in his sedan chair with six of his favorite wives who were buried alive. Hundreds of courtesans shared their fate, as rampaging palace guards, acting under royal edit, put them to the sword. Surely Bossa Ahadi's skull must sit atop Hell's Temple. I apologize for digressing about my hatreds for Bossa Ahadi. As a good Catholic, I pray for compassion to forgive him.

Mother and I remained at Azali almost a fortnight. Dahoman slave traders caused our delay by haggling with Ahadi's royal officials who set our price, and by waiting for a moonless night to commence our sixty-mile trek to Whydah on the African coast. The timing of our march seemed strange until I discovered that Dahoman slavers wished anonymity because of public scorn for their human trade. Nighttime movement also served our captors, keeping us Lucumís confused and compliant with their commands, creating deep despair among us. Mother and I battled this feeling without success.

My first experience with the use of a whip against a human being occurred when Dahoman traders burst into the compound where Mother and I slept with other Lucumís. They rousted us to start our walk to Whydah. Bravely Mother grabbed me and whirled around, shielding me from a lash catching her squarely across her back. We fell, as I saw terror in her eyes, but felt love in her embrace. We staggered to our feet, but Mother never cried out or even winced. I always knew about her big heart, but her quiet defiance filled me with a pride that I usually reserved for my warrior father.

Our guards herded us along the night-silenced streets of Abomey to a much travelled pathway to Whydah. You, John, called this route the most used by Europeans in West Africa. We meandered down it a short distance with Mother yanking me along. Turning a bend, I saw a campfire with several men standing behind it with faces glowing from the fire's shimmering flames. To a frightened little boy, they seemed like night monsters.

I stood in line clinging to Mother, as we filed by examiners who checked on our health conditions. Occasionally someone too old, too young, or too sick to reach Whydah caught their attention, and they pulled that person from the line with instructions to join other rejects by an open pit. I cringed when the "night monsters" scrutinized me. Mother squeezed my arm to comfort me, while assuring them that I could make the long journey ahead. They let me pass, and one of the investigators even patted my head, pretending to show affection.

As the last of our group passed inspection, guards quickly rounded up stragglers, and forced us toward Whydah. I noticed an uncharacteristic sadness in Mother's manner, while wondering about those left behind. She refused to answer my questions about their outcome, but other Lucumís did. They had become a burden to the Dahoman slave traders and had little market value. So our examiners ordered them killed and thrown into the pit that I had noticed. Quickly they buried their victims, some still clinging to life. This made me understand and share Mother's sadness.

As we moved toward our destination, familiar jungle sounds comforted me. Amusing were the big noises of tiny tree frogs or the many voices of roosting cicadas, all speaking at the same time. Even better was the panther's high-pitched scream, sounding like a woman in distress. Most of all, Mother and I sought the night-blooming moonflower whose white blossoms shone through darkness, God's sign for those who would be free. Already I felt slavery shrinking my soul, and had not yet met the whites who would shrink it further.

Dawn ended my eternal night, but not the burden of sadness that my narrow shoulders bore. Mother noticed my distress and used her adorable childlike side to pull me from my gloom. She challenged me to the "pebble game" where we extended our feet into the path to see how many pebbles we each could pick up with our toes. Usually I would win until she decided to give me a lesson in humility. Then she would stretch and spread her long spider-like toes bringing up more pebbles in one effort than I could in two, causing my standard acknowledgement of defeat: "You could empty a creek bed with those toes." A hardy laugh always finished our games. Without those playful interludes and Mother's optimism, my capture and losing most of my family would have overwhelmed me.

14

The snap of a whip ended our game. Guards hustled our group to a certain tree and made us circle it. This tree they called *Yemoja*, or in the Dahoman language, "The Tree of Forgetfulness." That an inanimate object contained a spirit was common among religions of the Slave Coast and later in voodoo. Our captors believed that Yemoja purged our African memories, making adjustment to the white man's slavery easier. But no damn tree could make me forget my longing for Africa. Mother reinforced my feelings, whispering to me an old African proverb: "No matter how far a river wanders, it never forgets its source."

When we entered Whydah, I was amazed. The Portuguese, English, French, and Dutch each possessed a large fort collectively dominating the port city. Some Dahoman slave traders brought their captives directly to one of these forts for auction. Upon sealing a bargain, buyers representing a large company from their nation, routinely deposited their human cargos in a fortress jail until their transportation to America. Other Dahoman traders sold directly to individual white buyers not connected to these four forts. A trader of this last type bought Mother and me.

As our guards marched us past the forts, I looked beyond the shore, and over the ocean, until the horizon and haze blocked my vision. I never saw the ocean before, or those massive vessels bobbing in a gentle breeze. Were these houses for sea spirits, and what did they have to do with us?

My thoughts ended when guards forced us into a holding pen, known as The House of Honnou, specializing in sales to private dealers. Honnou, its owner, enjoyed Bossa Ahadi's protection, and was Whydah's top public official. In preparation for the sale, Mother and I were lucky to have been parceled to the same lot. Less fortunate Lucumí families suffered broken hearts. Their wailings made me hold Mother's hand tighter.

Soon after our division into lots, our guards led us into Honnou's main courtyard filled with independent European slave dealers. Each merchant gave us embarrassing examinations to discover our health conditions. They even checked our anuses for signs of dysentery. On this point, they exercised careful vigilance, as a slave dealer weeks earlier had sealed the assholes of his merchandise with oakum to conceal their dysentery, known as the "red runs." This deadly killer could destroy a buyer's entire investment. Mother and I passed inspection and joined others of our lot faring as well as we had. The African slave dealers killed those who failed, because they were a drain on their financial resources.

A huge man bought our lot. He had a face worn into deep wrinkles like gullies on an eroded hill. He wore a red bandanna cocked over his left ear, which had been cut off in a fight. Black whiskers streaked with gray decorated his jaw, like a dying forest. But it was his deep cruel eyes recessed below bushy eyebrows which ignited those features, striking fear into others. Those eyes seemed predatory and ready to command enormous hands and forearms against anyone bucking his authority. Never did I want to spark his wrath. "Bull" was his name and the only one he ever used. A surprising intelligence brimmed behind Bull's overwhelming authority. At sea, he served as *La Marie's* navigator; on land, he purchased slaves for his captain. He spoke Ewe and Yoruba and, more importantly, translated Captain Pierre Leclerc's drunken orders to his crew.

From the House of Honnou, guards arranged our lots according to purchase order and placed us in a large windowless holding compound. Those native to Whydah called it *Zomayi*, or "The Place Without Hope," causing despair to grip Mother and me the night before we departed Africa. Before he returned to his ship, Bull announced that our destination was Saint-Domingue. Where was it? Was it near Africa? Were people there kind? These were my worried questions to Mother. Experience soon gave cruel answers.

A blast from a cannon on board *La Marie* ended our fitful sleep and our time in Africa. . As we stumbled toward the harbor, guards stopped us at a large tree, "The Tree of Spiritual Return."

Each touched it, and each realized that we would never see Africa again. Soon we joined other slave lots at a wharf called "The Gate of No Return." What a cruel name! Those who enslaved and sold us, and those who bought us, knew exactly our fate. Damn them!

Because of silting along the harbor shore, skilled African oarsmen rowed canoes, longboats, and small skiffs to slave ships, anchored a long distance from land. Mother and I joined about twenty others in a longboat. With each stroke of the oarsmen, we approached a new but dreaded destiny, and my senses took on an awareness, like a person about to die. Dipping oars creating salty swirls, small waves splashing our bow, shrieking sea gulls nose-diving for fish, garbled voices from other boats, slave ships growing larger as we approached them, all made me realize how wonderful life is when you expect it to end.

At last, we came along the starboard side of *La Marie*. Once our craft was lashed to her hull, our bobbing cradle stabilized, and our guards instructed us to climb the ship's ladder to the main deck. Those too weak could be hoisted topside, but our oarsmen warned against this. The captain, they said, might see it as a slave's unfitness to join his human cargo. I scurried up the ladder ahead of Mother, clinging to its rungs, while responding to her hard nudges from below but afraid of what awaited me from above. When we gained the main deck, the African traders who had auctioned our lot assembled us for a last buyer's right of refusal. Captain Pierre Leclerc strutted down from his perch on the poop deck like the little rooster that he was, inspecting us one by one. He had an aura of evil about him. Soon I learned to hate him.

The captain stood not much taller than five feet two inches or so. He wore a commodore's tricorn (three pointed hat), a self-appointed rank since slave ships often exercised the same independence as pirate ships. Leclerc's one facial expression was grim, like someone constantly constipated. He had thin lips often curled with anger, and when he spoke, the odor of rum would precede his first word, followed by a shower of tobacco juice. And in his beady cobra-like eyes, I saw a man ready to kill anyone opposing his will. Only Bull seemed unintimidated by this posturing little man.

Leclerc, his first mate, and Bull moved from fore to aft inspecting parallel rows of slaves. But Leclerc owned the show, as both Bull and first mate Louis Laroux seemed disinterested. Mother sensed danger in this final buyer's review and overcame her fatigue, warning me to stand up straight. She was like a doe protecting her fawn from a deadly enemy. As the captain passed down our line, he gave me a strange look that disturbed Mother but moved on, staggering a crooked path like a serpent.

Leclerc struck quickly. He rejected a handful of slaves whom he deemed unfit, ordering them promptly returned to their African traders who forced the rejects to board their boat alongside *La Marie*. Thank God for Mother's strong constitution! The disappointed sellers knew that their profit had just been reduced. Oddly, Leclerc selected only women. I later learned that Leclerc did not favor female slaves when trading with the planters of Saint-Domingue who sought males for strenuous short-term labor, a quick fortune, and a return to France.

As the African traders left *La Marie* with their flawed merchandise, they ordered their oarsmen to stand off near our vessel. They stabbed and pushed the women into the harbor. "No sale, no value" was the motto of these murderers, much to Captain Leclerc's visual delight. This horrible scene formed my final memory of the Dahoman Empire which had captured me, enslaved me, and placed me on a slave ship. With this episode, the curtain fell on my African enslavement. The curtain, however, would soon rise on my enslavement in Saint-Domingue. From a black to a white stage, my life got worse.

Captain Leclerc and his crew promptly set our routine during our ten-week voyage to Saint-Domingue in the West Indies. Shackling male slaves came first. Leg irons were particularly cruel, as two slaves were clasped together by joining the right ankle of one chattel to the left ankle of another. They bore these restraints

constantly, as Leclerc feared slave mutinies and suicides from jumping overboard. Women and children were rarely placed in irons,
except at night in the crowded sub decks.

After *La Marie* took on a cargo of rice, yams, and horse beans
for its enslaved passengers, the ship weighed anchor, and glided
toward the breakers beyond the harbor. Leclerc then ordered male
slaves below deck to a place between hell and purgatory. There they
entered into decks with three feet of clearance or less. So many
slaves crowded these spaces that they had to lie prone with one
slave's head resting on the thigh of the next. Four conical pots per
deck served as commodes, but depression so overcame some that
they relieved themselves where they lay. Sweltering heat mixed
with nasty odors made these confined areas unbearable. For relief,
sailors brought and supervised male slaves topside twice a day for
food and exercise.

Leclerc regarded eating and exercise essential to his human
cargo's health until he could sell it to planters in Saint-Domingue.
Consequently, he ordered that any slave refusing food should receive
five lashes to increase his appetite. For exercise, he commanded
his crew to make males dance two by two, chains and all. Some
sailors found this amusing, and played tunes on crude instruments
making the farce even funnier. But they did not notice, nor cared
to notice, the grievous sores that the vibrating irons rubbed on the
ankles of their dancing victims.

Our daily routine ended at sundown when the crew forced us
into the sub decks. I dreaded this moment, as Mother and I became
separated, increasing my torments. Descending into the sub decks,
rising heat and the smell of human waste met me. Temperatures,
I estimated, rose above one hundred degrees should portholes be
shut on a hot day. On my initial descent, I vomited and cried, but
was grateful that Mother had not witnessed my weakness. I soon
learned, however, that a person can become acclimated to almost
anything.

As time passed on our voyage, I established the practice of

climbing on the nearest shelf, assuming a side position at shelf's end, facing the bulkhead with my nose curled under my armpit, and using one of my arms as a pillow. This system reduced nauseous odors with my own, and kept me from resting my head on someone's thigh. But I never solved stifling heat keeping me awake.

Nights spent below never got easier. Of the at least 300 slaves on board, most slept only fitfully. They moaned, crying out in outbursts of loneliness and despair. I never got used to it. And the morning after a night in the hold was even worse, as survivors of the night watched for those who had died. Hardly three or four nights passed without at least one slave death—usually by suicide. In fact, suicide was Captain Leclerc's greatest concern, as each death reduced his profit. More than a few slaves attempted leaping into a waiting sea, a move that they thought would bring their spiritual return to Africa. This usually failed, as safety netting extended along the port and starboard sides of *La Marie*, and as sailors constantly guarded against slaves jumping overboard. Once I saw Bull tackle and hurl a pair of slaves shackled together at least ten feet in the opposite direction. He gave each man three lashes and sent them below for the rest of the day.

But desperate slaves sought desperate measures for relief—suicide by swallowing your tongue. A person would gather saliva in his (or her) mouth to the point of drooling. Then with the fluid behind his curled tongue, he would swallow and swallow until his tongue sucked down into his throat, cutting off airflow. Suffocation followed. Add those afflicted with fatal diseases to those who committed suicide, and the slaves of *La Marie* easily suffered a twenty percent death rate. Unceremoniously, the sailors of *La Marie* dumped their bodies overboard to hungry sharks. I once saw a shark frenzy around a floating body until one of the larger attackers dragged it into the deep.

Amid this horror, I still had a youngster's fascination with *La Marie*. I had never been on a sailing ship. This one was a three-mast, square-rigged merchant ship, like the one you, John, captained as a slave trader. Truth is, I never ventured beyond a few miles from my Lucumí village before my enslavement. I enjoyed watching sailors raising or lowering a sail, while being sprayed from lapping waves from a constant wind. Especially did Bull's use of nautical instruments to plot our course arouse my interest.

At first, Bull seemed indifferent to my interest. But he could not help hearing my questions, as he spoke Yoruba, native tongue of the Lucumís. When this hulk of a man finally turned toward me after days of my unanswered questions, a cold shiver shot up my spine. Had I awakened a sea ogre? I suspected that his massive arms might hurl me to our destination. Instead, he invited me to peer through a quadrant which he used to establish *La Marie's* position relative to latitude. Of course, I did not know the purpose of this instrument, and he told me that he used it to sight Africa. A cruel joke as it turned out, but also the beginning of our unexpressed friendship.

Exceeding Bull's softened attitude toward me was my discovery of a playmate. It started one night in the hell-hole below deck. Slave children were grouped together on the same shelves, and I had a cry-baby sharing my thigh for his pillow. Almost every night, I nearly cried myself, but hearing his sobs increased my resolve not to do the same. But somehow, I had to silence him, so I tried making him laugh. I pointed out that his tears soaking my loin cloth, might cause Mother think me a bed-wetter. Or, if he didn't stop, his tears would convince the sailors that the hull leaked, forcing them to pump the bilge. He finally giggled, and I told him my name. He responded that his name was Wésidéè Èjì (born on Wednesday, Second Born Child), and that he was nine years old. I told him my age, and now Saturday had Wednesday as a friend. I wondered if the other days of the week were aboard? We laughed.

Èjì and I became inseparable. He was small for his age, so some crew members thought us twins. Èjì had a more tragic story than mine, at least for a while. Dahoman warriors took his parents and

21

him captive, and forced them to journey to Abomey and then to Whydah, where they joined our group. When our division into lots occurred, Èjì's mother went to a different lot from his and his father's. Overcome by grief, his father committed suicide early into our voyage.

I knew that Èjì's nightmares about lost family were like my own. My warrior father's fate I found especially troubling. Years after my enslavement in Saint-Domingue, his outcome still tormented me. The image of him cowering under a driver's whip sickened me. I never learned his fate, but Lucumí captives from my village told me that a small band of our warriors fought bravely, but fell to overwhelming Dahoman numbers. Their deaths provided me a mental sanctuary, because I convinced myself that my father had been among them. As for my siblings, I searched for them relentlessly. Every new coffle of Lucumí slaves attracted my attention. I looked into their faces, but never discovered a brother or a sister. My efforts to find them continued until I finally realized that they could be anywhere in the slaveholding world.

Èjì and I expressed our sorrows differently, but we both were desperate to find family security and a parent's warm touch. This is why Mother became even more precious to me. She connected me to my once-happy Lucumí childhood.

Èjì and I always found each other after a night of hell, and joined Mother topside. At first, she did not want Èjì as an extra burden. But Mother loved children, and always had room in her heart for one more. She especially sympathized with Èjì's loss of his parents, but made it clear that as his "Ship Mama," he must obey her at all times. Èjì agreed but grinned, a signal to me that his obedience to Mother had space for mischief.

Nearly all day, Èjì and I would sit near Mother against the railing, watching the busy crew. Their skills of seamanship amazed us. Each crew member had his place, and each obeyed the commanding deck officer. First Mate Laroux should have relayed Captain Leclerc's commands to his crew, but clearly Bull ran *La Marie* in the captain's absence, as the shipmaster was generally drunk or doing something worse in his cabin.

This led to a shameless game that Èjì and I played: We gave each crew member an animal name representing that person's character. In our imaginations, creatures manned our ship. Bull was "Bull" because no other name suited him. Others were "Crocodile," "Vulture," "Crow," "Rooster" (the captain), and so on. But what should be the first mate's name? Laroux had too many meals at the captain's table, and fat swelled his upper body, making it seem that he had two sets of teats, one in front and one in back. We named him "Sow" (*ran* in Yoruba).

We whispered these names to each other, confident that the crew did not understand our Yoruba language. Still, Mother discouraged our game. She was right, because we whispered the first mate's nickname too loudly when Bull stood close by. He knew Yoruba, and leaned over us. We turned pale, but this man with an unsmiling, chiseled face whispered *erin* ("elephant" in Yoruba), then moved on with his usual air of indifference. Our near disaster caused Èjì and me to abandon the name game. Mother was relieved, replacing it with storytelling. Èjì and I did not know it then, but she was teaching us how to survive our bondage. Her tales came from African fables and oral traditions.

In many of these fables, the most clever jungle creature was a small spider named "Anansi." He was a trickster who sometimes got his way, and sometimes outsmarted himself and lost. Animal characters Anansi challenged included a tiger, an alligator, a firefly, and a turtle. Èjì and I loved these fables, but our favorite was "Anansi and Turtle." Mother liked to repeat it to illustrate an important point: Tricksters must pretend to be something they are not—to be weak before the strong, dumb before the smart, cowardly before the brave. To survive as a slave, you had to hide your intelligence from your master and nearly every mulatto and white in Saint-Domingue. If a slave ever carried the moment with his master, it required a trickster's cleverness.

In our favorite fable, Anansi is sitting down to a fine meal of yams, when Turtle shows up and invites himself to dinner. Anansi is polite and tells Turtle to join him, but has no intention of sharing his food with this hard-shelled intruder. He keeps Turtle from his table by continually having him wash for supper while he (Anansi) consumes the yams. Turtle leaves hungry, but thanks Anansi and invites him to supper at his creekside home. When Anansi arrives, he sees that Turtle has prepared a table of fine foods on creek's bottom. Turtle dives to this underwater banquet and begins eating his supper, but poor Anansi can only gaze at the bottom and see food disappearing into Turtle's mouth. Anansi is too buoyant to dive to the victuals. No matter how hard he tries, he fails. Deception brought both victory and defeat to Anansi and Turtle. In Mother's scheme, I played Anansi and Èjì played Turtle, but she warned us to play the trickster's part carefully.

The crew forced our first performance. They set up mirrors on the main deck, and had their Lucumí captives peer into them. Many had never seen a mirror before, and thought their reflection was their spirit or another person in the mirror. Some made faces or tried looking around the back of the mirror to see if someone was there. The crew howled with laughter at their antics. But most Lucumís figured out that they saw their own reflections—there's a difference between being stupid and being uninformed.

But the crew persisted in their game. That was when the crewman whom we nicknamed "Crocodile" selected Èjì and me to continue their show. He took our hands and led us to a mirror. Èjì went first, and did he put on a performance! He repeatedly looked into the mirror and grinned, showing all his teeth, while rolling his eyes. He knew how to play the fool and avoid the price which he might pay if the crew thought him "sassy." My following performance did not match his, but the crew laughed heartily at us, and so did we. But they thought our laughter acknowledged our own foolishness. Instead, we laughed at the fools who thought they tricked us. Anansi and Turtle had won a subtle victory, and we learned an important technique to survive as slaves with some dignity—thanks to Mother.

Just three days out from our destination, the greatest tragedy of my life occurred. Mother, Èjì, and I met at our usual spot after a long night of high seas and seasickness. We sat quietly, struggling to recoup our normal feelings. That was when we saw First Mate Sow walking slowly fore and aft, surveying the women and children. He did this periodically throughout the voyage. When he stopped, he would pat some male child on his head or rub his neck, then lead his unsuspecting victim to the captain's cabin. This seemed Sow's only first mate's duty during our loathsome journey to Saint-Domingue.

Mother became desperate, as our time had come. When Sow approached us, Èjì and I began our trickster routines by feigning seasickness and vomiting. He stood over us for a long time and finally left, heading for the captain's cabin. Èjì and I thought Anansi and Turtle had won again—but we outsmarted ourselves like our favorite characters in the fable.

Not long after, Captain Rooster strutted from his cabin of perversion, heading directly for us. Apparently Sow informed him of our defense, and Leclerc had none of it. His appetite for sodomy demanded either Èjì or me. He took my arm, making me stand up. I saw terror in Mother's eyes, and knew that the devil beckoned me. Rooster pulled me to him with his other free hand, stroking my hair, while directing me toward his cabin. An absolute fury gripped my soul. In my rage, I bit Leclerc's right hand, sinking my fangs deeper than a viper's. He yelled, pulled his bloody hand back, cursed, and then hit me. I slid across the deck, laying there while the captain regained his composure. Sow tried picking me up in preparation for my punishment, but tilted and sprawled on the deck, adding his humiliation to the captain's anger.

Death was upon me. One of the sailors scooped me up, slammed me against the main mast, extended my arms around the post, and tied my wrists on the other side. Rooster's lust for blood now outweighed his desire for sex. He ordered Sow to bring him a cat-o'-nine tails. Five lashes probably would have killed me.

Mother's intervention saved my life. She wrapped her arms around Leclerc's knees in a beggar's embrace, wept, and pleaded for my life. Leclerc could not understand Mother's Yoruba, but enjoyed her agony. Finally, she gestured to him that she take my place, and Leclerc pretended to accept her pleadings. He only connived to add her to his show. First, he would make me witness Mother's death, and then kill me. In the captain's twisted mind, no slave should ever draw a white man's blood, even in self-defense.

Mother died bravely. She moaned slightly after each lash from Leclerc's whip until she fell unconscious, but he kept beating her while I wailed and cried. In my fervent prayers, I begged God to either take the captain to hell, or let me die with Mother. Èjì shared my hysteria, but a sailor restrained him from helping her. When Leclerc finished beating Mother, Sow cut her bindings, and she fell limp upon the deck. On signal from Leclerc, no one stopped me from rushing to her. She was dying, and Leclerc enjoyed extending his bloody vengeance. I crouched down over Mother, as she struggled to speak. She whispered "no matter how far a river wanders…" and died, but I finished her sentence: "…it never forgets its source." Mother's soul had returned to Africa, or to Heaven, or to some other good place. I grieved that I was not with her.

I believed that God abandoned me, when Sow succeeded in picking me off the deck, and secured me to the mast. Let Leclerc's blood circus begin again! I did not care. I wanted death. At that moment, God exercised His style of mysterious intervention. Just as Leclerc raised his whip, a huge hand nearly enveloped the captain's entire right forearm. It was Bull! He held Leclerc's arm inside his huge fist, slowly bringing Rooster's arm to his side. The captain was furious, but Bull, in his unassuming manner, said that he needed a personal slave and asked my price.

Difficult choices faced the captain. He could order his navigator's arrest, but that would only get Rooster's neck snapped and those of several of his sailors before Bull could be brought down. That, thought cowardly Rooster, was not a good choice. On the other hand, he could set my price for an adult male slave (400 *livres*), making the crew believe that he had bested Bull in the deal. This way he saved face, and could kill me later. With the bargain struck, the still-angry captain staggered back to his cabin with Sow trailing behind.

Bull's mercy stunned me, but why did he not save Mother? This question mixed hate with my love for this giant man. As time passed, my hatred mellowed, because Bull must have felt conflicted between his duty to obey Rooster and his humane instincts. Besides, had he acted earlier, the outcome might have saved no one. Years later, I faced a dilemma like Bull's, and I forgave him completely.

Bull ordered a sailor to bring him an empty yam sack. Picking up a cannon ball, he placed it in the bottom of what became Mother's shroud. Then he gently lowered her body into the sack with Èjì and me holding the flaps back. With a large needle and wide thread used for sail repair, he stitched the flaps shut; then with Èjì and me saying goodbye, he dropped her body over the side, as we watched it sink quickly. No shark had a chance to carry her away. Later Bull explained that Mother deserved a sailor's burial, and did not want me to see sharks eat her body.

My first night following Mother's death seemed endless. Bull directed that I sleep near him on the main deck until we reached Saint-Domingue. Clearly, he feared that some sailor in the night might kill me. Main deck would be safer. He also allowed Èjì to stay with me until we dropped anchor at Le Cap François, main port for Saint-Domingue.

Because my previous nights were spent below deck, I did not know how mysterious the main deck became after dark, as *La Marie's* prow cut through briny, foam-capped waves. When I listened carefully, I heard vibrations from the ship's rigging caused by *La Marie's* constant speed and an ocean breeze. I swear that those sounds were like Mother's soothing voice after a harsh day. Loose objects left by some careless sailor now and then slid across the deck, reminding me of Mother's shuffling steps. Above was a full moon, enveloped at times by passing clouds, dimming its silvery flow across the water. In all of this, Mother was telling me goodbye. Bull and Èjì slept on.

In the final days of *La Marie's* voyage to Saint-Domingue, I became zombie-like. Even life's funny moments depressed me without Mother. Èjì´s sympathy failed to console me, and in self-pity, I forgot how deeply he felt Mother's death. In his own clumsy way, Bull tried occupying us with endless errands. But nothing helped except the passage of time.

On the last night of our journey, Bull ordered Èjì and me to his side, as he took the helm. He soon demonstrated his navigational skills, as *La Marie* began coasting dangerous waters along the island of Hispaniola. It seemed like a dream, as the moon cast its beams down mountain slopes that plunged to the sea, revealing dangerous crags which Bull deftly avoided, while mighty Mt. Cibao slept. From the port side, Èjì and I strained our eyes to discern silhouetted objects which a light-filled night seemed to touch with fairy dust. Gradually Hispaniola's high coastal mountains receded, revealing an ever-widening coastal plain. *La Marie* had begun paralleling the French side of Hispaniola.

But something strange defined Saint-Domingue besides a widening coastal plain and lowering mountains. These were the fiery dots in the distance that increased in size closer to shore, casting their glowing reflections across surf-washed beaches. Were these communal fires? Had *La Marie* returned us to Africa? Bull quickly dashed my fantasy. No! They were the eternal furnaces of plantation sugar mills during "Crop," a time when slaves worked an eighteen hour day and furnaces never shut down. Bull's comments were blunt, but they came from his manner, not from his heart.

I find irony in this moment. Only twice was I on a ship that coasted the North Province of Saint-Domingue. On my first voyage in 1767, I was a child on a slave ship, full of wonder about glowing sugar mill furnaces. My second occasion came when I escaped the terrors of the Great Slave Rebellion in 1791. That time, plantation houses themselves glowed in rising flames, as they fell to ashes. My entry came at the peak of plantation slavery in Saint-Domingue; my exit marked its fall.

During the night, Èjì and I clung to each other, remembered nice things, and hoped that the next day might be better than we feared. Not intending to, we fell asleep—a sleep so deep that we did not hear *La Marie* drop anchor near the entrance of Baye du Cap, harbor for Le Cap François; neither did we know that a pilot had come on board to guide us through tricky channels to our anchorage. But scurrying sailors brought us to our feet. Already, they were weighing anchor to take advantage of a rising tide that would sweep *La Marie* to her moorage in the harbor. They worked in an indigo light of rising daybreak, adding to the sad feelings which Èjì and I felt about our uncertain futures.

As *La Marie* eased into port, I became fascinated by how calm the waters were once we crossed the main sand bar and left breaking waves behind. As morning rose, the sky reflected itself on mirror-like water, and clouds appeared to float across its surface, rather than across the sky. With the rising sun, also came unbearable glare, especially from Le Cap's white-washed houses. Their intense radiance burned my eyes, making me look away.

When the pilot finished his duty, I swear that I heard every chain link click when the crew let out *La Marie's* anchors. We had arrived! But as the ship settled, Bull motioned Èjì and me to join him. He advised us: Save your names, because slaves lose their identity when their masters give them "cutesy" first names and their own last names. So he instructed Èjì to use the French word for Wednesday (*Mercredi*) and me to use the French word for Saturday (*Samedi*) when a master or overseer asked our names. Never use our African versions (Wésidéè and Kwambe) or that connection with our homeland would be lost. Like Mother's use of African fables, Bull helped us survive slavery. Besides, Anansi and Turtle would have approved our new disguises.

While Bull instructed Èjì and me, a yawl came alongside, and official-looking men came on board. They were from Le Cap to inspect the health of *La Marie's* human cargo, and to determine if we required quarantine. Bull ordered all slaves topside into two lines from fore to aft for inspection. Meanwhile, Rooster and Sow peered down from the poop deck in dress uniforms. Leclerc's uniform, however, bore no badges of a French naval commander like those that he wore during our voyage. His dress now was that of a simple merchant captain.

The inspectors hurried their investigations, as slave-hungry planters impatiently awaited us on shore. Their main concerns were dysentery and Pompey Disease (massive bleeding from pores, mouth, and anus). They found nothing. During these import-ant matters, Captain Rooster periodically whispered to Sow who responded with giggles, prompting Bull's Yoruba comment to me that "the captain must have had pork on his menu the night before." I did not smile again for a long time.

The sad moment arrived! Sailors began disembarking *La Marie's* slaves for shore and to a destiny more brutal than what they left behind. Rooster and Sow with an armed escort approached Bull and me. Sow reached for Èjì's arm, but Bull blocked him, sending the first mate squealing back to his captain. An animated conversa-tion followed between Leclerc and Bull that I could not understand. Apparently Leclerc refused to suffer another humiliation at the hands of his navigator, and demanded Èjì at all costs. Bull delivered a forceful but failed offer to buy Èjì, followed by Sow and Rooster gathering Èjì and heading for a slave-laden boat bound for the docks. The captain hastened to meet his merchant-sponsor and gather his pay. Watching Èjì leave broke my heart. My dearest childhood friend was gone!

Shadows from a lowering sun fell across the harbor when Bull and I reached Quai Saint-Louis, near the entrance to Rue

Saint-Pierre. The atmosphere was like a carnival. Planters some in field dress with wide-brimmed hats, others decked out as if expecting an audience with the king, wandering merchants, slaves suffering intimate examinations by prospective buyers, beautiful brown-eyed mulattresses with parasol umbrellas seeking a planter while he sought a slave, constant noise, and the bad smell of unwashed humans, combined to give me a glimpse into purgatory, or was it hell?

Bull and I pushed through the crowd to a long rectangular platform, covered with an open-air thatched pavilion. There in a row were important-looking gentlemen, sitting in wicker chairs, and enjoying air fanned by attending slaves. These were the wealthier planters of Saint-Domingue's North Province. First one, and then another, made a hand motion to a plantation manager buried in the crowd to push the bid higher, or hold the current one on slaves put on the block. These flesh mongers carefully avoided buying too many slaves from the same African nation. Mixing different African languages in the same slave gang disrupted their communications to plan a rebellion.

We seemed to wait forever. I was sad. I was lonely. I was angry. But mostly, I feared what lay ahead of me. Finally, the men on stage ended their bidding, and descended the steps near where Bull and I stood. The last man down appeared unimpressive. He was short, rotund, middle-aged, and walked with a cane. He claimed that his lame right leg came from a fall from his horse; others claimed it to be gout. He was Louis Pantaléon, Comte de Noé, the largest landholder in North Province, and a man who helped to save my life. Unlike most planters *(grands blancs)*, he was born in the colony and intended to die there. And unlike other planters, he opposed the more cruel features of slave treatment in the French colony, such as branding newly arrived Africans.

Bull hailed the Comte, and they began a friendly conversation in French which turned serious. I could not understand it, but I heard the word *Samedi* mentioned, and knew that they talked about me. Bull made his points repeatedly in the animated fashion of an Italian, only to be met by the Comte, shaking his head in disapproval. At last, they reached an accord, because the Comte opened his purse and handed Bull a roll of livres.

Bull walked over and explained to me that the Comte had spent all his own money for slave purchases, but that he did have money remaining from his uncle, the Comte de Bréda in France whose financial interests in Saint-Domingue he managed. Using his uncle's money, the Comte located me on Bréda Plantation in the care of Aunt Caroline who cooked for the manager's family. Choked with emotion, Bull explained that this was all he could do, since I would not be safe with him on a slave ship, especially should he continue serving Captain Leclerc.

The Comte hobbled over and guided me to his carriage. When I looked back, Bull had disappeared. I never saw him again, but I had a warm suspicion that Bull had saved other slave children. He was a good man on the wrong side.

When we reached his carriage, the Comte invited me to sit up front with old Uncle Solitaire, the coachman and a fellow Lucumí. He told me that his name meant "Lonesome" in French—one of those "cutesy" names that Bull warned me about, but I just smiled. As Uncle Solitaire guided our carriage through the streets of Le Cap and toward Plantation Row east of the city, the Comte leaned back, acting as if he rode in a royal parade. Nearly every passerby waved at him and he them, especially pretty mulattresses. But my thoughts were on Mother, Bull, Èjì and that awful Captain Leclerc.

Only Mother's fate did I know. Èjì disappeared from my life, but sometimes I imagined Turtle outwitting some overseer or plantation master. Even now, he remains in my heart as my dearest childhood friend. I never saw Bull again, but I did get snatches of information about him over the years. Sailors on the docks told me that he quit slaving altogether to run weapons to rebel forces during the American Revolution. That was all. But I have fantasized that Bull met a heroic end, locked into a deadly fight with British marines, killing several before being felled himself. Old Bull deserved the death of a gallant man and not as a drunk drowning in his own vomit, or as a stabbing victim along some remote water front. As for Captain Leclerc, my information is sketchy but rewarding. A slave ship captain of his description was taken over the side by a slave desperate to commit suicide. They sank immediately and drowned, sending one soul to Africa and the other to the Lake of Fire.

As our carriage wheeled toward Bréda Plantation, the drowsy sun fading behind Morne du Cap, west of Le Cap, reminded me of my uncertain future in Saint-Domingue. That part of my life's journey is the subject of my next letter.

Love to My Boys,

Saturday

When Philip finished reading, he saw Wahl facing him, while her eyes flashed deep anger.

"Hope your fuming is not intended for me, Wahl?"

"You have no idea, Massah. Saturday's terrors were like those of millions of other slaves. I saw what Saturday saw; I felt what he felt. His tears, my tears, the tears of our people could have swept over South Carolina like a tidal wave. Maybe you think you're a good man, Mr. Philip, but why would a good man enslave my people?"

Wahl fell silent again, only her eyes expressed the fury in her soul. A sense of his own shame kept Philip from comment. Her "why would a good man enslave my people?" haunted him. Phillip searched for words. "I'll return to read another letter" was all he could say.

"Yes, Massah," Wahl replied with her usual contempt for the man who had re-enslaved her.

Phillip started for the kitchen door, feeling Wahl's gaze heating the back of his neck, or was it his own self-questioning? Can a righteous man own slaves? He knew the rejoinder; Wahl had simply reminded him.

When Philip met Susan Elizabeth in the restaurant, he expressed remorse about excluding her from Saturday's first letter. His revenge hurt her, but she soon turned matters to her own advantage.

"Didn't want me there, I understand," Susan Elizabeth said tearfully, knowing that she had Philip by his heartstrings.

"Quit using your emotions to win an argument," Philip snapped. "I just resented your indifference to Saturday's passing."

What Philip considered a triumphant reply only hurt Susan Elizabeth, as a sorrowful look drifted from her eyes. "How could you expect me to have feelings for someone whom I never met?"

"Oh, I give up," Philip complained. "You women are too clever for us dumb males. Here, you might want to read Saturday's first letter, and join Wahl and me for the next reading."

Susan Elizabeth gave him a lover's look, signaling that she won their argument. No need for a trumpet's tinny victory blast when a simple, *I love you, Philip*, would do.

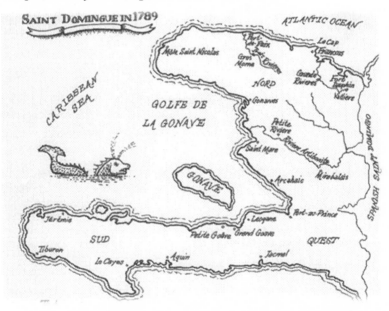

From Thomas O. Ott's *The Haitian Revolution*, 1789-1804

Copyright © 1973 by The University of Tennessee Press. Used by permission.

34

The Second Letter

Metallic sounds of ladles and skillets, as Wahl placed them on hangers signaled the end of her day. Now she could enjoy her fireplace and catch its warm glow. She found such delight poor compensation for her concern that Philip might not return. Had her rudeness discouraged him?

Her attitude toward Philip, she mused, did not include Susan Elizabeth, whom she had grown to like. No, her feelings toward Philip were deep inside her. She had gained her freedom in Cuba and moved to Limonar, but the purge following the Escalera Conspiracy forced her to leave. Even though John her former master and Saturday encouraged her to flee Cuba, it was Philip who returned her to slavery. He saved her life, but she felt humiliated, and the sight of him always re-opened an already festering wound. Still, she could not help staring at the kitchen door. Would he return? A turning door knob and squeaking hinges caused Wahl's excitement to surge. Philip was back with Susan Elizabeth!

Wahl tried speaking to Philip, but could only say, "Thanks Mr. Philip, I'm glad that you're back."

Her courtesy surprised Philip, as he and Susan Elizabeth took seats at the kitchen table. Befuddled, Philip began searching his pockets for Saturday's second letter, which he found and started reading:

15 Elliott Street, Southside
Charleston
May 17, 1806

Dear Philip and John,

I had fallen into a deep slumber during my carriage ride to Bréda Plantation. Anxious moments of the day had drained my energy, and memories of the evil voyage to Saint-Domingue lowered my spirits in an ebb tide of emotion. Sleep provided my only escape. I dreamt that waves striking *La Marie* were tossing me around, only to awaken and find two chubby hands shaking me. And when I looked up, I stared into the cleavage of two huge bosoms--like a valley between two mountains of flesh. I bolted up, and looked into a black face as round as the moon but with happy eyes. She was Aunt Caroline, the woman Comte de Noé selected to be my guardian. Over the next few years this short, fat, bossy but loveable woman taught me how to survive on Bréda.

Before leaving for his plantation, Comte de Noé instructed Aunt Caroline to let me sleep until the slaves took their noon break, have me join their mealtime, and then send me out with them to continue the sugar cane harvest. I had become a field slave! But I had no special skills for anything else.

When Aunt Caroline roused me, she shook her head in mocking amusement, encouraged me, and gently shoved me toward the door of her two-room hut. Already, the gentle toughness of this woman whom I called "Auntie" started lifting me from my despair. A bright Caribbean sun greeted me, as I stepped into a hot July day. There had been no rain for days, and dust rose from the slightest movement of man, or beast, or breeze. Not more than a hundred yards away, several hundred men, women, and children stood and squatted, covered in dust, like powder sugared gingerbread people. And their chatter seemed a veritable Tower of Babel, as I understood few words.

I could only identify two or three African languages among them, including my native Yoruba. Many conversed in Creole—a slave language born in Saint-Domingue, marking the first victory slaves scored over their masters.

Plantation owners sought to disrupt slave conversations, a

policy aimed at new African arrivals that they suspected harbored thoughts of rebellion. So the planters mixed different African nations into their slave gangs, creating a battalion of mutes. But the Ibos, Aradas, Asantis, Dahomans, Lucumís and others would not be silenced, as they developed a new universal slave language in the colony. The language is spoken swiftly. Its words are largely French with some African and local color thrown in, and the word order (syntax) is akin to Ewe, language of the Aradas. It is profane, pornographic, passionate, and beautiful. With Aunt Caroline's help, I eventually learned Creole.

My only thought was to reach a large kettle of boiled rice, with slices of yams and salted fish, the main meal of the day for a field slave. Hardly had I filled my belly, when the snap of a whip above my head startled me. It was the driver ordering us back to the cane fields. A second driver cracked his whip, and directed another group to the boiling house where skilled slaves processed cane into sugar, molasses, and rum.

A word is necessary about these drivers. These mostly black men served white overseers by brutally enforcing their bosses' demands on other slaves. Chattels not only faced their tyranny in the field but even socially, as drivers frequently grabbed a slave girl for a dance or for sex. Any male slave's intervention might bring a driver's whip across his back. Small wonder that slave rebels in the great uprising of 1791 sought to kill these minions of the overseers with as much enthusiasm as they did whites.

The driver commanding me, clutched my arm, and went into a pantomime, demanding my name. In my anxiety, I shouted: "Samedi!" Everyone froze, including the driver. The shadow of fear passed from me to them, because Samedi is an important *loa* (spirit) of voodoo, representing the dead. This spiritual aura protected me against drivers prone to violent behavior. Luck, not the gods, had blessed me.

Louis, our field driver, was short, broad chested, with a pock-marked face and the fiery red eyes of someone given to drink. He was a *creole* black (born in Saint-Domingue), and his savvy about slave habits and his willingness to deliver our overseer's commands to us had won him his job—a job he cherished. Over his surprise about my name, Louis yanked me next to another youth near my age, gesturing angrily that we were to bear water to the field slaves. He knew from our ceremonial scarring that we were from different African nations. My work partner was Ashanti and I Lucumí. He spoke Fon and I Yoruba. Louis gave him a malicious nickname: "Zèbre" (*zebra* in English) because his back bore zebra-like stripes. His Ashanti name was "Zuberi" (*strong* in English). Once again, I appreciated Bull's effort to protect my Lucumí identity. Zèbre, like many other slaves, had his stripped away.

Once in the fields, Zèbre and I toted water to the cane cutters. It fascinated me to watch them methodically cutting stalks off at ground level to preserve the bottom joint, especially rich in sugar cane juice. Another group of slave cutters cleared foliage from the stalks and piled them; a final group of mainly women and children tied the stalks into bundles, and then loaded them into oxcarts bound for the sugar mill. Watching others work sometimes slowed my water deliveries, bringing a shout from Louis: "*Chival, chival!*" Creole slaves aimed this term at newly arrived Africans, meaning that like a "horse" we were only fit for hard labor, and at the bottom of the social order in Saint-Domingue.

On my first day in the cane fields, I saw the evil of slavery. A cutter pointed to something between the rows of sugar cane. Other slaves joined him, followed by Louis and Michel Lajoie the overseer. Together they carried out a body to a clearing. The corpse was that of a slave, probably from Flaville Plantation since he wore its brand. Even more disconcerting, the deceased wore a locked metal helmet with places for his eyes, ears, and nose, but nothing for his mouth. In his pocket, Lajoie discovered a half-chewed joint of sugar cane, a cruel reminder of why he had been punished.

Lajoie ordered us to form a circle around him. He pointed out that the unnamed victim stole and ate his master's sugar cane, therefore reducing his owner's profits. Thus, he had to wear an iron helmet for punishment, causing his thirsty flight to elude slave catchers and their dogs, only to die in a Bréda cane field. Lajoie supported the punishment, and said he would impose it here if Comte de Noé and Gilly the plantation manager had not forbidden it. The Comte restricted punishment for this offense to two whip lashes and then only to adult slaves. The overseer finished by saying that the Comte could not always protect us, and that we would rue that day!

I hated Michel Lajoie from the start; our subsequent meetings made me hate him more. He stayed mostly out of sight, letting his drivers establish daily routines and apply minor discipline. But if a slave committed a "crime" on his list of forbidden transgressions, he appeared like a demon in human form. Lajoie had a pretty boy's appearance and fashioned himself a lady's man. His blond curly hair was thinning, and his scalp had a red glow, a Caribbean sun's price for his hatless vanity. His build and height were modest, but his temperament displayed a hard-to-restrain hatred and contempt for Bréda slaves, a common characteristic in his class of small whites (*petits blancs*). While owning no slaves themselves, they abused both mulattoes (*gens de couleur*) and slaves on and off the plantation, earning them the tag: "aristocrats of the skin."

When the lowering sun melted into a cluster of colors, I entered Aunt Caroline's hut. I looked like one of those gingerbread boys that I had seen earlier. Exhaustion had overcome me. Auntie hugged me, and introduced another member of her household. He was Jean-Pierre Bréda, a big child bordering adolescence. Both were uniformed for service in Master Gilly's kitchen and dining room. As they departed to attend their evening responsibilities, Jean-Pierre and I exchanged glances of mutual hostility. I was surprised at his presence, he resented mine. Our competition for Auntie's affection was instant. Our birthplaces made matters worse: He was Creole and I African. This explains his malicious humor in nicknaming me "Horse." Through the years, our sibling rivalry followed a tortured path until its final resolution.

Jean-Pierre was big for his age, had a round face, and a wide body frame which promised an accumulation of fat, a promise that he seemed to be keeping. His eyes belied his mood, as moments of emotion leaped from his deep brown pupils. Jealousy aimed at me was my first encounter with this trait. His father placed him with Auntie after his mother died. Ironically, Jean-Pierre's father played a bigger part in my life than did Auntie.

A conch shell's eerie sound called us weary field slaves back to work. Unknown to me, Bréda Plantation was in its last month of "Crop," a six-month harvest period from February to August. Masters, managers, overseers, and drivers worked desperately to process harvested sugar cane before it soured. This task required that slaves work an eighteen-hour day or more.

Auntie saw my fatigue, and sought my exemption from more field work on my first day at Bréda. She confronted Louis the driver on the subject. A violent argument ensued between them, but Auntie apparently won, as she signaled me to a straw-mattress. Why had she won? Was she under the protection of Comte de Noé? No. Her assumption of authority over the driver came from another source that I later discovered. But a fuming Louis got the last word, as he planned to give Zèbre and me a dangerous assignment.

Before sunrise the following day, Auntie jarred me awake with "*Reveye miven enpe gason*" (Creole for "Awaken my little boy"). This greeting began my day as long as we lived together. She also handed me a rough cotton shirt and short breeches to replace my loincloth. But my good fortune ended when Louis ordered Zèbre and me to join André's work gang, serving the sugar mill and boiler house. Less severe than Louis, this tall, lean black man was "all business," as those who managed Bréda feared yet another poor harvest for Comte de Bréda, the owner in Paris.

At the sugar mill, I observed young women unloading bundles

of cane stalks from ox-carts, cutting their bindings, and feeding them into a conveyor. At the top, a slave perched on a chair guided the stalks through grinding ox-powered millstones. Next to this "feeder," lay a cane knife for him to amputate any of his append-ages that might lodge in the machinery. From there, the extracted greenish cane juice flowed into a large cistern where another slave added lime to bring impurities to the surface which he ladled from the contents. When the liquid reached "clarification" standards for purity, he sent it to the boiling house.

Here I learned a mythological story that strengthened us slaves. About ten years before my arrival at Bréda, a slave named François Macandal served as feeder in a nearby sugar mill. He caught his left hand in the millstones, forcing him to amputate his arm at the elbow before getting dragged through the machinery. No longer could he work at the mill, so his overseer assigned him pastoral duties. Legend has it that a witch taught him to identify deadly herbal poisons, which he planned to use to pollute plantation water supplies.

Discovering his plan, planters chased Macandal down, and burned him at the stake. White authorities required slaves near Le Cap to witness their hero's execution. Whites assumed that Macandal's threat ended with his death. But those in bondage considered it only the beginning, because they believed Macandal became even more powerful in the supernatural world than in life. As a loa, Macandal would intervene in their troubles. Slaves often acknowledged his presence by saying "Macandal" when they saw a vigorous puff of smoke.

From the mill, Zèbre and I entered the boiling house, and a wall of oppressive heat struck us, making me feel faint. Over the furnace sat a series of heated copper boilers. The first and larg-est received "clarified" cane juice from the mill. A slave stood by each boiler with a ladle nearly as big as himself, skimming rising crust off the now-bubbling liquid. From the first boiler, the heated juice flowed through five others until reaching the last one where stood a "striker" who judged the correct moment for releasing the processed cargo into a cooling vat. After the juice congealed into lumps, slaves broke up the "cakes" with shovels, and placed the contents into large barrels, known as "hogsheads." Near the bottom of these hogsheads, slaves inserted cane joints into plug-holes to siphon molasses from the clayed sugar. The sticky fluid gathered in a porcelain gutter, some destined for shipping barrels and some for distillation into rum.

As Zèbre and I walked through the boiling house, we noticed lurking dangers for workers. Most complained about slaves fainting and falling into a tank of molten cane juice. For that reason, plantation managers usually rotated the boiling house crew every six hours. After a few minutes in this Satan's outpost, Zèbre and I felt our bodies swelling, our thoughts becoming fuzzy, and rivers of sweat poured into our eyes, soaking our clothes. I must admit that Louis got his revenge against me.

Over the next few years, my routine remained the same. During "Crop" from February to August, I worked the boiling house, seven days a week. After the frenzied harvest, we slaves prepared the ground for planting and replaced old canes with new cuttings. The labor was tiring and tense under Louis' supervision, but at least "off season" gave me a half-day on Saturday, all day off on Sunday, and a Monday through Friday work load of twelve hours daily.

Sundays in the off-Crop season became a pleasant time for many slaves. We attended Mass, and afterwards, adults with a pass from the plantation manager headed for the Negro Market in Le Cap to sell anything they owned. Some sold exotic birds that they had trained to city mulattresses who believed a bird-of-paradise in the parlor advertised the erotic arts of a Venus in the boudoir. Produce from a slave's garden also filled the bins at the Negro Market. Auntie traveled to the market every other Sunday during off season. For her and others, the Negro Market allowed time for gossip from neighboring plantations.

Masters ignored the Negro Market, but required our attendance at Mass. They knew that parish priests were advocates for slavery. Often, we listened to clerics deliver homilies, emphasizing that a "good" slave must always obey his master. But results were not what master and priest expected: We listened without hearing; we saw what we wanted to see. When we saw Saint Patrick with those writhing snakes at his feet, we saw Damballa the snake loa. When we saw the Virgin Mary in her purity, we saw Ezili Freda. When we saw the crucifix on the altar, we saw the sacred crossroads where resides Legba, keeper of the gateway between mortals and loas. We associated him with Saint Anthony. The Catholic liturgy further helped us to solidify our voodoo beliefs. Part of voodoo was pure folk religion, part violently anti-white and anti-slavery. Plantation masters virtually ignored this religion developing under their very noses. Clearly voodoo was a slave victory.

After Mass one Sunday, I met Toussaint Bréda for the first time. He stood inside Auntie's hut, sharing hilarious conversations with her and Jean-Pierre his son. She would smile, roll her eyes, and laugh, and I could see by Jean-Pierre's expression that he adored his father. I felt like an intruder and deeply missed Mother at that moment. But Auntie and Toussaint hugged and pulled me into their family circle, causing Jean-Pierre to despise me even more. In his view, I had stolen Auntie from him, and now sought his father.

Maybe Jean-Pierre's jealousy had merit, as Toussaint filled the hole my father left. But his role in my life was so much more. His ordinary appearance might fool you. He wore a red head bandanna as his trademark, possessed an angular face with a slightly protruding lower jaw, and one of his fingers on his right hand was terribly crooked from a poorly attended fracture. Barely five feet tall, he weighed about the same as a jockey, and bore the nickname *Fatras-Baton* ("Throw-Away-Stick").

Despite his unimpressive physical features, Toussaint the total man was awesome. His eyes communicated intelligence and depth of soul. He was instinctively kind but also conniving—conniving to gain personal power and conniving to construct a better world than slavery. His majestic bearing reflected his royal Arada heritage that earned both his father and him a *de facto* free status, known as *liberté de savane*. Under this designation, he maintained a private household, and possessed five slaves.

Toussaint's baptized name was François Dominque Toussaint, but he preferred Toussaint Bréda. He was creole-born, and had gained literacy from Jesuit instruction. He radiated a quiet authority that slaves feared and plantation managers respected. It was his friendship with Aunt Caroline that gave her an advantage over Louis the driver on my first day at Bréda.

Serving as the Gillys' coachman, Toussaint arrived at Aunt Caroline's hut one Sunday in a one-horse shay to offer her and Jean-Pierre a ride to the Negro Market. Good naturedly, he invited me to come along, but I refused graciously because I felt Jean-Pierre's blazing glare. Wisely, I gave him his father that day. Toussaint smiled, betraying his agreement with my rejection. But there would be other days. I left and looked for Zèbre with whom to spend the rest of my Sunday.

Soon I fell into a routine with my adopted family. My favorite time was the slow-season (September to February) before Crop, because Auntie gave me special attention at the end of my work day. She would hug me, take a large wooden spoon, point me to a chair near a window, and make me recite Creole words. She indicated different objects, and I supplied the correct words. I knew Creole for everything in her hut: *tab* ("table"), *fenet* ("window"), *pot* ("door"), *po* ("pot"), *kasann* ("bed"); and on a moonlit night she would point outside: *lain* ("moon"), *kann* ("cane"), *kanpe* ("star"), *lonbraj* ("shadow"). Invariably Jean-Pierre added another word to my growing vocabulary: *chival*; and I to his: *kochon* ("pig"). Our insults would escalate, and that was when Auntie employed her spoon to shut us up. Out of respect for her, we usually did, but our peace served only as a truce in our continuing dislike for each other.

Besides teaching me Creole, Auntie instructed me on the art of serving master's table. I practiced standing at attention behind my imaginary guest and the sequence of attending his or her every need. She taught me proper utensil selection, on which side to serve a guest, the proper way to cut food on a guest's plate, how to select and serve wines, and above all, how to keep my silence before master's guests. Look dumb, act dumb, but be proficient— sounded like Anansi's game; and I appreciated her efforts to take me from the cane fields into the big house.

Auntie also showed her sensitive side to Jean-Pierre and me and to the children of Bréda Plantation. She regularly "stole" kitchen food for her boys, and especially wanted us to feel the warmth of Christmas. She baked shortbread and tarts for master's table, some mysteriously appearing at our bedsides on Christmas mornings. She also loved weaving sugar cane dolls from discarded foliage, and made sure that every slave child got one of these ugly babies.

Auntie had a deep religious devotion as well. On Saturday night, she attended a voodoo ceremony and sometimes experienced pos- session, known as "a loa riding his horse." Her loa was Elizi Freda, which meant that she dressed like this spirit. Since her loa identi- fied with The Holy Virgin of Catholicism, Elizi's primary clothing color was white, and so was Auntie's. Her appearance dressed in white convinced her master's family that she was neat and clean. And she was. But Jean-Pierre and I knew the deeper meaning of her dress. On Sunday mornings, she normally worshipped at Mass to conclude her religious experiences of the night before. To Auntie and to other slaves, the word *Catholic* included the loas of voodoo plus the symbols and liturgy of the Church.

More than anything else, Auntie comforted me. When despair drained my soul, she refilled it with hope. And when I cried for my Mother, it was Auntie who held me, rocked me, and consoled me.

Zèbre made up the last member of my extended family. He spent almost all his spare time in Auntie's hut avoiding his mother. When I first met him, he displayed a cheerful personality, but it changed to somber, and most Bréda slaves knew why. Michel Lajoie the overseer raped his mother regularly, and poor Zèbre bore witness to her agony. When his mother saw him coming, she would send Zèbre to tend the small provisions garden behind her hut. Zèbre often heard her sobbing, and saw Lajoie buttoning his breeches as he left. All of us wanted to take a cane knife to his penis. Such sorrow moved Auntie to train Zèbre for kitchen duties as she had me, hoping that this change would lift his spirits.

When I was ten years old, Zèbre and I quit our mill and field duties for the big house. What a different world! Auntie in her starched white uniform stepped smartly: supervising cooks, moving quickly between kitchen and big house, and instructing her waiters. She served both as maître d' and head chef—truly remarkable in both skills. Her fledglings had not yet gained her confidence, even though she had spent long nights teaching us "table French" and a waiter's proper conduct. So she relegated us to toting food items from kitchen to dining room. From culinary delights cooking in the kitchen to Master Gillys' table, I knew every step. I carried baked hams, roast chickens, and lamb, as well as every cooked vegetable the colony produced. Zèbre and I worked hard and gained basic conversational French; after nearly two years, we finally graduated to massah's dining room.

The dining room! What a strange place for a young African. And what a telling place to discover a side of the master not usually revealed to a field slave. My job required that I stand by a sideboard, making sure food flowed to the Gillys' table on time with Auntie's standard of no heated food grown cold. Between courses, I used crystal rinsers to cleanse wine glasses for the Gillys and their friends. Zèbre's job included substituting for me and pulling the velvet cord of the "Shoe-fly" fan over the dining table for steady air movement.

The Bréda big house offered two levels of dining experience. In both, Madam Nannette Gilly assumed the air of royalty, even when only she and her husband "dined in." She was boisterous, pretentious, overweight, and sometimes unintentionally funny. When she became too overbearing or too drunk, Maurice Gilly, who matched her expensive wines with his cheap rum, would insult her. This would prompt Madame Gilly's profane response and her usual apology: "Pardon my French!" Even at an informal level, she displayed her expensive china, fancy candelabras, sterling silver place settings, and endless porcelain figurines. The Gillys often amused me. They were not bad, only sad.

Dining "in state" was the highest level of epicurean experience at the Gilly's table, and might have even blushed our good King Louis XV. For those serving, however, our required decorum created tension. This began with our decoration of the dining area and adjacent drawing room. We carefully placed priceless tureens representing God's gentle creatures: that of a swan being my favorite. Waiters set Madame's tables with Irish linens, Meissen porcelain candelabras, covered vegetable bowls, gold place settings, Danish crystal wine glasses, and exquisite collections of Meissen, Tingdezhen and Cantonese chinaware. God help a slave who broke an expensive object!

Our decoration included the drawing room. By the entrance, sat a sideboard with *tabatières* (porcelain boxes) equal in number to guests present, and filled with fine Swedish snuff. To symbolize planter wealth, every lid bore an emblazoned stalk of sugar cane with each master's name and coat-of-arms. Inside the parlor, visitors could enjoy billiards, gaming tables, or social conversation. My favorite game was a chessboard with porcelain pieces of historically important people in French history. On one side, King Louis XIII stood, protected by Madame Pompadour as his queen and by Cardinal Richelieu as one of his bishops. On the other side, King Henry II of England and Anjou stood, protected by Eleanor of Aquitaine as his queen and by Edward the Black Prince as one of his knights. Madame Gilly required us to recite their stories when a guest demanded. One of my most painful moments came during a recitation. Monsieur Turpin signaled me to his chessboard, calling me a *noir bête* (black beast), demanding that I give him each figure's biography. I did, but he said that a monkey could have done better.

When "dining in state" began, tension rose even higher for wait-ers and servers. A waiter dressed in white and trimmed in black with white gloves stood behind each diner, attending his every need. We waiters had to remain silent, making no facial expression beyond that of a servile idiot. Humor sometimes challenged our silence. Funny were moments when Madame Gilly flaunted her self-importance before her husband and guests. Monsieur Gilly usually sat slumped with the odor of alcohol emitting from his every pore, ignoring his wife. She would brag to visitors about some important person whom she had met in Paris and about Parisian fashion. Like clockwork, Monsieur Gilly would finally rouse himself, commenting that she was a drunken old cow who could not graze beyond the wine shops of Bordeaux and Nantes, much less make it to Paris. I found it hard not to smile.

When a diner made hurtful remarks, my emotions challenged my silence. One night, table conversation centered on Abbé Raynal's *History of the Two Indies* (1770). Guests agreed with Raynal that French colonialism had victimized them and that they needed more home rule. But from there, table conversation focused on Raynal's condemnation of slavery, making several diners angry. Monsieur Turpin made heated racist remarks justifying slavery, making Comte de Noé, his cousin Bayon de Libertat, Libertat's wife, and the Gillys uneasy. This thin man, looking like a plucked buzzard, argued that the black man lacked a soul. Refusing to tolerate more, Count de Noé blurted out a retaliation which I remember well: "That which God giveth, Monsieur Turpin, you can never taketh away!" We slaves fumed. I imagined myself a Lucumí warrior. My knife and fork were my spear and shield, and I was poised to cut Monsieur Turpin's throat.

Big house wealth gave me pause, because I knew that many of my people had perished for Madame Gilly's grand appointments and army of servants. Had Mother died for this? Rage and sadness drifted over me, but I could not suppress my optimism for long. Someday, all this would change. Someday, I would be free again.

The year 1772 began with a simple carriage ride that mended my strained relationship with Jean-Pierre. Papa Toussaint knew that "his boys" loved trips with him to Le Cap. So imagine my excitement when he reined his coach at Auntie's doorway and invited us to accompany him to the port city. I would experience only my third trip to Le Cap since my arrival at Bréda. He was taking the Gillys to Le Cap where they would take lodging until Madame Gilly boarded a ship for France. Our happy group left Auntie's that morning. Jean-Pierre and I sat up front, giggling with anticipation about new adventures. In the rear, the giggling Gillys sat. She giggled with thoughts about Paris, and he giggled because he could pursue unrestricted drunkenness and whoring in her absence.

Along the ten-mile run to Le Cap, we passed elaborate coffee plantations covered in white blossoms, announcing bountiful crops for the coming harvest. Their breath-taking panoramas almost made me forget the agony of those who cultivated them. On one of those estates, Mille Fleurs Plantation, I would later experience the most agonizing moments of my life.

While I looked at garden scenes, Papa Toussaint guided his coach like a Roman soldier riding his chariot into combat; soon we entered the southern limits of Le Cap. Trotting along Rue Gouvernement, he turned west on Ravine, stopping at the Hôtel de la Couronne on Rue Espagnol near the docks. The Couronne was both luxurious and convenient for those arriving and departing Le Cap. Immediately, Jean-Pierre and I jumped down to help the Gillys inside with their light luggage. The heavier trunks we left for groaning hotel porters.

We stayed with the Gillys to their suite of exquisite rooms. Jean-Pierre and I kept turning our heads, watching waiters pushing carts with fine foods, looking at expensive oil paintings hanging from hallway moldings, dodging people rushing to and fro, and feeling lush carpets beneath our feet. But mostly we ogled at the beautiful mulatto women whom we saw in every hallway that we strode. The sap of manhood crept up my trunk; in Jean-Pierre, it reached his crown and outer branches, and sexual desire blossomed in both his eyes. Our fantasies evaporated when Papa Toussaint ordered us to open the door to the Gillys' suite. We did, and settled the Gillys before leaving for the lobby with Toussaint.

Back in the coach, Papa Toussaint toured us around Le Cap. Starting at the wharves, he pointed out warehouses, inns, taverns, and waterfront billiard parlors. Then he wheeled along Rue Pen-thievre and Rue Gouvernement where there were long rows of small shops, each specializing in different French products. Sea captains owned most of these businesses, and each displayed a small sign listing contents for sale. Bathhouses were one street over where patrons enjoyed soothing waters, as well as any other pleasures they desired.

Then Papa Toussaint passed the Place d'Armes (Parade Ground) and the old Church of Notre Dame which showed cracks from a settling foundation. From there, we travelled Rue Saint-Sav-ior and Rue Saint-Francis Xavier forming the perimeter of the Government Buildings, once belonging to the Jesuits until France evicted them in 1763. The Government Clock stood above the second story of the main building. It struck each hour and played a tune for which city slaves invented the lyrics: "A good white is dead, only the bad ones survive."

Near these buildings, stood the pride of Le Cap—the theatre. The city had its own troupe of actors that performed every Sunday, Tuesday, and Thursday. Toussaint laughed and said that lonely grand blanc planters could always find male-seeking mulattresses in the audience. Past the theatre, he took us down Rue Marché to Whites' Market where every conceivable European import could be purchased, even pornography.

We passed street after street of small but attractive masonry houses, mostly one-storied with jalousie shutters. If a house had a slate roof, it came from Anjou; if tile, it came from Normandy. The Great Fire of 1743 inspired the city fathers to encourage construction of these stout residences. Unpaved streets packed with sand and shell fronted city houses, creating unbearable dust during droughts and disgusting quagmires during rainy periods. Our last stop was the Negro Market on Rue Anjou at Clugny Square. This is where enterprising slaves like Auntie sold fruits and vegetables. Originally, open only on Sundays and holidays, it now served its patrons daily.

Constant noise formed my final impression of the city. From carpenters hammering barrel staves into place, to stevedores rolling their barrels to the docks, to hawkers barking their wares, to wagons rumbling over rutted streets, Le Cap was a busy, prosperous place. It reminded me of Charleston upon my arrival there in 1791. And like Charleston, city slaves constituted a majority of Le Cap's population.

Dismounting his coach, Toussaint told Jean-Pierre and me that we had an hour to explore the city, and then promptly return to the market. He added that our adventure should not blind us to lurking dangers. Be especially servile toward whites and even mulattoes, he advised. Then he handed us each a few *sous* (five cents per), winked, and told us not to buy everything within sight. With cash in hand, Jean-Pierre and I headed for merchants' row on Rue Gouvernement. We both wanted a treasure for Auntie's approval. But sibling rivalry spoiled what should have been a joyous occasion. A silver chain dangling from a shop display caught my eye, and I felt compelled to buy it. I did, and Jean-Pierre bought one like it. Not that he wanted his purchase; he just feared that I might outdo him. A tie, he believed, beat second place.

Leaving the shop, we hurried to the theatre and Sunday's matinée performance. At intermission, Papa Toussaint said that mulattresses seeking lovers crowd the promenade outside the theatre. Of course, they desired grands blancs, not two teenage slave boys. But we could still enjoy their low-cut blouses, bulging bosoms, wiggling hips, and inviting lips. We just wanted to view the carnal ship, not sail on it.

In breathless anticipation of the flesh carnival, Jean-Pierre and I walked past a grand blanc without acknowledging that strutting peacock. He turned, cursed us, raised his brass-headed walking cane, and charged us. His first blows fell on Jean-Pierre's back, causing him to square up and look his assailant in the eye. I knew that my companion's temperament called for a furious retaliation. Then Mother's death on *La Marie* flashed through my mind. I had to act fast to stop Jean-Pierre from striking this white man and paying for it with his life.

Jean-Pierre made a load for me to defend. I stepped between them, restraining Jean-Pierre with all my might. Blows struck my back, but my excitement dulled the pain. Then Jean-Pierre lunged at his assailant, but toppled over as we hit the ground and rolled over with me on top, exposing me to our attacker. Satisfied that his precious ego had been avenged, the grand blanc uttered a few oaths, and walked away.

We lay on the walk bloodied, stunned, and embarrassed—embarrassed because the mulattresses across the street witnessed our beatings. They crossed to our side of the street, and crowded around us. But none applauded what had happened, and most condemned our plight. A lovely woman helped me up, while another assisted my fallen companion. She hugged me, and my face seemed a perfect fit for her cleavage. She then handed me her silk handkerchief that mulattresses carry as a prop for flirtations. I heard others curse Monsieur Lebrun, our assailant, and his habit of attacking unsuspecting slaves on his Sunday strolls. Never will I forget the compassion of these pretty females, and felt honored to have discovered in them a beauty far beneath their skins.

Jean-Pierre and I limped to the Negro Market, our clothes torn and bloody. But we sensed a new feeling between us. We were now brothers, or as we laughingly put it—blood brothers. From then on, we became close friends and shared our surrogate parents with only occasional spats of jealousy. To bind our new alliance, I gave him the silk handkerchief that the mulattress gave me, and that I so wanted to keep. He loved my peace offering, and wore it as a bandanna atop his head.

When we entered the Negro Market, Papa Toussaint gave us an angry stare that could have melted iron. We were late! But when we told him what happened, his fiery anger dampened to sympathy. Usually good at hiding his emotions, Toussaint let us glimpse his inner-self, because like us, an angry white man had once assaulted him. It had happened when an overseer near Bréda stopped him, searched his carriage, and found a book under the front seat. Accusing him of literacy, which was true, the overseer beat him severely. Toussaint believed that he might have killed the man in a fair fight. But he knew the consequences of retaliation, and just took it. With sage words, he advised us to do the best you can in the world you live in. Obey the rules, but never confuse obedience with acceptance of slavery.

When we returned to Bréda, Toussaint reined his coach by Auntie's hut. Our appearance alarmed her, and Toussaint's account of the day made Auntie furious. Some damn white devil had harmed her boys; then a look came over that jolly round face that I never will forget. Anger and vengeance shot from her eyes, like one of God's avenging angels. But Toussaint hugged her, and the jovial Auntie returned. She looked at us, shook her head, and said that we looked like two sailors who fought over a girl. Jean-Pierre told her every intricate detail, and at once she realized that our beatings had a silver lining: Her two boys were brothers at last.

Around mid-1772, my rising good fortune declined. Maurice Gilly finally drank himself to death. Madame Gilly left France after receiving word of her husband's failing health, but did not reach Saint-Domingue until nearly a month after his burial. She directed Jean-Pierre and me to accompany her to Gilly's grave site. For over an hour, she stood motionless with tears flooding her cheeks. It occurred to me that despite their combats, which they seemed to enjoy, they shared a real affection for each other—the type of affection that is re-emphasized at the end of a long relationship.

Returning to Bréda, Madame Gilly packed her belongings, and moved to a townhouse in Le Cap. She made a poor decision, because nearly everything in the city reminded her of Maurice. After two years of misery, she returned to France. Her departure for Le Cap opened a period of uncertainty for Bréda. Who would be our next manager? We soon found out.

All seemed well at first. Comte de Noé for years had overseen the welfare of Bréda for his uncle in France. So the uncle took his nephew's advice that Antoine Bayon de Libertat should be the next manager. Monsieur Libertat had treated slaves in previous managerial experiences better than his colleagues. The appointment seemed an easy choice, reinforced by Maurice Gilly's deathbed recommendation of Libertat, and that Comte de Noé and Libertat were cousins. But no one could have predicted the treachery of Monsieur Guillaume Delribal, or the sudden lack of confidence that Comte de Bréda directed at Comte de Noé.

Having served for a few months, Libertat resigned after facing severe drought and Comte de Bréda's criticism. The development of Bréda's attitude came from letters Delribal sent to him, accusing Libertat of being too liberal and too unbusinesslike for plantation management. Bréda needed little persuasion because of Comte de Noé's earlier appointment of Maurice Gilly and then Libertat to that position had turned into economic disaster. Thus, Comte de Bréda overruled his nephew with Libertat's removal. Delribal, he believed, would carry Bréda Plantation to prosperity. It brought instead a reign of terror.

Delribal strutted like a flamingo sneaking up on a fish, and enunciated his words deliberately. Bald and slender from shoulder to mid-section and from ankle to waist, Delribal's stomach stuck out like a mountain rising from a plain, making him appear pregnant. When he walked the grounds, a slave with an umbrella shaded his bare head. His face was long and mulish with eyes sunken inside dark rings, like someone recovering from an illness. His mood was sullen and nervous, as if he expected disaster but could not discern its shape. Much of his anxiety, he focused on deadly diseases that he just knew he had. His fear of yellow fever, a real threat in the colony, illustrated his excessive behavior. Even though he had lived long enough in Saint-Domingue to be "seasoned" against the disease, he took extreme measures to prevent the malady from reaching his doorstep. This included moving his bedroom to the second floor to combat dangerous earthly vapors, while directing his slaves to ignite large brush piles to purify the air.

On other occasions, he believed that his bowels suffered parasitic consumption, and examined his stool for wiggling critters. When this scourge no longer threatened him, then the dreaded Pompey disease took over. Widespread bleeding characterized this affliction, and his bloody nose one morning convinced him that he had it. Dr. François Truloc from Le Cap made more trips to his bedside than a mistress, and became a member of Delribal's extended family.

How Delribal connected with Comte de Bréda was anyone's guess, but the strongest clue rested with Delribal's Huguenot family near Carcassonne in southern France. As a middle son of a noble family, Delribal had a bleak future in France due to the laws of primogeniture. So like many other impoverished nobles, he went to Saint-Domingue to find fame and fortune. Comte de Bréda had lived in Carcassonne, and like Delribal, he was a Huguenot and knew Delribal's family. Thus, Delribal likely used family ties with the Comte to bolster his colonial ventures and to land the managerial job at Bréda.

This was the man who stood before us slaves on the fateful morning of his introduction. Noticeably absent was Comte de Noé, nursing hurt feelings at his Héricourt Plantation. This meant that he no longer protected Bréda and that Toussaint's moral influence may have shrunk as well. Others besides me sensed these changes, as Michel Lajoie the overseer smirked, while standing next to the slow-speaking Delribal. We knew that this was the day the overseer predicted we would regret.

And regret it we did! Delribal's new order on Bréda was the old order for most other plantations in Saint-Domingue. He decreased slave provision plots for more space to grow sugar cane. Time for social dances (the Calenda) he restricted to Saturdays during the off-season and none during Crop. A new slave code elevated his oppression more. Overseers and drivers had no limits on their use of the whip. For the first time, branding new slaves from Africa became standard on Bréda. Any slave caught munching sugar cane would suffer wearing a steel helmet with slots for eyes and nose but none for mouth. The worst he saved for runaway slaves.

Fugitive slaves threatened the master's authority and his property. Unchecked, these mavericks might unravel the fabric of slavery itself. The more serious danger came from runaways who permanently left the plantations to lead a resistance in isolated communities. Masters feared them because they drew new recruits from the plantations, and raided those same estates for women and portable objects. White authorities knew them as *maroons*, and believed them capable of starting a major slave rebellion. Less alarming were *petits maroons*, fugitive slaves fleeing plantation oppression, but planning to return when conditions improved. These runaways posed no physical menace to a planter but did threaten his "pocketbook," his main reason for being in Saint-Domingue.

Delribal had a whole menu of horrors for a fugitive slave. For his first offense, he would receive a branded Bourbon Lilly (*fleur-de-lis*) on both his cheeks. A second capture would bring amputation of an appendage, starting usually with a finger. Additional arrests would cost him more fingers, ending with his ears. As a last resort, his hamstrings were severed to slow him to a crawl. To enforce his system, Delribal employed the slave-catching *maréchaussée* to bulk up a practically non-existent Bréda slave patrol, and added a pack of vicious hounds to assist their tracking duties. The new rules took immediate effect.

Early one morning, I heard a commotion, as Auntie, John-Pierre, and I prepared for our kitchen duties. We ran outside, joining a crowd of curious slaves. It was Nicholas! Dragged feet-first behind a horse, his captors had arrested him just off Bréda Plantation. Two slave patrolmen dismounted, picked up poor Nicolas, and chained him to a post. Louis our driver warned us to stay away from the victim until after his punishment at sundown.

Beaten, exhausted, and thirsty, Nicolas suffered under a sweltering Caribbean sun. A simple fellow with simple needs, Nicolas was not a runaway, but instead had sought amorous adventures on the nearby Galiffet Plantation with his lover and companionship with their child. Every slave on Bréda knew his habit of sneaking away on Sundays to satisfy his romantic passions, and then returning on Monday mornings before the slave gangs assembled. This had been going on for nearly a year under Bréda's relaxed slave code which Delribal swore to fix. Lajoie and Louis knew that he had no intention of escaping Bréda. But Delribal demanded a quick example of his iron fist; overseer and driver gave him Nicolas.

Frightened Nicolas stood bravely before an audience of his peers late that afternoon. He squirmed and twisted in the grasp of two plantation policemen. Next to them, a red-hot branding iron pulsated, ready for application to a victim. Nicolas grimaced and sobbed, as Delribal himself branded both his cheeks. The smell of Nicolas' burning flesh sickened me. He passed out, but soon revived.

The plantation police taunted Nicolas with remarks that his scarified cheeks made him a member of the French tribe, or that his cooked face might go well with yams. Battered Nicolas staggered to his feet, laughing at their jokes. Then with all his remaining energy, he slowly raised one of his unchained hands, and pointed to smoke curling up from a lowering fire. They laughed, but we got Nicolas' meaning. He had called upon Macandal to avenge his injuries. None of the whites understood his defiance—none, that is, except Delribal who now became worried.

Others followed Nicolas in a parade of torture. Hounds tore one fugitive to shreds. Some lost fingers, others their ears. Severed hamstrings followed for third and fourth offenders. The threat of gruesome punishment only encouraged more slaves to escape. Within four months of assuming the manager's position, Delribal's slave gangs fell to half their normal size and the epidemic grew daily, as escapees entered into petit maroonage. The dark clouds looming over Bréda would one day break over the entire colony.

My eyes are tired and my hand painfully cramped from gripping my pen. It is time for this old man to retire for the evening. In my next letter, I will describe my last years at Bréda before going to Mille Fleurs, your mother's plantation.

Love to My Boys,

Saturday

When Philip finished reading, he saw Wahl shaking with Susan Elizabeth hugging her. Wahl lifted her head, tears streaming down her ancient cheeks. "Oh, my God," Philip muttered, "what have I unleashed? And I believed the old girl was beginning to like me."

"You don't understand, Mr. Philip," as Wahl tried expressing herself. But her words stuck in her throat, like leaves in a drain. Then she stood, turned around, lowered her blouse below her shoulder blades, and displayed an "F" that had been branded into the once velvet smooth flesh of a beautiful woman.

"Don't you see, Mr. Philip? I felt all the bad times in Saturday's letter. Especially did I know about that year of terror on Bréda Plantation. But the slaves on Bréda enjoyed a better life than I did. Every year on Flaville Plantation was a reign of terror for me!

"I once lived in Whydah with my mother, when priests serving the Cult of the Python, swept me up with other young girls, and forced religious instruction on us. After several months of being closeted as devotees to the Sacred Snake, they began returning us to our guardians for a fee. My poor mother could not pay, so they sold me into slavery to retrieve their loss.

"I arrived in Saint-Domingue in 1785, having survived The Middle Passage, only to be sold to Maurice Lebrun, master of Flaville Plantation. When I laid eyes on him, I knew that he wanted me for his bed. My beauty was both my curse and my salvation. That is why he branded a hidden part of my body to leave my appearance unblemished.

"I served Lebrun as his cook and his mistress—right under the nose of his wife, who probably felt relief from her previous sexual obligations, and whose only joy was how drunk she could get. We both were unhappy women because Lebrun sealed off all the sweetness and love that passion should unleash. I hated him.

"The things I saw at Flaville were the Devil's work. Hungry slaves locked into iron helmets for eating sugar cane, runaways branded on their cheeks, an aborting mother giving her unborn child the gift of death rather than life, waiters with pepper-swollen eyes punished for infractions of etiquette, all formed my awful memory of that place. I believed that my only escape was to kill Lebrun, and then poison myself."

An overwhelmed Susan Elizabeth sat down with more information about Wahl than she could absorb. "My God, Wahl, please stop," she begged.

But Wahl continued, "Just when all seemed lost, there was divine intervention. Whether it was Dangbe, Damballa, Jesus, or the Virgin Mary, I don't know. Maybe just luck. My choice is Our Lady of Sorrows, because only her stout shoulders could bear the grief of her Son's crucifixion, and only shoulders that strong could carry mine. The miracle happened in late 1786, when Lebrun demanded my company at the Hôtel de la Couronne in Le Cap, a favorite spot for masters and their mistresses, or for masters searching for the beautiful mulattresses filling lobby and hallways.

"As the evening progressed, Lebrun's interests switched from flesh to gambling in the Wine Room, a huge parlor filled with gaming and billiard tables. Lebrun had a passion for billiards, and considered himself unbeatable, an opinion many shared. Having dispatched several skilled players and winner of a tidy profit, Lebrun looked around and sighted your Uncle Philip, fearless, foolish, and half drunk. Philip was one of the wealthier planters in northern Saint-Domingue, making Lebrun's challenge high: Victory would gain Lebrun five hogsheads of sugar worth ten slaves or more; victory for your uncle would bring him me. The match favored Lebrun, and he only needed one more shot to defeat Philip. And then it happened. Our Lady of Sorrows had seen enough! Lebrun scratched his cue ball, and the triumph went to Philip. I was now his slave!

"Life with your Uncle Philip was not perfect, but better than before. Désirée, his wife, treated me well, and I became her attendant when not cooking. Philip and I only had one indiscretion, and it was as much my doing as his. Mostly, he remained faithful to the woman he loved, but not to me or to Désirée. If a faithful husband in Saint-Domingue has only one mistress at a time, as local saying goes, then Philip was faithful. But to whom?"

Susan Elizabeth and Philip left the kitchen, feeling honored that Wahl had opened her heart to them. Philip, however, sensed that Wahl held something back, but what it was he did not know.

In the depot dining room, Philip and Susan Elizabeth stopped by the window facing The Branch Oak. She amused herself with his game of making its limbs appear to move through the wavy glass. They kissed and moved on.

The Third Letter

Philip seemed lost in thought, as he stood on the freight platform with Susan Elizabeth, watching the Cotton Express rumble by. It hauled cotton bales to mills below Branchville, but most of its cargo headed to Charleston, destined for northern states and England. He had done his duty. He had set the station semaphore to pass the freight through. He felt the train's vibrations, and heard its metal wheels striking rail joints. Nothing, however, disturbed his concentration, not even the smell of acrid smoke trailing the locomotive, draping the depot in a diaphanous veil of ash.

"What's wrong?" said Susan Elizabeth, breaking their silence.

"What happens to the idealism of our youth?" Philip replied. "Slavery is an abomination. I've known it since I escaped the Great Slave Rebellion in Saint-Domingue. I saw bodies everywhere, burning cane fields, big houses in ruins, slaves being whipped, slaves branded like cattle, slaves executed, white and Negro babies mutilated, no hope only fear. That was slavery's legacy to Haiti. It destroyed my world and the world of thousands of slaves. I needed no intellectual treatise on the subject. My friend Bason and constant nightmares were my teachers."

"Bason?" Susan Elizabeth questioned. "Where did he enter in all this? He died before I met you. You seldom mentioned him."

"William Penn Bason was my closest Charleston friend whom I met in his late teens. His father abandoned him when Bason was only ten. He avoided the Orphan House by serving an indenture with Adam Tunno, a wealthy merchant who imported fine wines

61

and slaves. Tunno became so impressed with Bason's business acumen that he established his former servant with his own grogshop on Line Alley."

"So what does this have to do with your convictions about slavery?" Susan Elizabeth quizzed.

"Despite his dapper appearance, slicker than any Charleston dandy, Bason bore both a Quaker name and a Quaker heart," Philip responded. "He refused to leave Charleston when the Society of Friends ordered Quakers to exit South Carolina for the slave-free Midwest. Although no longer a Quaker in good standing, Bason shared the Society's strong anti-slavery position. I spent long nights in his grogshop, listening to his diatribes against slavery."

"So what happened to your anti-slavery convictions?" Susan Elizabeth asked.

"Greed," Philip lamented, "pure greed. I bought slaves to save a failing business. In the end it failed. Worse still, I failed myself."

Philip grew silent. Susan Elizabeth sensed that he had nothing more to say. She took his hand, led him down the freight platform steps, and across the narrow, grassless yard to the depot kitchen. She opened the door, gently ushering Philip into Wahl's domain. Philip smiled, as her warm, aromatic kitchen soothed him, like a child ending his day at his mama's stove, sampling her soup.

"Want some coffee, Mr. Philip and Miz Lizzie?" Wahl asked.

"Miz Lizzie!" Philip exclaimed. "Where did that come from, Wahl?"

Then Philip relaxed and enjoyed the developing friendship between cook and wife. But he still wondered if he and Wahl could ever bridge their differences. Suddenly, he caught them leering at him.

"We're playing with you, Philip," Susan Elizabeth teased, "that's what families do."

"Well, you sullen sisters nearly made me forget the matter at hand," Philip bantered. Leaning against a pie safe, he raised Saturday's third letter, broke its seal, and began reading;

15 Elliott Street, Southside
Charleston
January 3, 1807

Dear Philip and John,

Bréda slaves believed that Delribal's oppression peaked with his new slave code, but he went beyond our wildest predictions. The key to his behavior lay in his panic that some fatal disease would strike him down. There was yellow fever, then Pompey's Disease, followed by dysentery. There might have been more, but he lacked a medical journal. Dr. Truloc calmed his health fears, but not his suspicions that a slave had been poisoning him.

He knew Macandal's story better than most slaves: how Macandal lost his left forearm, suffered demotion to herdsman, learned a witch-woman's poison craft, planned to kill every white in Saint-Domingue, suffered capture and execution, and joined the loas protecting slaves in the very smoke curling skyward from the fire that had roasted him. Most slaves held this belief as part of their voodoo faith, and so did Delribal; only theirs rested on spiritual conviction, his on fear of revenge.

Guests at Delribal's table only accelerated his fears. The quality of table conversation diminished dramatically with the absence of Comte de Noé, Bayon de Libertat, and even the Gillys. Those now at our manager's repast held disgusting opinions about slaves: Turpin believed them soulless; the manager of Galiffet Plantation prescribed applying pork brine to wounds of freshly whipped slaves to deepen their pain; Nicolas Le Jeune supported the master's total power, later acting on his argument, when he tortured and murdered some of his own slaves.

For me, dinner time became a dreaded occasion. I had the distasteful task of standing behind Delribal's chair and attending his needs. Silently, I repeated Papa Toussaint's proverb: "Obey the rules of slavery but never accept it." Obedience was getting harder, and Toussaint never said when it should end; Anansi the clever spider now wanted to become Anansi the deadly spider. But I performed my duties as Auntie demanded, even listening to such tripe as Odeloc's that slaves on his Galiffet Plantation were happy, and that punishment made them love him more.

Invariably conversations shifted to a slave poisoning his master, his master's family, and even other slaves. Those around Delribal's table found it amusing when he became overwrought on the subject. They described every ghastly detail, saving the best for last: A poisoner might kill everyone on the plantation, saving the master for last to witness his own financial ruin. Financial ruin! Delribal cringed every time.

Had other events not coincided with Delribal's obsession about poisoning, this tempest might have blown itself out. But we were not so lucky. Several of Bréda's draft animals perished, including two oxen and a horse. Papa Toussaint had veterinary skills and told Delribal that drought conditions probably killed the oxen, and that overeating likely killed the horse. Delribal remained unconvinced.

A conspiracy to poison him grew in Delribal's mind. When Louis the husbandman reported several animals dead or missing, his fear deepened, and he arrested Louis for interrogation. When torture failed to loosen Louis' tongue, Delribal sent his shepherd to Le Cap, where authorities subjected Louis to a more professional cross-examination. Battered, humiliated, and hopeless, Louis committed suicide without revealing the plot that Delribal desperately sought to uncover. He cursed the constable of Le Cap as inept, swearing that in the future, his own officials would conduct torture. So Delribal ordered a chamber of horrors built on Bréda to his cruel specifications.

The Spanish Inquisition would have been proud: a rack for stretching body parts until joints separated and bones cracked; thumbscrews for tightening until pain knocked a victim out; a charcoal brazier where glowing-tipped pokers awaited the tender skin of the accused; an assortment of whips, each specifically designed for human damage. If these instruments failed, the inquisitor always had the sweat box. This all metal house had dimensions of eight feet by eight feet and four feet high, keeping its occupant cramped and unable to stand. Its front door could only be unfastened from the outside, and on the door were tiny slits for food, water, and conversation. Builders placed their human cooker to catch the full sun. Those entering this metal contraption either died, or suffered lifelong physical and mental damage.

Plantation panic spread when André, one of the drivers, failed to answer his morning call to duty. Members of his slave gang found him dead. He showed no outward signs of a struggle but his tormented facial expression, bulging eyes, and a saliva-soaked shirt from a frothing mouth, all suggested that someone poisoned him. Even Toussaint acknowledged this, but most of us believed that André probably fell victim to his own amorous misdeeds. As sensible as this seemed, Delribal disagreed and deepened his resolve to uncover the plot aimed at ending his life.

Delribal offered his dwindling slave gang a reward for anyone supplying information about the conspiracy. He would also award personal freedom to anyone stepping forward and "fingering" the evildoers. Never would we have reported a fellow slave for poisoning, and most would have embraced our own deaths to escape this place. So Delribal continued chasing the shadows of a non-existent plot.

Unfortunately a shadow fell across Auntie. Armand, food supplier for Auntie's kitchen, became entangled in Delribal's web of suspicion. Our crazed manager reasoned that Armand had delivered poison to the kitchen hidden in baskets of fruits and vegetables. He further deduced that Auntie, as kitchen cook, had ample opportunity to distribute toxins to his food. There could be no doubt; Delribal believed himself on Death's highway.

When armed guards hauled Armand to the torture chamber, Jean-Pierre, Papa Toussaint, and I knew that trouble headed our way. Two days later, Armand returned to Auntie's kitchen unmarked and emotionally unchanged. Now we became deeply apprehensive. Had he given names to his tormentors to escape their evil hands? We suspected that he had placed Auntie's name on Delribal's list of conspirators. Our dear Auntie! Convinced of Armand's treachery, Jean-Pierre became enraged and challenged him with a kitchen knife. Toussaint stepped between them, calming his son, pointing out that any attack on Armand would confirm Auntie's guilt in Delribal's eyes. Our only chance was to wait, and pray for God's intercession.

Where was God the night Michel Lajoie the overseer and two armed policemen arrived at our hut to arrest Auntie? Auntie seemed at peace, almost as if she expected this moment. She offered no resistance, because she sought to protect her boys and her neighbors who shared our love for this kind, generous woman. Quietly she boarded their carriage, and headed toward the plantation jail near the torture chamber. Even Delribal knew the danger of arresting this slave mama and inciting an uprising, so he ordered foot-mufflers for his carriage horses to prevent disturbing those sleeping.

Jean-Pierre and I were stunned. Debribal snatched our Auntie from under our very noses. Although Auntie begged our compliance with her arrest, why had we not attempted her rescue? We were cowards! We looked at each other, dried our tears, and knew instinctively what cowards do best. We ran. To the mile or so to Toussaint's cottage, we ran all the way.

I fell often, as a moonless night made our pathway treacherous. But each time that I fell, Jean-Pierre yanked me to my feet, displaying his enormous strength. We collapsed on Papa Toussaint's door, pushing it open, as we fell into a lighted room. There sat Toussaint at a table with a lantern casting shadows across his face, giving him the severity of a sitting judge. We wondered his ruling on our behavior. We told Toussaint about Auntie's arrest, as well as our failure to save her. He considered our comments, rolled his eyes toward the ceiling, and then brought them down staring straight into the windows of our souls. Were we guilty of failing Auntie?

His response surprised us. No, we were neither cowards nor

fools. Had we defended Auntie, results could have been devastating. Sure, we may have killed a plantation policeman, or even incited a slave riot which might have killed Delribal, but we would have lost. French colonial soldiers would have occupied Bréda and imposed martial law. Riot ringleaders (he meant us) would face summary execution. Military authorities would not stop there: They would have dispersed the Bréda slaves to plantations with reputations for mistreatment. So he consoled us, commenting that he had plans to save Auntie and stop Delribal. The best way to destroy that beast was to use the instruments of slavery against him. What did Papa mean? Like Anansi, he wove too much deception.

We talked deep into the night about Auntie. Toussaint believed her innocent of poisoning Delribal, and that interrogators could only establish motive, proving nothing since most of Bréda's slaves felt the same. Then Toussaint shared stories about Auntie which we never knew: how as a young cook on the Ducrosse Plantation she aborted her baby to avoid interrupting massah's meals; how the love of her life fell into a vat of molten sugar cane juice and died; how Madame Ducrosse had two slaves hold her in place, while she rubbed peppers in her eyes for serving her guests poorly baked pastries. It amazed us that Auntie still had a heart full of love for those around her.

With Toussaint's reassurance of Auntie's rescue, Jean-Pierre and I fell into an exhausted sleep. My sleep ended when boney fingers shook me awake. I thought it Auntie, but it was Toussaint, telling Jean-Pierre and me to hurry to Auntie's hut before the conch shell sounded and our absence discovered. We had a half hour to get there. We arrived in fifteen minutes.

Our tired bodies betrayed our hard night, as we entered Auntie's kitchen. Renée, Delribal's new cook from Millot Plantation, greeted us, dipping my and Jean-Pierre's spirits below our physical appearances. Her presence made me miss Auntie more. When we walked between kitchen and big house, Jean-Pierre and I would glance toward the torture chamber, and swear that we heard Auntie's screams. We wanted to run to her, and it took all our self-control to restrain ourselves. Papa Toussaint emphasized that such demonstrations would only make matters worse for Auntie, ending in our arrests. Warriors follow orders, he reminded us.

A distant tinkling bell signaled to those in the kitchen that Delribal demanded his breakfast in bed. I volunteered to deliver it, not sure if I would kill him or not. I loaded the silver service with all his delights: a pot of coffee, French pastries, a poached egg, squeezed orange juice with seeds removed, and a cup of vinegar for purging his system. When I entered his chamber, he had a lit lamp on each side of his bed, and warned me not to adjust his closed shutters. He waited for the full morning sun to burn off dangerous vapors from the previous night. My attention passed to his double, canopied bed which he alone occupied. No woman in Saint-Domingue wanted to share it, not even a mulattress seeking fortune and comfort. The only things next to Delribal were several large ledger books that he desperately sought to stop dipping in red ink for the summation of his balances.

He shoved his account books off his lap, and bade me to sit by his bed while he ate. He talked about Auntie, swearing that he only sought her best interests. She was sick, he added, and wished only for her recovery. Currently, those charged with Auntie's care had quarantined her. He knew that Jean-Pierre, Zèbre, and I missed her, and would order her "attendants" to let us visit her after our daily duties. He wore a smirk just like Captain Leclerc's before I bit him. The son-of-a-bitch had gone from sarcasm to sadism in the same breath. He seemed to relish my torment and servility. With serving tray in hand, I turned like a helpless fool, bowed, and backed out of his bedroom. Toussaint's plan needed quick execution, or else I might slit Delribal's throat.

More trouble brewed at dinner that night. All appeared normal, as we set Delribal's table, and brought in a cask of Madiera wine. At that point, Delribal entered the room with a large wine goblet, and began filling the vessel with Madeira. Then he ordered his waiters to their places at his table. He handed me the goblet first, made me take a deep swallow, passed it to the next waiter, refilled the chalice, and kept it going until everyone had partaken in what I called "The Devil's Communion." Since none of us hesitated, or showed signs of poisoning, he began laughing and said that we were the first niggers he ever served fine Madeira. His guests began arriving soon after, and he maintained a cheerful mood during the entire meal. A good host perhaps, but we became convinced of his insanity.

After the guests left, Jean-Pierre, Zèbre, and I hurried to Auntie and discovered the depth of Delribal's evil. As we walked into the chamber of horrors, Lajoie greeted us, and said that he attended Auntie, but that she had been a "bad girl" for rejecting treatment. His mocking behavior matched that of Delribal's earlier. But where was Auntie? We had expected to find her in chains, yet her disappearance alarmed us more.

"Not to worry, my little visitors" were the words falling from Lajoie's mouth, adding to our torment. He led us to the sweat box, where a terrified Auntie lay incarcerated. He knocked on the box, announced us, and said that Doctor Delribal would allow us thirty minutes with his patient.

We wailed, as if standing before the tomb of Jesus, but Auntie's sweet voice drifted through our tears. She calmed us, and we took turns talking to Auntie through the slits in the sweat box. Such strength she had, when we verged on coming apart! She told us to be proud, strong, and never surrender to Satan's minions. Someday God's Might would overcome the forces of sin. For now, we must endure the pain of slavery, but follow Toussaint's good advice. Then she promised us that she would soon be in her kitchen with her boys. We knew that she lied to keep us from attacking her guards.

When my turn came, I reached through the slit with my right hand, extending my finger tips until they touched Auntie's chubby fingers. Then she rubbed her cheeks against my fingers, and I felt tears flooding her face. But when I pulled my hand back, blood and not tears covered it. Our beloved Auntie was dying!

When Lajoie ended our visit, I felt the tension in Jean-Pierre's muscles, as he leaned on me to stand up. He crouched, preparing to attack Lajoie like a tree-bound leopard. Only instinct guided him, and the time was right. I'll never know how Zèbre and I got him away from the sweat box without his engaging Lajoie in a fight. We left on the overseer's order for us not to return until Auntie's release.

The walk to Auntie's hut was agonizing. Silently, we nursed an individual grief, as if Auntie belonged only to each of us. There was truth in our selfishness. She made her love so personal. When we stepped inside, Toussaint sat at a table, waiting for "Auntie's boys."

Only twice did I ever see worry on Papa's face. This was the first; the second was on the eve of the Great Slave Rebellion of 1791. He made us tell him about "The Devil's Communion," my serving Delribal's breakfast, and our visit with Auntie. My comments about Delribal's ledgers sparked an idea in Toussaint. He told us to take only the clothes on our backs, and make an inconspicuous exodus to his cabin. Stay there because the plantation police probably would soon be at Auntie's kitchen to make our arrests. Instead, he would deliver Delribal's breakfast tray.

The next morning Toussaint entered Debribal's bedroom with his food, gaining a clever impromptu interview with the plantation manager. I will never know exactly what transpired, but if Debribal respected any man on Bréda, it was Papa Toussaint. A business discussion followed in which Papa's deal likely raised Delribal's eyebrows. Toussaint's semi-free status permitted him to own slaves whom he trained to become coachmen. He would sell two, one to Millot Plantation and the other to Clement Plantation. With these combined sums, he would purchase Jean-Pierre and me from Bréda. Zèbre and his pregnant mother he would deal to the Mille Fleurs Plantation, where the Chaillot family needed a waiter. Toussaint convinced Delribal that these shrewd transactions would put black ink in ledgers mostly recorded in red. Profit! There could be no better way for Delribal to slow Comte de Bréda's wrath over his plantation's financial crisis. Delribal snapped up Papa's bargain.

A good judge of human character, Toussaint knew that once Delribal had his money, he would be like Pharaoh and not let his slaves go. So he acted forthwith. That morning, Toussaint drove Zèbre and his mother to Mille Fleurs. Jean-Pierre and I were sad, but relieved to see him go. When night fell, Papa Toussaint stood watch, while we slept. Later that evening, a stranger knocked and entered his cottage. Our arrests seemed at hand, causing Jean-Pierre and me to head toward a window to escape.

Papa Toussaint stopped us, but our terror left us trembling. He then introduced us to Canga, a maroon leader with a long history of hiding in the tropical forests above the plantations on the North Plain. Now and then, he and his band would sweep down and attack those same plantations, and then beat a quick retreat before local authorities could respond. These men were like trapping shadows, for they became invisible by day and like wild dogs by night. Toussaint told us to follow Canga into the interior. Stay by him. Learn from him. As soon as Bréda got rid of Delribal, he would send for us. He planned advertising in *Affiches Américaines*, Le Cap's main newspaper, that we were fugitives and post a reward for our capture. Toussaint's trick probably convinced Delribal of how lucky he had been to sell us before our escape, and that Toussaint had not deceived him.

Into the night, Jean-Pierre and I followed our new guardian, stumbling over roots and falling on pebble beds. Our guide led us up a dry creek into the steep hills above Bréda. Branches whipped back on our flesh, thorns tore our clothes, and our eyes strained to look into an unyielding darkness. Fatigue swelled our legs and ankles. Thirty minutes of this made us regret leaving the comforts of Toussaint's cottage.

But Canga moved with the deftness of an animal native to the bush. Lean and long of body, Canga seemed always sniffing the air, as he listened for enemy sounds. He expressed most of his conversations in hand motions, but when he spoke his manner was curt and his words few. His face was sun wrinkled, making him appear older than his age. Almost animal-like, he used his basic instincts to drive his behavior: Hunger made him steal, anger caused him to attack, fear made him retreat, and he would choose death over capture. He had been a maroon for twenty years, and he might have been born to a wild sow as to a woman. He was a human boar, his tusks a brace of pistols, and his targets those who would enslave him.

Up, up, up, we ascended until the creek bed became narrow. I thought we had walked at least two miles; actually only half that, when Canga halted us. We were far enough from Toussaint's cottage to avoid the plantation police. Canga took a rope from his tote-pouch, made a circle with it on the ground, reclined in its center, and motioned us to join him. We huddled together, our body heat warding off the chilling night. The rope deterred crawling and slithering creatures from joining our company. In the morning, we would ascend to the craggy outposts of Morne du Cap, overlooking North Plain.

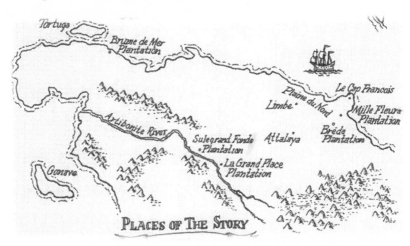

Map by Tim Stevenson

72

This first night made memorable impressions on me: So close was I to two other humans that I recalled the hold of a slave ship with my friend Èji; so dark that the only light came from twinkling stars, like tiny diamonds strewn across a black velvet cloth; so soothing that night sounds made me feel that I enjoyed God's serenade; so secure that I was beyond Delribal's reach; so sad that I did not know Auntie's fate.

As we trekked further up a mountain trail, Canga relaxed more, as we entered a tropical forest. He was in his briar patch, and no flat land hound had better follow. I saw uncultivated fruit trees, providing more than enough for Canga and his men to survive. Approaching Canga's camp, we encountered fierce dogs straining on ropes and acting as baying sentinels. About five hundred yards beyond these snarling mutts, earthen mounds stood with pits containing sharpened stakes fronting each. Behind these redoubts, small huts fronted a canebrake. Should they face assault, a rear guard would goad attackers into a charge, causing them to fall into the pits. Meanwhile, the main body of maroons would scatter behind a bamboo curtain.

On our first night in camp, Canga explained dangers Jean-Pierre and I faced and how to evade them. The maréchaussée posed our greatest threat. Officered largely by whites, this mounted unit of free blacks and mulattoes attacked maroons and other fugitive slaves with brutal enthusiasm. They so coveted the station of big whites that they took their ambitions to a cruel parody, fostering a popular proverb: "To be a slave of a mulatto was usually fatal." Avoid open space, Canga advised, because they fancied themselves as elite cavalry, and loved cutting down fleeing victims. The maréchaussée received a salary and collected a bounty for each branding initial that they sliced off a dead African slave, or the left ear off a creole one. He further warned against riding a horse, as it offended the maréchaussée. Only gentlemen, they believed, should ride horses, and any slave or maroon on one would gain their attention faster than a hawk on a sparrow.

Canga emphasized ways to avoid the maréchaussée: Travel in small groups of two or three, crawl when approaching a road or path, move by night and remain still by day, and finally, carry a forged master's letter for permission to travel. The best method of evasion, however, was blending. A maroon could slip into and out of any plantation if he acted like a slave. If trapped, bed down in a slave's hut, join the work gang the next morning, seek the fringes of a field, roll into the bush, and find a nearby hill or mountain for safety. He chuckled that when you see the white-necked crow you will have escaped, because that bird avoided the cultivated fields of plantations.

Canga added that he had a keen rivalry with Captain Gaspard Ardisson of the local maréchaussée. Outfitted in an all-white uniform lined with green taffeta, polished copper buttons, and a gold-hilted sword, the captain boasted to his superiors that he would have Canga's head on a pike in two weeks. Six months now, Canga smiled, and still no head for Gaspard.

Canga warned us to stay ready for frequent movements from one base camp to another. Maroons must guard against the laziness of convenience. This was why Monsieur Gaspard bladed only the air so far. Canga planned to operate in the radius of a hundred miles, making forays as far south as Jean Pebarte's Sulegrand Fonds. This fine coffee plantation with over a thousand slaves stood above the Artibonite River, near a Canga base camp. We would gather food there, visit favorite slave women, and even attend voodoo meetings. He laughed, adding that all blacks look like slaves. He finished by promising our protection but not at the expense of his band. Should one or both of us die, it would be for a good cause. He also promised Toussaint our return to near Le Cap after Bréda Plantation cooled off.

After a short rest, our journey began again. Jean-Pierre and I each received a cane knife and two leather pouches, one of pepper and one of poison. Should the hounds of the maréchaussée pursue us, we would sprinkle pepper to confuse their scent; failing this,

74

we would poison the dogs. As a last resort, we would poison ourselves to avoid capture. We carried no firearms, as they were in short supply.

A few days from Canga's mountain stronghold, we approached the road to Le Cap near Bréda. As we hid in heavy undergrowth to make a safe crossing, I saw a large carriage wheel by with two footmen in attendance. It was Delribal on his way to Le Cap! Canga put one hand on my shoulder and his other on Jean-Pierre's to keep us from attacking that evil man and exposing our position. Be patient, he reminded us, for our retribution against Delribal was coming.

By early nightfall, we crossed the road, heading south along the east bank of the Rivière du Haut du Cap. This route took us through swamps and bogs and out of sight of the maréchaussée. There were, however, two enemies: swarms of blood-sucking mosquitoes and hungry crocodiles. To remedy the mosquito problem, Canga offered me a homemade solution smelling like manure on a wallowing dog. I refused, but later accepted it. The mosquitoes began driving me mad, and I finally applied Canga's repellent. Had it been hog shit, I still would have used it. Saint-Domingue had no poisonous snakes, but crocodiles made up for their absence. To avoid them, Canga instructed us to stay clear from the edges of swamp ponds and lagoons.

Once we reached Ducrosse Plantation, we turned due east, approaching a second road to Le Cap and the Rivière Commerce. Here, burrowed in a grassy field, we spotted a small maréchaussée patrol. It was Captain Gaspard Ardisson with an escort of ten mounted men. Temptation overcame Canga, as he deployed his maroons to ambush the escort. Showing only enough force to bait his trap, Canga and five other widely spaced maroons sprang up, while the rest remained concealed.

Captain Ardisson thought he saw a foolish prey, aligned his men for a charge, peered through his spyglass, and recognized Canga. Sword drawn, he ordered a charge that would harvest his hated enemy's head. But Canga anticipated Captain Ardisson's rash response. By deploying half his men in front of a swamp to take the cavalry charge, our human boar braced for the fight. As the cavalry rode by, other maroons rose from the grass on either side of horse and rider, slashing with knives and machetes at the legs of passing steeds. This ancient infantry tactic against cavalry, the maroons had learned from their struggle to survive and not from history books.

Suddenly, Captain Ardisson realized that he was trapped. Then with one of his escorts dropping from his saddle, he charged Canga who waited to a split second before dropping behind a log. The captain's horse leaped as if clearing a low hurdle, while Canga rolled on his back, firing both his pistols at the airborne captain. For all his cunning, Canga was a poor shot, but one pistol ball struck Ardisson's shoulder, as his leaping stallion flipped in the muck. Sailing into the pond, the terrified captain landed amidst a log jam of floating crocodiles. No man ever moved faster through waist-deep water, and with a desperate lunge he reached shore before a pair of snapping jaws nearly retired him from the maréchaussée. Crawling to a safe distance from his amphibious attackers, the exhausted captain rolled over, bloody and muck-covered, awaiting the executioner's blade. But Canga knew better. The captain's escort had fled seeking reinforcements. Any delay might bring destruction to his band. So he ordered a retreat to his outpost near Pebarte's coffee plantation. A weary and muddy Captain Ardisson could keep his head for another day.

Canga, Yaya, Jean-Pierre and I moved into deep brush across the road. Yaya was Canga's son and about the same age as Jean-Pierre. He was thin, narrow shouldered, but with a youthful, friendly face and a brightness in his eyes that reflected a willingness to learn his father's skills. Although a piglet now, one day he would become another tough boar that the maréchaussée rarely rooted out. Jean-Pierre admired both father and son, and became envious of their adventurous life.

We headed toward our destination by climbing the slopes above the Artibonite Valley. Canga knew that the valley roads were easier, but oft-patrolled by a maréchaussée too lazy for mountain trails. The going got tough. I frequently slipped on pathways tilting to the contour of the slopes and slick with moisture. When we reached the northern end of The Montagne Terrible, Saint-Domingue's highest mountain, I learned how to walk across a log over a gorge. A steady wind swept the higher reaches, defoliating scrub cedars on their windward sides. This same force could blow a novice off a fallen tree trunk if he did not lean into the stout winds. Damp cold kept us moving, because huddled bodies could not prevent its assault on our persons. With Canga's other maroons, we finally positioned ourselves above Pebarte's coffee plantation and prepared for night forays against it for food, tools, weapons, and women.

Veterans went first. They ventured in pairs down the rocky slopes at dusk, using coffee trees, brush piles, wagons, outbuildings, and even slave huts for cover. The more skilled maroon at avoiding detection raided the coffee warehouses where piles of red and green pods gave concealment until he reached the processing area for drying coffee beans. Careful to avoid greed, he shoveled several handfuls into a pouch, and spread remaining beans over the bare spot left by his theft. Stealth got him in and stealth got him out. As Canga schooled, he left by a different route and abandoned his partner to fend for himself. Losing one man was bad, two much worse.

The other less experienced maroon split off from his partner and dropped into a drainage ditch for directing mountain rainwater away from Pebarte's plantation. He followed its course to the slave huts near this dry canal. In the first hut, resided big house cook Chéri with her young daughter Henriette. They were trusted accomplices. Because of her duties, foods stockpiled in Chéri's hut did not raise the overseer's suspicions. The forager arrived there unnoticed, collected his food in a sack, slipped around the hut, received his cargo which Chéri shoved through a hole in her rear wall, and returned to camp using the dry ditch for exit. Had he been trapped, he would have remained in Chéri's hut overnight, risen with the field slaves the next morning, and used them to conceal his escape. This "blending tactic" had a record of success.

Maroon duos trekked daily down the mountain slopes to Pebarte's plantation. There were no discoveries and no injuries, prompting Canga's decision to give his novices a try. Calling for Yaya and Jean-Pierre, he informed them that they would pair for the next mission. Elated in Canga's confidence in him, Jean-Pierre joined his new friend, as they left camp to their targets below, fulfilling their assignments like clockwork. Jean-Pierre's maneuvers to gather food at Chéri's had the mark of a veteran. When they returned to camp, Canga ceremoniously handed Jean-Pierre a pistol for conducting himself so well, an award usually reserved for seasoned warriors.

I came next. Canga himself partnered with me, realizing that his skills might be needed to guide me through my initial task. He was right. He moved down the mountainside ahead of me, as the half-fallen sun surrendered to night behind a distant ridge. He drifted out of sight, as he headed toward the coffee warehouses. I was on my own!

I hid behind whatever was handy: low palm fronds and banana trees being my favorites. Once concealed, however, I had to marshal all my courage to scurry to the next bush or tree on my way to the drainage ditch. Like a burrowing rabbit, I just knew that moments of exposure had revealed me to plantation guards, or worse to the maréchaussée. With sweat soaking my clothing, I finally reached the embankment-sheltered canal, my highway to Chéri's. Even here, I cautiously picked my way, always ready to flatten myself on the ground should I spot someone ascending the ditch. How did Jean-Pierre do this with such ease?

Slaves at Pebarte's plantation were in from the fields when I arrived at Chéri's door. Inside I met Chéri and Henriette, her twelve-year-old daughter. Mama looked to be a woman in her late twenties, pretty, shapely, with a nearly perfect coal-black complexion. She seemed amused at my ruffled appearance, and at my handing her a sack soaked with my perspiration. She stuffed yams into it, and placed the bag in the rear of her hut, ready for her to jettison it to me once I was outside and in position. Then she laughingly gave me a nickname: her "Littlest Maroon."

So far, so good, but I still had to exit through Chéri's front entrance to get to the rear of her hut. With nothing in my hands, I would look like any other plantation slave. Leaning out, I stuck one eye beyond the door frame. I froze! Close by were two white men, probably the plantation manager and the overseer. I jumped back. Chéri consoled me by saying that she would check on what was happening, but returned with a disquieting report: Three slaves had escaped. The manager ordered his slave catchers into action. He also notified the maréchaussée. Damn my luck!

Chéri told me to spend the night and use blending to escape. She would stay in or near her hut until time for her and Henriette to attend their kitchen duties. It would be night then, and I could hide under a blanket in the rear of her hut. Even a plantation guard's shining lantern would miss my presence amid all the casting shadows. But I had to remain motionless until she returned. Her instructions were clear, but my confidence was low.

Meanwhile, I stayed close to mother and daughter until time came for them to leave. For a distraction, I began noticing Henriette's budding beauty that probably would bloom into a gorgeous rose like her mother. Desire for her boiled in my veins, but not returned. Every time we made eye contact, she turned her head away, as if she wished someone else might take my place. I was such a beginner: not quite a maroon and not quite a lover.

Time came for them to leave and for me to hide under a blanket. I heard their footfalls, first loud and then fading, as they walked to the plantation kitchen. I tried to remain motionless, but found this impossible, as cramping required me to shift my position. Every sound outside Chéri's hut shivered my spine. Any moment, a plantation guard's heavy hand might yank my camouflage away, bringing me to a terrible end. I even imagined my severed head for others to see considering desertion from the plantation. I felt a bolt of terror when my nest was finally exposed, but it was Chéri's soft touch, announcing her return.

After our meal and short conversations, we prepared for bed. Even in darkness, Henriette undressed behind me, because she did not want me to glimpse her silhouette. Chéri bedded down near her door, guarding against anyone's sudden entrance. I bunked in the rear of the same room, and Henriette slept in a small adjoining alcove. I fell asleep praying for Auntie and for my own safety.

Soon after, a hand slipped over my mouth, and a woman's sweet whisper asked my silence. It was Chéri! She lifted my blanket and slid next to me, her warm body against mine. Her firm breasts and erect nipples rubbed my chest, arousing my passion. With groping fingers, she found my manhood, causing her to tease that she might have to reconsider my nickname. Then she rolled on top of me, and her willing thighs performed the rest.

For those denied a childhood, first sex is more memorable than first kiss. Chéri launched me like a comet across the night sky, a night fraught with fear of discovery, serving to heighten my rising crescendo of sensual gratification, so that even Eros might have blushed. What a ride! I could not decide which was worse: my capture by a plantation patrol or an enraged Henriette finding me with her mother. In any event, neither happened, and Chéri returned to her bed. I am still grateful for her generosity. She took nothing from me, because my childhood wonderland ended with my enslavement.

Next morning, I arose before reveille to wait for slave assembly, reinforced by a hug from Chéri, and shamed by Henriette's suspicious stare. When the slave gang filed by Chéri's door, I joined them until I ducked behind Chéri's hut, grabbed the bag of yams, and jumped the embankment bordering the dry ditch. Like a small merchant ship in dangerous waters, I set sail to ascend the drainage ditch to Canga's camp.

I rode a calm sea until I saw about three hundred yards below me a hurrying man, whip in hand, like a frigate in full sail. Despite all the canvas that I unfurled, he kept gaining; soon we would engage in a battle that I could not win. I spun around with my cane knife to inflict what damage I could, when Canga swooped down from a bank in a cloud of dust, pistol in one hand and blade in the other. He had trapped my pursuer as slick as a royal ship falling in behind a pirate's corsair. The hunter had become the hunted.

Canga had hidden all night behind Chéri's hut. My guardian had witnessed the man following me. So he trailed him, and reacted to his apparent attack on me. My alarmed stalker dropped his whip. His name was Renaud and a driver on Pebarte's plantation. He swore that he meant me no harm, and knew that I was a maroon. He saw me carrying a sack, scaling a levee, and descending into the drainage ditch. Slaves rarely carried sacks, especially not in the morning, and especially not seeking exit from the plantation. He followed me to join the maroons. He felt heartsick about injuries that he had inflicted upon Pebarte's slaves, and sought redemption by serving the maroons.

Canga bought his story, perhaps because killing Renaud without just cause might frighten recruits from joining his band. But Renaud bore watching. A veteran maroon would shadow his every move to guarantee that he was not Pebarte's spy. For further safety, Canga ordered that we break our camp and move near another of Pebarte's plantations in the Artibonite Valley. We had stayed too long, and Renaud's desertion possibly alerted Sulegrand Fonds that maroons were nearby, making Canga apply his "laziness of convenience" rule. Renaud's loyalty to our leader over time made the annoyance of changing camps worth it.

We encamped on high ground above Pebarte's La Grand Place in Mirebalais Parish, where waving green cane fields provided better concealment than the more open coffee plantations. This position moved us further north and closer to Bréda Plantation, still far away. Homesickness overtook me, as I tormented over Auntie's fate. Then I heard cheering sounds of distant drums rhythmically beating out invitations to the Chica and the Calenda, favorite slave social dances, but my soul needed feeding first. Observing my mood, Canga invited me to a voodoo ceremony down in the valley.

Canga, Yaya, Jean-Pierre and I reached the outer limits of Pebarte's plantation. The lush growth and poor vision led me to wonder if Canga knew his destination. Then breaking into a clearing, we saw a low fire surrounded by jungle forest. There we joined other slaves from Pebarte's work force. In the center of this nocturnal gathering stood a tall man dressed in red, wearing a red bandanna and blue sash. He served as the *papa-loi* (*houngan*), or high priest, accompanied by a female *mama-loi*, or high priestess. Like her male counterpart, she wore mostly red, symbolic color of voodoo. Sometimes these servitors called themselves "king" and "queen."

No drum beats beckoned us, because snooping masters, their managers, or the maréchaussée might discover the meeting's location. White leaders suspected that these secret meetings could turn slaves against their masters, or even spark a rebellion. This explained the papa-loi's troubled look as he approached us, but he gave a broad grin when he recognized Canga. His old maroon friend had arrived to celebrate their ceremony, make an offering of coffee stolen from Pebarte's plantation, and spend time with Rose, his "best girl."

Now certain of their security, the voodoo faithful continued their ceremony. The papa-loi removed a cage containing a boa from an improvised altar, placed it on the ground, and put his foot on its lid to gain the sacred snake's spiritual strength. Touching the mama-loi's hand, he transmitted the serpent's gift to her, while she shook the cage, making attached bells tinkle to heighten her power. Soon she fell into a trance, while Damballa the snake loa spoke through her. Worshippers lined up to ask her questions, leave offerings, gain advice, and receive her blessings. Sometimes she flattered a person beseeching her aid, and sometimes she scolded him. Most wanted her intervention into their lives: a jealous lover seeking revenge, a barren woman wanting a baby, a mother begging her sick child's recovery, a slave imploring Damballa to grant him control over his master, and my entreating for Auntie's deliverance. With supplicant needs met, voodoo dancing began.

It commenced without drum accompaniment. The dancers slowly and rhythmically promenaded in a circle, intensifying with each rotation until they burst into a frenzied peak, some wiggling like snakes, others flicking their tongues reptile-style and hissing, and still others shaking and trembling in an unconscious state. These last worshippers were in Damballa's possession, known in voodoo as a "loa riding his horse."

The Calenda followed. This social dance was a favorite among slaves, and provided a deception against any spying eyes viewing their gathering. Now the voodoo votaries broke out their drums, sounding out sensuous rhythms. The Calenda used two drums, as performers formed two lines facing each other, one female and the other male. The player of the larger drum picked up the dance beat, while the player of the smaller drum tapped out a far more rapid beat, generating passion in the dancers. And passion there was! Clapping spectators surrounded the dancers, chanting a refrain to the male lead who composed a spontaneous, bantering song. The lines advanced toward each other, skipping and turning left and right in perfect cadence with the music. Closer and closer they came, and further and further they retreated in time with the drums. But with every new advance, the nearer the two lines approached each other until they struck thighs, and retired with a pirouette to their original positions to do it all again. Their synchronized movements would have pleased a choreographer.

After a long night of social dances, Yaya ordered Jean-Pierre and me to return to our mountain camp. He added that Canga would join us the next morning. Jean-Pierre and I chuckled. We had seen neither Canga nor Rose for nearly an hour, and assumed that they had found a spot for romance. Canga's weakness for women would later prove fatal for this ghostly legend.

83

Like an old boar that had inexhaustibly spread his seeds the night before, Canga struggled through bushes surrounding our camp, slumped down before the breakfast fire, and took a cup of Pebarte's coffee. Canga had a euphoric demeanor and kept laughing and smiling, as he yawned and stretched. His love for this Rose would never wilt.

Late afternoon shadows fell over our camp before Canga arose from his bed, ready to assume command. On his signal, Jean-Pierre and I joined his band for his instructions. We dared not continue following the Rivière du Artibonite, because, as Canga pointed out, the valley had become too wide and adjacent mountains too low for safe cover. This included us not attacking the de Rossignol family plantations on the Rivière du Ester, especially L'Etable. We had to pass them up. Too much open space, giving the maréchaussée an advantage, and too many alligators on the approaches to L'Etable ruled out a night raid. Ending his short commentary, he ordered us into higher mountains, setting a course north and west of the Plaine du Nord to the village of Limbé, then turning east to Morne du Haut du Cap overlooking Le Cap, near Bréda Plantation. We would stay together until Attalaya, and then break into separate four-man squads to follow the Rivière du Limbé north to Limbé. Jean-Pierre and I would accompany Canga and Yaya because of dangerous low country above Attalaya.

Crossing the mountains along the Rivière du Artibonite to Attalaya tested my nerve to cling to ledges above steep ravines. Our journey crept, as Canga taught Jean-Pierre and me to stand motionless to know Nature's sounds, and sounds of intruding humans. Animals will scurry into hiding when noisy humans invade their domain, and so did we. No wonder Canga seemed like a ghost to the maréchaussée.

Several weeks passed before we reached Attalaya to break into small squads to follow the Rivière du Limbé north. Near the village of Limbé, we turned east and passed through dangerous open ground. We slept by day and moved by night, like nocturnal animals avoiding daytime predators. Our most dangerous incident came when we crawled close to the western road from Le Cap and waited for the cover of darkness to cross. Several maréchaussée patrols passed our hiding place, and one commander wore a white uniform, dangling a sword from his hip in a golden hilt. It was Captain Gaspard Ardisson! But our old boar did not stir. My and Jean-Pierre's safety were his only concerns.

Upon reaching the heights of Morne du Haut du Cap, I was bone tired, but Canga denied us rest. He ordered a new campsite since the maréchaussée might be at our old one, waiting there in ambush. Not until we had dug pits, implanted them with sharpened stakes, caught and tied wild dogs near our battlements, and built crude huts, could we rest. By then, I could not sleep and sought a stony crag overlooking Le Cap and its harbor. From my rocky perch, I peered down upon a moon-dazzled scene, missing only a fairy ballet to make it complete. Sparkling light-drenched harbor waters flickering between seas of dark onyx veils, etched silhouettes of Le Cap's distant homes and buildings, and a constellation of pin-pointed glows from lighted windows and street lamps, all served to remind me of my good fortune to be alive and of Auntie's terrible circumstance. Every night while in camp that rock ledge became my favorite spot.

Days later, Canga stopped me on my way to my cherished evening location. Papa Toussaint had arrived to escort Jean-Pierre and me to Bréda in the morning. Jean-Pierre beat me to Papa before I could race into his warm embrace. He rejoiced at seeing us, but became sad when he told us about Auntie. Delribal released her from the sweat-box about six days after we left Bréda. Her incarceration in excessive heat had caused her severe mental and physical damage. When he arrived for her release, she emerged with a drooping face, glazed eyes, and speech restricted to *home* and *boys* and a few other words. Since her release, she continued to decline. She would sit for hours, never changing position, speak, or even blink an eye. She only gave a vacant stare. Papa finished his terrible news, telling us that old Josephine had Auntie in her care.

Papa's news bolted through my heart, and all night Jean-Pierre and I shared our sorrow and our wonderful stories about Auntie. Christmas season approached, and I could not help smiling about her ugly cane babies that she gave to children. She rescued me from the cane field, taught me Creole, and had patiently waited for Jean-Pierre and me to bond as brothers. Only Mother could match Auntie's big heart. Blessed is the person with one good mother. I had two. Just before dawn, sleep finally draped a veil over our grief.

Papa Toussaint nudged us, as Jean-Pierre and I struggled to our feet. Despite little sleep, returning to Bréda energized us. We could, however, not leave without thanking Canga and Yaya. They kept us safe, and we experienced the adventure of a maroon's life—a life that Jean-Pierre had adapted to better than I. Canga smiled without comment, but made strong eye-contact with Jean-Pierre, the look a pack leader gives to a new member.

On our way to Bréda, Toussaint instructed us to remain in his cottage until he came for us. He had clean clothes for us on his bed, adding that our obedience would be rewarded. Rewarded? What had Papa Toussaint contrived? Finally, we reached Papa Toussaint's cottage, washed ourselves in a horse trough, dressed, and settled down to await our reward.

We did not have long to wait. Papa reined Delribal's coach at his doorway, complete with the mad manager's coat-of-arms on its sides. He motioned us aboard. We assumed that he wanted us to sit next to him. Instead, he directed us to take back seats reserved for Delribal and his honored guests. Two slave boys recently on Delribal's death list, on the way to some mysterious appointment, and acting like plantation masters filled us with wonder. Soon our wonder turned to joy, when Toussaint stopped near the big house, and we witnessed a scene beyond our wildest dreams.

The Comte de Noé, Bayon de Libertat, and the constable from Le Cap with his deputies stood at the main entrance. They supervised the evictions of Delribal and his hated overseer Michel Lajoie.

For months, the Comte de Noé had written to his uncle in Paris, using a declining balance sheet to make his argument. In a letter to his nephew, Comte de Bréda recognized his error of Delribal's appointment, restored his nephew's authority, and reinstated Libertat as plantation manager. With this letter in hand, the Comte de Noé arrived at Bréda, gruffly ordered Delribal from his bed, told him that his epidemics were over, and that he needed to start packing. He had assembled a crew for that purpose, and would personally watch that he took nothing belonging to the big house, especially the silverware.

By mid-afternoon, Delribal and Lajoie boarded a shay that the Comte donated for the happy purpose of getting rid of those villains. Their furniture and personal items had already departed for Le Cap. Soon they followed with Delribal's tall figure made taller by the damn umbrella protecting his bald head. These evil men living the lifestyle of city nobles on money stolen from Bréda disturbed me—hardly the justice for Auntie. With their departure, the Comte de Noé permitted the slaves to celebrate. We danced the Chica and the Calenda deep into the night, ending in spent pleasure, as slaves returned to their huts, liquored up on rum, and anticipating the Comte's promise of an off-day. Jean-Pierre and I staggered to Auntie's, and stretched out on the floor, anticipating yet dreading our visit with Auntie the next day.

Thankfully, Toussaint prepared us for our first visit with Auntie. There she sat with a melted face, glazed eyes, and saying nothing. But Jean-Pierre and I each held one of her limp hands, and spoke to her as if she was normal. We reminisced about our funny times together, and thanked her for improving our lives. I swear that she squeezed my hand slightly, or did I imagine it? We kissed our unresponsive Auntie goodbye, as a mounted maréchaussée galloped past us, heading for the big house to deliver terrible news to Bayon de Libertat, our new manager. News masters and managers might not like, but great for Bréda slaves. Justice for Auntie at last!

Bayon de Libertat stepped onto his piazza to receive the

messenger whom he probably saw from a window, advancing and trailing dust for almost a mile. The maréchaussée made such an abrupt halt that he nearly sailed upon the piazza. His antics amused Libertat, as he began listening to the rider's message. Late on the previous evening, a maréchaussée patrol came upon a shay which appeared abandoned, but on approach, they saw two bodies slumped forward, one had been quickly dispatched, the other mutilated. The first, Michel Lajoie, had his throat cut, but showed no other signs of struggle; the second, Monsieur Delribal, had multiple shallow cuts over his body. His broken umbrella shaft had been shoved down his throat, causing such profuse bleeding that he may have drowned on his own blood. The horses had their traces cut, and grazed lazily when the patrol rode up. Evidence pointed to a maroon attack. His commander, Captain Gaspard Ardisson, believed that the hated Canga had done this and guaranteed his capture. Expressing concern but not surprise, Libertat thanked the messenger for his information, and promised to be on the lookout for maroons. Our new manager then turned and walked into the big house completely unruffled.

I have often wondered if Papa Toussaint, Bayon de Libertat, or the Comte de Noé had planned the assassination of those despicable men. They wanted justice for Auntie, prosperity for Bréda, and a boost to slave morale. Especially did I consider Toussaint's possible involvement because he had maroon support, as well as a magical way of making things happen. Even Jean-Pierre admired Papa's style, but in the days ahead, he would tire of Papa Toussaint's oblique methods. A direct, straight-ahead son was bound to conflict with a father who manipulated outcomes.

Every day before and after our new jobs in the Bréda stables, Jean-Pierre and I joined Papa at Auntie's. Each visit only renewed our sadness, as Auntie continued fading from life. After nearly a month, Josephine met us at her door, choking back her tears to tell us that Auntie's breathing had become rapid and shallow, sure signs that she was dying. We stood by her bedside as she passed.

This moment drew me even closer to two men whom I had come to love. It forged the last link of a chain that bound us together for the rest of our lives.

We knelt around Auntie, as her spirit left her mind-dead body. Papa and Jean-Pierre each kissed her frozen lips, and hugged her corpse, but I could not touch her. I wanted to remember her as the warm, vibrant person whom I met on my first day at Bréda, not a cadaver awaiting burial. She was now with Elizi-Freda, voodoo patron of female purity, who may have already placed her in the arms of Jesus where all good spirits go. Auntie would never be lonely because Jesus has lots of good people in his embrace, Mother included. What funny stories Auntie and Mother must be sharing about me! All my life, I've struggled to become a better person. When my feet began slipping and my knees bending, those two joyous spirits always made me stand stronger.

Auntie's funeral became a celebration of a wonderful life passed into the next world. Bayon de Libertat allowed Bréda slaves a full day to pay Auntie the respect that she so richly deserved. Drummers led the procession to her burial site with emotions running so high that a few hysterical women tried jumping into Auntie's grave. We found Libertat generous, if not endearing, for letting us practice our African burial traditions. We laid Auntie to rest in a Catholic graveyard, a right that baptized slaves had under the French Black Code of 1685. Auntie devoted herself to the Catholic faith, and despite her voodoo beliefs, no other place would have been suitable for her.

Jean-Pierre and I moved to a hut near Toussaint's cottage. We were his slaves now. This story continues in my next letter.
Love to My Boys,
Saturday

Susan Elizabeth looked at Philip when he finished Saturday's letter. Her eyes expressed amazement. "How could human beings be so cruel to other humans?" she asked. "How could Delribal kill Auntie?" Then with swelling emotion, she slammed her fist on the table, shouting: "I only wish that I had killed that bastard myself, and rammed that umbrella down his throat until it came out his asshole!"

Trying to soothe Susan Elizabeth, Philip glanced at Wahl for support. Wahl smiled, and said, "Don't worry, Mr. Philip, your stirred-up women won't attack you. We're just angry at those who brutalize others. There's no one here like that. Guess you'll just have to do." Her humor brought laughter, and broke the tension created by Saturday's story.

Wahl began a new line of conversation after they sipped their coffee, and took big bites from one of Wahl's delicious peach pies. She grinned at their culinary satisfaction and remarked, "Apple season isn't far away, and if you like my peach pie, wait until you taste my apple pie."

Disarming Philip and Susan Elizabeth with her friendly air, Wahl began commenting on Saturday's letter: "I used to hate every master and every white person. That's what slavery does to you. Makes you despise everything not suffering and not black. Some of those whom I've hated deserve my scorn. But after meeting Bull, the Comte de Noé, and Bayon de Libertat in Saturday's story, I need to re-examine my hatreds, and not base my estimates on skin color. Lord knows that those black drivers in Saturday's story deserve my loathing too." Then displaying her sense of humor, she looked at Philip and giggled, "Him, I don't know about yet." Her joking manner relaxed Susan Elizabeth, and even Philip began feeling comfortable around Wahl.

The clatter of horses' hooves and grinding metallic sounds of iron-rimmed wagon wheels near the loading dock ended their visit. Local farmers were arriving with their vegetable-loaded wagons. It was a community event that ran through the summer. From late May until late September, farmers seeking the Charleston market routinely came to Branchville twice a month to unload their produce on the freight platform. Standing guard over their cargos in open air to maintain freshness, they would load a freight car around 3 a.m., ready for the Charleston Run at 5 a.m. The Branchville car was one among several from small towns served by the railroad. Waiting for the train became a social event, as farmers stayed the night, told embellished stories, traded knives, chewed tobacco, drank whiskey, got a little loud, and a little drunk. Philip dreaded these events, because they kept him up all night.

Philip finished complaining about his station duties, when John Gilbert, Malcolm Lawson's indentured servant, brought in a box of ripe tomatoes to Wahl's kitchen. Philip had sharecropped his farm to Lawson who was shipping his share of the produce to Charleston. Young John was not so young anymore. Lawson bought his indenture from the Charleston Orphan House when John was eleven. Now twenty, he approached freedom under the terms of his indenture.

John handed Wahl the tomatoes, bringing her remark to Philip that "on the morrow, I'll make you a fine tomato pie." Philip nodded, opened the kitchen door, and headed for the raucous farmers on the loading dock.

The Fourth Letter

A tired Philip walked into Wahl's kitchen. A sleepless night and a hard workday were the cost for a night of socializing with his friends. Both cook and Susan Elizabeth faced the door, waiting for him.

"How was your night?" Wahl asked.

"Long, but fun," answered Philip. "Except that I tired of O.H. Ott, my future son-in-law, hounding me about selling him my remaining land from my inheritance. He even suggested its inclusion in my daughter Harriet's dowry. What a bore! He never considered that I might need my land to grow food for the depot kitchen. More important, what about my slaves working there? Give them to him? I think not. I don't trust him to be a kind master."

"Now, Philip," Susan Elizabeth sympathized. "Your whole night didn't concern O.H.'s greed did it?"

"No," replied Philip. "I relished the hunting and fishing stories my neighbors told, especially those of Emanuel Fairy and James Berry." Then Philip began a laugh that soon became a belly-shaker.

"What's so funny?" Wahl questioned. "Or are you as mad as Delribal?"

"I just can't stop laughing at James Berry's tale," Philip answered.

"Well, let's hear it," Susan Elizabeth complained. "I'd rather the story drive us mad than your damn laughing. Save us, Philip, please!"

"Berry's story began," Philip said, "with his 'upnawth' relatives who came to Branchville to fish Lake Marion, South Carolina's natural and largest lake."

"'Upnawth'?" Wahl questioned.

"Yes," Philip teased. "It's local jargon for 'Yankee' territory north of Virginia. Hardliners argue anything above South Carolina."

"Get on with Berry's story," Susan Elizabeth interrupted.

"On Lake Marion," Philip continued, "there was a time-tested safety procedure for entering the cypress swamps lining its shores. Their shallow waters teemed with bass, crappie, alligators, and cottonmouths. Gators didn't concern fishermen much, but cottonmouths did. Now a cottonmouth is a clever beast and uses Spanish moss to conceal himself. To counter this crafty critter, each boat carries a crew of three fishermen: one at the bow, one in the middle, and one at the stern. The one in front looks for floating obstructions, the one in back paddles, and the one sitting mid-ship watches limbs for cottonmouths. If one drops from the forest drapery, he has a canoe paddle to deflect him from the boat. It worked every time. But Berry's 'upnawth' relatives figured to outsmart the Branchville local yokels."

"Meaning what?" Wahl asked.

"I mean that they replaced the canoe paddle with a shotgun," Philip continued. "Their cousin Jim Berry did nothing to discourage his 'Yankee' relatives: Never told them about Francis Marion's encounters with marsh creatures during the American Revolution; never told them of his own encounters with cottonmouths; never explained their aggressive behavior; never told those know-it-alls anything. He just played the dumb country cousin. He even loaned them his shotgun."

"His shotgun?" Susan Elizabeth interrupted. "You mean Berry's pride-and-joy that had been his grandfather's?"

"Yes, Jim Berry would risk anything for a good joke." Then Philip returned to his story. "So off went Jim's 'upnawth' relatives, as proud as Daniel Webster after winning a debate. They pointed their bow for the nearest cypress swamp, poles and lines ready for fish, and gun ready for snakes. Hardly had they entered the swamp, than out of the Spanish moss dropped a big moccasin. The middle man

93

fired both barrels at the invader hitting their deck. Snake dead, boat sunk. The 'nawthuners' abandoned their craft into waist-deep water, perched themselves on a log, and awaited rescue. None other than Cousin Jim showed up, laughing so hard that his own boat nearly capsized. He couldn't quit howling, even when his relatives told him that his shotgun was lost in the ruckus. Knowing Jim as I do, he probably accepted its loss as the price of a good joke."

While Wahl and Susan Elizabeth laughed at Berry's story, Philip's thoughts turned to Saturday's next letter, putting brother John and himself on stage for the first time. Rumors had long circulated about his parents. Did Saturday clarify them? Did he even want them discussed? Saturday's comments were sure to be painful.

Food from Wahl's stove softened Philip's fears, as he began eating the old cook's tomato pie, along with cornbread, country butter, and greens with pot-liquor.

"You know, Wahl," Philip observed, "this might be a man's last meal." Wahl said nothing, but sensed Philip's dread concerning the next letter.

With their repast over and dishes soaking in a tub, Philip looked across the table at "his girls" and knew that they anticipated Saturday's fourth letter.

15 Elliot Street, Southside
Charleston
September 11, 1810

Dear Philip and John,

Jean-Pierre and I moved into a hut on Toussaint's side of Bréda Plantation. There were four others, housing those who worked Papa's blacksmith shop, the stables, and coachmen in training. As novices, Papa gave us the tasks of assisting his blacksmith, wheelwright, and farrier, and cleaning his stables. One day we might become coachmen, but for now our learning had to start at the bottom. So he pointed us toward the horse stalls, and told us to start digging manure.

On our way to our smelly assignment, we detoured through the blacksmith shop, and met Chisulo, Toussaint's slave smithy. He was skinny, of average height, with enormous forearms built from years of pounding his anvil with his four-pound hammer. I believed then, and do now, that he was the strongest man on Bréda Plantation. Neither blazing sun nor heated forge deterred him from his duties, as he looked up at us grinning through rivers of sweat. After welding two pieces of wrought iron together, he doused them in the slack tub by his forge, causing hissing puffs of steam to rise.

Striding toward us, Chisulo barked that we must be Toussaint's "boys." We assured him that we were, and he began instructing us about the functions and rules of a blacksmith shop. Inside the shop, his orders took precedence over those of the wheelwright and farrier. Then emphasizing his authority, he told us that "Chisulo" meant "steel" in Ewe, the language of the Aradas. He took deep pride in his Arada heritage and blacksmith skills. Both Marc the wheelwright and Frédéric the farrier were Aradas, revealing Toussaint's preference for slaves from that nation. The Arada reputation for intelligence and hard work may have been his reason. More likely Toussaint's royal Arada blood influenced him.

Chisulo listed the small items his shop produced: shutter hinges and fasteners, door hardware, square nails for carpentry and horseshoes, kitchen utensils, andirons for the hearth, tongs including pipe tongs for smokers, most shop tools, bits and rings for horses, and carriage bolts. Then he switched to larger items: iron tires for wagon wheels, metal framing for carriage and wagon repair, and trip hammer parts for the large one serving the blacksmith shop.

Like a new father showing off his baby, he hurried us outside to show us more. He pointed to a thirty-foot tall chimney serving as a furnace, producing up to a ton of cast iron per year. Bréda never reached peak level due to shortages of skilled furnace workers and resources. Consequently iron salvage on the plantation became critical. Metal scrap and cast iron bars purchased in Le Cap all went into a pile behind his shop. Any blacksmith worth his weight, Chisulo added, regarded as treasure his heap of iron and carbonated steel.

From his "treasure," Chisulo guided us to a smoldering, earthen mound, where hardwoods were converted into charcoal. Duty here was strenuous, dirty, dangerous, and ours. We would be under Marc the wheelwright, an experienced "burner." He showed us how a wood pile should be covered with dirt, ignited, vented, and when to run before dangerous gases exploded. Then Chisulo prophesized that cutting hardwoods to expand cultivated fields and make charcoal would one day turn those beautiful green hills behind his shop into heaps of mud.

Chisulo made our last stop the work benches of Frédéric and Marc. I found Frédéric the more interesting. Papa Toussaint had purchased him to rescue him from a cruel overseer whose beating of Frédéric mentally damaged him, but not so damaged that he could not perform routine duties. Frédéric was small with a perpetual smile and good humor. Even though he spoke with a lisp, his cheerfulness became contagious to those in Chisulo's shop who, in effect, became his family. Part of his charm came from his innocence that he demonstrated with his model of a thatched village on a shop shelf. For people, Chisulo periodically gave Frédéric three nails welded together resembling human form. But no one performed the duties of farrier better than this man-child with his wooden tool box. Most impressive to me, however, were the love and trust between horse and farrier. Maybe there is something to the African belief that mentally diminished people are on a higher spiritual level than normal humans.

Marc the wheelwright had a different personality, and had the distinction as the first slave Toussaint owned. He was joyous, teasing, and loved a good joke, which generally kept shop members smiling until his humor became tedious, causing Chisulo to order him back to work. He had first-rate carpentry skills, and even built carriages matching the finer ones from Europe.

The time that I spent at the blacksmith's shop provided me with lasting memories. I especially enjoyed coffee and breakfast at Chisulo's forge, while watching our master smithy rekindle his furnace. His forge's fiery stage brightened, and charcoal sparks took flight from their iron host, reaching a welding heat. We slaves were like that, getting hotter with each passing year.

Although Jean-Pierre and I continued serving Chisulo's blacksmith shop, Papa Toussaint emphasized our stable duties. No one in Saint-Domingue could outdo his knowledge of horses, nor his reputation for training competent coachmen. That is why planters across Saint-Domingue sent him horses to train and slaves to drill into drivers. Many different breeds arrived at his stables, but he preferred Arabians and American Quarter horses for the saddle and French Percherons for the carriage. By 1780, Toussaint estimated that he had trained twenty active coachmen serving plantations across the Plaine de Nord. By 1791, he believed that number doubled. I did not realize it then, but Papa Toussaint used his coachmen as his spies. At plantation events, he and his "graduates" conducted conversations that gained Toussaint information about the mood of slaves across the Plaine du Nord.

Toussaint began our training by teaching the nature of young colts. Get them used to human touch, he demanded. We rubbed them with the flat of our palms, talked to them, communicated with them through eye-contact, and once we won their confidence, we could lead them with a halter or bridle. Never, Toussaint instructed, ride your colt. It would hurt him. No colt could be ridden until he was a late two-year-old. Then he looked at the hulking size of Jean-Pierre, and chuckled that his horse should be a four-year old.

Realizing his remark hurt Jean-Pierre, Toussaint told him that planters sought big men like him for coachmen to impress their neighbors. Why just a year ago, he had trained a seven-foot slave from the Turpin Plantation. He was Boukman Dutty. The same Boukman Dutty, I might add, who later joined the maroons, became a voodoo priest, raised the slaves of the Plaine du Nord in the Great Slave Rebellion of 1791, and called upon the God of the blacks to avenge wrongs done to them by whites.

Training a horse to bear a saddle takes patience, and watching Papa Toussaint made me appreciate his well-deserved reputation as a horse trainer. Near his stables was a circular corral fifty feet in diameter, where he taught colts obedience. It was not easy, since Papa had to stay out of the colt's kick zone, while maintaining eye contact with his equine pupil at the same time. Eventually, the colt would "join up," meaning the colt's acceptance of Papa. In the "follow up," Papa got the colt to accept a saddle. I have always wondered if Toussaint learned his mastery of men from his mastery of horses.

Papa taught me to love horses, but learning a coachman's decorum suited Jean-Pierre and me more. Decked in the red livery of footmen, we watched Papa's every move. Once when he delivered the Libertats to a plantation ball, he heralded his approach by blowing a brass coach horn with a tinny tune uniquely his own. After stopping his carriage in the plantation yard, he got down with grand elegance, standing to Madame Libertat's left with her husband on her right, and walked with them toward the big house steps with Jean-Pierre and me following behind. At the steps, Toussaint stopped and the Libertats separated. Colorfully dressed servants guided Madame through the double doors of the plantation house to accommodate her wide-hooped dress, the fashion of the day. Another servant guided her husband through a single door on the right, and the couple reunited inside the ballroom. While the Libertats danced on the inside, coachmen and footmen on the outside socialized; a few even mocked those in the big house by dancing to the melodies of Viennese waltzes floating into the night air.

After Delribal's departure, the positive changes on Bréda gained my attention: Runaways who escaped Delribal's insanity began returning, work assignments became more reasonable, food allotments increased, severe discipline declined, and recreational time increased. These improvements translated into profitable balance sheets, pleasing the Comte de Noé's uncle in Paris. These changes, I believe, directly resulted from an unusual friendship and work partnership that existed between Papa Toussaint and Bayon de Libertat. Their friendship began before Libertat's arrival at Bréda, when Toussaint delivered messages to him from the Comte de Noé.

Antoine Bayon de Libertat came from southeastern France, near the Pyrenees. He arrived in Saint-Domingue, seeking a fortune that primogeniture inheritance laws denied him at home. But a planter's life failed to suit him, and he turned to estate management as a better choice. The Comte de Noé liked him, not just because they were cousins, but because they had liberal, progressive views about slavery—views rarely shared by other Saint-Domingue masters and managers.

Libertat was tall, stocky, and bearded, with piercing brown eyes as focal points on an otherwise sad face. But his infectious, sunrise smile illuminated his countenance and warmed those around him. As a husband and father, he devoted himself to his wife and two daughters. Vanity seemed his only vice.

Fronting his secretary's desk, a portrait hung of his most illustrious ancestor—Pierre Bayon de Libertat. He never tired of telling about Pierre's attack on Marseille to support French King Henry IV's suppression of a local Huguenot independence movement. Henry IV rewarded his loyalty by ordering a statue of Pierre be placed in front of the Hôtel de Ville de Marseille. No guest ever escaped Bayon de Libertat's study without hearing his ancestor's delicious story. He avoided repeating it to fellow masters and managers, but to those beneath his station, he retold it endlessly.

I learned more about Bayon de Libertat from studying Pierre's portrait in his study and from another one over the dining room mantel. Bayon de Libertat bore a strong resemblance to his ancestor. Both radiated arrogance and self-confidence, like Spanish conquistadors lording over Indians whom they had just defeated. I wondered, however, if the Libertat on the wall shared the compassionate traits of his descendant. Over time, I learned the biography of Bayon de Libertat better than my own, for as I grew older, slavery filled my memories, and those of Africa faded. Celebration of a personal history is freedom's gift denied a slave.

"The wolf shall dwell with the lamb...," said the prophet Isaiah, and their names were "Libertat" and "Toussaint." Even Isaiah might not have predicted this relationship, so adored by Bréda slaves, but so despised by the masters of the Plaine du Nord. From a modest seeding before Libertat's arrival on Bréda, their friendship grew into a seventeen-year working partnership. Libertat directed Bréda's fiscal policies, while Toussaint executed them as overseer. Both agreed that Bréda slaves should be treated humanely but firmly. With Toussaint giving orders, we found "Crop" and other demands easier. Papa gave Bréda slaves more time off, while restricting use of the whip. No Bréda slave could be disciplined without Papa's approval and presence at the punishment. Libertat further established a better balance of female to male slaves for Bréda, hoping to increase his slave population through natural propagation rather than through importation. Few masters did this because women having babies fouled their scheme to accumulate rapid wealth; thus only heavy importation of African males could sustain their plantation slave population.

The Libertat-Toussaint partnership brought prosperity to Bréda. Within three years, Bréda had the highest rate of sugar production per acre of any plantation on the Plaine du Nord, and a peace fell over our land. In 1776, a happy Libertat rewarded Papa's performance by granting him his freedom with Comte de Noé's approval. Despite this grand event, Papa remained at Bréda, overseeing its slave gangs and training horses and coachmen. He and Libertat grew even closer, as they labored together, whored together, travelled together, and argued their social views.

I witnessed the intellectual side of their friendship. Toussaint valued education, as first his godfather, Pierre Baptiste, and then Jesuit missionaries gave him the gift of literacy in his late teens. Libertat even invited his use of his plantation library, a forbidden gesture in Saint-Domingue. Papa's first book from his friend's library seemed innocent enough. It was Denis Diderot's *Encyclopedia of Trades and Industries* (1767) full of vocational information, including blacksmithing, which inspired Papa to improve his own shop. But next he read Abbé Raynal's *History of the Two Indies*, which condemned European colonialism, and called for a black leader to liberate his people.

After Papa Toussaint gained his freedom in 1776, Libertat pried open more doors for him, including his membership in Saint-Jean de Jérusalem Écossaise, a liberal Scottish-rite Masonic Lodge, noted for its belief that all men are brothers. Even though Masonry enjoyed popularity in French intellectual salons, it also swore its members to secrecy, thus denying me much knowledge about this part of Papa's life. But he became a high degree Mason, and hobnobbed with a class of people whom he secretly despised. No Mason could hide his feelings better.

Libertat's complete disregard for the oppressive code of most masters benefitted Jean-Pierre and me. Toussaint determined that we too should have "the gift" of literacy. He chose as our primer Diderot's *Encyclopedia* because its innocuous contents would restrict our crime to achieving literacy. He added that his "gift" included only us and none of his other coachmen. All massah wanted, he emphasized, was a nigger schooled in carriage driving, not one who could read.

Learning exited me, Jean-Pierre less so, for my brother's intelligence lay outside of books. We also had visitors who assisted Toussaint's teaching. One was Pierre Baptiste, Papa's aforementioned godfather, whose worn body disguised a good mind for mathematics and Latin. For relief between his intense lessons, he shared stories about Papa's youth which embarrassed Papa. We even teased him about being a skinny runt when he was a child. An angry glare from Papa usually stopped his tormentor. My favorite tutor, however, was Father Laurent Leclerc, a defrocked Jesuit priest.

Our crestfallen cleric instructed us mostly on Roman Catholicism and Jesuit history. Papa's friendship with Father Leclerc began years ago when both worked at a Jesuit hospital, and the Leclerc of those early times had a deep faith and dedication to the pope. He lost his faith when Louis XV of France evicted the Jesuits from the French Empire in 1763, followed by his own defrocking when he refused to leave Saint-Domingue with his Jesuit brothers. The final blow to his faith came when the pope disbanded the entire Order of Jesuits in 1773.

Nothing, however, could destroy his compassion for the downtrodden. If anything, it intensified. He told us how the Jesuits in South America joined their Indian wards against Spanish and Brazilian slave hunters; in the French West Indies, they taught slaves vocational skills, despite menacing masters. His model for Jesuit behavior in Saint-Domingue was Father Pierre Boutin who, in 1714, blazed pathways that his order followed. Boutin studied African languages and customs, conducted classes for slaves, and encouraged the founding of Providence Hospitals for men. He taught us that Jesuits must maintain a military-like discipline, take commands only from the pope and their order's leader, oppose tyrants, and even support tyrannicide.

At times, Papa looked at Leclerc with the sadness one has for a sick friend. Being a devout Catholic, Toussaint knew that Leclerc was a fallen cleric, making it necessary for him to monitor his teaching. When Leclerc suggested that we might read Molière's *Tartuffe* and Voltaire's *Candide*, Papa forbade it, saying those books might damage the faith of young men seeking The Almighty. Leclerc knew Toussaint's forceful nature, dropped his recommendations, and continued teaching us Jesuit history.

Two distinctly different masters formed the Toussaint-Libertat alliance. Libertat's type was rare in Saint-Domingue, but common in South Carolina where masters believed that material improvement would create a happier slave, more willing to endure his enslavement. Libertat was wrong. Nothing redeems the human spirit more than soaring in the heady heights of freedom. Until we escape slavery, my people will remain unhappy, restless, even tormented. Toussaint, on the other hand, was a master by circumstance who loathed slavery. His situation compared with Moses' who bided his time as Pharaoh's advisor, unsure of his destiny until God burdened his heart to lead His people to the Promised Land. Moses' mission to free the Children of Israel began with plagues sent from God to embattle Pharaoh. Toussaint's began with those from France.

Despite the improvements the Libertat-Toussaint alliance brought Bréda, the tempest of slavery still tore at the shores of our plantation. The sudden appearance of newly promoted Major Gaspard Ardisson and his maréchaussée unit made Bréda slaves aware that they stood on a tiny island in a sea of evil. The major acted on complaints from neighboring planters that Bréda had become a safe haven for their runaway slaves. None were present, as both Papa and Libertat only accommodated runaways with food and safe passage into the hills near Bréda. Both knew the severe penalties for helping slaves escape. Magistrates would have judged it as theft of property.

Ardisson ordered Toussaint to muster Bréda's entire slave gang into formation immediately. Papa's anger seethed, as field hands dropped their tools to follow Papa's grudging orders. Ardisson walked down the line of assembled slaves, examining each as he went. Finding no runaways, he became anxious to justify his invasion of Bréda. That is why his mood became sinister by the time he reached Papa's blacksmith shop.

With Papa and Libertat close by, Ardisson shouted for the slaves to step lively to assembly. We did, but the frustrated major eyed Jean-Pierre, and asked where he had seen him before; my brother replied that he was uncertain, but maybe it was at a swamp pond where he used to work. The major lifted an eyebrow, preparing to speak, when he rose up in his saddle, and stared at a human shadow in the recesses of the blacksmith shop—it was Frédéric hovering near his village display. Sword drawn, Ardisson dismounted, screaming for him to step forward. When he failed to respond, a fury gripped Ardisson, and he raked his sword across Frédéric's village, scattering his nail people and straw huts. Tears flooded Frédéric's cheeks, as he doubled over on the floor, and began rocking himself like a troubled child. Quickly Chisulo stepped between them, hammer in hand, and the flintlocks of ten maréchaussée muskets clicked back in unison. The confrontation escaladed, as plantation field hands with their hoes and cane knives gathered behind the major's escort.

A bellowing voice pierced the tension. It was Bayon de Libertat, playing the part of the proud warrior portrayed in his study. He had become Pierre, his ancestor, and demanded to know who in hell authorized Ardisson's inspection of Bréda's slaves? Where was his search warrant, or even his superior's written order? Now Ardisson cowered, as he ordered his guard to "stand down," followed by the disordered clicking of flintlocks being released from their firing positions. Libertat pointed at Frédéric, swearing that he had his mind damaged by one of those planters claiming that he harbored fugitive slaves. Frédéric, he said, was simply a frightened child who meant no disrespect. With anger firing up his flue, Libertat told Ardisson that he would not tolerate his behavior, and would report him to his commander and civil officials in Le Cap. I fully expected that the major himself might join Frédéric on the floor. Instead, the humiliated commander apologized and left Bréda with his unit.

Good to his word, Libertat complained bitterly to the Le Cap Superior Council about Ardisson's actions, and several councilmen accompanied him to the headquarters of the maréchaussée commander, adding their chorus to Libertat's repeated complaints. The Comte de Noé held a considerable lien on the commander's plantation, making him a willing audience. The commander then ordered Ardisson to stay off Bréda unless he obtained Libertat's permission. He added that if Ardisson violated his orders, he would lose his rank, and suffer reassignment to the isolated island of Tortuga, off Saint-Domingue's northern coast. Libertat returned to Bréda in triumph, and most slaves bore him a smile, including Frédéric now busy reassembling his display and tending his farrier's job. But Papa cautioned Libertat that shame had wounded Ardisson, making him more dangerous than before.

This event was followed by a gentle tapping on Papa's door during one of our study sessions. It was Yaya. Jean-Pierre and I rushed to greet him, and then realized that our friend bore bad news. Papa got him a chair, and our sad maroon began his story. He spoke slowly words that we dreaded to hear. "Rose, Rose, I warned Canga about Rose," I remember Yaya saying. Canga stayed too long near Pebarte's La Grand Place. Each visit to Rose's bed, he promised to be his last; but each new day brought another broken promise. Love boggled his mind, clouding his military judgment that had for so long kept the maréchaussée at bay. Compounding his dalliance, local plantation owners offered a huge reward for his capture or death. Proof of death required his killer's presentation of his head to the local maréchaussée. If the killer was a slave, the sponsoring masters would purchase his or her freedom including the reward. God's forbidden apple was no greater temptation.

Choking on his tears, Yaya accused a slave on La Grand Place of betraying Canga, driven by greed and by the promise of freedom. It was neither a jealous suitor seeking Canga's place with Rose, nor a beguiling female seeking Rose's elimination from Cupid's competition. No. It was Moreau, a voodoo houngan. He intrigued with the maréchaussée to send them a signal when Canga was in Rose's hut. He did this by replacing the amulet of Damballa hanging from his neck with a simple red scarf. Those passing Moreau's hut probably failed to notice his wardrobe change or its timing. Only maréchaussée agents took note. Six nights ago, Moreau alerted the maréchauséee, which promptly encircled Rose's hut. A young captain, instead of Major Ardisson patrolling near Le Cap, ordered Canga's surrender.

Canga must have been too entwined with his African goddess to know what was happening. The maréchaussée opened with a fusillade, ripping through Rose's hut, killing her and wounding Canga. With the instinct of an injured boar, he ran from Rose's hut, and sprang upon the captain's horse, while the fumbling maréchaussée desperately reloaded their muskets. Canga knifed the captain, dropping him off his saddle. In the same motion, he turned the captain's horse across a stream and up a slope. Lead balls flew, striking trees and bushes along his way, several hitting his back. Falling off his horse, he crawled into underbrush, feeling no doubt the juices of life flowing from his body. It might have ended with the maréchaussée taking Canga's head, except for Renaud.

The person whom I once thought would kill me, Yaya described as Canga's most devoted follower. Concern for his leader made Renaud place pickets along the pathway Canga frequently took to his mountain outpost. These guardians opened a return fire that struck down two of the maréchaussée who beat a quick retreat to the flatlands. Renaud found Canga half-burrowed into deep brush, like an old dying boar, determined to deny his body to a pack of pursuing hounds. Renaud pulled him out, but Canga had neck wounds denying him speech. With frantic hand gestures, the old warrior made it known that the maréchaussée should not take his head. He died as his hands fell away. Renaud and Yaya honored Canga's request by dumping his body into an alligator infested marsh, and then retreating with their maroons before a reinforced maréchaussée renewed their attack.

Moreau fared less well than Judas. He did not even get thirty pieces of silver, as those sponsoring the reward refused payment, claiming there was no proof of Canga's death. Even worse for Moreau, he remained a slave at La Grand Place, and workers there suspected his part in the plot to kill Canga. Many resented Moreau's mellowing treatment of Pebarte and his plantation officials in his voodoo ceremonies. Stranger still, maréchaussée raids ceased on Moreau's gatherings. Had Pebarte used Moreau's voodoo ceremonies to turn voodoo's sharp blade against the very victims of slavery? If this evidence did not enrage the slaves of La Grand Place, the timid observation of a six-year-old boy did. Of all who passed Moreau's hut, only he discovered the signal for betrayal. Three nights after Canga's death, three burly slaves entered Moreau's hut, strangled and beheaded him, spiked his head on a pole, and erected it near Pebarte's big house. To the slaves, it announced the price for betraying a brother or sister; to the grands blancs, it announced that the quiet war between master and slave continued.

Yaya's news stunned Papa Toussaint and me, but crushed Jean-Pierre. Tears rarely came to his eyes: Aunt Caroline's death was the first time, and Canga's the second. Since our return to Bréda, he felt himself derelict for not joining the maroons. In his mind, the time had come to correct his mistake. Besides, he had lost patience with Papa Toussaint's oblique approach to fighting slavery; it had no end in sight, nor was he sure it ever had a beginning. He loved the maroons because they were direct and fighting now. When Yaya left Papa's cottage, Jean-Pierre might as well have left with him. After three weeks of pining and staring at distant hills, he left. Not a word to me or to Papa, but on the foot of my bed, he left half of the handkerchief that I had given him after our beatings in Le Cap. It symbolized the beginning of our enduring brotherhood. When Papa discovered that Jean-Pierre left for the maroons, he was furious. He had wasted all that time teaching him coachman's skills. But like any good father who opposes his son's decision to fight, Toussaint took deep pride in Jean-Pierre's courage.

My time to leave Bréda came in August, 1781. Papa hesitated to tell me that he had sold me to a neighboring plantation; so he set the stage carefully with an all-day outing with Chisulo in Le Cap. I boarded a large wagon with us three sitting up front. Toussaint and I accompanied Chisulo to help him gather salvage from a warship that had blown up in late July, killing over a hundred sailors, and raining its pieces on the town. Some residents had cannon balls fall on their houses, and metal fittings strewn in their courtyards. For Chisulo it was a joyous time, as metal prices dropped severely. From house to house, we went along the harbor, accumulating within a few hours a wagon load of "treasure" for Chisulo's metal pile at Bréda. We ended our day at a grogshop, where Papa revealed the reason for our trip to Le Cap.

Toussaint explained that your father purchased me as a wedding gift for your mother to serve her as coachman and personal attendant. I would remain at Bréda until they returned to Mille Fleurs following their honeymoon. In a rare gesture of affection, Toussaint hugged me, commenting that he would miss our friendship. Then he added that he planned to marry Simone Baptiste who would bring her young son Placide with her. In his early forties, Papa wanted a settled life with Simone who would bring order to his household and bear his children. Someday, he said, I would understand a man's need to leave a few footprints on this earth before he goes away. But I was the one going away and very sad.

I left for Mille Fleurs in early December, 1781, fearing a return to a tyranny like that of Delribal. Out of character, Papa attempted cheering me with superficial conversation. He called my attention to the plantation's beautiful entry and its main avenue with trees overhanging both sides, forming a tunnel of green to the big house. Intricate English gardens bordered the mansion, featuring statuary of Roman gods and goddesses. The house was two-storied with a wrap-around veranda on the first floor. Overhanging the veranda roof on the east side were two enormous trees, one a royal palm and the other a live oak. Your grandfather Matias had once ordered his overseer to fell both trees, but rescinded his order because of a troubling dream.

When I stepped from Papa's carriage, John Chartrand (your father) smiled at me, one of the few that he ever gave me. He was excited. I was his gift to his unsuspecting bride at her writing desk

108

on the second floor. I followed him, while looking back at Papa which irritated your father. He led me into the plantation ballroom that impressed me with its elegant beauty: carved mahogany walls and a beautiful winding double staircase leading to a second floor gallery. Climbing those stairs, your father ushered me to a small alcove with a large window overlooking coffee groves and distant low mountains. There was Catherine, your mother, gazing out the window, but responding to the sound of our footsteps by slowly turning around, and acting surprised at his gift, me. Your mother was a beauty: auburn hair, blue eyes, peaches and cream complexion and a perfect figure. My first glance into her eyes told me that your father's gift pleased her; one glance more told me that your mother and I would become friends.

You may not know much about your mother's childhood, but I will tell you what I recall. She was born to Matias and Veronica Chaillot of Le Cap on December 5, 1761. She was the last child and only daughter of this Huguenot couple. She was in essence an only child, as her older brothers, Claude and Augustine, completed their education in France at her birth. Both brothers remained in France where they found employment at Romberg and Bapst of Bordeaux, the same company their father served as its agent in Le Cap. Catherine did not rock in a pauper's cradle, as Daddy Matias had amassed a fortune, owned three plantations, and purchased two townhouses, one in Le Cap and the other in Plaisance.

Catherine grew up in Le Cap at Number 7 Rue Saint-Pierre where neighbors waved at her sitting atop her parents' patio wall, watching ships pass on the sun-silvered waters of the Baye du Cap. These moments also stimulated Catherine's overactive imagination. When not pretending a better world than the one she lived in, her next favorite routine was visiting her busy father's office on Quai Saint-Louis.

Your mother told me that her joy was the trip itself, because crowd movement and noise combated her loneliness. She loved hearing barrels rolling across quay planking, grunting stevedores toting large coffee sacks, a trip hammer's ringing sound, and squawking gulls scooting for food. Someone was always cursing, someone always angry, someone always happy, and someone always shouting orders. Every human emotion and every noise, whether human or gull, soothed a little girl heading to her daddy's office.

Your mother became a "daddy's girl," much to Veronica's chagrin who let this small irritation become a canker, even after Catherine became a beautiful woman. But your grandmother concealed her jealousy with a smile, pretending to encourage their father-daughter relationship which was simple and pure. Long afternoons in Matias' office found little Catherine under his desk, rolling paper wads across his carpet, while he advised a client. When your mother's self-amusement grew dull, Matias would clear a spot at his office window for her to watch harbor activity. At day's end, father and daughter walked the quay to their home. Her self-confident stride inspired your grandfather's nickname for your mother: "Cock-of-the-Walk."

Mille Fleurs' name came from little Catherine's imagination. When she was seven years old, Matias bought a coffee estate near Bréda. Routinely the Chaillot family took long winter visits there after yellow fever season diminished. Little Catherine could hardly wait for nighttime carriage rides with her parents under the moon's guiding light. On one occasion, when servants had packed for the return to Le Cap, your mother begged your grandparents for one more ride.

The full moon that night sent cascades of light across the coffee groves, illuminating their white crowns in full bloom and looking like a fairyland to your mother. Years later, she still remembered spreading her arms apart and telling her father that there was this many white blossoms out there. About a thousand, she told him. Her father lacked the heart to correct her, and instead joined his daughter's fantasy when she renamed the Chaillot Plantation *Mille Fleurs* (Thousand Flowers). Even Veronica liked the change, and so Catherine named the plantation that would one day be her dowry.

110

Though treated as an only child, nothing was special about your mother's education. When her best friend and one of Libertat's daughters studied in France, she stayed home to attend a female academy, sharpen her French, and hit debutante balls to "announce" her willingness to marry a "suitable" husband. Catherine was in shallow water, but was not herself shallow. Boundless energy combined with her inquisitive mind, as she read the philosophers and other best authors of her day. She refused to play the pampered, useless role of a grand blanc female. A kind heart topped off her strong character, as suffering animals and humans found an advocate in Catherine who instinctively protected the weak. Any brute fell under her spell, as her musical voice alone soothed anger and cleared heads.

"Catherine Chaillot, Catherine Chaillot" was a name on the lips of nearly every eligible dandy. Her beauty was stunning, her wit captivating, her family respected, her father rich, and her dowry bulged with title to Mille Fleurs. But her fruit hung too high for grasping suitors, until she met John Chartrand, your father.

The Chartrand brothers came to Saint-Domingue, seeking fortunes denied them in France under the laws of primogeniture. Your Uncle Philip amassed a fortune and settled in Le Cap. John lacked his brother's entrepreneurial talents, but instead used romance as his road to wealth. He landed at Gonaives armed with charm and good looks, hoping to marry a rich planter's daughter in the Artibonite Valley. None did, but the wealth of the great valley plantations excited his greed.

At L'Etable and at des Dunes fil, John coveted their "à *la creole,*" a local saying for extravagant lifestyle. At des Dunes fil, where he resided for a week, he saw alternate squares of black marble and sterling silver flooring, gold hardware, and hundred-candle chandeliers. Your father left the Artibonite Valley wifeless, but determined to marry wealth, as he went to Le Cap to be near his brother. That is where he romanced your mother into marriage. For their honeymoon, your father took his new bride to

111

the Artibonite Valley as guests of Louis de Rossignol at L'Etable Plantation, hoping to inspire her to material excess. But underneath it all, your mother had simple tastes and wants. Love and children were her intended luxuries.

My time at Mille Fleurs coincided with your parents' marriage. Your father demonstrated his greed from its beginning. Under his direction carpenters, tile masons, painters, cabinet makers, plasterers and decorators converged on Mille Fleurs. Noise filled the big house: hammers striking square nails, saws ripping, boards dropping, and scooting sounds of mortar sliding into wetting troughs. Odors of wet paint and plaster did to the nose what noise did to the ears. The once graceful Mille Fleurs became gaudy, a gaudiness built upon a plunging debt your father gained from his growing slave gang, struggling to cultivate more acreage to acquire more debt. Ornate mahogany staircases, Italian rose marble floors, gold hardware, hundred-light chandeliers with hanging crystal prisms, Chinese porcelains, and fine French figurines could not change your mother or your father. He was a King Midas in search of gold; she an Aphrodite in search of love.

After my interview with your mother, Zèbre waited at the foot of the stairs. Old friends reunited! Zèbre had left Bréda years ago, and so much had happened since then. He had grown from a small child into a small adult, while I became a lanky six-footer. We both blinked at Nature's changes, and then we started laughing and hugging each other.

Our conversation turned serious. I told Zèbre about Aunt Caroline, my time with maroons, Delribal's fate, Canga's death, and Jean-Pierre joining Yaya's guerrillas. His news was less action-packed than mine. His mother died trying to abort Lajoie's baby. Just as well, he growled, because Delribal's right-hand man robbed his mother's self-respect. When I questioned Zèbre about Mille Fleurs, I paid close attention. How were slaves treated here? Was it better or worse than Bréda?

Zèbre's anger exploded! No other plantation in Saint-Domingue was like Bréda, certainly not Mille Fleurs. Atrocities common to slavery in Saint-Domingue were all here: branding newly arrived Africans, maiming captured runaways, whippings for minor infractions, the sweat box for major ones, insufficient food, too few women, overwork, and little free time. Most of all, he hated the overseer (Louis Blanchard) and his two drivers (Félicité and Christophe) who took any slave woman they wanted, and committed rape with only a coffee tree for privacy. The manager (Césare La Porte) tried restricting their behavior, but lacked the will to stop them. Zèbre finished by saying that the Chaillots were decent, but absent from Mille Fleurs six months per year. They simply came for vacations and to glean profits from their plantation. He doubted that the Chartrands would change conditions. He was wrong. Conditions got worse.

The high lifestyle of planters and the agonies of slaves seemed everlasting. But beyond the sight of the joyous and the hopeless, off behind distant hazy mountains, God began raising a storm so angry that even the Devil himself would take cover. Retribution was coming!

Love to My Boys,
Saturday

When Philip finished Saturday's letter, he saw Wahl leaning back in her chair, looking him square in the eye, half-smiling and saying, "You sure you're your father's child? You're too good to be his. John and you must take after Catherine."

Then Susan Elizabeth chimed in: "I wouldn't be here if Philip was like his father who took self-indulgence to an art form." Susan Elizabeth left her chair, went to Wahl's woodstove, poured herself a cup of coffee, and waited for Philip's response.

"I don't know what to say. What I read about my father in Saturday's letter is far beyond what others told me. You must realize that he made extended visits to France when I was only a child. If Saturday called him a scoundrel, he probably was. Oddly enough, I remember Uncle Philip more than my father." Philip felt defensive about his father, but had nothing on which to base an argument. All he could do was change the subject.

"Malcolm Lawson, who sharecrops my land, told me that he would release John Gilbert from his indenture if I hired him," Philip explained. "I need help here at the restaurant and depot, Wahl needs kitchen assistance, and Susan Elizabeth needs her workload reduced." Philip took a deep breath, saw them nodding their approval, and said, "Good, I've hired him with the title of assistant stationmaster; he starts tomorrow."

Slightly piqued, Susan Elizabeth asked the urgency of John Gilbert's hiring, and Wahl jumped in, "I bet it has to do with the delegation bound for the Nashville Convention. I've read about it in the Charleston *Mercury* on the stationmaster's desk."

"So you're the one taking my papers," remarked Philip. "You must know then that Robert Barnwell Rhett is the delegation's leader. He is an intellectual lightweight, self-appointed leader of the secessionist movement, and wants to wear deceased John C. Calhoun's mantel. I cannot stand Rhett, his ideas, or his posturing, but Branchville loves him. Our Orange Parish promises a big turnout to greet him when his train from Charleston rolls in here for lunch. A new engine and crew will take the delegation to Hamburg to connect with points west to Nashville. Our good citizens plan to display a large banner on the station platform saluting Rhett, and two town dignitaries plan short speeches supporting him.

"Hell, Rhett scares me, because he could turn South Carolina into another Saint-Domingue. I also find annoying his contention that national policy opposing slavery in the territories oppresses the Southern gentry. He never considers the oppression of slaves. I hoped that my old friend Joel Poinsett might be a delegate to offset Rhett. No chance! Poinsett is a unionist and, though a slaveholder, he questions its morality.

"I'll deal with all this tomorrow, but I can't speak out because I'd lose my restaurant customers and my job as stationmaster. We'll

return to Saturday's letters after things calm down around here."
Philip walked over to Susan Elizabeth, and they left the kitchen.

The Fifth Letter

An amused Philip stood at the window facing the Branch Oak, peering through the wavy glass. He wished that the window the Nashville Convention afforded South Carolina's future might be as clear. Yesterday he avoided criticizing Rhett, even with old friends and neighbors. But he survived the ordeal, and Susan Elizabeth and Wahl sealed their lips too. He found consolation in their loyalty to him.

He moved through the depot's backdoor to Wahl's kitchen. There they sat, sipping coffee, eating pie, and waiting for him like old friends. "Make much money from serving the delegates and their supporters?" Wahl asked, breaking a friendly silence.

"Yes," replied Philip, "at fifty cents a plate, I made a hundred dollars. Damn nearly lost it though when Malcolm Lawson proclaimed to Rhett's audience that I might want to donate my profits to reduce delegation travel expenses. I could have strangled Malcolm for putting me on the spot. Delegates and their friends suddenly quit talking to hear my response. A "No" might have identified me as a unionist. So I replied that I'd like nothing better, but I must save my money to buy uniforms for men like Malcolm, ready to stand for South Carolina. They laughed at Malcolm, and I kept my hundred dollars."

"We shut our mouths for you, Mr. Philip, but Mr. Rhett's stew needed a little spicing," said a smiling Wahl. "Couldn't find the right root for pig poisoning." They all burst into laughter.

Philip's mood turned somber, knowing this letter promised

more information about his mother and events leading to the Great Slave Rebellion. "How many of those at yesterday's rally," he asked, "might one day write about a similar holocaust in South Carolina?" With this horrible vision etched in his mind, Philip began reading Saturday's fifth letter.

15 Elliott Street, Southside
Charleston
December 1, 1812

Dear Philip and John,

There was a proverb in Saint-Domingue that described your father's relationship with your mother: "Romance gets a man inside a woman's heart, marriage kicks him out." Truly John seemed intent on alienating Catherine. His extravagance deepened each year, and Catherine's father who represented Romberg, Bapst and Company gave into his son-in-law's pleadings for extended credit, driving him into deeper debt. By 1783 John had mortgaged the entire Mille Fleurs' coffee crop to Romberg and Bapst.

Your father's uncontrolled behavior extended to his lust for women. In a land where the standard for faithfulness is a husband with just one mistress, John still failed that definition. His multiple affairs lifted the eyebrows of those who knew him, and established his sexual fame among those who didn't. Widespread rumors about your father made Catherine avoid being seen with him. Whispered comments about your father, and some not so whispered, inspired another of his bad habits: dueling. Anyone smearing his name, he challenged to a match on the field of honor.

Constant fighting became the hallmark of your parents' relationship, but Catherine did not shrink from John's tirades. Finances and John's affairs dominated their arguments, but a particularly violent conflict involved Zèbre, who served as your father's personal attendant. In a hot moment, Catherine remarked how fitting that his attendant should be named Zèbre because only a zebra could

117

attend a jackass. In a flash of temper, your father retorted that from now on "Zèbre" would be known as "Jupiter," and stormed from the room.

A few days later, I forgot your father's demand, and I called him "Zèbre." He accused me of insolence, and ordered me whipped. Immediately Catherine interceded, forbidding my punishment because I was her slave. In an outrage, he ordered that Zèbre should take my punishment: five lashes from Félicité, his driver. Catherine felt humiliated, and Zèbre's hatred for your father deepened.

Through these tumultuous times, your mother and I became friends. Enduring friendships rarely begin suddenly, and that certainly happened between your mother and me. Catherine tried to salvage her marriage, but your father's affairs and long periods in France killed any rally. Though a strong woman, she did her share of crying on her pillow until she reconciled herself to her circumstance, and even anticipated his absence from Mille Fleurs. During those times, she relaxed her husband's restrictions on Zèbre (alias "Jupiter") and me. When she dined informally, I would deliver her food tray to her bedside; often I lingered and had long conversations with your mother. I told her the odyssey of my enslavement, while she expressed her love for her father Matias, and recalled her wonderful childhood.

Your mother had a difficult pregnancy with you, Philip. In her seventh month of term, Dr. Truloc, Delribal's former physician, ordered her to bed. Your grandparents moved into Mille Fleurs to nurse their daughter, while your father left on yet another voyage to France. Days and nights seemed endless for Catherine, and although she appreciated that Matias and Veronica tended to her needs, she demanded privacy, except times when I read to her.

Her favorite book was Defoe's *Robinson Crusoe*, a book her father read to her as a child on the Quai Saint-Louis, overlooking the harbor. Nostalgia was not the only reason that she chose this book: Crusoe's endurance inspired her, as she clung desperately to a sinking marriage. Late at night with breezes and sounds drifting through her bedroom jalousies, Catherine would prop up on her pillows, pull her silk sheet to her chin, and let the flowing air rearrange her beautiful auburn hair; then with the innocent expression of a child, she listened to my reading of Crusoe. Sometimes your mother interrupted me, commenting that if Crusoe could have his Friday, she could have her Saturday. Your mother frequently fell asleep, after which I extinguished her lamps and left her room.

Near the end of her pregnancy, your mother's ankles and feet swelled. Veronica sent for Dr. Truloc who arrived with a companion named Aunt Vermeille (Scarlet), a short slave woman about as wide as she was tall. Grandmother Veronica demanded that Truloc bleed your mother to relieve her swelling. To his credit, the doctor advised against it, arguing that Mother Nature would purge her daughter's excess fluids at delivery. Then he motioned for Aunt Vermeille.

So many women and babies in Saint-Domingue were lost by fumbling attendants that the French Crown in1775 appointed a "lying-in doctor" to train midwives, and Aunt Vermeille was Truloc's best pupil. When she waddled to Catherine's bedside, I lacked confidence in her. That quickly changed when she thrust her chubby hand under your mother's sheet, felt her vagina, and announced that she would birth Catherine's baby at the next full moon. She smiled at her audience, and followed Grandfather Matias to the nursery where she took up temporary residence. For the next two weeks, I slept outside your mother's door. When the grand moment came on March 15, Aunt Vermeille's presence confirmed Dr. Truloc's decision to have her stay with Catherine. She turned you, Philip, in delivery, or else you would have strangled on your umbilical cord.

Catherine enjoyed several good months following Philip's birth. I slept on the nursery floor after Vermeille departed Mille Fleurs, and made sure that wet nurses maintained their schedules. But just when your mother sailed into calmer waters, new storms churned her life. In August, Matias died at Romberg, Bapst and Company. His death devastated your mother. Her best friend was gone. She hardly had time to grieve, when your father returned, and a depressed Grandmother Veronica moved into Mille Fleurs, swearing Death beckoned her to join Matias on the "other side."

Despite Grandmother Veronica's melodrama and demand for your mother's attention, she shielded her from your father's abuse. Veronica had a square jaw, tight thin lips, and faded rusty hair streaked with gray tied in a bun. She had the habit of leaning forward and peering through glasses which made her squint when she spoke, like an old lioness ready to defend her realm. She and John hated each other, and she returned his verbal blows with those of her own. Their stalemate benefited your mother because your father knew that Veronica would intervene in their arguments, giving him another reason to leave for France.

Catherine could no longer tolerate bad behavior. Her moment to deal with a domineering mother and abusive husband came when John departed for France in early 1786. She plopped down at your father's writing desk, collected his ledger books, and called for me to drive her to your Uncle Philip's office in Le Cap. When Veronica injected her comment that wives needed to leave business to their husbands, Catherine replied that she loved Mille Fleurs too much to leave its fate to her spendthrift husband. When Veronica tried to respond, your mother told her to mind her own business. Her nod to me put a spring in my step to get her carriage. As I left, I tried not to let your grandmother see me smiling; only Catherine did. "The Cock-of-the-Walk" was back!

When I reined Catherine's chaise by Uncle Philip's office, the carriage door immediately swung open, and a determined Catherine stepped down holding a stack of ledgers. She handed me a few, and commenced a stride to her brother-in-law's office that I found difficult to match. A surprised Philip sat behind his desk, the landing spot for our ledgers. Awkwardly, he stood up and offered Catherine a chair, while I remained standing. No business association ever had a more abrupt beginning, or any friendship a more gradual start.

Your Uncle Philip and your father seemed unlikely brothers. Both suffered disinheritance under French law, and both came to Saint-Domingue seeking their fortunes. In every other way, Philip the older and John the younger were different: Philip was tall, John short; Philip's demeanor was modest, John's boastful; Philip was clumsy around women, John debonair; Philip worked hard, John hardly worked; Philip knew how to accumulate wealth, John how to lose it. Even their marriages were different: Philip appeared devoted to Désirée, his wife; John seemed dissatisfied, even unhappy with Catherine.

Our trips to Philip's office became constant. Slowly your uncle and mother worked Mille Fleurs from under bankruptcy. Following Philip's advice, she ended her association with Romberg, Bapst, and Company with its unlimited credit to your father. She increased acreage under cultivation at Mille Fleurs, reduced her slave gang, and provided those who remained with more and better food. Uncle Philip advised her that a well-fed, better-rested slave works harder. When bankers refused loans to Catherine, your Uncle Philip co-signed her notes. Failing this, he usually granted your mother an unsecured loan, but only if it served to save Mille Fleurs. There was no better business partnership in Le Cap.

Twice yearly, Catherine made trips to Philip's home or office to select both a market and a shipper for Mille Fleurs' coffee. Your Uncle Philip ruled out big French merchant houses, like those in Nantes or Bordeaux. He said that they often lured clients into expenses beyond simple shipping and selling. When Catherine inquired about the small American ships riding anchor in Baye du Cap, your uncle replied that "Yankee Peddlers" were a tempting risk. But everything relied on a handshake with one of those Yankee captains and faith that France would keep her colonial ports open to them. No. It was too risky, and he would not jeopardize your mother's coffee crop. Instead, he recommended a local shipper of high reputation who did steady business with France and occasional business with Charleston. His choice was Vincent Ogé, wealthy mulatto owner of Le Cap real estate and a fleet of cargo ships.

On "contract day" I would escort your mother to Philip's office, where your uncle and Ogé awaited Catherine's arrival. Ogé had gracious manners, and attended to your mother's comfortable seating, after which he would pour her a glass of wine, and engage her in trivial but socially polite conversation. Your uncle seemed socially awkward, and often relieved his tension by motioning to me to get a notary, a person who constructs a legal contract between the shipper, sender (seller), and buyer. He also arranged for the shipper to receive a "bill of exchange" from buyer to seller, which allowed the seller to draw a specified amount of money held on account in a Le Cap bank.

Rarely did Philip send Catherine's coffee anywhere but to Nantes, France, where Guillaume Barbot acted as her factor. He knew Barbot when he acted as a commercial agent in Plaisance, Saint-Domingue. When Philip went elsewhere, he chose Charleston for Mille Fleurs' crop. This is when I first heard the name "James Macomb" mentioned. Serving as both vendue master (master auctioneer) and factor, Macomb had uniquely positioned himself to sell Catherine's coffee and to provide credit for those products her plantation demanded. Although Uncle Philip believed Macomb did not always get "top dollar" for coffee on the Charleston market, he considered the vendue master's reputation for honesty worth the lower price. Once when Philip selected Catherine's crop for Charleston, Ogé objected, reminding him of the dangers of trading with a non-French port. His ships might end up as prizes in an admiralty court. Then overcoming his fear, Ogé selected the schooner *La Normandie*, his most expendable ship for such duty.

There are two kinds of love. One is electric and travels on passion, but rarely bores deep. The other kind of love sinks a slow but deep foundation, almost unperceived by those experiencing it. But once established, it becomes durable, long-lasting, comforting, and at times passionate. Your mother and Uncle Philip experienced the second of these. For Catherine, Philip was more the man she wanted than your father. She felt safe with him, as she once had with her father. For Philip, Catherine's charm and beauty captivated him, and her need for him excited him even more. He was falling in love with Catherine and out of love with Désirée.

Both your uncle and your mother sensed their deepening relationship, and so did Désirée. Frequently she stayed in her bedroom when Philip and Catherine transacted business at her home; or if jealousy overcame her, she would leave her townhouse altogether. Even I felt the same feeling when Uncle Philip handed me "wandering around money," so he could visit with his sister-in-law. I would stay until your mother nodded agreement, because I served her, not him. As far as I could tell, however, your mother and Uncle Philip controlled their feelings, but wanted Fate to change their circumstances.

When your father returned to Mille Fleurs at the end of the year, he seemed pleased that Catherine had named their first-born after his brother. That Catherine and Philip had spent so much time together in his absence seemed not to trouble him. Did he underrate his brother, or did he consider Catherine a worn-out possession, ready to be discarded? His only discord with Philip came from his demand for a larger stipend from Mille Fleurs' profits, claiming that his lifestyle required more. But Philip replied that he would have no lifestyle without Catherine's hard work. Money, and not misplaced romance, divided the two brothers.

The year 1786 brought many changes to your mother's life, and delivered a dramatic one to my own. Zèbre and I began attending voodoo ceremonies more than we did Catholic Mass. Night after night, we slipped into the woods surrounding Mille Fleurs to locate a gathering. More often than not, we found one near Bois Caiman (Alligator Wood), not far from Bréda Plantation. A sort of magnetic force pulled us there, and into audiences of suffering slaves expressing their woes and anger to a voodoo houngan. These meetings brought me back to my African origins, if only in my mind.

There appeared infrequently a sixteen-year old priestess from Whydah, where the Cult of the Python flourished. This sensuous beauty made her tall, slender body writhe in a fashion pleasing to Damballa, the snake spirit; and pleasing to me were her shining alabaster form, perky pear-shaped breasts dripping sweat like dew drops, and a pretty face convulsed in a religious trance. Had she been one of those goddesses that devours her mate after sex, I wanted to be her victim. Her name was Alisha (or "Mysterious" in the Ewe language), but known to voodoo worshippers as "Witch Woman."

At first, we joined our lives like two gentle breezes preceding a hurricane. After her possession by a loa, I helped others carry her to a quiet spot for recovery, while drums rattled and voodoo worshippers danced to the rhythm of the Calenda. When others left her side to join the dance, I remained. To explain my presence when she awakened, I kept a red cloth for her to wrap around her shoulders and bare, heaving bosoms. Alisha became wild under Damballa's spell, but her normal behavior was modest, even bashful. Initially my presence irritated her, but my persistence softened her resistance to me.

I discovered much about Alisha: How priests of the Cult of the Python in Whydah trained her to become a priestess, and then sold her into slavery; how she barely survived The Middle Passage; and Maurice Lebrun's purchase and abuse of her in Saint-Domingue. Alisha did not mince many words, as action fueled by emotion was her loudest voice. Imagine my surprise when as I handed her the red wrap, she sprang up with the agility of a cat, half-flipped, half-rolled on top of me, and began humping me with the driving force of a blacksmith's trip hammer. As a child I loved hearing an African panther's high-pitched scream, but I never thought of having sex with one.

Too exhausted to regain my feet, I saw the moving spokes of

a fiery wheel, casting shafts of light and shadows between slaves dancing around a fire. From where Alisha and I lay, it seemed as if all the spirits of voodoo celebrated my communion with Witch Woman. She quietly gathered herself, and headed toward the dancers. I, on the other hand, believed that I might be under the Snake Spirit's spell, and needed to slither home. But I got up, joined her, and danced until Zèbre found me to head back to Mille Fleurs.

Alisha invented ways to escape Lebrun to attend voodoo meetings. His drunkenness, whoring ventures, or obsession with billiards provided those opportunities. I never knew when would be our last time, because Lebrun planned to take Alisha with him to Paris in the fall. But with each encounter, our renewed passion deepened into love; stated simply, Alisha had stolen my heart. As lovers do, I concocted a secret nickname for her. She liked my calling her *Wahlawahla*, a Ewe word meaning "the way a woman walks." I thought it too obvious, so I contracted her nickname to "Wahl," a name that always filled my heart with music.

Never did my love for Wahl blind me to the fact that she was a powerful woman. On one occasion, the maréchaussée routed our voodoo congregation. We suspected betrayal by one of our own, and the houngan lined us up for interrogation voodoo-style. Out stepped Wahl from the priest's hut, wielding a wand and wearing a gruesome look. Wahl had become Witch Woman again. She wove in and out of the suspects, crouching and entwining herself around each one, like a snake climbing a tree, until she made direct eye contact. With a wave of her wand, she would move to the next person. This "evil eye" method caused the informant to fall out, begging the voodoo spirits for mercy. Killing him became unnecessary, for later that night he hanged himself.

Forlorn is life without love; mine seemed lost on a ship sailing for France. Two months without Wahl apparently confirmed my fears. I imagined her standing on a deck, tall, beautiful, and beside Maurice Lebrun, a man whom she hated. Maybe she saw Saint-Domingue growing smaller, and guessed where I might be? Easy!

Looking for eastward-bound ships, and wondering if one might be hers. My dread gave me "the blues."

Catherine noticed that gloom had settled over my good nature, and suggested that we deliver ledgers to Uncle Philip. It was the longest ten miles to Le Cap that I ever remembered. The horses seemed like lead ponies and my arms polished marble, but we finally arrived at 22 Rue Jean. Inside, Catherine handed her ledgers to a smiling Uncle Philip. He quickly informed us that he had won Lebrun's cook at the Hôtel de La Couronne. Then he clapped his hands, saying that she had prepared desserts for us. The cook making delivery was Wahl! Wahl! I blurted out her secret name, and our exchange of glances signaled to Catherine that Uncle Philip's new cook and her attendant shared a passion for each other. Now your mother felt a tinge of jealousy, but nothing challenged our friendship. We had something more durable than romance; we were family.

No matter how bad conditions became in Saint-Domingue, Wahl, Catherine, and you boys comforted me. But sometimes my sanity became marginal, like the time your father ordered a carriage for me to take Catherine, his attendant, and him to Le Cap. What was in store for us? As we entered the city, he directed me to the Negro Market. There, atop a pole, was the head of Yaya! I nearly wept, but refused your father that pleasure. He clinched his fist, shouting that this would be the fate of any nigger daring to take up arms against white men. Catherine and Zèbre sat like chiseled statues.

The boastings of the maréchaussée and general hearsay gave me a picture of what happened. Yaya had made two forays against the Galiffet Plantation, looting storehouses and injuring a driver. The third raid proved fatal, as Yaya failed to vary his routine, a Canga cardinal rule. Halfway to his target, the maréchaussée pulled an ambush, killing three maroons and surrounding Yaya's band. The maroons appeared doomed, as the maréchaussée closed in. But a large maroon rallied some of his brothers, and escaped their encirclement into the cover of heavy woods. This unnamed hero snapped the neck of one maréchaussée, and slashed another with his machete. Yaya, though trapped, fought like a desperate animal facing death. Cornered, he took his brace of pistols, shot a maréchaussée with one and turned the other on himself to avoid capture. Major Ardisson then took his head for a trophy, and brought it to Le Cap for public display. The major's turn was coming, however, because I suspected who the unnamed maroon hero might be.

Not long after the appearance of Yaya's head, public alarm swept the Plaine du Nord and Le Cap. According to rumors, Major Ardisson had led a maréchaussée unit to attack slaves at a voodoo ceremony, but maroons were waiting, disguised as worshippers. Springing their attack, they focused their efforts on capturing the major. This maneuver cost the lives of two maroons, but the maréchaussée took flight, abandoning their commander. Whites dwelling in Le Cap, plantation masters, and colonial authorities failed to find the major, and then expected his head to appear on a pole along some road leading to Le Cap. But no head appeared, only a mysterious rider.

Jean-Pierre provided the rest of the story about Ardisson's fate. He had the major stripped to his underwear, bound, and dragged stumbling into the hills with his band. Not one for torture, Jean-Pierre recited the major's crimes against slaves and strangled him. He then directed a careful disposal of Ardisson's body to begin an ingenious plan. After a week or two passed, he donned the major's uniform, and rode his white stallion into a moonlit-night. On the first night, he followed the road from Dondon to Le Cap. When he got close enough for guards at the gate to see his white uniform and stallion, but not his face, he reared his steed, brandished his sword, and with gifted horsemanship galloped off in the opposite direction. On the following two nights, he repeated his deception on different roads to Le Cap.

Rumors excited the city's slave population that Major Ardisson had become a zombie serving Ogun, voodoo's most warlike and anti-white spirit. The slaves at the Negro Market believed the rumor, and spread it across the Plaine du Nord. Jean-Pierre's trick empowered slaves, like Macandal's death years earlier, and girded them for the deadly struggle sure to come. My maroon brother said that his biggest regret was killing and disposing of Ardisson's white stallion. The maréchaussée's discovery of the beast would have revealed his deception, which he still promoted by appearing as a zombie near plantations.

The last year of unchallenged white rule was the year 1788. If you were a grand blanc or a well-to-do mulatto, you might have thought that the gentle breezes of the good life might blow forever. Le Cap competed with America's more sophisticated cities of that time in culture and in population. The *Affiche Américaines*, its main newspaper, found an audience for news from France and local interest; the Cabinet Littérature provided the wealthy an elegant reading room with newspapers from Europe and America; intellectuals took mental exercise in the Cercle des Philadelphes and in launching hot air balloons; those prone to secrecy and social progressivism might join the Scottish-rite Masons; and an active theatre with mainly European productions and salt water bathhouses provided the core of leisure for upper class city dwellers. On the plantations, the display of wealth reached gaudiness. And should the wealthy become bored, they might sail to France for an extended visit.

Despite grand blanc and rich mulatto lifestyles, disquieting signs indicated that they might end. The wealthy's obsession with France drew their attention away from the dangerous world in which they lived. In Le Cap, they ignored a rising defiance among slaves: like slaves hurling rocks at city clocks to make them ring, minor brawls between slaves and between slaves and white sailors spilling onto Quai Saint-Louis from adjacent grogshops, and at night the unhappy kept the happy awake and complaining. The city constable grumbled that his twelve deputies lacked sufficient numbers to maintain the peace. Outside Le Cap, slave poisonings, maroonage, voodoo ceremonies, and suicides concerned plantation masters across the French colony.

The case of Nicholas Le Jeune in 1788 illustrated the extremes planters took to protect their authority, while deepening the despair of slaves to whom they denied legal protection. Long professing total control over body and soul of his slaves, Le Jeune even shocked fellow planters when he put his claims into practice. When his slaves began falling to unidentified ailments, Le Jeune blamed it on two female slaves, whom he accused of poisoning his work gang. He had them chained to his torture chamber wall, where he used scissors and knives to extract their confessions. Even those most hardened to torture found these two cases sickening. For days, both women hung from Le Jeune's wall, gangrene spreading, barely conscious, and barely alive. Fourteen of Le Jeune's own slaves went to the inspector general in Le Cap to file complaints under the *Code Noir* of 1685, attempting regress by petition rather than by sword. Its outcome sickened all bearing the name "slave."

Louis XIV devised the Code Noir primarily to defend a planter's right to rule his slaves, even with violence and oppression. But there were limits on his power. Excessive torture was this boundary, and clearly Le Jeune had crossed it. Investigators upheld the petition of Le Jeune's slaves. Then all hell broke loose, as the entire planter community threatened the inspector-general's office and court judges, bringing Le Jeune's acquittal. The petitioning slaves received only lashes for their courage.

Most slaves, however, held on to a thread of hope. Slaves had no faith in colonial whites and not much in mulattoes to enforce a just law. The great king of France was another story, as African justice frequently came from a powerful ruler from above to those below. They considered the planters' refusal to enforce the righteous laws of Louis XIV and subsequent kings of France a betrayal of their powerful "father" from above. This may explain the wonderment of those observing slave rebels marching behind the Bourbon flag in the beginning days of the Great Slave Rebellion.

In Early 1788, your father once again left for France and left your mother once again pregnant. So your Uncle Philip suggested to Catherine that she seclude herself until delivery at his beautiful plantation on the northern coast of Saint-Domingue. There at his Brume de Mer (Sea Mist) Plantation she could take the salt air, enjoy ocean breezes, watch the violent crash of waves against the rocky shore by day, and listen to the soothing sound of the surf by night. Your mother readily agreed because the Mille Fleurs of her happy childhood had become the Mille Fleurs of an unhappy marriage. We made the trek to Brume de Mer in early March: Catherine and young Philip, Uncle Philip and his wife Désirée, Grandmother Veronica, midwife Vermeille, Wahl, Zèbre, and me.

Time spent there had its good moments. Cupid's arrows found their mark, whether Wahl and I were in the pantry, laundry closet, pathways overlooking the seascape, or in the carriage house. And when Cupid wasn't firing his love missiles, he guided me through darkened hallways to Wahl's bed. This was the best time that Wahl and I had while in Saint-Domingue.

Grandmother Veronica added to our good times as well. True, she dominated your mother, despised your father, and demanded everyone's indulgence. But the old lady could tell a good story and loved her grandchild. Customarily, I attended to young Philip's evening meal, including his table manners. Usually a "little peasant" could not join his parents' table until twelve years of age or older. After Philip finished his supper, I routinely delivered him to Grandmother Veronica, seated on the veranda. She would begin by staring at him for a moment, and then asking him if he wanted a story. Philip always did, and had he not, I would have. I loved the old lady's stories as much as you, Philip.

Her oft-repeated tale about buccaneering ranked as my favorite. Adjusting her spectacles, she would dramatically raise her right arm, point northward, saying that out there in the sea, but not far from here, lay the island of Tortuga, once home to motley sea wanderers, runaway indentured servants, and an occasional fugitive slave thrown into their mix. They were America's first democratic society, she emphasized, because if a man could carry his weight in battle, and do his share of work, he gained equality with his comrades-in-arms. At first, their enterprise carried them to the very spot where we sat to slaughter cattle and swine abandoned by the Spanish. After stripping their animal victims of their skin or hide, they cut their flesh into long narrow pieces, and placed them on a *boucain* (Arawak for "barbecue grill"). They sold their smoke-cured product to captains of passing ships, angering Spanish authorities who swore to expel these "meat smokers" (buccaneers) from His Catholic Majesty's empire. Then flourishing her glasses in her right hand, as if she brandished a sword, she shouted the old Spanish conquistador war cry: "¡*Santiago y a ellos!*" The soldiers of the Catholic king had just dispatched their own runaway livestock, forcing the buccaneers to starve or leave.

Those dastardly Catholics, claimed your Huguenot grandmother, had underestimated the buccaneers who took to their boats to attack Spanish treasure ships plying the Caribbean. The buccaneer technique required a one-mast boat, marksmen who could shoot with deadly accuracy, and a daring captain sometimes given to insane behavior, like chopping a hole in the bottom of his own craft to inspire desperation in his crew to board an enemy vessel. With this "sink or win" method, our crude buccaneer capitalists usually won, and afterwards divided their loot into individual shares. A few got rich, most did not, as they squandered their money in taverns and on whores.

Buccaneering produced famous pirates, according to Veronica. Jean-David Nau once sat near our porch, planning an attack on the Spanish. Cruel Rock the Brazilian, who chopped off the limbs of anyone who caught his fancy, lurked in our vicinity as well. By this time, your grandmother had become so much a part of her own story that she giggled when introducing her favorite buccaneer: Henry Morgan. This Jamaican scoundrel spent time in Tortuga recruiting his crews, and raiding Spanish ports, especially Panama City. France tired of these ocean warriors late in the seventeenth century because they disrupted colonial society. So Louis XIV decreed that the buccaneers must leave Saint-Domingue, be hanged, or marry Parisian whores dumped there and become plantation masters. Those who made the third choice, concluded Veronica, wished that they might have chosen the second one.

On July 10, 1788, your mother gave birth to John. His entry was unusually smooth after Philip's hard delivery three years earlier. I attributed this to Vermeille, and to second deliveries that are often easier than first ones. By mid-November, John was four months old, and Catherine wanted to return to Mille Fleurs before Christmas. Homeward bound, I witnessed a long line of Philip's slaves under the driver's whip, heading for nearby limestone quarries. He rented them out between plantings and harvest, never wasting the brawn of his slaves.

At Mille Fleurs, Vermeille with you boys and Zèbre headed for the big house, while your mother and I waved goodbye to Philip and Wahl on their way to Le Cap. We both knew that we wished for something that we could not have. Then she squeezed my hand to follow her to her sitting room where an unopened letter from your father awaited her.

She began reading the message, postmarked early October. She smiled when your father apologized for his decision to remain in Paris another six months. He wrote that duty made him join other planters in France seeking a voice in the coming Estates-General to convene on May 1, 1789. The determination of French nobles to defend their purses from a bankrupt monarch and to re-establish their power lost to Bourbon rulers provided the planters of Saint-Domingue a golden opportunity for more home rule. He argued that French nobles and the planters of Saint-Domingue shared a common destiny; they would rise or fall together. Hoping to loosen the King's grip on colonial rule, your father joined planter agitators to form the Colonial Committee, dedicated to a generous seating in the Third Estate. Unfortunately, not all his colleagues shared the views of the Colonial Committee, but he believed that the heavy boot of crown oppression would change their minds. He closed by sending his love to his children, although he didn't know the health, or even the survival, of his second child. Your father also enclosed a copy of Abbé Sièyes pamphlet, *What is the Third Estate?*

Your father's letter disturbed your mother, and she invited my comments. I advised her that we ignore the tremors under our feet, go about our business, and trust that changes in France will benefit Saint-Domingue. Perhaps I spoke too boldly when I told her that her husband had waded into a slow-moving stream that might become a raging torrent, making him wish for higher ground. She nodded agreement, and I left her with the thought that her husband knew nothing about oppression, just ask a slave!

Subsequent letters from John reflected his confidence that the grands blancs would control Saint-Domingue; that is, until Catherine received word from him in mid-November, 1789. An ill-wind disturbed your father, and threatened the planter elite. All began well enough when the Colonial Committee supported the Third Estate's claim to represent the French nation. On June 20, The Third Estate became the National Assembly with Louis XVI's reluctant approval, but only six of the thirty-seven delegates from Saint-Domingue were seated. Then public hysteria gained momentum when the Bastille fell on July 14, followed by The Great Fear that swept the French countryside, stripping the nobles of their privileges. A growing panic flowed from your father's quill, as he lamented the defeat of the very ones starting this revolution. On August 20, the Colonial Committee disbanded and joined the Club Massiac, a Saint-Domingue pressure group dedicated to protect their colonial interests from rising republican values.

It did not stop here, your father complained. On August 26, the National Assembly passed the Declaration of the Rights of Man. Its emphasis on inalienable rights did not include slaves since they were property, but what about mulattoes? If the National Assembly applied it to them, the exclusiveness of the plantation elite in Saint-Domingue would be compromised, an outcome John found intolerable; he denounced the mulattoes as nothing but niggers pretending to be white men. To press their demands, he continued, the mulattoes gained support from the *Amis des Noirs*, a powerful anti-slavery society, and the *Colons Américaines* that advocated for mulatto rights. Then your father blamed Catherine: Did she know that Vincent Ogé co-led the Colons with Julien Raimond? Why had she ever done business with that son-of-a-bitch? He then poisoned any chance of gaining your mother's sympathy, threatening her with more about Ogé when he returned to Mille Fleurs.

John concluded his letter with dreary news concerning Louis XVI and his queen, Marie Antoinette. A mob had marched on Versailles, occasioned by bread riots in early October. The situation might have exploded if the Marquis de Lafayette had not intervened with troops loyal to the King. But the safety of the royal couple came with a price. Louis and wife agreed to leave Versailles for the Tuileries, where the Paris mob, some dubbed *sans culottes*, would have easier access to them. Denied both royal and noble support, John likened the cause of the planters to a sinking ship, and ended his letter.

When I drove Catherine to Uncle Philip's office in late November, I knew your father's nightmare had spread to our colony. Nearly every white wore the revolutionary tri-colored cockade, and spewed the one-title-fits-all salutation: "citizen." The grands blancs were first among these farcical rebels, concerned only to defend their privileged position against the mulattoes and their royal allies. In 1790 they forced Governor Comte de Peynier's flight to France, accusing him of disloyalty to their class.

Another group of small whites, the petits blancs, menaced white class unity even more. Made up of small businessmen, overseers, small farmers with few slaves, and others who did menial jobs, the petits blancs challenged grand blanc control of Saint-Domingue,

even writing a constitution in 1790, making the colony independent and in their grasp. Later they recanted this bold move.

But it was the Mulatto Question in 1789 and 1790 that sparked
white unity on at least one point: The people of color must remain
non-citizens. Often the issue generated violence in Le Cap, as
a grand blanc with a mulatto wife suggested tolerance toward
and citizenship for mulattoes. An angry white mob stormed his
house, dragged him to the street, and ripped him apart. Simply
put, colonial division between the royal bureaucracy, big whites,
small whites, and mulattoes created anarchy, causing neglect of
their slaves. Their neglect was our advantage.

Slaves had a different view because the jargon of the French
Revolution failed to move us. How could we take seriously a doc-
trine that the hated petits blancs, those "aristocrats of the skin,"
professed so easily? How many times had they abused my brothers or sisters only because of their skin color? Slaves needed no
ideological priming before making a violent move. Years of abuse
and sorrow pepared us for the opportunity to break our chains.

Leaving Uncle Philip's office, Catherine told me that Grandmother Veronica intended taking passage on the *Léopard*, bound
for France the following Monday. I would drive your grandmother
to Quai Saint-Louis for boarding, but Catherine would not accompany us. A prolonged argument over your mother's relationship
with Uncle Philip fueled Veronica's decision to leave, and not
her intention to visit family in France. Part of me realized that I
would miss that old autocrat. Her strength of character had been
her undoing, and perhaps her greatest gift to her daughter.

At the entrance to Mille Fleurs, Catherine said that she had
a troubling conversation with Philip . She asked me to rein her
chaise and listen to what she had to say. Philip, she began, converted
most of his assets to cash, even selling Brume de Mer. He told
her that the situation in Saint-Domingue had become dangerous,
and a rebellion of the mulattoes, or even the slaves, could not be
ruled out. He planned on keeping his townhouse and accounting

business in Le Cap, but now sought safer areas for his capital. To that end, he purchased two plantations near Matanzas, Cuba, and a fourteen-hundred acre land tract in Lowcountry South Carolina.

Your mother invited my response. For now, I assured her that we were fine, but no one knew God's plans for our colony. It had thrived too long on the agonies of a downtrodden people. Did she know Pharaoh's fate? She told me that I bordered on insolence, but appreciated my honesty. I loved your mother, and I wanted her to see the gathering storm.

The colony's strife reached the slave population with the plantation balls before Christmas, 1789, and ending before Lent, 1790. Carriage drivers traditionally gathered in the plantation yard to exchange yarns, gossip, news, or to dance to musical tunes floating from the big house. With our bright livery colors, we looked like roosting parrots, and our assembly was joyous, even exuberant. That changed by late 1789. Our meetings became somber, our conversations serious, and tempers grew short. Most of all, Papa Toussaint's social manner changed. No longer did he offer rum to coachmen, while he led them in light conversation, or challenged them to outdance him to a tune from a European minuet. Now he became Toussaint, leader of men, as he flitted from driver to driver, gaining essential information about plantations on the Plaine du Nord. Already Papa began constructing plans in case of a slave rebellion.

More than plantation balls, voodoo ceremonies indicated changing slave attitudes. Never at peace with slavery, voodoo worshippers traditionally expressed a hope for vengeance against plantation masters; but now their voices reached a higher level, and Ogun the war spirit frequently appeared at their meetings. They chanted over and over *Eh! Eh! Bomba heu! Heu! Canga bafio té. Canga, mourné de lé. Canga, do ki la. Canga, li!"* (Creole for "We swear to destroy the whites and all they possess. Let us die rather than fail to keep our vow!")

At voodoo gatherings near Mille Fleurs, worshippers generally arrived from short distances. But now, strangers attended from distant places. Some, like Biassou, were practicing houngans. Stranger still, Papa Toussaint appeared. Why would a man with serious reservations about voodoo be there? It occurred to me that Toussaint joined these newcomers in a war council. The white elite ignored this, content to sniff their snuff, pirouette to a waltz, sip French cognac, treat their slaves badly, and bow only to God, and some not even to Him.

The French National Assembly's March Decree (1790) permitted all colonial male property and taxpayers twenty-five years of age or older to vote and hold office. But the gens de couleur remained unnamed in this law, giving the Club Massiac in Paris and white-controlled colonial assemblies the power to suppress them. The table was set for a mulatto-white civil war.

The Assembly's disregard for improving mulatto rights in Saint-Domingue infuriated Vincent Ogé and the Colons Américaines. With support from French abolitionists, Ogé left France in July, determined to do with his sword what he could not do with his pen. In early October he landed near Le Cap after an extended visit to Charleston, South Carolina. With support from Jean-Baptiste Chavannes, Ogé raised a small army, demanding that the Provincial Assembly at Le Cap apply the March Decree to mulattoes. Its refusal led to a brief civil war in which Ogé's forces suffered defeat at the hands of avenging whites. Ogé and Chavannes fled to but were extradited from Spanish Santo Domingo. Early in March, 1791, white authorities broke both men on the wheel, hanged them, and impaled their severed heads on poles at separate entrances to Le Cap.

Ogé's death deeply affected your mother because she remembered him as the gentleman who had helped her export her crops. I believe that the depths of racism in Saint-Domingue shocked her. How could she, with such a good heart, have been on the wrong side of the slavery issue? One day the Catherines of this world will cross to the side of freedom; when they do, slavery will die.

Indirectly, your father became a casualty of the Mulatto Question.

He constantly plunged into heated arguments with members of the Colons Américaines, piquing his elevated sense of honor; especially did Colons' member Monsieur Ducasse offend him, and he challenged the mulatto to a duel outside Paris. Even though John was a good shot, Monsieur Ducasse was better. Your father fell on the field of honor on August 22, 1790.

Catherine learned of her husband's death in early October, and played the grieving widow. For a whole year, she mourned and wore black. She did not want to overdo her obligation to the social customs of Saint-Domingue's elite. So she backdated her mourning to August 22, reducing her widow's isolation by six weeks, while planning a huge "announcement party" ending her bereavement. She even paid deference to Grandmother Veronica in Bordeaux by using the word *widow* in her return addresses in letters to the old dowager. French Catholic society distinguished between socially acceptable widows and divorcees whom the Church considered fallen women. Catherine publicly looked sad, but privately rejoiced and praised The Almighty for her new life. Fate had removed one obstacle keeping Philip and her apart, only Désirée still stood between them. But a tidal wave of human blood would sweep away their chances.

Love to My Boys,
Saturday

Wahl grinned at Philip when he finished Saturday's letter, betraying a shyness one expects in a young girl. "Mr. Philip now you know why I'm called *Wahl* and my sweetheart: S-a-t-u-r-d-a-y! I'm happy to share my joy with you and Susan Elizabeth, but maybe not my sex life."

"Oh, don't worry," chimed in Susan Elizabeth, "what Saturday writes won't leave this kitchen. Besides Saturday's descriptions might inspire my always-too-tired-man."

Now Philip blushed. "Damn," he complained, "could we change the subject?"

"Your mother?" said Susan Elizabeth.

"What about her?"

"Just this, her strong character and spirit got her through hard times. Her concern for others made her sparkle. She must have loved you and John very much."

"I believe so, my dear, but I remember so little about her. That is the beauty of Saturday's letters. I felt her presence, as I read them."

Before the personal melodrama of Philip went further, John Gilbert entered the kitchen dragging metal garbage cans. Their clatter could have drowned the sounds of a passing freight. Feeling awkward for having interrupted their conversation, John Gilbert backed through the kitchen door, while expressing his apology.

"Hard to train indentured servants," Wahl teased. "Give me a slave any time."

Wahl's self-effacing humor punctuated the departure of Susan Elizabeth and Philip for the depot. But before leaving the kitchen, Philip turned toward Wahl and promised to read Saturday's next letter after he met the needs of the returning South Carolina delegation to the Nashville Convention.

"God bless you, Saturday, my mother and Susan Elizabeth," Philip said in a whispered voice, unsure of Wahl's response.

"God gave us mortals to love to remind us that only His love is everlasting," replied Wahl in a pious moment.

The Night of Fire
August 22, 1791

The Sixth Letter

Philip spent all day accommodating the boisterous South Carolina delegation. They tried his patience because of their complaints about not carrying the Nashville Convention.

Moderates had dominated and accepted the bills crafted by Henry Clay, collectively known as The Compromise of 1850. But Robert Barnwell Rhett ranted at Philip, claiming that the slaves-as-property issue in national territories remained unsettled, and would prove it before a Charleston audience. Then he boasted to Philip that he would popularize the word *traitor* among Southerners.

After these trials of the day, Philip sat down in his office chair, waiting for Susan Elizabeth, and fell asleep. Fitful dreams became nightmares, nightmares that once filled his head as a boy. Flames, smashing glass, howls of vengeance, screaming victims, blood-covered bodies, bodies chopped apart, dead babies spiked on poles, burning cane fields, roaring cannons, and the popping sound of musketry formed a battalion of misery that captured his mind. Marshaling all his will, Philip pried open his eyes and re-entered the world of the Branchville depot. Susan Elizabeth stood over him, but even her sweet smile did not ease his terror.

"Why are you so upset?" Susan Elizabeth consoled.

"For over fifty years," Philip complained, "I suppressed the horrors of the Night of Fire, the first night of the Great Slave Rebellion. Now Saturday's letter will reopen old wounds.

"Don't go to Wahl's kitchen today," Susan Elizabeth suggested,

141

"if reading Saturday's letter will upset you; in fact, we can cancel reading the letters altogether."

Philip blinked, and said, "I have to read Saturday's letter. He expected it of me, and I expect it of myself. How else am I going to know my mother?"

With that comment, Philip and Susan Elizabeth entered Wahl's kitchen, and entered the arena echoing Saturday's past. There sat Wahl. She and John Gilbert had cleaned her kitchen. Wahl waved at Philip to start reading Saturday's sixth letter. "I need it," she said. "Every old woman needs to remember her season to be loved."

Philip grinned and began reading the letter.

15 Elliott Street, Southside
Charleston
March 12, 1816

Dear Philip and John,

God set the timing for Moses to lead the Children of Israel out of Egypt and toward the Promised Land. That moment came when Pharaoh and Egyptian families lost their first-born sons. God's timing in Saint-Domingue had a different cadence. Incessant warfare between the royal bureaucracy, grands blancs, petits blancs, and mulattoes plagued the colony, leaving no one in control. Only those burdened with their chains found encouragement: the slaves.

By June, 1791, the sands of time were running out for us. The mulatto faction suffered a severe setback with Ogé's defeat and execution on March 9. Four days earlier, royal government in Port-au-Prince collapsed when the King's Troops mutinied, executed the garrison commander and joined the petits blancs in occupying the colonial capital. Governor Blanchelande barely escaped to Le Cap, avoiding his general's fate. Even though the governor had the loyalty of royal soldiers near Le Cap at Fort Dauphin, their allegiance was fragile and French authority nearly non-existent. Adding further strain, white colonial unity verged on happening.

In July, 1791, news of the May Decree reached Le Cap. The French National Assembly specifically cited Saint-Domingue mulattoes, giving full citizenship to a few. The National Assembly's gesture of saluting Ogé's martyrdom infuriated large and small whites alike. They realized that their disunity left them vulnerable to social changes from growing radicalism in France. Both factions met in early August, called for a provincial assembly to govern Saint-Domingue from Le Cap, and adjourned to a later date. A white colonial coalition threatened our chances for freedom.

Had God not passed the mantel of Moses to Papa Toussaint, our chances to respond would have been nil. Years earlier, he had placed his coachmen across the Plaine du Nord to provide him information, and to contact Negro *commandeurs* (overseers) and drivers. Slave gangs under these commanders lent essential strength to rebel legions attacking and burning hundreds of plantations on the first night of rebellion. Papa further merged his secular organization with voodoo's spiritual force. Though deeply Catholic, he appreciated its potential political power. He knew influential houngans, gained their support, and together they posed a significant threat to white colonial control.

On August 14, in woods known as Bois Caiman bordering the Leonormand de Mézy Plantation, Toussaint met with black overseers and houngans from the Plaine du Nord. Under Papa's guidance, they chose their leadership. With his persuasion, the gathering picked Boukman, a former coachman, voodoo priest, and ex-maroon, to lead the rebellion. On top of his seven foot stature and broad shoulders, rode a head with a face twisted with permanent anger. Second in command went to Jean François, another former maroon. He possessed uncommon good looks, attracting women with little effort on his part. This aspect of his life interfered sometimes with his military duties. But he had a keen sense of battlefield maneuver, and treated those whom he captured better than Boukman's other lieutenants. Georges Biassou filled third in the chain of command. He had worked at a charity hospital in

Le Cap where he knew Papa; later he became a voodoo houngan. He demonstrated valor on the battlefield, but frequently relied on superstition rather than on sound military judgment. Jeannot Bullet, a commandeur on the Bullet Plantation, gained the last staff appointment. Small, thin, but with facial expressions betraying vicious intent, Jeannot later unleashed a blood purge that sickened his most ardent followers. Unfortunately, his zone of assignment included Mille Fleurs.

Why had Papa not assumed command? Perhaps like Anansi the spider, Papa moved in a dangerous world. He had much to lose should the rebellion fail: He was a free man with a wife and children, commandeur on Bréda, and a slave owner with three small plantations. He planted one foot firmly in his current life, while stepping boldly forward with the other into the uncertainties of a slave revolt. That meant letting Boukman and his lieutenants assault the palisades of slavery; and should they succeed, he would pull his rear foot forward in a full commitment to lead his people. Papa knew the history of failed slave rebellions, making him justifiably cautious. But caution meant delay, and might cost him his moment in history. As he once said, "You can't avoid a galloping stallion by standing in front of him." Not only did he miss being trampled, but he mounted the fiery steed of revolution.

I doubt that those planning to attack the plantations on the Plaine du Nord imagined where it might go. Beyond calling for the gods of Africans to wreak vengeance upon whites, Boukman lacked vision; Jeannot settled for licking the white man's blood off the blade of his knife; Biassou, Jean François, and Toussaint at the beginning restricted their dreams of freedom to their own followers. But only Toussaint's vision grew into a crusade to free all his people.

Pretending to deliver fliers about horses for sale at Bréda, Papa Toussaint looked me up at Mille Fleurs following his Bois Cayman meeting. He expressed concern for our loved ones. If the Libertats stayed at Bréda, he could protect them because he controlled the slaves there. But how could he save loveable old Comte de Noé? Then I broke in, stating my anxiety for the safety of your mother and you boys. But I felt conflicted. I understood the justice of the coming rebellion, but at the expense of murdering our loved ones? I couldn't. I planned to protect my family with my life. Toussaint assured me that the outcome need not be so drastic. Together, we concocted plans to save our families and friends from The Angel of Death.

We had ten days to prepare for the onslaught, scheduled for Wednesday night, August 24. Papa would prod Bayon de Libertat to invite the Comte de Noé to his plantation as an overnight guest for the fatal Wednesday. For my part, I would convince Catherine to spend time in Le Cap following her "coming out" party on Monday. My argument was that she needed a different setting with her boys, and could satisfy her longing to see Philip. Your uncle notified her earlier that he would miss her party because his appearance without the ever-ill Désirée would be a display of bad manners. Violation of social etiquette had a sin rating far above adultery, which many coming to your mother's celebration considered a virtue. Catherine agreed to my suggestions, and the Comte de Noé, with equal speed, accepted his cousin's invitation. After all, the old gout-ridden Comte could never pass up an evening at Libertat's table. All fell into place. Too simple, you say? It was, as our plans began unraveling.

Just a day after Papa and I made our scheme, the maréchaussée apprehended slaves setting fire to a plantation outbuilding. Their impromptu arson caused a police investigation, and one of the slaves confessed to a plot to burn every plantation on the Plaine du Nord, killing every white in the path of destruction. But investigators found no evidence to support his story, and dropped the matter. Fearing their secrecy compromised, the rebellion leaders moved the date of the uprising to Monday, August 22, at the very time of your mother's party! What a mess! Now Toussaint and I set about devising a new plan.

Libertat simply changed the Comte's invitation from Wednesday to Monday, but how could I save Catherine and you boys? I could not confess to your mother my knowledge about the coming attack, because I refused to betray my people. Besides, I doubted that she would have believed me anyway. I felt totally confused. Then a scheme occurred to me, bringing even Papa's praise.

I planned to lead you boys and your mother from your room on the second floor, across the veranda roof, and down an oak overhanging the big house porch. Live oaks have low trunks, giving us easy access to the ground. Once down, we would crawl into the maze of statuary and shrubs in Catherine's English garden. Once we reached the row of hedge adjacent to the avenue leading to Mille Fleurs, I would shepherd my group through a hole which I had cut earlier. Once across the avenue, we would hurry into the coffee groves and walk toward Bréda. The cane fields presented our greatest danger, because we had to cross them to reach our destination. If they were ablaze, we would be forced to the road, and faced with a possible rebel encounter. Toussaint promised to meet us at Bréda, and escort us to its big house. In a day or two after rebel rage receded, he and Bréda slaves under arms would guide us safely to Le Cap.

For four days, I made every conceivable preparation to make our plan work. Under your beds, I stored a cane knife and clothes appropriate for slaves that your mother and the two of you could wear. I also had shears for Catherine to crop her hair near her scalp, as well as extra lanterns for enough oil soot to blacken your white skins. I climbed down the oak and walked the escape route each day before the rebellion.

My scheme had a weakness. How could I get Catherine away from her guests and into your room before the beginning of the slaughter? This was when Zèbre joined my escape plan. After you boys told your mother "good night," I would take you to your bedroom, wait ten minutes, and send Zèbre to the ballroom with a note for Catherine: "Come quickly, Mrs. Catherine, John is sick—Saturday!" Such a message would have brought her bounding up the stairs to John at approximately thirty minutes before sundown. We desperately needed that time before springing our escape into the falling darkness. Zèbre and I had a long-standing friendship, and he liked Catherine. He readily agreed to join our escape to Bréda.

Two beautiful grandfather clocks stood in your mother's hallways, but I hated their swinging pendulums, reminding me that time was running out. Would my boys die? Would Catherine die? Would Wahl die? Would I die? The night of August 22 held answers to these deadly questions. Now I could only wait, and guard against something setting off the slave rebellion before Monday and wrecking my arrangements. For this reason, I slept on the floor between your beds to evacuate you boys and your mother should Mille Fleurs suffer an attack.

On Sunday, August 21, I remained at Mille Fleurs to protect you both and Catherine. Word reached her slaves of a huge voodoo ceremony set to begin at Bois Caiman soon after dark. Zèbre went. So did Wahl. So did many slaves from the Plaine du Nord. I spent the evening watching your mother's preparations for the ball and her hairdresser's labors to make her coiffure the most admired among her guests. Woven into her headdress was the revolutionary, tri-colored cockade. To keep her frizzled hair in place, she slept upright in a parlor chair. Your gay, giddy, and talkative mother and I conversed all Sunday night about many subjects. She never mentioned Uncle Philip's name, but when I did, a look of love flowed from her eyes. Her party would start her new life, better she was sure, than the one left behind.

When Zèbre returned from Bois Caiman, he could not contain his enthusiasm. He told me that Boukman presided as high priest and green-eyed Cecile Fatiman served as high priestess. Why Boukman even promised that a black god would avenge wrongs that a white god had committed. I told Zèbre that the high priest's theology was erroneous, but agreed that the moment of atonement for whites had arrived. My friend continued: Ogun speaking through Boukman named the rebellion leaders (after Papa's approval, I chuckled). Boukman further argued how evil advisers around King Louis XVI took him prisoner, preventing him from improving slave conditions. The audience responded by waving the Bourbon flag to salute their captured king.

Heavy humidity and dense fog shrouded the rising sun, struggling to announce Monday morning on the Plaine du Nord. Hard rains the night before probably created these conditions, but I fantasized that God maybe changed His Mind about starting this day. While Catherine applied final touches to decorations for her "coming out" ball, I rechecked everything for our escape, including walking you boys from your bedroom window to the live oak where later we would climb down. I repeated my instructions to Zèbre to deliver my message to Catherine, and then follow her so that we might escape together. Since I had no time to show him our escape route, I told him to stay close to me.

With the falling rays of an afternoon sun, I stood on the veranda, watching Catherine's guests arrive. Each carriage had a coachman and two footmen in colorful livery, with a smartly dressed Mille Fleurs slave announcing its arrival in a baritone voice. It was the last promenade of the pampered privileged that ascended the steps of your mother's mansion. The women wore coiffures so high that their heads seemed too tall for their bodies, and into their headdresses were woven eye-catching ornaments. Most wore chemise gowns in the style of Marie Antoinette. Their male escorts were no less colorful with perfumed powdered wigs, silk jackets with lace cuffs, silk knee breeches and stockings, and shoe buckles with diamond studs. Some "men" seemed prettier than their women. This haughty assemblage ended an epoch best described in Saint-Domingue as "à la créole." I just hoped that its victims might find a better world than the one they were leaving.

When the orchestra struck up the *Marseillaise* before its repertoire of minuets and waltzes, I re-entered the ballroom, and there

148

stood the most gorgeous woman in the room—your mother. Her beautiful auburn hair featured a headdress decorated with a blue, white, and red ribbon representing the French Republic, and she wore a blue and white chemise gown. Her blue eyes picked up the colors of her dress, and her smile gave her an aura of kindness. The people in her house were all about appearance; only I knew your mother's good heart. God should have put her in a different time and place.

Catherine leaned forward, saying that an old man needed help into her halls. He was Comte de Noé! Why wasn't he at Bréda with the Libertats, his only sanctuary from the coming slaughter? When I reached his chaise, sadness overcame me. He explained that he could not go to Bréda without first calling at Catherine's for a glass of Madeira. Here was the man who contributed much to my salvation upon my arrival at Le Cap years ago, chose Aunt Caroline as my guardian, and conspired with Papa Toussaint and Libertat to bring Delribal to justice. The Comte always bore me a smile, and treated me with respect. Now our every step to the big house became a funeral march. Surely he would die. Already my fragile plan began breaking up.

Time came for me to climb the staircase to your bedroom. I had left Zèbre there to make sure that you youngsters did not wander off. John especially liked to play hide-and-seek in armoires. When I got there, music from the first minuet silenced the chattering guests below. Both of you wanted to witness the festival in the ballroom and to bid your mother "good night." At the foot of the stairs, your radiant mother stood, arms extended to embrace her wide-eyed children running to her. Was this "good night," or was it "goodbye?"

We returned to your bedroom, and I dressed you in tattered clothing and smeared you with lantern soot to look like slave children. You started giggling, and I explained that we played a game called "slave escape." Did you remember that oak with its limbs touching the veranda roof? To climb down it, John would hold on to my neck, while Zèbre would assist Philip. What a surprise for your mother's guests when we re-entered the ballroom and climbed upstairs to bed.

Clearly ten minutes passed, when I handed Zèbre the note for Catherine, telling her that John had fallen ill. I emphasized that there could be neither detours nor distractions until he delivered my note; afterwards, he needed to be in the boys' room soon after Catherine. Time was life, I told him, and time was running out. Zèbre hugged me, smiled, and left carrying my note. Ten minutes went by, no Catherine, no Zèbre; twenty minutes passed, still no Catherine, still no Zèbre. After thirty minutes, I knew something had gone wrong. Now I had to deliver my message myself, and then pray that I had time to get to my boys. I told you to stay put and keep silent, and when I returned, we would continue playing "slave escape." I shut your door, and ran for the stairs.

Halfway down the hall gallery, I heard the gates of hell crash open, bringing hundreds of machete-swinging, cane knife-stabbing slaves into the midst of Catherine's guests. Their demonic howling only accelerated their instruments of death, as their screaming victims scattered in every direction. Overturning tables, smashing crystal, spilling wine bowls, crashing chandeliers, and the pleadings of those about to die raised a Satan's chorus. Frozen by fear but desperately hoping to help your mother, I ran full speed to your room where I blocked the doorway. Miracle of miracles, here came your mother, racing up the staircase with half her gown torn from her back, with four slave rebels right behind her. Each step she got closer to me; each step they gained on her. Not more than twenty feet from me, they grabbed her, and I knew that it was over.

I shut and bolted the pocket doors to your room. Sounds of your mother being hacked apart, and hacked some more, tore at our hearts. The merciful hand of Death led Catherine away; the only noise came from the snarling wolves unleashed in her hall. A tide of grief and fury swept over me. Even as I write, the sorrow of that moment has not receded from the flood plains of my soul.

I had no time to mourn, maybe not even enough to save you boys.

Finished with Catherine, they began beating on your bedroom doors. That was when I took the two lanterns hidden under your beds, splashed their oily contents on the entry, and set it ablaze. Flames and smoke stopped your mother's killers, but, more importantly, Mille Fleurs became her funeral pyre. Maybe God interceded to at least prevent the desecration of her body.

Quickly, I led you boys to the window for our escape. Then I noticed something strange: Though fear-struck, neither of you cried; neither of you ever did, at least not in my presence. We reached the oak's limbs overhanging the veranda roof, and had our first bit of good luck: Our silhouettes were obscured, as casting shadows from the fronds of a nearby royal palm fell over us as we climbed down the oak. John did remarkably well with his arms around my neck, and Philip stayed near me until we touched ground. Then we crawled under the veranda deck, near the English garden, and remained motionless for long periods. Heavy footsteps of intruders vibrated the floor above us, while we saw pairs of legs run by in the yard. Shrieking and yelling from anguished slave rebels made us uneasy—but not a peep came from my boys.

When I thought that most rebels, like ants, had clustered on the dead body of Mille Fleurs, we crept into the English garden and slowly worked our way to its center, where stood a magnificent fountain of "Latona Pleading to Jupiter." In Roman myth, peasants had insulted her, and the goddess wanted Jupiter to punish them for their insolence; he did by turning the offenders into frogs. If only Catherine had been Latona, she might have asked Jupiter to change those seeking to kill her children into frogs, or at least into turtles, so that we could outrun them.

When we reached the opening that I had cut through the garden hedge, we hid, waiting for stragglers rushing to Catherine's now flaming mansion to run by us. When I thought the coast clear, I pushed you boys through the hole and followed. When we prepared to dash into the coffee grove on the other side, we blocked a machete-wielding slave. He charged us, brandishing his weapon. I drew my cane knife and slashed at him with my weapon before he could use his. Shocked that I was not an easy victim, he backed up, and our eyes locked; he saw in mine my determination to save the lives of two little boys; I saw in his the sufferings of a lifetime. He made a half-circle around me, and continued sprinting to Mille Fleurs. Latona had not interceded, but God and luck had.

Once in the coffee grove, I carried you, John, in my arms and gave you, Philip, frequent respites. On a knoll, nearly a mile from Mille Fleurs, we looked upon the flames shooting from its doors and windows and through its shingled roof. Over the sad manor hung a glowing crown of destruction, and even at our distance, we heard rumbling flames out of control. But across the Plaine du Nord, for as far as we could see, sister mansions repeated this scene of devastation. No plantation house stood unkindled; no cane field without waves of wind-driven flame churning a fiery sea. So much smoke rose from the holocaust that the stars and the moon were blocked from view; only a Milky Way of sparks spewed across the Plaine du Nord, giving off a dim glow like a prelude to a deadly storm. Nearly three hundred other plantations on the Night of Fire shared Mille Fleurs' fate, and were buried with her in the graveyard of history.

We spent the rest of the night advancing toward Bréda and then backtracking, avoiding the revealing glare of a burning cane field. For long periods, we lay motionless when we heard marauding slaves. With morning's early glow, through hanging smoke and falling ash, we reached Bréda's entrance. But not more than a hundred yards down the plantation avenue, three shadows advanced through a wall of haze. They were Papa Toussaint, Jean-Pierre and Renaud. Our saviors looked for us all night, while protecting Bréda from destruction. My boys and I had reached safety!

On our way to the big house, I noticed that Bréda appeared untouched. Jean-Pierre explained to me that Toussaint had armed Bréda slaves, and assigned them the duty of defending Libertat's plantation from overzealous rebels wishing its destruction. Even Bréda's cane fields remained intact, as their long green leaves waved in a gentle breeze. In a sea of destruction, Bréda indeed had become an island sanctuary. In defending Bréda, Toussaint not only protected Bayon de Libertat's interests, but also his own in case he had to return to the old order.

Upon reaching the big house, I took my boys to an upstairs bedroom, the same one that Delribal once occupied. For the next four days we rested, while I visited with Jean-Pierre. He told me that he led his maroon band down from the hills to defend Bréda on Papa's request. Despite his loyalty to Papa, he still felt confused about his position on the rebellion. Then he growled that Toussaint needed to lead his people before they passed him by.

On August 26, we left for Le Cap. Our expedition consisted of a carriage driven by me for the Libertats, their daughter, and my boys; the rest included a wagon carrying household items from Bréda, nearly one hundred armed slaves under Papa's command, and about forty maroons led by Jean-Pierre. Toussaint had reports that Jeannot blocked the main roads into Le Cap to wreak further havoc on retreating refugees, serving his boast to destroy every white on the Plaine du Nord. Papa knew that trouble was likely, and handed me a pistol with a stout brass butt to stick inside my belt.

Barely beyond Bréda's gates, we witnessed Monday night's tragedy. Decaying human carrion littered the road: Here a disemboweled white man tied to a carriage wheel, there a dead white woman with her dress pulled above her head, further along a dead mother cut in half with her lifeless infant still clutching her breast. The stench of dead flesh and buzzing bottle flies became intolerable, while buzzards cleaned up the carnage; I did not know that the Plaine du Nord had so many of those foul-looking creatures, but God bless them because Nature had more compassion for the fallen than pitiless man.

Near Le Cap, Toussaint's worst fear came true when we encountered Jeannot. Two men stepped out ahead of us, holding ignited stalks of sugar cane as improvised flares to warn their chief of our approach. There followed the din of hideous sounds, as Jeannot's rebel band used cast iron cauldrons for drums and anything metallic for drumsticks. They accompanied this melodic disaster with a war chant that sounded more like wild dogs howling at the moon than anything African. Soon Jeannot's ragged army appeared, some wearing their victims' garments, some half-dressed, some naked. They numbered close to six-hundred; a few carried muskets, more cane knives and machetes, and even more hoes. Papa's greatest concern was two cannons mounted on wagons substituting for gun carriages. A three-man crew sat by each field piece; their wild-eyed intensity betrayed their willingness to fire them at us.

Toussaint and Jean-Pierre ordered us into battle formation. Our smart movement and the sun's rays reflecting off our muskets gave Jeannot pause. He spoke first, asking why we took the road to Le Cap? Did we not see signs of danger, or had buzzards carried them away? He meant no insult to Toussaint and his black escort, and they could pass, but not the whites whom he protected. After all, Jeannot said that he needed them for his collection. Then his soldiers dragged before us three white women fettered together. One of them, I recognized from Catherine's party. All three had the dazed looks of the insane.

Then Toussaint spoke. He told Jeannot that their conversation ended here if the gunners did not abandon their wagons. If they failed to do so, they would be gunned down before they could touch-off a cannon. Jeannot obeyed; already he felt his authority withering before his rival. Toussaint then not only refused to give up the Libertats and my boys, but laid claim to Jeannot's three white women. Bringing whites safely to Le Cap, he emphasized, would improve the atmosphere for negotiations with French colonial officials. Jeannot backed down, surrendering his female captives to Papa.

Then I saw him! Next to a rebel sporting the Comte de Noé's distinctive walking cane, stood Zèbre! He stepped toward my carriage, as Jeannot opened his ranks letting us pass. I reined my horse, halting our entire procession, as I awaited the traitor's arrival. The brass knob of my pistol pressed on my stomach, urging revenge. Fury filled my being, as he handed me the note for Catherine. I faced a critical decision because shooting Zèbre would start a melee, and my boys might be killed. Caution silenced me, but not little Philip. You waved at Zèbre with the sweet innocence of a child, expressing your pleasure that he had survived. Your words shamed Zèbre more than I could have. Our column began moving again, but to this day, I feel cheated that I spared Zèbre's life. The note, I folded and placed in a pocket over my heart, where it still remains to this day.

When Le Cap came into view, Papa dispatched a rider under a flag of truce to the central gate. He instructed him to inform the garrison commander that we had white refugees, including injured women requiring immediate medical attention. Riding out with a detachment of dragoons with your Uncle Philip at his side was Colonel Louis Tousard, French commandant of Fort Dauphin and director of martial law in Le Cap. Uncle Philip had spent four sleepless days and nights searching for Catherine. Not seeing her among the three women in Papa's care, he listened to my story and was crushed. But Tousard had a different purpose: He had come to extend Governor Blanchlande's invitation to Papa for a conference.

As a courtesy, Tousard would provide an escort for the Libertats, my boys, and me to Uncle Philip's townhouse, while Papa conferred with the governor. Papa agreed with Tousard's request, but with the proviso that Jean-Pierre and another maroon accompany him with only one pistol each. Sly old Anansi! Papa avoided some nosey white in Le Cap spotting Ardisson's sword dangling from Jean-Pierre's side. Leaving Renaud in charge of his camp, Papa, Jean-Pierre and a maroon left with Tousard and his escort for Blanchelande's residence at Le Gouvernement. The two dragoons left behind directed me and Papa's whites to join the people filing into Le Cap.

As I guided our carriage through the city's main gate, salvos of rolling thunder from Fort Dauphin's heavy cannons shook the earth, as rebels pressed Le Cap's defenses. Substitute drums for those instruments of death, and I might have heard a giant Calenda. This was, after all, the dance of thousands of slaves breaking their bonds and those before them for almost two hundred years. Their hopes rose on a high tide of human blood, spilt by whites and mulattoes but mainly their own, only to find in time, less than they expected.

Our carriage and escort rode the streets of Le Cap slowly, picking our way through people in every state of despair, dodging fire brigades dowsing an arsonist's blaze, and staring at lampposts bearing the burdens of lynch victims. Hysterical white mobs sought free Negroes and mulattoes for their vengeance, convinced that these poor souls collaborated with the slaves who torched the plantations on the Plaine du Nord. Swaying with other lynch victims was Madame Lujoie, mulattress keeper of Le Cap's public baths and friend to many city whites. Mob violence fortunately died down when we arrived, but it still smoldered. Even in this uneasy lull, smoke and ash from ruined plantations fell upon streets clogged with refugees moving toward Le Cap's main wharf serving their evacuation. Our entourage halted at 22 Rue Jean, Uncle Philip's and Aunt Désirée's residence. Your uncle awaited us, as he had preceded our arrival.

A lump swelled in my throat, as we touched ground. Was Wahl alive? Uncle Philip's deep grief over Catherine made me hesitate asking him about Wahl when we first met. Now my anxiety drove me wild, as Uncle Philip's stone-cold face revealed nothing about my love. But when we entered his townhouse, I saw her! She had survived the hurricane of human destruction. I raced to embrace her, oblivious to everyone else's sorrows, even your uncle's. Soon, however, our joyous reunion gave ground to the sadness of your mother's death filling the house. Now Uncle Philip asked me for every detail of her last moments. After everyone left but us for the courtyard, I obliged his request. When I finished, an emotionally defeated Uncle Philip wept for his beloved Catherine. His only consolation came from watching my own tears for your mother. When I entered the courtyard, Wahl came over, and leaned her head on my shoulder. My love's safety gave me great celebration, but Catherine's death paled my happiness.

Philip joined Désirée, bedridden by depression and withered by drink, in her bedroom. Apparently they discussed changing their plans for exile. I am convinced that had Catherine survived, we all would have sailed for Matanzas, Cuba, where your uncle owned several plantations. But the torment of Catherine's fate darkened his heart. He did not want any reminder of your mother, including you boys. Instead of going to Cuba as one group, he now divided us into two. He, Désirée, and Wahl would sail for Cuba. For the second group, he directed you boys and me to Charleston with a letter of introduction for his old business associate, James Macomb. Your uncle placed you boys in his care with a stipend for your expenses deposited in the South Carolina Bank of Charleston.

Uncle Philip called me into Désirée's bedroom. Upon entering, I saw Désirée embracing a crestfallen Philip. Despite the emotional distance between them, despite her perpetual sadness that Philip did not love her, and despite her suspicion that your uncle had an affair with Catherine, she felt overwhelmed by her husband's loss of a love that she never had. She became your mother's proxy to tell your uncle "goodbye." Perhaps more than men, it is inborn in women to understand the tragedy of fallen romance.

What your uncle offered made me realize the helplessness of a slave. He knew the damage he did separating Wahl and me, and as an empty gesture he offered me my freedom—a freedom that he knew I would reject to stay with my boys. How could I abandon them in their voyage to Charleston because a six-year-old and a three-year-old would likely fall to Fate's lightest blow? Once in Charleston, city whites might treat my free status as a threat to their security, and keep me from my boys. As their slave, ironically, I could see them freely. Your uncle accepted my argument, but knew that I longed for Wahl. His grief had turned him into a lesser person than I believed him to be.

Philip, with tears filling his eyes, hugged me. He told me how grateful he was that I rescued you boys, and how he regretted that he placed me in an impossible position by granting me freedom. He added that Désirée's poor health precluded her handling two active boys; as for him, recouping his fortunes in Cuba required all his time, eliminating fatherhood. Then he told me to remain with my boys at his home until he arranged passage for us to Charleston. For expenses, he handed me a fifty livre note, enough for my room and board in Charleston for six months. Now I had to explain Uncle Philip's new plans to Wahl.

Grimacing at my message, Wahl burst into tears. Our dream of a life together had become a nightmare. If I had not restrained her, Wahl might have attacked your uncle. As it was, she only trembled in my arms, uttering words in Creole that would have blushed the spirits of voodoo. Finally Bayon de Libertat calmed her with a proposal.

He announced his family's decision to remain in Le Cap to see if French forces could restore order, making it safe to return to Bréda. In any event, they would leave within the hour for their townhouse on Rue Espagnol. Then he asked Wahl and me: Why not spend our remaining hours together honeymooning? We could stay in the hut for household slaves attached to your uncle's patio wall. Philip quickly consented, and said that he and Désirée would stay in their house except to draw water from their well. Fatalism is a slave's companion, and we agreed, knowing that we could expect nothing more.

When Bayon de Libertat and his family began leaving your uncle's house, I graciously stood, bowed, and hugged each one as they left. They were good people, and Libertat ended the terror on Bréda, and lightened his slaves' burdens. He even broke rules required of a plantation manager; foremost was his encouragement of my and Jean-Pierre's quest for an education. Libertat gave Bréda slaves the thin hope that the humanity which he implanted might tear at the conscience of masters, forcing them to ask an essential moral question: "What right permits one human to own another?" The Libertats later fled to Baltimore when insurgents stormed Le Cap in 1793; Libertat left his safe haven in 1797 on Toussaint's invitation to resume his management of Bréda, only to be murdered by those failing to overthrow Papa.

Wahl and I devoured our short "honeymoon." Echoing blasts from big naval guns, rolling cannonades from Fort Dauphin, rattling musketry, clanging bells announcing yet another fire, striking horses' hooves on nearby streets, and noisy refugees should have raised a chorus of distraction for Wahl and me; but inside, the fleshy explosions of passion became the only sounds we heard. A deep, peaceful slumber followed our exhaustion, my first since the first night of the slave rebellion. Only Papa's commanding voice awoke us. It was time to go. Uncle Philip booked passage for my boys and me on a ship sailing with the tide for Charleston. Another ship on the same tide would carry Philip, Désirée, and Wahl to Cuba.

We stepped into the courtyard to the smiles of Jean-Pierre and Papa. The morning sun struggled through clouds of gun and wood smoke hanging over Le Cap, but enough shone to indicate the time of day—our last day together. The four of us walked inside the townhouse where Uncle Philip and Désirée had assembled eight men to double as porters and bodyguards. Mostly they carried trunks belonging to Désirée.

Before our departure an irrepressible Jean-Pierre told me about Papa's meeting with Governor Blanchelande. Delicately, Papa refused the governor's request that he form a black auxiliary militia to support Tousard's regulars. He opted out, said a smiling Jean-Pierre, under the guise of needing to pacify the area around Bréda before joining the French. Then Papa interrupted Jean-Pierre with a metaphor saying it all: No longer could he stand before the racing stallion and not be trampled; instead he must get the powerful steed to accept a saddle with himself as the rider. It only remained for him to return to Bréda, provide for his family's safety, and join the rebels in the hills. He and Jean-Pierre finally became brothers-in-arms and their records became legendary. Papa even shed "Bréda" for "L'Ouverture," a name he forever chiseled into history.

Once our motley parade headed for Quai Saint Louis, I noticed a marked difference in the Le Cap that we saw earlier. Gone were scenes of utter chaos, as soldiers lined both sides of the street; gone were looters, dragging their stolen treasures from a townhouse; gone also were bloodthirsty lynch mobs, seeking the neck of a free Negro or mulatto to stretch from a lamppost. Terror now became more organized, more deliberate, as Le Cap fell under martial law. Doses of grape shot dispersed lynch mobs; firing squads dispatched looters; summary trials awaited those inciting panic or riot. Calm appeared only on the surface, like a boiler with no valve, ready to explode into new violence. Despite our unease, we reached the docks of Le Cap with our grunting escort, struggling with the trunk-laden valuables of Uncle Philip and Désirée.

Barely had we stepped onto the planked quay filled with refugees, than three soldiers blocked our way. They demanded our trunks, explaining that each trunk filled a space that denied someone's escape. Over the quay's edge the chests must go, they ordered, and at gunpoint directed execution of their orders. Horrified, Désirée ran after her cargo of a lifetime with one trunk alone filled with all her shoes. Uncle Philip ran after his furious wife before a soldier might consider her behavior sufficient reason to shoot her. With soldiers now chasing Désirée, she reached her last trunk, flipped its latches, reached in, and grabbed her dearest possession: a silver cognac flask, the trophy of her drunkenness. Her antics caused a hail of laughter from soldiers and nearby civilians. Unruffled, she put this companion of her loneliness inside her shawl and huffed back to Uncle Philip, pretending nothing had happened.

Why had Papa Toussaint not foreseen this embarrassing moment and warned the Chartrands? This incident could not have surprised him. It dawned on me that maybe he orchestrated this event to grant me a little revenge against Uncle Philip. Then Désirée did something that amazed me. She stepped to pier's edge, watching the military guard toss her luggage into the harbor. The first seven trunks sank almost immediately, the eighth one with her shoes sank more slowly, one end up pointing skyward and the other end submerged, like a sinking galleon. Just before it passed into the deeps, Désirée threw her cognac flask into the harbor, and watched its silvery shimmers, as it joined her chests in their watery graves.

She seemed angry, like an infant just out of the womb. She had nothing but herself, only age and a few clothes separated her from the beginning of life. Hurling her flask had set Désirée free. Until then her life had been empty, hopeless, and loveless. Only Death sat in her audience so far, applauding her poor performance, and to Death only had she played. But no more! Before the final curtain call on this poor play, she pledged herself to a better role. What she left in Saint-Domingue did not follow her to Cuba. In Cuba, this sickly, sad dame, whom Uncle Philip considered near Eternity's Gate, regained her health, outlived her spouse, and lived to a very old age. Even her relationship with Philip improved, as they gained mutual respect and affection for each other, although short of love. Of greater importance, alcohol no longer ruled her life.

A musket's loud blast ended this dockside farce. A refugee standing behind us panicked and headed for the lowering longboats packed with passengers. He elbowed his way forward, pushed the first guard aside, but the second one shot him, and pushed his body over the side of the quay; there the dead man joined other cadavers bobbing in the tide for having violated martial law. Calm settled over the crowd, and our line moved mechanically forward, like theatre patrons handing their tickets to an usher.

With us were Jean-Pierre and Papa Toussaint; dear Wahl was with the Chartrands in another line for transportation to the *Crépuscule*, a French packet ship bound for Matanzas, Cuba. As we moved forward, something besides losing Wahl troubled me, and Papa Toussaint sensed it. Staying and fighting with my brothers for freedom or leaving for Charleston with my boys ripped at my soul. Papa put a hand on my shoulder, looked into my eyes, and put my conflict to rest. He told me to leave Saint-Domingue with my boys, adding that I was no coward. He and Jean-Pierre would remain and probably die, but someone needed to survive to write our story, explaining what drove our people to rebellion. I still recall his words: "You will do this! That is my command." I promised Papa that I would—a promise that I almost forgot until an incident at Colonel Alston's mansion in Charleston jolted my memory, inspiring me to fulfill my pledge.

Time arrived for our departure. Jean-Pierre squeezed me hard, stood back, and pulled from beneath his shirt a mahogany amulet representing Ogun, the voodoo war spirit. Pressing it over his heart with his right hand, he handed me a second amulet of Ogun with his left. Both images he had carved. We were truly brothers, born out of rivalry, danger, and eventually love. Even though I never saw Jean-Pierre again, I put his gift on the chain which I had acquired from our boyhood adventure in Le Cap, and put it around my neck where it still remains. Toussaint gave me a heartfelt farewell. He had become the father that I lost back in Africa.

I struggled with you boys to board the longboat carrying us to the *Sundown*, a Jamaican merchant ship evacuating refugees from Le Cap. I strained to see if Wahl might be in one of the outward bound boats disappearing into banks of haze. Nothing! First Catherine and now Wahl! Both gone from my life! Suddenly, I felt cold and hugged you boys, as we shared a common grief.

When we reached the *Sundown*, her crew hoisted women and children on board first; then the rest of us clambered up the ship's netting, white males first and blacks last. My appearance on deck signaled the captain of the *Sundown* to weigh anchor and for me to find you boys. Alone for nearly an hour, there you stood like soldiers, following my orders and awaiting more. Our safety depended on your cooperation with me, a burden you both bore well.

Hardly had the *Sundown's* prow set course for open water than

I realized her type. She was a slaver! Stowed in the gunwales, both port and starboard, were instruments of bondage: manacles, fetters, chains, and whips. How ironic that one of Satan's fleet carried me to Saint-Domingue, while another took me away. Sad memories returned, especially my loss of Mother. Fortunately a mariner's voice penetrated my grief. It belonged to Captain Samuel Gamble. He explained that he and your uncle were business associates. As a favor to Uncle Philip, he promised to take us on board the *Sundown* sailing for Charleston. But his responsibilities as commander limited his ability to protect us. He warned that our greatest danger might come from a grieving white, taking offense of a master-less slave accompanying two white boys.

I thanked Captain Gamble, as the *Sundown* left Le Cap on a turning tide. Disappearing first were people on the docks, then houses and buildings, and finally the spire of Notre Dame Church; but never disappearing were thoughts of loved ones—especially Wahl. Her ship meant *twilight* in English and mine *sundown*, the omen seemed obvious. I'd never see her again.

I will continue describing our voyage to Charleston and our life there in my next letter. For now, my heart and wrist have grown tired.

Love to My Boys,
Saturday

Philip ended the letter lost in thought. His mind carried him back to his escape from Saint-Domingue. Gratitude for Saturday's rescue of John and himself filled his heart, but vied with his anger over his mother's death. He remembered the *Sundown*, heading for Charleston, as if only yesterday. Two long bony arms squeezed Philip, snapping him back into the present. It was Wahl hugging him.

"Feels good, but why—" as Wahl placed a finger over his lips.

"It's just something from my heart. Human suffering touches me, even if it falls on a massah's child," said the old cook. "Don't say something silly like my warm heart came from sitting too close to my stove. Just accept my sorrow for your misery. You're not easy to love, but I'm trying."

"You never cried about your mother's death?" Susan Elizabeth inquired.

"Saturday just never saw John and me crying. The *Sundown* could have floated on our tears. We wept plenty when Saturday slept."

"Now I know the sadness in your soul. Why didn't you tell me before now?" Susan Elizabeth scolded tearfully.

"A man doesn't always express his feelings," Philip retorted. "Some subjects are best left alone. Talking about my mother's tragedy makes me feel sad again."

Wahl motioned the fussing lovebirds to her table for pie and coffee when the kitchen door swung open. With his back to the entry, Philip assumed the intruder was John Gilbert, attending to his duties.

"John, come back—" Philip said, as a gruff voice cut him off.

"Ain't no John, suh; I be har tah git ma' niggurah. Joe be his name. Hiz ownuh en Chawlstohn dun sen' me tah collect'um," said the man at the kitchen door.

The voice belonged to C.M. Jones, known to Lowcountry folks as "Moccasin" Jones, perhaps the state's most notorious slave catcher. Moccasin was of average height, portly, with a sun-withered face, and an unkempt tobacco-stained beard. He had a coiled whip in his right hand and a whistle to call his dogs in his left. Not one to trifle with, Moccasin sensed Philip's fear of him.

"Iz ya seed um, stationmassah?" Moccasin growled.

"Seen whom?" Philip replied.

"Damn, yo knows who I be talkin' bout! Jes told yo. I gets ma niggurah ever' time. Jes axe dat boy I dun got down on da Edey-stoh."

Philip knew that Moccasin referred to a fight that he had with two fugitive slaves escaping by rowboat on the Edisto River. Just as the runaways shoved off, Moccasin leapt into their small craft, but, toppled overboard. As he fell, he grabbed both young men,

164

carrying them over the side with him. In the ensuing fight, Moccasin drowned one and captured the other. Incidents like this one created the legend that no slave could outrun Moccasin's pursuit. Like the cypress swamps' deadliest snake, Moccasin dangled over the head of any fugitive attempting flight, and his bite could be fatal.

Moccasin warned, "yo bettuh not be hiden' no utter man's niggurah. Dat be stealin'. Dems dat duh go tuh dah hooscal."

Turning his reptilian gaze on Wahl, Moccasin asked, "duh yo kno' whar Joe be, old niggurah?"

"Duh not kno', suh, but look en dem pots. Joe ain't en nun uf dem," Wahl replied, making Moccasin's temper flare.

"Yo ain't gonna giv' me no sauce, niggeruh!" Moccasin shouted. "I'll whoop da sass off'n yo ass!"

Faster than a striking snake, Moccasin uncoiled his whip, and Wahl edged toward a knife on her table. Wahl's temper smoldered, but Susan Elizabeth moved quickly, grabbing the knife and slicing more pie for herself.

"Delicious," remarked Susan Elizabeth, licking the knife blade. "Wahl makes the best pies in Orangeburg Parish. Have some, Moccasin." But the ill-tempered beast rejected her offer.

Now Philip confronted the man whom he feared. "Wahl is *my* slave. I will not allow your whip across her back, Moccasin. If you do, you're in for a fight. But I do recognize her insolence toward you, and she'll be punished for it."

Moccasin relaxed, while gathering his whip. Wahl still fumed, while Susan Elizabeth anticipated the tipping scales of the conflict. She still held the pie knife, but would its use be for eating or fighting?

Leaving the kitchen, Moccasin whirled around and pointed at Philip, "yo be niggurah luvah. Why duh yo tink I be har'? Mos' folks 'round har kno' dat. I got ma eye un yo. Bettuh giv'up Joe if'n yo be hidin' him."

Ignoring Wahl, Moccasin tipped his hat to Susan Elizabeth and stormed out; Susan Elizabeth felt relieved but embarrassed over the slave hunter's courtesy toward her. But Moccasin's exit brought Philip no relief. He knew that his adversary would be watching the depot with a serpent's patience. After a few minutes, Philip checked outside, circled the depot, and even searched two vacant freight cars on a siding. No Moccasin lurked, at least for now. Philip dashed back into the kitchen, and began questioning Wahl.

"Do you know anything about Joe?" he asked. But Wahl said nothing. "I've long suspected that you aided fugitive slaves," Philip added. Wahl continued her silence. "Remember Phillis four years ago?" as Philip homed in on Wahl with a prosecutor's focus. "You assisted her, didn't you? Her master suspects that I participated in her escape."

Wahl could stand no more, "Yes, yes, yes! Do you think that I could ignore runaways needing my help? And yes! I know where Joe is. He stepped off a passenger train from Charleston with a forged pass from his master. But like a poker player with a weak hand, he decided to end his bluff. So he took to the woods, waited for nightfall, and climbed into the water tank. He's there now, setting for a chance to make a run."

"Hell, Wahl!" Philip snapped. "You could have ruined everything for us. A slave owner is president of the railroad, and slave owners sit on his board. Plantation slaves along the road's right-of-way and railroad-owned slaves built the South Carolina Railroad. What will happen to Susan Elizabeth and me if railroad officials suspect us of harboring fugitive slaves? Proslavery locals might damn well lynch us before the railroad could fire us."

"Sorry, Mr. Philip," Wahl replied. "I didn't mean to cause you and Susan Elizabeth trouble. But I've watched countless trains passing here with cattle cars loaded with slaves. Mournful songs and sad faces told me that many were uprooted from their families and probably headed west to plantations in Alabama and Mississippi. And I endured Mistuh McElveen arriving here with coffles of slaves for rail shipment west, or for auctions in Charleston. I can't help it! I have to stand with my people if one escapes."

Philip considered Wahl's defense and replied, "I understand your feelings, but your timing is awful. There is a mood favoring secession in South Carolina, and the political atmosphere is more heated than a skillet full of your hot biscuits. The eyes of the law are on this depot, forcing me to deny your further involvement with fugitive slaves."

Anger contorted Wahl's face, and she felt her old hostility toward Philip returning. Then Philip gave her reason for hope.

"I don't want you anywhere near where Joe hides," Philip emphasized. I'll assist his escape, but for now, I want you either in your kitchen or in your bed. Moccasin will turn us over to the sheriff on the slightest provocation.

"I be yo niggurah. Why, I duz yo work, Mas' Philip. I be good en mak' yo proud," said Wahl, back to her old sassiness.

"Thanks, I'm glad that you'll do my work and make me proud," said Philip, returning her sarcasm. "We won't meet again until after the Fourth of July. Maybe by then, the fire-eaters will have burned themselves out, making safer any decision I make about our helping fugitive slaves. Until then, you will attend *only* to cooking duties, while Susan Elizabeth and I will avoid your kitchen. No point giving Moccasin material for a conspiracy theory. We just need him to grow tired of watching us, and move on down the line."

Wahl's temper still fumed, as the couple left her kitchen. With no one to talk to, she spoke to her reflection in the kitchen's only window. "Is Philip just another white man unmoved by my people's sufferings? Why didn't Susan Elizabeth speak in my defense?" Her image in the glass listened, but gave no answer.

Late that afternoon, Wahl sat on her kitchen steps with a cooling breeze soothing her temper. She saw no sign of Philip's promise to save Joe; only John Gilbert passed with a wide-brimmed hat shielding his head from the sun. He had his tool box, a bucket of oakum, and a spool of cotton cord. John waved at her, apparently on his way to seal leaks in the water tank. She watched him scale the ladder and disappear into the tank. A little later, Wahl saw a man descend the ladder with his toolbox, wave at her again, and disappear. That night, a shadowy, hatless figure climbed down from the tank, heading for the depot kitchen. Wahl toiled at her duties when John Gilbert walked in bareheaded and soaked to his knees. Philip had kept his promise.

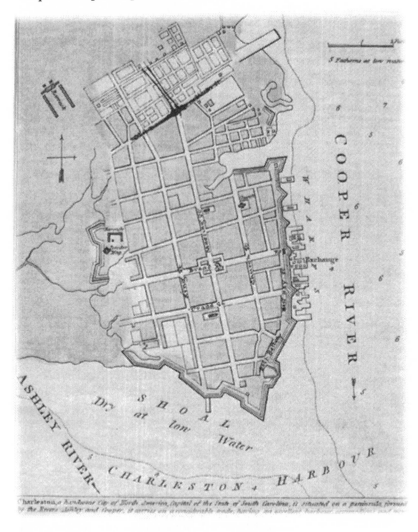

Charleston in 1800
John Luffman, Cartographer

The Seventh Letter

Philip stood at the sorting table, pigeonholing the afternoon mail. He sought a particular letter since the Fourth of July. Then he found it, an envelope addressed to him from the South Carolina Railroad. He tore it open, and began reading:

Office of the President
32 South Carolina Railroad Street
Charleston, July 11, 1850

Dear Mr. Chartrand:
    I am pleased to announce that on your and the superintendent's recommendations, Morgan James has my and the board of directors approval to fill the position of stationmaster at Lewisville. Mr. James has given the South Carolina Railroad long and faithful service as section boss on the Hamburg Branch; the board members and I are confident that he will continue his good service in his new assignment. The selection of a new section boss as his replacement, we leave to your discretion.
Sincerely,
H. W. Conner,
President of the South Carolina Railroad

Armed with new information, Philip hurriedly collected old copies of the Charleston *Mercury* from his desk top, as Susan Elizabeth joined him. Together they would state their position to

Wahl about assisting runaway slaves. Philip knew that his credibility with the old cook had grown thin, as they entered Wahl's kitchen. She looked up, as she trimmed excess dough from her pies. Back was her old scornful stare.

"What want me fo' massah?" she mocked. "I be here fo' sho.' Only in ma kitchen or in ma bed, like yo' done sade."

"Mock me if you like!" Philip replied. "But damn it, you're going to listen to me. And knock off the Gullah. You speak it poorly." Then Philip dropped the stack of Charleston *Mercury* newspapers on her kitchen table.

"We live in dangerous times," Philip began. "South Carolina verges on secession. A man wishing to live out his years here would be crazy to help a runaway."

Then Philip started reading testimonials in the *Mercury*.

"Here's one denouncing the Union as a source of Northern oppression of the South. Here's another by William Gilmore Simms who believes South Carolina must defend its liberties with sword and rifle. Another from Orangeburg inspires its citizens to stand against Northern aggression like they had in 1832. Here's an interesting one that calls African slavery conservatism's last stronghold. My favorite, however, comes from B. F. Brown in nearby Barnwell. He calls the Barnwell Artillery Carolina's devoted sons, defenders of Southern rights. Funny, I served in the Barnwell Artillery five years ago. Training involved firing six-pounder rounds into a dirt bank and digging them out for the next drill. Now that ought to frighten a federal army," Philip laughed.

"Make your point," Wahl growled. "If you're this slow having sex, I'd fall asleep."

"Well, stay awake," as Philip summarized Conner's letter. "Morgan James has gained the appointment of stationmaster at Lewisville and out of our way. I selected John Gilbert to replace him as section boss on the Hamburg Branch."

"So what?" Wahl injected.

Philip continued, "Helping runaways at the depot is dangerous, and Moccasin seeks our arrest. Public opinion is bound to intensify its support for a new fugitive slave law in the making. So I will not permit fugitives to hide near the depot, but instead I'll send them on to Gilbert's section gang camp near Hamburg. Since his crew is mostly railroad-owned slaves, Gilbert will give them new names, adding each to his role. When conditions permit, fugitives will move from Gilbert's camp to their contact at the Carolina Hotel in Hamburg by following Big Horse Creek. They must avoid the tracks because slave catchers patrol the rails closely."

Despite her renewed confidence in Philip, Wahl expressed her doubt: "Can you depend on John Gilbert's loyalty?"

"John Gilbert," he reassured, "not only rescued Joe, but suffered oppression as an indentured servant. He knows the yearning to be free and is anti-slavery. Besides, we have a close friendship. I guarantee his loyalty to me and to our purpose."

When he finished, Philip's eye caught the wall calendar behind Susan Elizabeth. "July 23rd!" he blurted out. "Tomorrow I make my annual trek to my friend Bason's gravesite. It'll be my twentieth since he fell to yellow fever."

Then Philip wondered what he would tell his old friend. He still owned slaves from his Tivoli Gardens venture in Charleston. South Carolina blocked his manumitting them, making it likely that he would die a slaveholder. Adding to this irony, his best friend had been a Quaker. Then Philip noticed Susan Elizabeth's subtle beauty. Normally he suppressed feelings of adoration, but not this time.

"I really love how sunlight and shadows etch your good looks," Philip said adoringly.

"Must want something," Wahl giggled.

They laughed, and even Philip joined in at his own expense. A relaxed mood settled over the trio. With his girls smiling again, Philip began reading Saturday's seventh letter:

Labyrinth Plantation
Matanzas
April 4, 1823

Dear Philip and John:

I ended my last letter as the *Sundown* left for Charleston on a fair wind. We stood looking at Le Cap with smoke rising from the Plaine du Nord behind it. Many white dreams floated away in that troubled sky, making way for the new dreams of a freshly liberated people. I further caught the irony of white people crowded on board a slave ship. I wondered about their reaction had they worn those shackles stowed along the gunwales. I did, however, regret the grievous losses of some. Slavery stole from hearts on both sides.

My thoughts ended when a distinguished looking man, accompanied by an old dame, pushed through the crowd to where we stood. He was chatty: Would Le Cap fall? Would the sea turn heavy? Would Charleston receive us well? I had no answers. Then he introduced himself and his companion. He was Monsieur Dainville, actor and comedian. The lady was the Comtesse d'Offermont, patron of Le Cap's theatre. He traveled with the Comtesse to Charleston to find her a suitable residence, and then return to Le Cap when the slave rebellion ended. After I introduced myself and you boys, he urged me to tell our story. I told them everything to the moment of us sailing on the *Sundown*. They were deeply moved, causing Dainville to wonder what Shakespeare might have written about us. They even seconded Captain Gamble's warning that some grief-stricken planter might vent his rage on me.

Their apprehension soon became reality. An angry planter approached me, demanding to know why I chaperoned two white boys without a master. He had watched us since our boarding. Was I going to kill you boys? Was I saving you for a voodoo sacrifice in South Carolina? He said that *bêtes noires* (black beasts) killed his family, and that he had been helpless to save them before his desperate escape. The dried blood stains on his shirt belonged to his lifeless little girl whom he carried for miles before realizing that Death had shut her eyes. I might have sympathized with him, but now a crowd gathered and echoed my assailant's anger. He raised his cane, while I braced for his blow, knowing that any retaliation might get me lynched from a yard arm.

Then a loud voice pierced the man's violent diatribes, as another cane parried my attacker's. My savior had arrived. He was Monsieur Dainville, pretending to be the Marquis de Mascarille, wealthy planter from Limonade. The character came from one of Molière's comedies that he had played on stage. With the haughty affectations of an offended noble, he performed his part beautifully. What right, he shouted, allowed my assailant to damage *his* property? Any further discourtesy, he would settle with the sword sheathed inside his cane. Then turning to me he said, "the Comtesse requires your attention." I nervously moved with you boys to where the Comtesse d'Offermont stood, and she pretended to scold me.

Monsieur Dainville later settled the Comtesse in a townhouse on George Street, and returned to Le Cap. But his optimism about a short slave rebellion faded, and he returned to Charleston where he joined the French Theatre, and starred in Rousseau's *Pygmalion* beginning the 1794 drama season. On those occasions when I passed him on a Charleston street, he would quip, "The Comtesse requires your attention," and I always replied, "Yes sir, and how is she today?" Never have I forgotten his brave performance, or that he and the Comtesse remained in character until we docked at Charleston.

No more bedraggled, beaten group of people ever landed at Gadsden Wharf, except African slaves, than the Saint-Domingue refugees arriving in Charleston in early September, 1791. Warm-hearted Charlestonians opened their homes and purses to those descending the gangways. Many among our rescuers were Huguenots, proud of their French ancestry and proud of their part in the first great republican experiment in modern history—the United States of America. They aided us individually and through their benevolent organization, The Two Bit Society. Those refugee children without guardians, the society sent to the Orphan House, where they learned a trade or skill to prepare them for indenture.

Our group crowded into East Bay Street near The Exchange, where months earlier George Washington attended a ball in his honor. I revered President Washington, and later saw a parallel between him and Papa, as each guided his country through perilous waters. Standing in our midst was Jean de Ternant, French consul, who uttered meaningless consolations to desperate people. Mainly he advised us to avoid causing a political upheaval. He need not have worried, since most refugees were Royalists. Republican or Royalist, Charlestonians welcomed us because a "French craze" had swept the port city. France, they believed, followed the American example by declaring itself a republic.

Some refugees resorted to desperate measures to recover their fallen statuses. Such was the case of a wealthy white woman who came to Charleston, left her children with friends, returned to Saint-Domingue's Artibonite Valley, and located her hidden treasures. Death did not miss his second chance to claim her, and the orphanage got her little ones. More fortunate were those who left with their portable assets and a cadre of slaves. One sold a fortune in diamonds to an Alston to buy a rice plantation. Equally fortunate were the La Chicottes who recouped their wealth and social standing with Cedar Grove, Wellbrook, and The Tavern rice plantations on the Wando River.

But for the majority, a menial lifestyle characterized their lives in Charleston. Some became coiffeurs, teachers, dance instructors, jewelers, milliners, innkeepers, proprietors of coffee shops, theatre directors and actors, and owners of public "gardens," like Vaux Hall Gardens. Their shops were mainly on King, Union, and Archdale streets, while most lived on Queen Street. As a group they enjoyed a good time, as they established "long rooms" at taverns and coffee houses for dancing, music, and socializing. They also acknowledged human sexual needs with their establishment of brothels. The most famous was The Sailors' Boarding House which drifted from neighborhood to neighborhood, riding out waves of protest from the self-righteous. Charlestonians loved them because they were French and good-natured. These attributes more than offset local concern that the holy Sabbath was slipping away at the hands of these jolly heathens, and that their fear of slave rebellions made the Carolina planter class edgy. On balance, the refugees taught Charlestonians to have fun, or "à la mode française," as they called it.

Near our crowd of exiles, stood a man holding a child in one arm, while motioning me with his other. He asked in French if I were Samedi, and if you were John and Philip. He was James Macomb, your Uncle Philip's friend and prominent vendue master, a status he earned auctioning slaves "on the block" for high prices. We followed him to his house on Meeting Street, our home for the next few years. Macomb said that he received a letter from Uncle Philip concerning our arrival on the *Sundown*. This meant that Uncle Philip probably sent the message the day after the slave rebellion in Saint-Domingue, and before he knew Catherine's fate. Our suffering never entered his calculations. Why should I have ever trusted a slave owner?

During our Charleston years, the Macomb family figured heavily in your upbringing, as well as two other families, the Esnards and the Pebartes. While with the Macombs, John forged a bond with James, Jr., the Macombs' only child. Young James had a reserved personality, or so thought the Macombs until my raucous little John brought him into the playful world of children. Two loud children running and laughing through the Macomb household challenged the Charleston standard that little children should be little adults. You, Philip, by contrast, seemed reserved with an inner sweetness that once characterized your mother. I privately dubbed African nicknames for both of you: John was "Sunjata" ("Hungry Lion"), and Philip was "Garai" ("Calm One"). In the years ahead, John made friends easily with his peers and led a tight circle of associates which I named "The Pirate Gang." Philip, however, had few "growing up" friends. Mostly his friends were much older, men like Joel Poinsett and Philippe Noisette, who nurtured his interests in horticulture and public gardens.

After "settling in" at the Macombs, I wandered the streets of Charleston, a city bearing striking resemblances to Le Cap. Both places had populations close to seventeen thousand, more slave than free; both places had busy harbors encumbered with shifting sand bars; both places relied on a healthy carrying trade of exported commodities and imported finished goods; both amassed great fortunes from the slave trade, even though Charleston temporarily stopped hers; both places considered their cultures European in an American wilderness; and both places employed double standards regarding race. Oppression of slaves was the order of the day in both Le Cap and Charleston, but those same orders allowed free Negroes and slaves to occupy dwellings in the better white neighborhoods.

As in Le Cap, there were two Charlestons, one ordered, the other disordered. Ordered Charleston belonged to the whites. It secured their lives through laws, discipline, and a systematic tyranny of slaves and free Negroes. Disordered Charleston was the black world beyond white control. It flourished in alleys, tippling houses, the city after dark, and behind spiritual walls beyond white control. I once felt that the slaves of Le Cap verged on an explosion; I had the same feeling about Charleston.

My port city tour began on East Bay Street, paralleling the Cooper River. Here were the main wharves; here too were the home offices of Charleston's richer merchants. Proceeding down East Bay Street from The Exchange, I passed the intersections of Broad, Elliott, and Tradd streets, main location for retail stores. The better residential streets were Broad, King, Meeting, Queen, and Church streets. On the corner of Tradd and Bedon's Alley rested The Carolina Coffee House, named after its London parent. Here city moguls sealed financial and shipping deals; it further served as a well-to-do boarding house and as a club for social events. At the end of East Bay Street, I came upon East Battery and White Point, affording a wonderful view of the confluence of the Ashley and Cooper Rivers and the harbor beyond. Above The Exchange, I passed Prichard's Shipyard, where later I gained employment, until I reached Boundary Street, the effective northern limit of Charleston, and where wagon yards received Upcountry cotton.

Only East Bay Street was partially paved with cobblestones. Others were packed down in a mixture of crushed shell and sand (much like Le Cap). Charleston had four markets run by slaves, and for street cleaners were flocks of buzzards that locals affectionately called "Charleston Eagles." A city ordinance protected these winged agents of sanitation. Like Le Cap, Charleston in 1791 had several architectural gems: The Exchange, and St. Michael's and St. Philip's Episcopal Churches.

I made one more stop before returning to the Macombs. At the corner of Magazine and Mazyck, I saw a plain building. It was the Workhouse, home to the punishment and torture of slaves. Its warden served as a sort of city driver who whipped captured runaways and domestics incurring a master's wrath. For fifty cents, he would "give a nigger a little sugar," an expression derived from a sugar warehouse where this torment began in the city's history. Even gray-haired little old ladies, wishing not to soil their hands with their slaves' blood, found this service a convenience. The Workhouse, like the maréchaussée prison in Le Cap, was a monument to human sufferings.

When I arrived in Charleston, in 1791, Charleston verged on great prosperity following British occupation of the city during the American Revolution. Charleston acquired its first banks in 1790: the South Carolina Bank on Broad Street and the National Bank on Church. A new generation of merchants sat on a pile of gold with a generation of older ones, led by men like Adam Tunno. Two inventions accelerated Charleston's economy: the rice mill and the cotton gin. This caused cotton production to spread into the Carolina Upcountry, rice production to double, and Charleston to move away from the carrying trade and toward crop exports. Wealth also became concentrated in the hands of the rice barons, creating a proliferating demand for more slaves and a lifting of South Carolina's ban on the infamous African trade.

My first responsibility in Charleston was to find work. Thomas Bacot of the South Carolina Bank acted as trustee for funds which Uncle Philip had provided for you boys and for me, your slave. But this stipend soon ran out. James Macomb, "Uncle" James by now, agreed to provide us room and board, but beyond that, he emphasized his obligations to his family. He suggested that your education begin at the St. Philip's Free School for indigent children and orphans. Orphans? You weren't orphans! We were family! I appreciated Uncle James' financial position, because Uncle Philip had cast him into an awkward situation. I suggested that I become a contract slave, earning as much as two dollars a day. A good month might bring me fifty dollars. Out of my earnings, I would provide for my boys' education, clothes, their spending money at three dollars each per month, and for my own room and board at the Macombs' home. Uncle James readily agreed, and even paid for my annual work licenses totaling three dollars.

And so I hit the streets of Charleston looking for work. My blacksmithing skills landed me a job at Pritchard's repair shop at Gadsden Wharf. Impressed by my work performance, Pritchard further assigned me to his shipyard at upper East Bay Street. When free from tongs and hammer, I hired out as a domestic for special events at Colonel William Alston's 27 King Street address. On opening day of Race Week, I drove him and his family to the Washington Course attired in bright green livery, and accompanied by footmen and outriders who matched my uniform. The Colonel loved a damn good show. My most enduring friendships in Charleston came from these labors: Two were blacksmiths (George Wilson and Tom Russell), a third, a caulker at the shipyard (Gullah Jack Pritchard), and the fourth, a boatman at Gadsden Wharf (George Lining).

The history of Charleston was in the faces of its people: an old slave withered by time and toil; a prime slave staring angrily at a world that he hated; a Negro woman grimacing under the weight of Massah's clothes basket on her head; a bored white woman whose only place was in her home; a drunken sailor with a drooping face, wondering what had happened to his last dollar; a trollop with a painted face who had his last dollar; a young white face beaming with hope; a young black face with no hope.

Soon after my arrival in Charleston with my boys, I realized that the "French craze," which struck Le Cap, had followed us here. It was easy to understand: Charlestonians still resented British occupation of their city during the American Revolution; French assistance to the rebel cause still generated a warm feeling among townspeople; and the French Revolution raised a popular republican pride in a city governed by conservative Federalists. Foremost, perhaps, were the powers of fad and fashion.

City dwellers wore the revolutionary cockade as part of their daily dress, while salutations to a neighbor began with "citizen." If they shared a meal with friends, they circulated the "*bonnet rouge*" (red hat) for each to don and shout "*viva la révolution*" before passing it on; at public events, the American and French flags flew side by side, while audiences sang the *Caira* and the *Marseillaise* with as much heartfelt pride as if they themselves pulled down The Bastille. The craze got out of hand, when in early January, 1792, Charleston honored the French National Assembly in a public ceremony: The bells at St. Michael's and at St. Philip's chimed, a thirteen-cannon salute sounded, followed by a parade of French and American citizens to St. Philip's to hear a sermon. The service concluded with the congregation singing the *Te Deum* and the *Marseillaise.* That a church hosted the event, seemed ironic, given revolutionary France's attack on religion.

A tone of pure silliness entered the craze. Ladies of high society patronized a local hairdresser, not so much for his coiffures but for his radical politics. He was Monsieur Dubard, self-proclaimed *sans culotte* (Parisian rabble) and witness to Marie Antoinette's execution, which he shared with his customers in every juicy detail. Other hairdressers competed with Dubard's popularity by claiming that the human hair in their wigs came from those in France who fell to the guillotine's sharp blade. But nothing could top the beheading of a famous local statue.

Expressing their gratitude to William Pitt, the Elder (Lord Chatham) for opposing the Stamp Act, Charles Town in 1770 erected a marble statue to him at the corner of Broad and Meeting streets. The city's hero fame faded with the American Revolution and British occupation of Charleston. Never mind that the statue suffered damage when a British cannon ball blew off its right arm. The popularity of Pitt-in-marble fell further during the "craze," prompting little public sympathy when workers dropped it, snapping off its head. One joyful republican newspaper editor quipped that the statue's fate should initiate the guillotine's use in Charleston against those opposing the French Revolution. The Great Commoner's statue became "nobody's child" and eventually found a symbolic resting place in the courtyard of the Orphan House. These incidents of public mania seem funny now, but at the time, they mirrored the fractures of a society that I had just left.

Into this atmosphere stepped Edmond Genêt, French ambassador to the United States. Charleston feted this little man with parties, which only inflated his self-esteem. He displayed the haughtiness of a French aristocrat, while challenging President Washington's policy of neutrality. Even the Russian Court had earlier expelled him. For Catherine the Great to drive any man away, indicated his intolerable manner. With the assistance of the French consul in Charleston, Monsieur Mangourit, Genêt set about challenging American sovereignty.

He and Mangourit recruited Charleston's manhood for privateering against British shipping, or for attacking Spanish Florida. French privateers wandered Charleston streets, menacing passing citizens, entering gambling houses, and attending Jacobin Clubs that they founded. Genêt lost support from Charleston's elite when he acknowledged his membership in the Amis des Noirs, a French abolitionist society. Eventually Genêt left Charleston for an interview with Washington in Philadelphia. Washington demanded his recall; a then radical France wanted the ambassador's return to feed him to The Terror. He resigned, gained asylum, and moved to New York.

The "craze" calmed when the French Revolution cooled in 1795, and when the French navy began seizing American ships trading with England. By the time of the XYZ Affair in 1797, Charlestonians expressed a strong nationalism that only slavery weakened in the years ahead. Citizens met at St. Michael's to demonstrate their patriotic support for the Quasi War against France, and for a public subscription to build a frigate for the fight. In late 1798, workers at Pritchard's Shipyard laid the keel of the *John Adams*, a thirty-two gun frigate launched in June, 1799. I worked at Pritchard's during that time. I found interesting that the ship's Federalist name signaled the end of the craze.

An even greater outpouring of nationalism, while I lived in Charleston, came during the War of 1812. Charlestonians opened their pocketbooks to construct two small frigates at Pritchard's Shipyard, the *Decatur* and the *Saucy Jack*. Despite the British blockade of Charleston, Captain Chazel of the *Saucy Jack* made ships flying the Union Jack pay a heavy price. Chazel had escaped Saint-Domingue, and became an American hero.

Nationalism in Charleston crested following the destruction of Washington in August, 1814. A British army torched the city, and scattered the American government like scurrying rabbits. Charlestonians braced themselves, certain that the ravaging Red Coats had them in their sights.

Undaunted and defiant, the whole city rushed to build defenses. Working the battlements became fashionable in Charleston. Every morning, a band or orchestra assembled in the streets playing waltzes and martial music; behind them gathered Charlestonians of every walk, parading to construction sites. Even Charleston's wealthiest joined in, followed by their slaves carrying their tools and trays of refreshments. The well-built defenses of Charleston impressed military experts, but Charleston avoided attack; perhaps a spy suggested to the British that New Orleans was an easier target.

Amid the rising grandeur of Charleston, you boys grew up. I tried governing you like a strong father should. When your friends visited the Macombs and later the Esnards, I wore my white linen suit, and served tea to your little clan. I enjoyed mocking Charleston's "civilization of the tea table," a cherished upper class social event. If it "civilized" them, maybe it would you. Constantly, I reminded your guests to sit and speak well and not be "little peasants." And on Sundays when we walked to church, I taught you to greet strangers with the cheerfulness expected of gentlemen. When you or your friends acted unkindly to others, I meted out punishments. Remember when one of your group insulted a passing slave? I turned my carriage for home, and cancelled our swim at Cannon's Bridge on Coming Street.

My religious guidance of you gained less success than my lessons in civility. Although I am Catholic, I took you boys to the Huguenot Church, despite my having to sit in a separate section for slaves and free Negroes. Christ's Sacrifice impressed neither of you. I felt then, and still do, that you blamed God for the loss of your mother. When we lived with the Esnards who were Catholic, I took you to White Mass, which followed Black Mass for slaves and free Negroes. But The Holy Virgin had less success with you boys than had her son Jesus. Hardness of life will one day open your eyes to God's Kingdom. Why do you think so many of my brothers and sisters see it?

"The Pirate Gang" gave me moments of pleasure and concern. There were nine of you: Laborde, Huard, Haunurd, John and Peter Pezant, young Macomb, Pierre Cournand, and you boys. Philip unofficially belonged, but generally just tagged along to avoid loneliness. They were spirited and not easily controlled. The youngest, but also the leader, was my John. Your command rested on your charm, quick wit, and willingness to fight anyone challenging your authority. Cournand once made intemperate remarks about me. John took him on and received a thrashing. Philip jumped in and received an equal portion of thrashing. Both of my boys had bloody noses and busted lips. Never did I see either one back down from a fight; never did I see either win one. By Charleston standards of masculinity, a fighter was judged on spirit rather than outcome. Spirit! My boys had plenty. Of the members of "The Pirate Gang," two became bankers (Laborde and Huard), one a Cuban planter (young Macomb), one a horticulturalist (counting Philip as a member), and the rest (John, the Pezant brothers, Cournand, and Haunurd) took to the sea as privateers and slave traders.

Pierre Cournand, "The Pirate Gang's" eldest member, troubled me most. He and his mother came to Charleston from Martinique in 1793; she quickly deposited him at the Orphan House and disappeared from his life. When he was ten years old, the orphanage indentured him to Irving Whitehead, a sail maker at Vanderhorst Wharf. My boys made his acquaintance on our walks and soon fell under his influence. He was a tough, bitter young man near Philip's age. But it was John who idolized him. When Cournand ran off to sea at the age of fourteen in 1797, John could hardly wait to imitate him.

On the more formal side of parenting, I emphasized your education. Madame Fugas, a friend of the Chartrands, directed your early education. After that, Father Gallagher instructed you both at his Athenian Academy held at St. Mary's Catholic Church on Hassel Street. Gallagher found nothing exceptional in Philip who daydreamed too much. John, however, used his charm to gain advantage over other pupils. While John lacked academic interest in most subjects, Gallagher found his grasp of *The Iliad and The Odyssey* impressive, but felt that John's only interest in the classic seemed to be his love for the sea.

Our domestic lives changed when we moved in 1796 from the

Macombs to the Esnards on Queen Street. Jean Pierre Esnard had fled Saint-Domingue after witnessing trusted household servants slaughter his family; the victims included his parents and his brother Lacomb Esnard. Never mind that a slave hid him, and drove him to safety in his wagon; Esnard's scarred mind made it impossible for him to acknowledge any acts of kindness by his slaves. That is why when he and his young bride visited the Macombs, he found my story of our escape fascinating. He predicted that his life might have been different had I served the Esnard household during the Great Slave Rebellion. Perhaps, but I understood those who killed his family. They were torn as I was torn, but simply made a different choice.

Uncle James found our developing friendship with the Esnards a convenience for his plans to move his family to Victoria Plantation in Matanzas Province, Cuba, which bordered Uncle Philip's coffee plantation. He told the Esnards that he would soon leave Charleston, and suggested that we live with them. Jean Esnard jumped at Macomb's offer. Separation would permit the Macombs to regain parental control over young James; separation would further end their boy's association with John. But the scheming parents could not have foreseen that you, John, would one day acquire a plantation next to their own in Cuba and renew your friendship with James, Jr.

Not long after settling into the home of Jean and Anne Esnard, we met Jean's father-in-law, Jean Pebarte, a refugee planter and his unmarried daughter from Saint-Domingue. She was Françoise and Anne's twin. Once a coffee and sugar baron, Jean Pebarte saw his slaves torch his plantations, and arrived in Charleston destitute. This was the same Pebarte who once owned Sulegrand Fonds and La Grand Place plantations in the Artibonite Valley, where Canga's maroons raided. I drank his coffee, and had sex with Chéri, one of his slaves. These memories made me smile, but then I recalled that Canga had been killed at La Grand Place. Hatred filled my heart, as I now served survivors of a society which angry slaves had destroyed.

With a pauper's desperation, old Pebarte had but one purpose: marry his daughters to men of means, a matrimonial binding in Charleston known as "an alliance between families." Jean Esnard had been his first successful target. Slave rebels chased Esnard out of Saint-Domingue but not out of money. With determination and sufficient capital, he bought plantations near Matanzas, Cuba. Esnard embraced the future; while Pebarte clung to the past.

Living with the Esnards proved a better arrangement for us than living with the Macombs. James and Mary Macomb cared for your physical needs, but James seemed too rigid, and his wife too protective of young James, to enjoy two active foster children. The Esnards, on the other hand, quickly embraced you both, dropped "foster" from their thinking, and made you full members of their growing family. It warmed my heart that Jean Esnard never tired of spending time with you, nor did he complain when you interrupted him at his office on East Bay Street. That you called the Esnards "Papa" and "Mama," further endeared them to me. Even after you boys grew up, the Esnards always welcomed you and your friends to their table until they immigrated to Cuba in 1816.

My feelings conflicted concerning the Macombs and the Esnards. I felt grateful that they treated my boys and me well, but I could never forget, nor excuse, that they were in the business of enslaving my people. I fervently believe that one day all good people will "stand in the light" and dispatch slavery. But the Macombs and the Esnards illustrated that day is still far away.

Part of Pebarte's matrimonial plans fell into place when his daughter Anne married Jean Pierre Esnard in a Catholic ceremony in early 1795. For a dowry, she had only a few pieces of her dead mother's jewelry and a transfer of claims to one of Pebarte's lost plantations in Saint-Domingue. Uncommon to this type of marriage, love overwhelmed pocketbook, as the couple shared a deep affection for each other. Eventually, Anne bore Esnard a daughter and three sons. The daughter, Anne Marie Antoinette Esnard, was born in 1800 and later married John's best friend, Antoine Barbot.

185

Now Pebarte faced the greater challenge of marrying off Françoise, widowed by the Great Slave Rebellion.

I regularly visited Pebarte's home at 17 George Street to pick up you boys who had grown fond of the old planter. Small in stature, with dark hair streaked with gray and blue eyes, Pebarte seemed a typical grandfather. He had few friends and welcomed my arrival. He generally offered me coffee, and I usually smiled and told him that his drink recalled times when I enjoyed good Saint-Domingue coffee (his, of course). How could a man so decent have been a slaveholder? How could a man so decent mourn only his own losses, and not those of his own slaves? Neither Pebarte nor Esnard voiced any remorse for owning or mistreating slaves. Had I challenged them, they would have sent me to the Charleston Workhouse.

Getting Françoise married to "Mr. Right" became Pebarte's obsession. The prospect of Françoise remaining at his side until the Angel of Death claimed him was not an altogether unpleasant thought for the old man. But imagining her as a destitute, lonely widow disturbed him. So his assault on her condition began with "the tea table," an old Charleston tradition. He invited guests after their breakfasts to join Françoise and him for afternoon tea. Françoise's sister helped bait this trap by bringing fancy tureens and other expensive porcelains from her household to her father's table, making a wealthy display. I played my part by serving my imaginary massah's guests for a fee which Esnard provided. This plan failed because Pebarte's guests were usually couples and old friends; those eligible to marry Françoise respectfully declined his invitations.

Pebarte's next offensive came during Race Week, a socially festive occasion in Charleston in early February. Those in high society especially anticipated The Jockey Club Ball held on Friday. There "alliances" were made between well-established men in their thirties and teenage females from respected families.

Françoise dreaded the ball which strained her father's meager resources to provide her an appropriate dress. But a "decked out" Françoise made beautiful, escorted by her father, and driven in a carriage by me were not causes of her opposition. Sheer boredom and embarrassment drove her attitude. Upon entering the ballroom floor, surfaced with chalked silhouettes of horses, she passed middle-aged men dancing with young teenage girls, while navigating herself to a distant wall. Quite often matrons, who came only to be seen, sat slumped in chairs around the floor, while their husbands ignored them to enjoy the company of other men.

Françoise sat and sat, while eligible men spun a cotillion with teenage girls. And so after eight balls, she only came home with an old father and chalk-scuffed shoes. She wanted to give up the game, but on her ninth ball she met "the man," Andrew Lechais, a banker and refugee from Saint Domingue. They wed in late 1804.

I liked old Pebarte. Maybe it came from his gentle nature, sweetness toward my boys, or love for his daughters. Maybe also our friendship provided me some satisfaction: His defeat made me feel like a Greek warrior sitting upon and enjoying the ruins of Troy.

Most Charlestonians did not share Françoise's dread of Race Week. For many, it crowned the social season running from January to March. More than lathered steeds running heats, more than the new Union's greatest horse race, it signaled Charleston's rising prosperity in the 1790's. King Billy (William Alston), William Washington, Andrew Johnson, Richard Singleton, and other wealthy planters of the Jockey Club were back on the race track after devastating losses of their fortunes and thoroughbreds to an occupying British army. Colonel Tarleton of the British cavalry stole so much of their prized horseflesh that his name became forever snarled on their lips. A new track (Washington Course) opened in 1794, and provided them a stage for their wealthy displays and fast horses. The trumpets sounded; the jockeys steadied their horses. Charleston was back!

Race Week drew spectators from around the world. Taverns, coffee houses and later hotels (after 1800) bulged with racing fans, and when they reached capacity, private homes accommodated the overflow. The whole city buzzed with excitement, and its mood became friendly. Charleston's elite led this social parade, but visiting whites of good character often went as guests to their social functions. A sort of democratic spirit prevailed in an otherwise closed society. A massah might make friends with a slave if he knew anything about racing; and little children of different colors gathered in Charleston streets to cheer a favorite rider and his horse, as they walked from stall to track.

On opening day, I drove King Billy's carriage to Washington Course in a strutting promenade of Charleston's richest and most powerful. This beginning ceremony reminded me of competing roosters, crowing challenges to their competition. I found amusement in driving King Billy's carriage past his most pretentious rivals and gaining their reaction. Targeting Captain Reid especially tickled my sense of humor. There were his driver, footmen, and outriders dressed in yellow livery, while the Captain himself donned silks fit for a coronation. And then there was our entourage in green livery, surrounding King Billy who sat dressed to dazzle his challengers. As our group passed theirs, the Captain and the King turned and faced each other, exchanging scowls, like competing judges pronouncing the other's execution.

Social events of Race Week started on Monday with a dinner sponsored by the Jockey Club, followed by the Bachelors' Ball, various parties at private homes, and concluding on Friday with the grand Jockey Club Ball at St. Cecilia's Society Hall. No guest went undanced and unliquored. John and Philip, you glided the dance floors with beautiful women at your elbows. The pretty Louise Dubois impressed me most; your courtship of her leading to marriage pleased me, John.

During Race Week, gambling and drinking attracted companions of both colors, while planters recruited black jockeys and trainers with reputations for winning races. Cornelius was one. He prepared the horses of Colonel Richard Singleton, his master, for competition. Sometimes Mas' Singleton hired him out to another owner if he lacked a strong horse, as his trainer's skills could match even Papa Toussaint's. As Cornelius' preparation of race horses intensified, I assumed his other equestrian duties at Singleton's plantation.

Race days were Wednesday, Thursday, Friday, and Saturday. Horses ran races of two, three, and four heats with heavy betting before each contest. Ownership of land, slaves, money, and mistresses flowed with the ease of the rivers in rice country. Viewing these spectacles were the pampered females of Charleston's elite, sitting in their own grandstands, wearing fine silk dresses of every color, twisting their white parasols against the sun, and giggling with excitement. Those little women blown up with self-importance reminded me of a hot air balloon regalia, rising in bright reds, blues, greens, and yellows, amid white puffs of clouds. White males, free Negroes, and slaves sat where they could, many of my race preferring the rail-and-post fence surrounding the track.

There were cruel and funny moments at Washington Course during Race Week. Cruel was the planter who affectionately rubbed his horse's nose, commenting that he wished slaves were as bright as his thoroughbred. More brutal were slave auctioneers who sold their human flesh for intermission entertainment. I painfully recall a slave mother and her two children on the auction block. Their forlorn expressions brought to mind my own helplessness on board *La Marie.*

But the funny moments I remember well, some still making me smile. My favorite came as I wandered among tent concessions surrounding the track outside the fence. Some dispensed food like the one near the starting gate, advertising mock turtle soup. Other tents housed exhibits to amuse the strolling public, but none intrigued me more than "The Learned Pig." For fifty cents, I could watch the owner put his porcine scholar through exercises of adding, subtracting, multiplying, and dividing. The man hawking his animal's skills even claimed that his porky pupil could read and count his audience. I kept passing the canvas flaps of temptation, but as sure as a suckling piglet goes for a teat, I gave in and gave up my coin. I must admit that the prodigy in question seemed brighter than others of his breed, but I've never known many pigs. When "The Learned Pig" oinked and squealed responses to his handler's math quiz, I became distracted in my own amusement. Seeing my distraction, the show's huckster asked me if his pig furnished correct answers. Too embarrassed to admit my lack of concentration, I could not in good conscience say "no," so I said "yes." Easy "marks" like me helped to establish this long-lived hoax at Washington Course.

After Race Week, Charlestonians found other sources of self-indulgence. The city's gardens were favorites. Some, like the Charleston Botanical Garden, pursued experimental plant development, but most combined nature's beauty with public entertainment. Vaux Hall Garden typified this type. Modeled after an English garden by the same name, Vaux Hall showed its customers a good time. For a small admission, a patron could stroll in the garden, take refreshments, relax in a public bath, and view a fireworks display, but in 1809 it went broke. Other gardens followed with even more gaudiness.

When we walked Charleston's gardens, Philip became fascinated, and often begged me to drive him to Michaux's French Garden and Champney's The Garden, north of town. Serious botanical work progressed in both places: André Michaux introduced the camellia, japonica, and gingko tree to Charleston, while John Champney specialized in roses, especially hybrids. Their research efforts impressed both Philip and his friend William Penn Bason, but Philip was drawn more to the show business side of public gardens, and found employment at Vaux Hall Garden in 1803.

In nearly every other way, 1803 burned itself into my memory as a bad year. Every morning I walked the length of Gadsden Wharf, amid rising mist from the Cooper, hearing boatmen songs behind foggy curtains, and seeing sudden swirls around pier pilings, as one of God's sea beasts chased a school of mullet. Gulls were everywhere: some diving, some swooping, and some expecting a sea beggar's handout. Pelicans atop every post chaperoned this nautical party with smirks of disapproval. Heavy boots striking deck planking often interrupted Mother Nature's performance, as stevedores rushed to their jobs. Gadsden Wharf reached well out into the Cooper, and could accommodate thirty ships at a time. It was the longest wharf in the United States, perhaps in all the Americas.

But I was not out to view natural wonders or laboring stevedores. Instead, I sought a small square-rigged brig out of Rhode Island, the *Charming Sally,* captained by Edward Thompson. Captain Thompson made regular voyages to Saint-Domingue as both arms supplier to and friend of Papa Toussaint. Thompson, more than Charleston newspapers, kept me abreast about Papa's progress and setbacks in Saint-Domingue. First news had come from him about Napoleon's invasion of the tormented colony and Papa's surrender and imprisonment which left me thunderstruck. But was Jean-Pierre still alive? I believed that the captain might know.

After months of morning walks, I finally sighted Captain Thompson disembarking the *Charming Sally.* The old shipmaster greeted me with all the endearing gruffness of a New Englander. He told me that Saint-Domingue was aflame again, following Napoleon's restoration of slavery, and a man named Dessalines responded with a new uprising against French authority. Then he handed me a letter, apologizing that he had it for several months. He blamed his delay on President Jefferson's support of Napoleon's invasion of Saint-Domingue, slowing his trips to the embattled colony. In it, Papa Toussaint described the fierce Battle of Snake Gully in 1802, in which Negro soldiers under his command ambushed and seriously damaged the French army. When his forces finally withdrew, Jean-Pierre led a rifle company that stood like a wall against the advancing French. Papa's army escaped, but Jean-Pierre fell. My brother was gone! My mind flooded with wonderful memories of our time together. He gave his life to fight slavery.

The bad year continued. Charleston merchants hustled to prepare for the economic bonanza sure to follow South Carolina's lifting of the ban on foreign slave trading. Even those reluctant to become involved in illegal trading, joined the rush. No longer would they have sleepless nights worrying about government seizure of their investment and trial in a prize court. With restrictions temporarily lifted from the flesh trade, Charleston merchants built, bought, and refitted ships of all descriptions. Skippers in the illegal trade followed suit by bringing their vessels to Charleston to be careened, refitted, and prepared for the race to my homeland. One ship was the *Africa*, long involved in slaving. She went into dry dock, while carpenters replaced worm-eaten boards, and blacksmiths forged her new metal fittings. While under repair, the *Africa's* crew found housing in brothels, taverns, and coffee houses. Among them was Pierre Cournand, the runaway John so admired.

Cournand stopped me on the wharf, swore at me, and demanded to know where he could find John. My anger tempted me to teach him the lesson my boys once attempted. But this was Charleston, where every Negro stood in the wrong before every white, even a cursing ragamuffin from the sea. I lent him no assistance, but he found John anyway. They became inseparable, while John's attitude toward me hardened.

When the *Africa* slid back into the sea, her crew included two young men: Cournand and John. My John was a runaway at fifteen! My heart broke. I knew *Africa's* destination. Why would "my boy" enslave "my people," the Lucumís? Where did I fail? Why had John's experiences not led him away from slavery? Why did God punish me? These were questions defeated parents often ask when their children stray from the straight ways of life. John had chosen badly. I did not love him less, but felt compelled to love him more.

With Philip spending most of his time at Vaux Hall Garden, I announced to the Esnards my intention of performing contract work on a rice plantation and to find my own housing upon my return. Besides, I could not bear being in Charleston to see my brothers and sisters arriving in chains.

In my next letter, I will describe my long stay in the heart of rice country.

Love to My Boys,

Saturday

When Philip ended Saturday's letter, he felt disturbed that his girls were whispering and giggling to each other. He checked to see if he buttoned his fly. But he had. He wondered if their conversation had something to do with Saturday's humor about "The Learned Pig?" Or was it about Pebarte's matchmaking efforts? Then their convivial expressions changed to frowns, as they shook their heads in disagreement. Philip knew that they must be talking about John, and why he ran off to sea.

"Wahl and I disagree," said Susan Elizabeth. "She believes that John was just another white Charlestonian who sought Africa for its human wealth. Nothing motivated him more than that which attracted the others. But I sense something that Saturday left out."

"Wahl is partly correct," responded Philip. "My brother was driven by forces around him and by his own restless nature. He also loved the sea, and Pierre Cournand played upon that longing. Remember his other friends, like the Pezants, craved the sea as much as John. My brother left partly because of the sea and slaving, but Saturday excluded the part Cuba played in his story."

Susan Elizabeth broke in, "I knew that—"

Philip stopped her in mid-sentence, "Let me finish my comments! Saturday deeply resented Uncle Philip for not taking us to Cuba where he and Wahl could have been together. Instead, we went to Charleston and Wahl to Cuba. I think that his bad feelings toward Uncle Philip mellowed, but in 1800 our uncle's long arm reached from Cuba, disrupting our lives again. With the appearance of generosity, Uncle Philip gave me well over a thousand acres of undeveloped land near Branchville on the Edisto. To John, he gave a plantation and slaves in Cuba. John named it "The Labyrinth" from Greek mythology. And even though Thomas Bacot held our properties in trust, uncle's "gift" made John a massah at twelve.

"There is more. Why did our uncle separate his gifts, mine in South Carolina and John's in Cuba? It appears that Uncle Philip took John away from Saturday and me to establish a relationship with him. Rather than uncle-nephew, they would become more like father-son. When Saturday spoke about this, I felt his anger. First Wahl, now John; Saturday's good nature was overwhelmed. He wrote nothing about Uncle Philip luring John to sea and to Cuba because of his Christian values. He believed that God forgives those who forgive others. That hatred might cast a shadow across his soul, constantly worried him. At St. Mary's, he went to many confessions, hoping to free his heart from Uncle Philip's meddling and Zèbre's treachery."

"I knew John well," said Wahl, breaking into the conversation. "There was goodness in him. He loved his wife and children. He protected Saturday and encouraged my freedom. He had only favorable remarks about you, Philip, but he was still a massah and at times acted like one. I never considered killing him, but I would have cut his throat had his neck stood between me and my freedom!" Realizing that her she had gone too far, Wahl blushed and shut up. Philip was taken aback. After all, Wahl talked about *his* brother.

Susan Elizabeth ended their impasse by commenting, "Last time I looked, John still had his head on his shoulders. I'm sure Wahl meant to express her hatred for slavery, and not for your brother." Philip and Wahl nodded agreement; the threat to their friendship had been averted.

Susan Elizabeth knew that it was time to leave. But as they walked toward the kitchen door, she turned and reminded Wahl of their intention to return soon.

The Eighth Letter

The late afternoon sun bore down on Branchville, as Philip walked the dirt road to the Ott Cemetery. He seldom travelled this pathway, and then only to pay respects to Lavinia his first wife and to Bason his friend. He couldn't ever recall walking to be this heavy. Even birds didn't sing, animals didn't move, moisture-laden Spanish moss drooped from every limb, and he could hardly breathe. Thoughts crossed his mind about the dangers of such conditions. Deadly vapors from nearby Berry's Bay were high and bound to bring someone down with yellow fever in "Frog Town," local nickname for marshy Branchville.

Concerns aside, Philip reached the cemetery's fenced enclosure for Chartrand burials. A marble bench fronted Bason's grave, flanked by Noisette roses, transplanted from Tivoli Gardens. Philip began reading the inscription on his friend's tombstone, a sort of invocation for the ceremony to follow:

> *Pause, reader, pause, nor in haste pass by*
> *Interred here lies William Penn Bason*
> *Remember'd ever be his worth*
> *Of guileless heart—of playful mirth*
> *No foes, he had but many friends*
> *For his faults his virtues made amends*
> *To his memory a tear. Too soon you'll be*
> *Taken forth mortal trouble freed.*

"Hello old friend," Philip said, bowing his head. "Another year gone. Our Charleston days seem like yesterday, our public garden barely taken flight. We had so many dreams, all gone. Time is like sand, and will eventually bury us all.

"Saturday's passing this year has been hard on me, even though he lived to a very old age. I wanted him to live to see me free my slaves. But South Carolina law and my own caution killed that ambition. The slaves whom I bought for Tivoli Gardens burden my soul, but I can't free myself from them, any more than a Calvinist can rid himself of Original Sin."

"Changing the subject, Saturday's letters have lifted the curtain of secrecy from my childhood. My mother was wonderful, my father a villain. There is some question if he is my father, so I've decided to register as a mulatto in the forthcoming federal census. Whether Saturday sired me or not is a moot question, for in every way, he was my real father. I'm guessing about my birth, but I have an even chance of being correct."

Philip turned and saw Susan Elizabeth driving up in their chaise. "Goodbye, William. Rest easy. I'll be back next year, if my neighbors haven't lynched me."

"Hurry, Philip," Susan Elizabeth urged. "Wahl is waiting for us in her kitchen."

Philip climbed into the chaise, annoyed that Susan Elizabeth invaded his sanctuary, but relieved to avoid the walk back to Branchville. Susan Elizabeth snapped her reins, and they headed for the depot.

When the couple approached Wahl's kitchen, they heard a deep-throated, baritone voice singing, as a clattering freight hurried by. Its clicking wheels drowned most of the verses, but important words carried through, words like *Zion, gospel timber, true-hearted soldiers,* and *King Jesus.* When they opened the kitchen door, the powerful voice inside overwhelmed the noisy freight. It was Wahl singing *The Old Ship of Zion* with the force of a hurricane in the song's last verse: "She has landed over thousands, and can land as many more."

196

Susan Elizabeth chirped in with a soprano's voice, "Oh, glory, halleluiah; oh, glory, halleluiah!" Caught off-guard, Philip realized that spiritual matters had not crossed his mind in a long time.

"So where is the old ship taking you?" Philip asked, mocking the old cook.

"Away from here, away from South Carolina, away from slavery," she replied. "Our souls look the same to God, Mr. Philip, and slaves have only their souls. All vanity and all possessions have been stripped away. White folks would do well to remember that everyone stands naked before God."

While Philip's humor failed to turn Wahl away from discussing her faith, her baking pies provided a better chance to change the conversation. "What is that wonderful aroma?" he asked.

"My pies?" Wahl replied. "Have you forgotten that this is camp meeting week? Late July is our revival time every year, when the late peach crop and early apples make possible these fine pies. We fill our stomachs while feeding our souls. James Belin, a white minister from Murrells Inlet, and Soloman, a slave from the Santee Delta, will preside as evangelists. Belin will lead the white congregation; Soloman will lead the segregated blacks. You know all this, Mr. Philip. We're even holding our meeting on your land by the Edisto. Don't you remember? I even arranged for my replacement until I return."

"I forgot about revival week," a blushing Philip replied. "This has been your main event since you arrived at the depot. I don't know what good it does, but I admire your dedication to your faith."

"So what are you looking for, Wahl, or is this simply a vacation with your friends?" a curious Susan Elizabeth asked, "I understand the social aspect, probably my only reason for going to church occasionally."

"Searching," replied Wahl; "Searching for The Holy Spirit. Wesleyan Methodists believe in The Second Blessing after salvation in which The Holy Spirit guides your life. But The Holy Spirit won't come until you rid your devils. Preaching at daytime camp meetings inspires my emotional responses, but nighttime becomes a different matter. That's when the whites take to their tents and we to ours that my brothers and sisters seek The Holy Spirit with full intensity. By day, we sprinkle a little African on our Christianity; by night, we administer a full dose.

"Camp meetings are all the same. I first find my praying ground, and beg The Almighty to cleanse my heart from hatreds wrought by slavery. Forgiving your enemies takes a mountain of praying. Sometimes I wrestle my demons all night, with my sisters surrounding me in prayer, and holding me down when I go into a trance or convulsion. But I've never gained 'coming through,' the moment The Holy Spirit enters a person's heart. So far only Ogun, voodoo war god with sword in hand, has possessed me to avenge the hatreds in my soul. At my age, vengeance offers no comfort, but the tranquility of The Holy Spirit does. Now, I just want to board that Old Ship of Zion with a clear heart. Forgiveness isn't easy, as Saturday discovered, but maybe this year I'll find spiritual victory."

Philip never knew how deep the scars of slavery ran in Wahl, but then he remembered his own losses to the evil realm: his mother murdered at his doorway, and his brother lured to sea and to a planter's life in Cuba. Slavery spared no one. Maybe his own wounds made him cynical about God. He admired Wahl's determination to experience The Holy Spirit, but lacked her singleness of purpose. And then he remembered old Saturday's love for himself and his brother. A slave did this; then he realized that God heals in mysterious ways.

"Philip! Philip, stop staring at Wahl with Saturday's letter in your hand. What are you thinking?" Susan Elizabeth demanded.

"Thinking?" replied Philip. "Women not only want to know what's in a man's mind, but also what's in his soul," Then he realized that he had crinkled Saturday's letter. Meekly, he started reading:

Thomas O. Ott

Labyrinth Plantation
Matanzas
August 4, 1824

Dear Philip and John,

My education about the great rice plantations of Lowcountry South Carolina came from hiring myself out. With his master's approval and often encouragement, a slave would contract for a specific job. "The lion's share" of his wages went to his owner. Most of my hiring out took place within Charleston. Some required my domestic skills; most called upon my experience as a blacksmith, especially at Pritchard's repair shop and shipyard. But I always anticipated assignments carrying me into the Lowcountry. Thomas Bacot, director of my boys' trust and my temporary master, generously waived his right to share my profits, only requiring that I pay my own expenses to and from a job.

One of my out-of-city assignments carried me to Santee Plantation on the Great Pee Dee River in the heart of rice country, a land echoing the Allston name. Nearly all the plantations which the Allston clan owned were on Waccamaw Neck, between the Atlantic Ocean and the Waccamaw River. From Calais Plantation in the south to Wachesaw Plantation in the north, this extended family owned over a dozen estates, some matching the elegance of the once-great ones in Saint-Domingue. I worked those places and The Oaks, a less luxurious plantation that Joseph Alston owned. But it was "King Billy" Alston of Clifton who displayed a level of wealth matching the Rosignols in Saint-Domingue's Artibonite Valley. Here "*à la* Créole" lived again, and King Billy even struck an "l" from his name to distinguish himself from his less wealthy relatives.

The rice planters followed rigid patterns of acceptable social behavior. On Sundays they attended church, either Anglican or Huguenot, because God dare not be anywhere else. Those Huguenot sailed on the tide for the Huguenot Church in Charleston, earning it the nickname "Tidal Church," as rising and falling tides governed service times to accommodate the rice barons. Those Anglican either worshipped near home, or took a coasting vessel to Charleston for worship at St. Michael's or at St. Philip's.

In April, they took flight from their plantations like birds of magnificent plumage, hoping to avoid the talons of Death. Their barely visible enemy they dubbed "miasma," polluted vapors rising from swamps and flooded rice fields. They roosted on the Carolina coast, Upcountry South Carolina, Charleston, New England, and Europe. Generally they returned to their plantations after "black frost," the third heavy frost of late fall when leaves fall, grass turns brown, and vapors recede. Only household servants joined their plantation exodus, but field slaves remained to face disease and the driver's whip.

Participation in the Charleston social season from January to March was a major requirement for rice planters and their families. Race Week highlighted this period, and an invitation to the Jockey Club Ball meant one's acceptance into high society. In between, during, and after Race Week, formal and informal parties were widely held. For those seeking formal, there were concerts and receptions at the St. Cecilia Society. For those desiring informal, there were townhouse parties, like King Billy's on King Street. "The King" could guzzle most of what a small vineyard could produce.

I served at The King's parties, and received his instructions to lock his doors at midnight and to keep wine flowing to his guests. At dawn, I unbolted the doors, allowing Charleston's finest to escape their liquid confinement. Without fail, the champion of the night's imbibing was King Billy who stood at his front entry, wishing his guests a speedy return, as some crawled toward a rising morning sun. These were the consumers of the great rice fortunes (Carolina Gold), resting on the brawn of their slaves.

When I stepped onto the wharf at Santee Plantation from Captain Eddy's barge (or flat), I was greeted by a tall old man, wearing a Scottish bonnet, making him seem even taller. He was Old Daddy

Andrew, head carpenter and director of the blacksmith shop at Santee. Africans generally embraced old people holding titles such as his, because they respected the elderly. In his late sixties, Old Daddy bore his age well, except that he leaned forward, reminding me of an old oak about to fall. Though time had rutted his face, his eyes danced when he spoke, like a twenty-year-old anticipating the adventures of life. Together we picked up my bags, and headed to his wagon. From that February day in 1804 until my departure from Santee in December, Old Daddy directed my labors, and taught me about a slave's life on a rice plantation.

We arrived at the carpenter shop where slave cabinet makers were fast at work. Behind them were racks of hardwoods for furniture and fine interior appointments. Outside their shop were stacks of cypress, locust, heart pine, and poplar for exterior work. Some workers sawed lumber to Old Daddy's specifications, and then numbered each with a Roman numeral; this way he could re-assemble Mas' Choiseul's summer house on the coast in proper sequence. Inside again, I watched Old Daddy's work crew use their planes, each with a specific purpose. Curled wood shavings gave the work area a pleasant odor, especially planed Cherry. Old Daddy took pride in his shop, and in the big house, which he and his workers had built from architectural drawings. He not only read them correctly, but skillfully altered them to suit the Choiseuls. What he did at Santee, other slave master builders did for plantations across rice land.

Next, we arrived at the blacksmith's shop where I would produce hardware for the summer house: doorknobs, locksets, hinges for doors and shutters, wrought iron work, and masses of nails, screws, and bolts. A blacksmith working the forge smiled at me. He was George Wilson, my friend from Charleston, who had contracted to work for the Choiseuls. While at Santee, George and I bunked in a slave cabin for contract workers.

From the shops, Old Daddy wheeled our wagon down "the street," running through the three slave cabin districts at Santee.

Each district had twelve slave dwellings on each side of "the street," with two or three rooms on a single level. Some had lofts, most had porches, and all had fireplaces. While the exterior of these cabins were weathered cypress, all had window sashes, door frames, and porch posts painted indigo blue to repel roaming spirits. Stands of fruit trees bordered each dwelling. At the end of "the street" stood the overseer's residence from whence he kept "his eye" on Mas' Choiseul's slaves.

Elmer Stadler, a not-too-nice Rhode Islander, filled this position at Santee. "Mistuh Stad," as slaves addressed him, had worked on a slave ship, stayed in Charleston seeking a better job, and soon found employment at Santee. Weather-beaten from years at sea, Mistuh Stadler reminded me of Captain Leclerc of *La Marie* had he turned landlubber. Like the captain, he took delight in abusing slaves. Unfortunately for George and me, our cabin was next to his.

More than a master craftsman, Old Daddy Andrew served the slave community as their patriarch. His influence ran through the plantation workers right down to their children. Ironically, the Scottish Balmoral Bonnet, which Mas' Choiseul awarded Old Daddy to symbolize his authority, had a broader meaning to the slaves of Santee. It stood for leadership, but it also stood for the yearnings of the Scots for freedom. Like the Scots, Old Daddy embraced this feeling with all his heart.

Each evening, Old Daddy routinely visited a different slave cabin. There by the hearth, he gathered household children for Gullah tales. Some stories seemed clearly African; others were his concoctions from local experiences. All sought both to entertain and to instruct listeners. Gullah, by the way, became a universal language among Lowcountry slaves from different African nations. It was their common denominator, and their way around massah's attempt to limit their communication with each other. Based on the oral traditions of Santee slaves, my best guess is that the Gullahs were an Angolan people who arrived in early colonial South Carolina, and adapted their language to universal use in the Lowcountry. By altering English words, joining them with some clearly African, and placing them in an Angolan syntax (word order), the Gullah set the foundation for a new language to which other African nations contributed. This collective slave effort succeeded in South Carolina, as it had in Saint-Domingue.

Sitting by the fireplace required effort on the part of Old Daddy, as arthritis encumbered his limbs; "chilluns," however, listen better to a storyteller at their level. He spun his wonderful yarns only by the hearth, emphasizing its importance in African family tradition. Old Daddy once told me of an old slave woman at Mt. Arena Plantation who kept the flame alive in her fireplace—a fire her great grandfather had set over one hundred years earlier. Old Daddy then began his Gullah stories, as Buh Rabbit, Buh Fox, Buh Bear, Buh Gatuh (Alligator), and Buh Cooter (Turtle) all frolicked across Old Daddy's imaginary stage, but especially the tale of Mas' Snake and Sistuh Doe. It was an Old Daddy original.

As I recall, he told it this way: A fine-looking ten-foot rattler once roamed the rice lands of the Great Pee Dee River. Arrogant in his power, he slithered da cow-prats (cow paths) of his domain, choosing his victims. Within his realm, he was king. Buh Ottuh and Buh Rokkoon (Raccoon) even took to the swamp when they saw his approach; and though Mas'Snake avoided Buh Gatuh, he knew that few creetuhs (creatures) could withstand his deadly venom. Could anything be more lethal and beautiful than he? When he came to a clear crik (creek), he stretched out his long body, admiring it in the water's reflection. Delighted wid (with) himself, he couldn't stop shaking the butt'ns (buttons) on his tail. Ah, such sweet music. Truly he was wicked; truly no ruler more absolute.

After sunning himself for a while, Mas' Snake felt hungry because he had not eaten since his light chipmunk brekwus' (breakfast) that mawnin (morning). Now middle day (noon), the pangs of hongry (hunger) guided Mas' reptile's thoughts, but nothing excited his appetite or even his flicking tongue. His stomach called for a feast, but what could it be, as he slithered along under a hot sun?

Old Daddy paused to look at the chilluns. Not one squirmed, not one word from their lips, and all hung on his every word. The evil snake had charmed his way into their imaginations. Then Old Daddy asked if they wanted more: "Fo' go' sa'ke! We wantuh mo" was their excited chorus. And so Old Daddy continued.

Now Mas' Snake looked, but saw no suitable victim. He slithered into a harvested rice field, hiding and spying for any creetuh venturing from adjacent woods. An hour passed, then two, and three, still no victim for his snare. The sun melted into a pool of gold, making way for night. That's when rustling savanna grass revealed Sistuh Doe and her fawn. A repast at last! The doe might be nice thought Mas' Snake, but her speckled fawn could be better. He would invite other reptilian massahs to his domain to feast on fawn 'til dawn. Such wild parties in the past had earned him the title of "King Willie" from his overstuffed pals.

Now Sistuh Doe detected the snare, but not in time. She and her chile (child) stood at the reptile's gate. After a low curtsy, she braced herself for his lightening bite, but his charming gaze instead was fuh (for) her baby. A fury rose in her breas' (breast). Her broken will mended; eat me, but not my child, she snarled. Then her fawn approached Mas' Snake, obeying his come' yuhs (come heres); her speckled darling had become a slave to his gaze. Sistuh Doe would have no mo' (more). She bunched her razor-sharp hooves together, and with cat-like agility, sprang up and down upon Mas' Snake's long back, avoiding his every strike. First she chopped off his prized buttons, then chunks of his body, and fin'lly at las' (finally at last) his head. Da King Willie wuz (was) stone dead.

When Old Daddy finished his story, he asked its meaning. His eager audience offered many incorrect answers: Sta' way frum dem snakes; stay wid yo maum in da woods; don liss'n to no snake; weiz lik' da fawn. Then a brown-eyed cutie lifted her head, and said: "Me'Go' (God), Sistuh Doe be one uh we." Old Daddy smiled, and asked, who was the fawn? "Freedom," she replied.

Old Daddy sent me to inspect the sluice gates governing water levels in the rice fields. My inspections gave me an appreciation for rice production, which normally began in late February when slaves planted rice seeds encased in dried mud to keep them underwater.

Flooding the rice fields followed. Since Santee was on the tidewater, rice fields could be inundated, or drained with rising and falling tides. When the river rose after planting, gatekeepers opened the sluices, an event known as "sprout flow." After three days, they drained and entered the fields at low tide to clean them of debris and weeds, working in rhythm to their songs. The second flooding was called "long water," when fields were again submerged. After two days, they were half-drained, allowing tender rice plants to become stout. After three weeks, gatekeepers finished draining the fields, and slave gangs moved in under unbearable heat and mud to continue cultivation. Mid-July brought a final freshet which submerged fields for two months, allowing rice plants to mature. This was the "harvest flow." In late August, harvest began when plants reached "in the milk" (full maturity) and fields drained one last time.

A little yellow and black bird, the bobolink, forced master and slave to defend the rice fields. These menaces came in swarms rather than flocks, stripping a field faster than slaves using rice hooks. Overseers posted slaves with horns and shotguns to frighten these winged invaders, while the more inventive defenders flattened lead pellets to sound like a hawk's wings. Not until September, when the bobolinks migrated south, did this plague end.

Once slaves harvested a field, and bundled stalks into sheaves, they loaded them onto flats (small barges) for delivery to the threshing yards where African techniques of threshing, winnowing, and pounding refined the raw rice. This technology helped to spark Lowcountry's first great rice boom before the American Revolution. In the 1790's, plantation masters added Jonathan Lucas' new invention to this traditional African technology, leading to an even greater rice boom.

Lucas built his rice mill along the South Santee River,

revolutionizing rice processing. The whole procedure of winnowing and pounding were done at the mill, and finished rice went into its attic, barreled, and shipped out. One mill could do the work of a hundred slaves. Lucas' invention also created planter demand for more rice land, raising their demand for more slaves, pressuring South Carolina to re-open the foreign slave trade in 1803.

In May, Old Daddy Andrew ordered four flats (barges) loaded with building materials for the Choiseul's summer house on the coast. The first three carried cargos of numbered cypress and locust boards for the first floor deck. Secured on the fourth flat, were blacksmith products and even a carefully crafted weather vane. Each flat carried a helmsman with six oarsmen who rowed and poled their laden craft across the shallows on Squirrel Creek, connecting the Great Pee Dee with the Waccamaw River. The journey of the Squirrel Creek fleet provided crews a welcomed relief from plantation life. The trip to the Waccamaw lasted from sunrise to sunset, roughly forty miles. On the Waccamaw's far bank, a caravan of wagons awaited to transport us to the beach.

A party atmosphere began on Old Daddy's command to shove off, followed by splashing oars, laughing, and boatmen bursting into song. Soon we entered Squirrel Creek and Nature's Cathedral, as branches from hundred-year old water-oaks interlocked, forming a green canopy above our heads, with Spanish moss swaying in a gentle breeze. The fragrances of water lilies, yellow jasmine, Cherokee roses, wisteria, and myrtle competed to provide incense for our leafy temple. Swamp creatures lined the shore: rows of sunning turtles, curious alligators launching themselves into the creek, land snakes wiggling on the water's surface, moccasin heads popping up and looking like young cypress knots, and timid otters breaking up their swamp party as we approached. Above us, choirs of song birds tweeted their serenades, or were they Carolina mockingbirds, teasing us with their "four hundred tongues?" When dusk turned to night, we left Squirrel Creek under an arbor of blooming moonflowers, and entered the Waccamaw. My mind flashed back

Journey on Squirrel Creek

to when Mother and I looked for this flower, as our captors pushed us along to Whydah.

Once across the Waccamaw, we crawled into wagons on loan from Waverly Plantation, and slept until dawn. When the sun rose, so did we, as we took a quick breakfast, and headed to the beach. At the construction site, the industry of earlier slave workers impressed me: ten-foot piers from bricks fired at Santee kilns supporting heart-pine sills with floor joists in place and ready for planking. The tall piers were to keep the sea out, while heart pine's hardening resin repelled termites. After a month of raising walls, installing door sashes and window frames, flooring the piazza, and nailing on a cedar-shake roof, our supplies ran low. Every nail driven, every board put in place, had Old Daddy's supervision, while Mas' Choiseul pretended to be in charge. In early June, we left for Santee Plantation to collect specified materials needed for completion of the summer house.

Porch-sitting in early evening was an institution among Santee slaves. On our first evening back, George Wilson and I relaxed with Old Daddy on his porch. We figured that we deserved a rest, when Old Daddy pointed to his neighbor across "the street." An industrious slave woman hurriedly brushed on indigo paint to recoat her cabin's faded blue door frame, window sashes, and porch posts. She raced to finish before nightfall. But something besides falling darkness bothered her.

Old Daddy explained that she was Maum Sarah who lost her husband, Old Ben, to a *hag-hag*, a witch who could slip her skin, enter a person's dreams, and "ride him" all night. Often this spirit drove her mortal dream partner to insanity, even death. In the beginning, Ben woke in the morning in a cold sweat, but it got worse when he squirmed all night, and humped like a man having wild sex. Maum Sarah had enough. She declared war on her invisible rival luring her husband to a predictable fate.

She sought a conjure doctor's intervention. He used charms (*roots*) to dissuade the invader, even spreading spirit repellant on yard boundaries, across the doorway, and around Old Ben's bed. Then to keep the spirit from roosting, the conjure doctor sawed off Ben's bedposts, and removed other resting spots. He even sealed the front door keyhole, and placed an indigo blue plank across the foyer apron to block the hag-hag's re-entry into the cabin. Nothing worked, but Sarah became deeply jealous when Ben demanded that she leave his dream mistress alone. Sex had been better with her than with Sarah. Years earlier, a young slave girl named Nadine had competed with Sarah for Ben's affections. Sarah appeared the loser when Nadine suddenly disappeared. Some on Santee believed that Sarah murdered her. Was the hag-hag Nadine, returning for her lover? Sarah thought so.

Old Ben slowly slipped away, while neglecting his duties. Mistuh Stad whipped him severely, claiming that Ben was just plain lazy. Frustrated, Stad sent Ben to the plantation hospital under the care of the master's wife. She put Ben to bed, sent word to Dr. Ellery, and awaited his arrival and diagnosis. The white doctor found nothing wrong with Ben except malingering. So Old Ben returned to field work in declining health, and finally died.

At this point, we watched Sarah becoming desperate. She sloshed paint on her porch posts faster than a boatman splashing his oars on the Great Pee Dee. Old Daddy believed that Sarah's frenzy came from her fear that the hag-hag might come back for her.

Ben's funeral was a big event, as slaves from Santee and surrounding plantations gathered to bid Old Ben goodbye. From inside Old Ben's cabin, slave mourners viewing his body backed all the way to "the street." At midnight, the procession to the slave cemetery began. Pallbearers carrying torches strode next to Ben's coffin, with the sorrowful trailing behind, celebrating the deceased's departure from worldly burdens. Slaves in rice country believed that a body is best buried at night to prevent the departed from wandering and causing mortals harm. Night funerals suited most plantation masters, because slaves would not lose field work time.

At the slave burial ground, pallbearers set Old Ben's casket down, and motioned his two children to step over it. That way, his spirit would not haunt the two little boys whom he loved so much. After burial, Sarah laid Old Ben's favorite clay pipe on his grave, and crushed it under her feet, symbolizing the end of life. Following this slave liturgy, pallbearers circled Old Ben's grave with conch shells to confine his spirit to his burial site. The conch shell represented an important life cycle: "From the sea you came, and by the sea you shall return," meaning Old Ben's spirit headed back to Africa.

George Wilson chuckled at Old Daddy's story, and then quipped that maybe Old Ben might not return to Africa, if it meant giving up sex with Nadine. Old Daddy and I didn't laugh, but George meant no harm, and his infectious good nature soothed Old Daddy's feelings. But slaves had reservations about George. He was a mulatto and too close to his master and the white world.

After Maum Sarah's frenzy ended, Old Daddy invited us to join him by the riverside where slaves gathered secretly after dark to express their spiritual feelings. This violated plantation protocol where masters attempted to control slave worship with chaperoning white preachers. Religion for Santee slaves, however, meant defiance and healing injuries that masters inflicted on their souls. Using both Christian and African imagery, they built a spiritual bastion that white masters never conquered, nor even understood. I understood and joined Old Daddy on a pathway to the river. George declined, claiming that fatigue made him bone weary.

Night's heavy veil had fallen when Old Daddy and I reached a trail to the river. Our only encounters were with nightingales, tree frogs, screeching owls, and unidentified things scurrying across our path. A mile or so from the river, Old Daddy ordered us off the pathway and our torches extinguished. Only shards of moonlight falling through tangled undergrowth allowed me to follow Old Daddy. When finally we entered the deep tree line bordering the Great Pee Dee, I saw a little man standing by a hollowed stump, surrounded by sitting slaves. He and the stump flickered, as a lowering campfire gave a mystical glow to both. At his back, an industrious moon spread its silver across the shimmering river. He was a conjurer who carried the title "doctor," a mark of respect that slaves bestowed on this type of spiritual leader. The stump serving as his pulpit, slaves had bored out to pound rice stolen from Santee. Similar stumps were located along the Great Pee Dee, and slaves generally knew which one on what evening had designation for a spiritual gathering.

Our priest was one of the area's more feared and respected among slaves. Baptized as "Ezra" on Santee, slaves knew him as Doctor Claw. Short and thin, and sporting a snow-white beard, Claw reminded me of an Old Testament prophet. His fame came from his control over ghosts, witches, and *plat-eyes* (malevolent spirits) residing at crossroads and in graveyards. All three were evil. At birth, Claw had a membrane (caul) over his head, giving him the gift of seeing spirits on "the other side."

Like most conjurers, Claw kept a bag of sacred objects and charms. In his magical sack were peanuts, grave dirt, black cat bones, an eagle's beak and claw, a snake's head, and other items empowering him to enchant his followers. A rumor that death would strike anyone looking into Claw's sack without his permission protected his supernatural stash, inspired perhaps by the biblical story of The Ark. Many slaves believed Claw could cure or kill you, give you love or a lover's scorn, make you rich or keep you poor, condemn your soul or save it. Claw also treated the sick. Among his prescriptions were licorice potions to cure coughs and fevers, while others medicated sores, stomach aches, constipation, and depression. Those whom he chose not to cure, he could easily destroy with his herbal poisons.

The service which followed vaguely resembled Haitian voodoo. Supplicants begged Claw for roots granting them romance, vengeance, control over their master or overseer, and putting hexes on or taking them off. Some experienced trances and spirit possessions. Most of the worship was Afro-Protestant as opposed to Afro-Catholic in Haitian voodoo, explaining their differences.

In Haitian voodoo, loas are identified with the Virgin Mary, The Cross, and the saints; whereas in Afro-Protestant slave religion, these attributes are missing. In a word, slave religion in Lowcountry South Carolina lacked the liturgical development of Haitian voodoo. Despite Doctor Claw's powers, he lacked the strength of the houngans who incited the Great Slave Rebellion in Saint-Domingue. All said, Claw and his fellow conjure doctors might one day raise their followers against Lowcountry planters.

Ending our ceremony, Doctor Claw's followers lifted themselves in songs which reverberated across the silvery Great Pee Dee, as the breeze-rustled palmetto palms seemed to keep time. Most hymns beseeched deliverance from slavery: One begged the Lord to "come by here," another called for Moses because "time is a-rollin' on." As we left for Santee, I asked Old Daddy if he was that Moses. He said "no," but nearly twenty years later, Denmark Vesey heard and answered the call.

This brings me to slave treatment on Lowcountry rice plantations. It *appeared* that slaves had better treatment here than on the West Indian sugar islands. Materially, Lowcountry slaves fared better: cabins rather than huts, more clothes and shoes, more and better food, and a better ratio of men to women. Human emotional needs were better met here as well: more time off for Christmas, endearing exchanges between slaves and master's family on Christmas Day, and formal slave weddings. But these cosmetic features only disguised slavery's ugly features in rice country.

As in the sugar islands, Lowcountry absenteeism gave overseers the power to punish slaves for trivial reasons. The task system of slave labor illustrates this. A slave failing his or her assignment was frequently "shut up' in a plantation outbuilding and severely whipped. A nasty overseer, like Stad, often gave a healthy slave more than could be accomplished for many reasons, but revenge and forced sex were frequent.

Owners frequently justified abuse of their slaves by arguing that they were animals with no rights, or "walking property" as some

212

put it. Thus, a slave's value might be compared to that of a good dog—ads in Charleston newspapers generally offered more for the dog. And if Saint-Domingue had its Le Jeune who tortured his slaves, rice land had its Magill who hung six runaways on his plantation. Tribunals in both places exonerated both men.

Though terrible, these brutal dimensions of slavery in Lowcountry bore me less concern than more subtle ones. Masters even of good hearts were oblivious to their complicity in the sin of slavery. With a gentle smile and a spirit of condescension, they sugared their poison. Unlike the Stads of Lowcountry who cut black flesh with leather whips, these tyrants snapped word-whips that lacerated the human heart. Often they made revealing comments: "They can't help being black," "they're almost human," or "never call a Negro female a lady." These overseers of the soul might be decent, even sweet people, while relegating black folks to God's lesser creations. Mis' Lisa de Choiseul, whom slaves at Santee called Mis' Lisa, makes my case.

Mis' Lisa was Master Choiseul's aunt who came to Santee after retiring from managing her own plantation. A large, jolly woman, Mis' Lisa brought order to master's household and obedience from his slaves. In many ways, she was a loveable woman who stood against the brutal treatment of slaves, while failing to appreciate her own ironic behavior. Her Wednesday "audiences" on the piazza of Santee bears this out.

With the solemnity of a queen, Mis' Lisa, attended by Chloe her body servant, sat upon an overstuffed chair serving as her throne. Around her, household slaves anxiously anticipated receiving a trinket from a bag on the porch queen's lap. Each slave took a turn at making Mis' Lisa laugh. Some danced, some curtsied, some sang, some made funny faces, and some recited a funny tale. All wanted a prize from the queen's treasury. Most got one.

I found it hard to witness this farce. It reminded me of when Èji and I looked into mirrors on a slave ship, and incited the howling laughter of the crew who thought us fools.

A special occasion revealed more about Mis' Lisa's attitude toward slaves. Slave weddings at Santee were celebrated events, but the nuptials of Mis' Lisa's body servant outdid them all. When Chloe announced her intention to marry Lafayette, carriage driver for Santee, a determination gripped Mis' Lisa to take over wedding arrangements. For a woman given to few steps, Mis' Lisa now moved with a wedding planner's enthusiasm.

On the big day, the ceremony took place on the piazza, as Mis' Lisa refused having it in the plantation yard where most slave weddings occurred. Nothing but the best for Chloe! She even hired a white minister to preside. After Chloe and Lafayette exchanged vows, they mingled with their guests, eating small white cakes that Mis' Lisa had so carefully prepared. Then the new couple presented Mis' Lisa and the Choiseuls a full-sized cake and a bottle of wine in appreciation for their efforts.

Genuine affection often existed between maid and mistress as between some masters and their slaves. At times like Christmas and funerals, mutual good will flowed in abundance. Undeniably touching, these displays of kindness were also undeniably shallow. No relationship with a slave could keep a master from doing what masters do. If in their economic best interests, the Choiseuls would have likely sold Chloe and Lafayette to different masters. Nothing trumped the master's financial interests; nothing overrode a slave's desire for freedom.

My final thought about slave treatment in rice country came when George Wilson and I sat by our hearth. I thought about my boys and my return to Charleston. His thoughts were deeper, as he considered his life as a slave. He asked if I thought a slave's life better in Lowcountry than in Saint-Domingue? I knew that George was an apologist for slavery in the Palmetto State, and loved his master. I gave a comparison to spare his feelings: When considering the deadly force of two snakes, you don't judge them by the length of their bodies but by the strength of their venom. Truth is, either snake can kill a human soul.

214

One more voyage to the Choiseul beach house in late November completed my work at Santee. I told Old Daddy that I planned leaving before a cannon fired near Charleston. He seemed miffed. Then I told him about my holiday tradition of taking my boys to The Elms Plantation to witness its massah fire a small field piece from his piazza commencing his estate's Christmas celebrations. But I added that our friendship would always be in my memory. Old Daddy drove George and me to the Santee dock, where we boarded a flat bound for Georgetown. As our oarsmen pushed off, I saw Old Daddy with his Scottish bonnet cocked to one side, standing like a monument to my people's resistance to enslavement.

Upon returning to Charleston, I found quarters at 15 Elliott Street near Pritchard's repair shop at Gadsden Wharf. On this wharf and others, wooden sheds had been erected, as unhappy human sounds filtered through chinks left from careless construction. These were holding pens for newly arrived African slaves. No longer were quarantines held at the Pest House on Sullivan's Island as in colonial days. No! Massive planter demands for human flesh made quarantine a mere formality. Then around mid-morning slave dealers brought their victims to the front of The Exchange for auction. Buyers examined their every aspect for evidence of disease and discipline. Signs of either might squelch a sale. The auctioneer's loud call, the raucous responses of buyers, the smell of unwashed bodies, the ever-building crowd of curious spectators, all reminded me of when I was kidnapped as a child-captive to "the trade."

Seeing my brothers and sisters on the blocks, Irealized that Charleston slaves and free Negroes had not advanced much beyond those up for auction. In one way, a city Negro had it harder than a plantation slave where encounters with massah and his family were less frequent. Here, we experienced daily torture. Here, Charleston slaves and free Negroes often lived near or next to the elite. Here, we faced strict regulations. Here, the law ignored whites stepping out of line. Here, we faced white ministers seeking to control our religion. Here, whites enjoyed religious freedom. Here, self-improvement was only a fingertip away, but for Charleston slaves and free Negroes, it stood an ocean apart. Here, Muirs Book Dealers near my residence on Elliott Street stocked books forbidden for me to read. Here, the Workhouse loomed over every Charleston slave and free Negro. Here, we witnessed freedom's joys, while mired in slavery's gloom. In a word, here, you can easily understand the fueling of the Denmark Vesey Conspiracy nearly two decades later.

Christmas, 1804, saw King Billy (William Alston) hire me as maître d' for his annual December party. He paid me a good wage: ten dollars for eight hours' work, more than blacksmithing for a whole week. His guest list included Charleston's "upper crust:" Pinckneys, Manigaults, Alstons with one and two "ls," Reids, Izards, Westons, LaBruces and others. But most curious to me was King Billy's son, Joseph, and his pretty but mysterious daughter-in-law, Theodosia Burr Alston. She had spent long periods with her father in New York before his famous duel with Hamilton in mid-1804. Until then, I had only glimpsed this absentee bride once while blacksmithing at Joseph Alston's plantation on the Waccamaw River. Who was this mystery woman? I soon found out.

Awkward is the word describing King Billy's 1804 Christmas party. The King never dodged a juicy subject, nor ducked interesting gossip, especially the licentious sort. While guests sipped fine wine and ate gourmet food, the flow of Madeira matched the flow of trivial conversation because no one at the King's table dared to discuss Burr's duel with Hamilton, or even the Election of 1804. Despite the powerful guests at Number 27 King Street itching for a response from Theodosia, they bowed to their more powerful host by avoiding these touchy subjects.

A feature of a King Billy party was a culinary surprise, a *pièce de resistance,* if you will.

This time featured ice cream for dessert. Colonel Alston became acquainted with ice cream at Washington's presidential levees at the Federal Mansion in New York and later at the President's

House in Philadelphia. Washington had an insatiable appetite for ice cream, so he bought a *sorbetière*, a French ice cream machine. King Billy could not stand it. He bought one to excite both the envy and the palates of his guests. Ice posed no problem for the King because New England ships transported tons of it to supply city and plantation ice houses. With waiters carrying trays of ice cream scooped inside pastries, the dimming table conversation suddenly brightened. Pierre Rossignol of Cedar Hill Plantation triggered the change.

Rossignol had fled Saint Domingue to the banks of the Wando River where he regained his wealth. He wondered, he said, what King Billy thought of "Emperor Brute" of Haiti who carried the former French colony to independence after Toussaint's fall? Ugly comments flowed across the King's table: Haitians were lazy Africans and incapable of self-rule; wanted their masters back; comfortable only when wearing manacles; ungrateful black beasts. Those in silence nodded their approval, including Theodosia. Guests at King Billy's finally agreed: Negro slaves should stay slaves because they were nothing more than draft animals. The back of my neck blazed, anger filled my being. That was when Theodosia motioned me to her chair, and mockingly asked me to tell about my escape from the Great Slave Rebellion. She had heard snatches from others, but wanted the whole story from me. My prize, she said, was her half-eaten dessert. King Billy foiled her little game by saying that I previously agreed to tell my story for an ice cream dessert in his kitchen.

I presented a version sure to please my white audience: generous whites and unreasonable slaves. Fantasy cannot replace history. Too many slaves drowned in rivers of their own blood, and too great were my own losses, for me to bury the truth. I resolved never to be another darkie at a social for whites, misshaping his story to their specifications. That is when I started writing these letters (epistles) to you boys and to honor my pledge to Papa Toussaint.

John came home in 1806, while Philip left. Philip had an

enduring ambition to see the world-famous Tivoli Gardens, east of Rome, built by an extravagant Catholic cardinal. To finance his adventure, Philip sold some of the land that his uncle had given him. This funding method continued in his other business ventures, ending in bankruptcy. But in 1806, Philip had a young man's confidence, and later established his version of Tivoli Gardens on Meeting Street, near The Lines. Philip's obsession with his version of Tivoli later caused him to make other bad decisions, including buying slaves to lower labor costs. I felt deeply disappointed that he "bit the apple," and joined his brother as a slaveholder.

No sooner had Philip left for Italy than *Africa*, John's ship, dropped anchor in Charleston Harbor. This was *Africa's* third successful voyage since South Carolina lifted its embargo on foreign slave trading. The first two were to Havana, the third to Charleston. When John strode down *Africa's* gangway, I saw a sea dog without scruples about the "flesh trade." My anger at John smoldered, but never did my love for him waiver, or my prayers that he might end his evil ways.

In the spring of 1806, Esnard, "Papa" to you boys, asked me to attend Pebarte on Sullivan's Island because the old man had grown feeble, and might benefit from sea air. Anna his cook and Amos her young son would assist me on my only paid beach vacation. During my summer there, Anna and I developed a brief friendship, something missing in my life since Wahl. Although just a dalliance, I still remember Anna fondly.

We departed Beale's Wharf by packet boat one sunny afternoon, bound for Sullivan's Island. The same vessel returned to Charleston early the next morning. Sullivan's Island is one of many barrier islands along the Carolina coast. Barely above sea level, it had once been covered with sweet myrtle and scrub palmetto thickets. But defenders of colonial Charles Town cleared the island. As a final defensive measure, the British built Fort Sullivan there to intercept enemies approaching Charles Town by sea. When South Carolinians captured and then defended the fort against a British attack in 1776, they renamed it Fort Moultrie for their commander.

Another symbol of British colonial rule was The Pest House, a quarantine station for those seeking to enter Charles Town. After ten days of isolation, colonial officials either granted or rejected an immigrant's entry into the port city based on his health condition. Thousands of slaves arrived in Charles Town this way; many others died on the sandy isle and were buried there.

Sullivan's Island began changing into a vacation spot at about the time when we landed at Charleston in 1791. Two of the Pinckneys and Colonel Magwood built early summer houses there. Others followed. By the early 1800's, Charleston's elite crowded its beaches.

Esnard rented a modest cottage for his father-in-law on a slightly elevated half-acre lot with three bedrooms and a tiny detached kitchen. Beach Street fronted it, with a long, expansive shore extending to the surf. Only widely spaced palmetto palms, low sand dunes, and clusters of sea oaks, interrupted an otherwise clear view of the ocean from our porch. At night, creaking palms and lapping waves reminded me of my time on the deck of a slave ship. Only a noisy prow splitting the sea was missing.

Every morning, Anna and I carried Pebarte to water's edge in a heavy wooden porch chair, with Amos lagging behind with a raised umbrella, shielding the old man from the sun. Spent waves poured their salty foam over Pebarte's withered feet, making him smile. Anna and I stayed close by to keep him in his chair. After an hour or so, I generally carried Pebarte back to our cottage in my arms. Occasionally, he tried expressing himself but couldn't. His soul wanted to speak, but his lips wouldn't move.

Afternoons belonged to Anna and me. Leaving Amos with Pebarte, we walked the beach, sometimes reaching Breech Inlet, separating Isle of Palms from Sullivan's Island. Shore scenes fascinated us: sandpipers retreating from a spent wave, small fish popping out of churning surf, gulls squawking, kingfishers diving, all participated in Nature's Opera. Once we were interrupted when two white boys and two black boys splashed past us, knee deep in the surf, oblivious to each other's station in life, just enjoying the natural friendship that exists between children. I knew that the blacks had to be slaves, because only Negro servants attending white vacationers were permitted on Sullivan's Island.

Those times when we reached Breech Inlet, Anna and I would plop down in the sand, giving me time for reflection. In 1776, a British regiment once stood in formation on the Isle of Palms side, ready to cross the apparently shallow waters of Breech Inlet. Their arrogant commander believed victory would be his when his Red Coats attacked Fort Sullivan from its land side. Only he never measured the depth and currents of the inlet. Unable to wade across, the Red coats were left stranded. Without their support, the British navy failed to dislodge the fort's defenders, resulting in an American victory. Masters take note. Arrogance caused a British general's mistake, and arrogance causes masters to underestimate their slaves.

While I was on Sullivan's Island, the Esnards moved into Pebarte's home on George Street. They planned a more intensive care for him when he returned, but knew that he faced the inevitable end of life. He lingered almost two months. The Esnards sent for me, and I met Father Gallagher, who had just performed last rites for the old man. When I reached Pebarte's bedside, he whispered thanks for me being his friend. He closed his eyes and went away.

Soon after Pebarte's death, Old Daddy Andrew passed. He had worked against slavery all his life. "Time warrior" described him best, because he had hurled fables like lances to inspire a new generation of slaves to seek freedom. He fell on the highway to a better life for his people. Pebarte, by contrast, fell on the dead-end road of those defending slavery.

My lamp's flame grows low. Next time, I'll tell you about the heavy clouds over Charleston in 1822, reminiscent of those over Saint-Domingue before the Great Slave Rebellion.

Love to My Boys,

Saturday

When Philip finished Saturday's letter, Susan Elizabeth blurted: "How could Saturday befriend Pebarte? Wasn't Pebarte behind the ambush that killed Canga?"

"Saturday never forgot Pebarte's sins," replied Philip. "But he found something redemptive in most people, and perhaps figured that a defeated Pebarte had suffered enough. Besides, hatreds are like acids, too much burns the holder."

"And you, Mr. Philip, were a master gardener," Wahl giggled. "I've never seen you plant anything, except maybe a kiss on Susan Elizabeth."

"Gardening and gardens for public entertainment were ambitions of my youth," Philip responded. "I worked for John Champneys at Rentowles on the Stono River and for Philippe Noisette in Charleston. They inspired my botanical interests, but not until Alexander Placide employed me at Vaux Hall Gardens did I see how public entertainment and gardening could be combined."

"What about Joel Poinsett?" Susan Elizabeth interrupted. "I've heard you mention him in connection with your plans for Tivoli Gardens."

"Joel Poinsett," Philip responded, "inspired my dream of a public garden more than anyone else. I saw him when Saturday took John and me to the Huguenot Church. By the time that we met at Noisette's nursery, he had an education, and had become a world traveler. Though only six years my elder, he seemed much older, much wiser. Our common denominator was our love for horticulture."

"Let's see, Philip, didn't he have something to do with the poinsettia that we associate with Christmas?" Susan Elizabeth butted in.

"Yes, he popularized the Mexican plant in the United States. Now please, may I continue? Joel Poinsett told me about his wonderful travels and his collection of botanical specimens, but his story about Tivoli Gardens near Rome fascinated me more.

"The Minti Tiburtine Hills, where Tivoli is located, had once been the ancient playground of wealthy Romans. Emperor Hadrian outdid them all with his luxurious Villa Adriana; outdid them all, that is, until the cardinal son of Lucrezia Borgia came along in the early sixteenth century. Rejected for the papacy, Cardinal d'Este gained the Tivoli Diocese to compensate his loss. It didn't matter. The lavish tastes that he would have carried to the papacy, he now carried to Tivoli. He directed the construction of a magnificent palace below the town of Tivoli, and garnished its interior with appointments fit for royalty. But the palace gardens were more dazzling. Drawing water from the nearby Aniene River, his engineers built the world's greatest water garden, surpassing ancient Babylon's. I couldn't stand it; I had to see Tivoli.

"With a full wind in my sail, I sold some of my Branchville property to finance my voyage to Italy. In late 1806, I left Charleston on a ship sailing for Naples. Once at Tivoli, I never tired of its fountains. The Water Organ's cascading scene would have fascinated anyone with the senses of the living. A fountain shaped like a Roman galleon, spewing water in every direction, was Poinsett's favorite. Mine was the Owl Fountain, where warbling birds synchronized their escape with a predatory owl's appearance.

"When I came home," sighed Philip, "I sold more of my Branchville land to buy a ten-acre lot at the upper end of Meeting Street. When Tivoli opened in 1816, I found my finances running low, and decided that public popularity might fill my coffers. At first, large crowds assembled to witness side shows, culminating with gigantic fireworks displays; but sensationalism fades quickly."

"So what did you do?" Wahl injected.

"I resorted to desperate measures to solve my financial crisis. To reduce my labor costs, I purchased slaves, and I advertised for a higher class clientele. More Branchville land sales paid for an opera house. I hired the director of the Charleston Theatre to stock it with accomplished performers and to oversee productions there. I totally revamped the gardens of Tivoli, featuring the Noisette rose, Charleston's own creation. I even made room for an experimental crop of sugar cane at Tivoli. Momentarily, I thought that I might succeed when in 1826, Tivoli hosted the Palmetto Day Society's fiftieth year celebration of the city's famous victory over the British on Sullivan's Island.

"My changes failed," Philip continued. "I went to my old friend Antoine Barbot for a loan, but he turned me down. So did Leborde, a childhood friend. Losing hope, I turned to Poinsett, but he offered only advice. He tried to compensate by inviting me to his famous breakfasts at his mansion, so that I might plead my case before his guests. They offered me no money, only more advice. In 1830, I closed Tivoli, and moved to Branchville where I bought this restaurant, and later became a stationmaster. Bason accompanied me to manage my ever-dwindling farm and produce food for the depot kitchen."

"That's not all you got from Tivoli," Susan Elizabeth teased.

"You mean my first wife?" a blushing Philip replied. "Damn, why do you always want to know about my love life, dear? In 1829, a beautiful young woman and her father rode their carriage past Tivoli's main gate, raising the floodgate of my passion and sense of adventure. I followed them through the streets of Charleston and across Goose Creek, as they headed home to Branchville. She was Lavinia Langstaff. Our courtship lasted a year, our marriage fourteen years until her death in childbirth. I have only fond memories of our life together, our four children, and that damn doorknocker from Tivoli mounted on the depot wall."

"Some story, some disappointment," Wahl sympathized.

"Not really, without my defeats, I would not be standing here with you and Susan Elizabeth, reading Saturday's letters."

"See you after the revival, Wahl," Susan Elizabeth promised. "We'll continue reading Saturday's letters then."

Wahl nodded and smiled; Susan Elizabeth took Philip's arm, glad that Fate had brought her this man. Together they left Wahl's kitchen, heading for the depot.

The Ninth Letter

The day seemed brighter for Wahl, as she had just returned from the Methodist camp meeting on the Edisto. Her brothers and sisters had "prayed her through." She had found salvation, but worked on forgiveness to stay in Jesus' embrace. Still she was happy finding what generations of slaves before her had discovered: Massah had no control over the spiritual world of suffering slaves.

As she busied herself in her kitchen, she spoke her thoughts: "Philip and Susan Elizabeth are late. It's a bit unusual." She began humming a spiritual, keeping the song's time with the sweep of her broom. Then she stopped, leaned on her broomstick, and whispered: "Hard to pretend you're busy when your sack is full of anticipation."

When stationmaster and wife stepped into her kitchen, Wahl noticed a sour look on Philip's face. "What's wrong, Mr. Philip? Where is your grin? I'm not used to seeing you this way, especially when I want to share my joys from the camp meeting."

Philip forced a smile and replied: "I'm just a little preoccupied with a sad visit that I made to Statesburg to visit my old friend Joel Poinsett. He resides at the home of Dr. W. W. Anderson, a physician who treats Poinsett for consumption; both know that Poinsett's life is ebbing away."

"Sad," replied Wahl, "but that's life's cycle. Death comes to all of us. We just need to be ready to stand before God."

"I know that, Wahl," Philip agreed. "I don't know Poinsett's standing with God, but he is a good man. That's not what bothers me."

"For heaven's sake, Philip, tell Wahl what troubles you, and don't spend an hour getting it out," Susan Elizabeth injected.

"Oh, all right," Philip capitulated. "I'm disgusted that a son of Charleston, and one of South Carolina's great men, faces removal from the state's historical memory. Poinsett stood for many things: republicanism in Latin America, promotion of horticulture and the poinsettia, and critic of slavery. Poinsett owned slaves, but believed that the rising commercial revolution in the South would kill slavery; that is one reason Poinsett supported railroad development. But this not why white South Carolina turned on Poinsett."

"Then what did?" Wahl broke in.

"White South Carolinians believe that Poinsett betrayed the state with his pro-Union stance in the Nullification Crisis of 1833. He blocked secession at the Greenville Convention in Upcountry South Carolina. Once a state hero, Poinsett became a villain in the eyes of the good citizens of South Carolina because he challenged the states' rights philosophy of John C. Calhoun, Charleston's adopted son and flower of manhood."

Pausing because of his mounting anger, Philip continued, "South Carolinians, Charlestonians especially, have deified that damn Calhoun. Upon his recent death, eulogies were piled so high that had they been marble slabs, he could have stood higher than a Greek god. But with the state's elevation of Calhoun has come the lowering of Poinsett into an abyss of ingratitude. Why, when Poinsett dies, I bet Charleston will barely notice, and not even bury him there."

Embarrassed by his diatribes, Philip opened Saturday's ninth letter and added, "I hope that something in this letter will relieve my anger."

With that comment, he began reading.

Labyrinth Plantation
Matanzas
May 1, 1826

Dear Philip and John,

Since my escape from Charleston years ago, I have evaded your questions about my part in the Denmark Vesey Conspiracy. Now I am ready to talk about it.

The tolling of St. Michael's bells in the spring of '98 began this part of my story. Alarmed citizens rushed to the church, concerned that America's undeclared naval war with France might bring their enemy's frigates into Charleston Harbor. But something else fired their fear: the specter of Haitian soldiers liberating Southern slaves. The crowd extended from the chancel of St. Michael's out into Meeting Street. I squeezed myself into position near the sanctuary doors. From my perch, I saw the whole proceeding.

There by the altar, stood the militia commander, the intendant (mayor), and Governor Charles Pinckney. The solemn crowd readily responded to the governor's call to order. He began by explaining that word had reached him that Toussaint L'Ouverture planned to invade South Carolina to incite a slave rebellion. Angry remarks followed, rippling across the agitated audience: "Damn those French niggers!" ricocheted from every corner. Then one person stood, shouting that he would pay for rope to lynch every French Negro in Charleston. Another screamed that there was a good start last year when authorities hanged three black bastards from Saint-Domingue for planning a slave rebellion. For at least ten minutes, the governor failed to silence the angry crowd.

Finally he did. He explained that South Carolina, Charleston especially, was on military alert to respond to any invasion. The militia commander agreed, adding that troops had been mustered, while others stood ready if needed. The intendant injected his comments, saying that he had tripled the City Guard and imposed a sundown curfew on Charleston's black population. Any Negro breaking the curfew risked being shot—especially a French Negro. I thought that if I had a sign on me, "French Negro," the crowd would have hanged me from the steeple.

The invasion panic turned out to be empty. It had come from The French Directory's colonial agent, Theodore Hédouville, who schemed to exhaust Papa in foreign adventures and reinstate French authority in Saint-Domingue. I'm sure that Papa saw the agent's trap. Besides, Papa had his hands full in a war against mulattoes.

So just who warned South Carolina about an impending invasion? I believe that Papa Toussaint did it to draw the American government and Yankee merchants trading with his regime even closer. It must have worked, because soon after, the *Constitution* and the *Nathaniel Greene*, the pride of the pugnacious but small U. S. Navy, made ports of call at Charleston. The two warships soon assumed stations off southern Saint-Domingue to support Toussaint's invasion there. Hédouville, the sly French commissioner, was up against the king of foxes.

Charleston's fear of French Negroes subsided, but never quite died. Occasionally, an incident reignited this feeling. Such happened well after the Quasi War with France ended. James Negrin, who normally published almanacs and city directories, printed copies of the Haitian constitution. An independent black state so near home angered Charleston authorities. They jailed Negrin and confiscated his press. When he gained release, he sought safety in only printing almanacs and city directories again. He had learned his lesson.

As time passed, whites probably realized that French Negroes were old and small in number. But as whites feared us less, Charleston Negroes revered us more. I spent many nights in a Charleston grogshop, telling my story to its black patrons for free drinks. My account of the Great Slave Rebellion attracted a giant listener. He was Denmark Vesey, who held French Negroes in high esteem. Some of his conspiratorial plans came from information that I gave him about Saint-Domingue's blood bath.

The Methodist Movement added more to Denmark's plans for attacking and then escaping Charleston. Sometime around December, a tattered figure routinely appeared in Charleston. This ordinary man wore a long frock coat, knee-breeches, shoes with tarnished buckles, and donned a wide-brimmed hat, capping his long gray locks; ordinary in every way, except his penetrating blue eyes, which could look into a man's soul. He was Francis Asbury and his horse Spark. Free blacks and slaves found an advocate in this pioneer of American Methodism. He had come from England before the Revolution, riding horseback across the American colonies and later the new Union, sowing radical Protestantism, and saving souls for Jesus. Country folk and slaves adored this saintly man.

Asbury maintained vows of poverty and celibacy better than a monk. Every year in the late Eighteenth Century and the first decade of the next, this man relentlessly rode a five thousand-mile circuit, became a bishop, and emphasized the well-being of my brothers and sisters. Year's end usually found him in Charleston, recouping his energy for the next circuit season. While preaching in Charleston, he concluded that Negroes were better listeners to his message and more spiritual than his white congregants. His sympathy for the enslaved fed his abolitionist convictions, making him hammer home his Maker's command: No Methodist could own slaves, and those who did must set theirs free. Many of Asbury's circuit riders echoed the bishop's call for freedom, while frequently suffering persecution.

Storytelling was my favorite time with the bishop. His dull sermons could make any congregation drowsy, but he was warm and winning when presiding over small groups. Sitting amidst his Negro audience, he usually began by making direct eye contact with each of us, as if each was his dearest friend. Then he would tell a story that emphasized his attack on slavery. Our most cherished was our "ragged bishop" versus the unrepentant master.

His tale began with the bishop soliciting a guide to lead him to Charleston through Lowcountry swamps. No one volunteered because of Asbury's outspoken views on slavery. Finally one master relented, and offered his services to the bishop. Halfway through a bog, Asbury had to be Asbury, as he witnessed to the planter about the evils of owning slaves. The angry planter abandoned our bishop in the swamps. Asbury still reached Charleston. One of God's angels must have led his way.

Even better, was an exchange I had with our "ragged bishop." This happened when we traded stories about our Lowcountry experiences. He listened intently to Old Daddy Andrew's efforts to instill a love for freedom in slave children, bringing tears to his eyes. For his part, he told me about how unwelcomed he was at big houses where hospitality to strangers had a long tradition. Massahs even denied him lodging in their slave quarters since he might infect their chattels with thoughts of freedom. Then he made an interesting comparison: Treatment of Lowcountry slaves paralleled the horrible treatment of sailors in the Royal Navy. One was a floating hell, the other a standing hell.

I loved the old bishop. He not only "stood in the light," he glowed. Not since Bayon de Libertat, did a white man so work himself into my heart. And his ministry went well beyond Charleston Negroes to Philadelphia, where free Negro Methodists struggled against oppressive white elders. One man in particular championed black Methodists there. He was Richard Allen, a former slave whom our "ragged bishop" embraced.

Richard Allen and Francis Asbury had a long-standing friendship. Both were stanchly Methodist and anti-slavery. When Allen led a free Negro religious revolt in Philadelphia, Asbury shielded him from avenging white clergy by giving critical support to Allen's small Negro church on 6th Street. In effect, Asbury became a sort of spiritual midwife to "Mother Bethel," Allen's church which grew into the African Methodist Episcopal Church (AME) by 1816, the year Asbury died.

Charleston blacks closely followed the black Methodist revolt in Philadelphia, especially Morris Brown and Henry Drayton, respected free Negro ministers. They journeyed to Philadelphia in 1816 to explore a Charleston affiliation with AME, but faced basic differences: Freedom budded in Philadelphia, while slavery flourished in Charleston. Moreover, neither Brown nor Drayton shared Allen's separatist views, nor his fascination with Haiti as a Caribbean utopia for American Negroes escaping white oppression.

In 1817, Brown and Drayton returned to Charleston and to a seething rebellion within city Methodist churches. Black resentment exploded when an important white Methodist official tried removing Negro collection from black control; white trustees further insulted their black membership by proposing construction of a hearse barn at a black cemetery, causing black Methodists to bolt white churches by the thousands. They formed two African Churches, Zion on Anson Street and Cow Alley in the largely black Hampstead neighborhood. Brown and Drayton pastored the churches. For an instant, all of black Charleston became Methodists. I was never so proud of my people. White Methodists demanded the return of their Negro prodigals. Hell, no! The spiritual war was on.

White Charleston kept pressure on Brown and Drayton to return their sheep to the fold. Maybe this pressure provoked them to disregard the Charleston slaveocracy's warning to stay away from Allen and the abolition-infested AME. The two ministers affiliated their churches with AME anyway, and incensed white opposition further by inviting an AME delegation to Charleston. Intendant (Mayor) James Hamilton met this challenge by suppressing AME services, jailing many of its congregants, and running the Philadelphia AME clerics out of town. From1818 to late 1821, the religious war raged, a war Charleston AME was slowly losing. While this turbulence brewed, the Vesey Conspiracy shaped a more dangerous storm. But don't just focus on Denmark Vesey; also pay attention to Richard Allen in Philadelphia, as unrest intensified.

White opposition to AME correctly viewed it as a source of

abolition and abolitionist propaganda. It came not from the pulpits where Brown and Drayton soothed white Charleston with mellow sermons, but from a lower Methodist hierarchy, known as class-leaders. Technically, a class-leader led his members in prayer, Bible study, song, and preparation for church membership. Most followed the rules; some did not. One maverick was Denmark Vesey who used his class-leadership to scatter seeds of rebellion among his audiences at Cow Alley AME. It is no coincidence that nearly half of those convicted in the Vesey Conspiracy came from Cow Alley.

At this point, I need to explain how my life trickled into the rising flow of rebellion in Charleston. Other than unfolding events, two friends influenced my growing discontent over my *permanent* slave status. The first was my closest friend during my time in Charleston.

When I worked at Pritchard's Shipyard, I always listened for a distinctive baritone voice, sometimes singing and sometimes cursing. The voice belonged to boatman George Lining, slave of "Colonel" Charles Lining. George dutifully delivered his master's naval stores to Pritchard's twice a week. He was thin but tall, and at a distance, we had look-alike physics; up close, however, he had much larger biceps than mine, made rock-hard from poling shallow creeks and rowing the mighty Cooper. Not one to waste words, George had few conversations with workers at Pritchard's, so any chance of us developing a friendship seemed remote. Remote, that is, until the Great Fire of '96.

Heading for a grogshop near Lodge Alley, I noticed flames engulfing Queen Street and quickly spreading. The fiery tide became wind-driven, threatening to level Charleston. Five hundred homes had kindled, and some of the city's finest buildings were lost. In desperation, firemen retreated down Church Street before their roiling enemy. But they had one last reserve to throw at this storm of fire and smoke—barrels of black powder. They packed the Huguenot Church near St. Philip's with the stuff, and exploded it to build a firebreak. Their enemy's advance stalled, but spewing sparks filled the air, like fiery arrows shot from General Vulcan's bow, landing on St. Philip's roof and sending up tiny puffs of smoke.

At that moment, a man raced from the crowd for St. Philip's. It was George Lining. He entered through a steeple doorway, as the crowd pushed near the church. Then I followed practically unnoticed. George kicked out a vent, cut down a section of pull-rope to the bell tower, secured it, and climbed down to the roof. Then he began pulling off flaming shingles and tossing them to the ground. When he finished, his badly burned hands kept him from gripping the rope. So I yelled to him to tie the rope around his waist. With help from several men, we hoisted George back into the tower. He had saved St. Philips!

There was much speculation about the fire's origin. Some accused French Negroes for wanting to torch Charleston, as they had once done to Saint-Domingue. Others alleged other sources: careless burning of trash, a drunken sailor, or a child lighting fireworks. But all agreed on one thing: George Lining was a hero.

Brave George! Blacks cheered him, whites applauded him, and "Colonel" Lining bragged on his slave. But the colonel's enthusiasm cooled when the St. Philip's vestry offered to buy George's freedom. Master Lining wanted to keep his hard-working boatman. So he set his price so high that he thought the vestry would withdraw its offer, but the vestry opened its purse and met his demand. The colonel hid his bitterness, and accepted the money. Not used to losing, Colonel Lining had to blame someone. He blamed George for being brave.

The colonel's acrimonious behavior toward his former slave flared up faster than the flames which nearly destroyed Charleston: George could neither work for him, nor could he continue living on the colonel's plantation since a free Negro might incite a slave rebellion. This last restriction fell hard on George who adored his wife and children. The colonel added that if he sneaked visits to his family, he would have him shot. George's tragic circumstance reminded me of my good judgment not to accept Uncle Philip's offer to set me free. "Free Negro" is slavery but by a different name.

George became embittered, as each year brought heavier restrictions on free Negroes in Charleston. In a nutshell, South Carolina treated them as agents of abolition, and sought their expulsion. The state restricted their travel from South Carolina, and threatened them with loss of freedom should they return. More importantly, the state made manumission impossible. By 1820, only the legislature could free a slave, and eventually slaves could not even gain freedom by will. South Carolina's repression of free Negroes and slaves forced them to seek a common cause: their freedom.

I grieved for my declining friend. More and more, George and I spent long hours together in grogshops. When I rejected his invitation to "liquor up," he went alone anyway, and brooded over the unfairness of life. Then one morning in 1821, George loaded poles (masts) onto a hoist at Gadsden Wharf. Whether distracted by his thoughts, or simply not paying attention, he forgot to secure one of the lines. The hoist tilted its load over George's head, dumping its contents and crushing him to death.

Lining's life had ended long before his fatal accident. For him, freedom meant losing his family; for him, freedom meant facing unending white suspicions; for him, freedom meant constant threats of re-enslavement; for him, freedom meant lingering sadness; for him, freedom meant nothing. George's fate caused me to reconsider my own. Would good people ever bring slavery down? I found myself questioning my course through life. Should I have raised the sword? What Denmark Vesey had to say deepened my doubts.

An unlikely little man influenced my joining the Vesey conspirators. He was Gullah Jack, sold on the block in Charleston in 1806. From the Congo Kingdom of Lunda, he came from a long line of priests, once serving the rulers of that Bantu-speaking nation. They bore the royal title of "Lords of the Viper." In Bantu, his name was "Quaco" (Wednesday), which Paul Pritchard, his new master, mispronounced and then Anglicized to "Jack." A mere teenager when sold near The Exchange, Jack held onto his proud priestly ancestry. Captain Kingsley, who bought Jack in Madagascar, noticed that the young man guarded a little bag of African charms. And guard it he did, indicating Jack's determination to become a conjure doctor.

Because of Jack's tiny hands, Paul Pritchard assigned him the job of caulker in his shipyard. He became expert in lining the chinks of new and old ships with cotton filler and sealing them with oakum. Paul admired his work ethic, and allowed him to rent quarters near Gadsden Wharf. At first, I found him arrogant and aloof, even though I was thirty years his elder.

Gullah Jack never tired telling George Wilson and me about his powers as a conjure doctor. Often he showed us charms from his bag and indicated their special powers: a viper's head to inspire aggression, peanuts to gain Mother Earth's bountiful blessings, crab claws for protection against injury, and potions for love and revenge. He told George and me that he could see the invisible world of ghosts and spirits. More important, he claimed that he could command those "on the other side" to protect the living, making them invincible. No white man could kill him, Jack claimed, and anyone with his conjured crab claw in his mouth would enjoy this same protection.

"Hogwash," I thought, but something happened in 1812 that changed our relationship. Jefferson's Embargo (1807-1809) and the slow recovery which followed all but closed Pritchard's Shipyard. With no new keel on the stocks, Paul Pritchard dismissed his white labor force, and farmed his slave workers to other construction projects. But in 1812, he landed contracts to build two men-of-war, *Saucy Jack* and *Decatur*. Work became plentiful, as war with England began, requiring Pritchard to reassemble his slave workers and all but two members of his former white labor force. The two were bullies who had tormented Jack. They accused the little conjure doctor of stealing their jobs, and swore their revenge.

Those thugs stood near Gadsden Wharf almost every afternoon when Jack left work. They began by heckling, but soon threatened to thrash him. Any retaliation by Jack might cost him his life.

Refusing to stand idly by, George Wilson and I acted to keep those two buckras from dismantling our co-worker. We concocted a plan to save Jack, but unwittingly contributed to his reputation as a conjure doctor. Jack agreed with our scheme. When we reached the main shipyard gate, Jack and I pretended a violent argument that George could not mediate. Jack suddenly pulled from his bag a viper's head, and pointed it at me, while I feigned a convulsive trance and began writhing like a snake. Inansi and Turtle would have been proud.

The two white men approached us cautiously, but jumped back when they witnessed my convulsions. And Gullah Jack added a masterful touch by giving me the "evil eye." The bullies acted unafraid at first, but their fast-moving feet confessed their terror. It was only a ruse, but I swear that I felt the presence of spirits. Maybe the gods of Africa had helped us after all.

Word of our performance circulated Charleston quickly. Some whites surely feared the little conjure doctor, but among Charleston Negroes, Jack became a legend. Charleston's own Dr. Buzzard and Cotton Eyes, themselves conjurers, stood in his shadow. Only he, they believed, could bring down white men. Even Jack himself bought into his fame, growing a bushy black beard attended with the meditative gaze of a holy man. He had become Charleston's most famous conjure doctor.

Jack appreciated what I did for him, and tried putting me under his spiritual influence. But I had seen them all, whether voodoo houngans or conjuring doctors. I could not be moved, nor did Jack ever quit questioning my Catholic faith. Nevertheless, I regarded Jack like a son, and enjoyed traveling with him to Bulkley's Farm, north of Charleston, where his conjuring awed "countrymen," a name city Negroes gave Lowcountry slaves. Once he even ate a half-raw chicken, and drank its blood to excite his audience.

Unlike my relationship with Gullah Jack, were his with George Wilson and Tom Russell, both blacksmiths at Pritchard's. George and Jack kept trying to proselytize the other. George rested his case with Jesus; Jack rested his with conjured African spirits. George loved his master and his class-leadership at Cow Alley AME. Jack hated slavery, and despised the master class. With no chance of victory for either, they settled for a distant friendship. I loved George's happy demeanor, but never quite trusted him. Much different was Tom Russell's relationship with Jack.

Tom had a coal-black complexion, dancing brown eyes, and teeth as white as ivory piano keys. Tall and lean, he had a natural athletic build and a vivacious personality. He found small things funny, and teased his friends endlessly. When he sensed that he had gone too far, he would shove all four fingers on his right hand into his mouth, suppressing his laughter; only his eyes seemed to laugh on. Tom was intelligent, but lacked concentration, causing him to flit from task to task. A little lazy, but kind, Tom was the perfect companion well-met for us at Pritchard's.

When Gullah Jack joined our little group, Tom quickly fell under his spell. Gullah taught him the art of conjuring, and as the doctor's reputation grew, so did Tom's. He became, in effect, the sorcerer's apprentice. With his rise as a conjurer, Tom's bubbling personality turned somber. No longer did he stick his fingers in his mouth, as he had quit laughing. More than once, I restrained Tom from attacking a white man who had offended him. So thoroughly did he stand under the wizard's cape that Gullah Jack once remarked: "If you see Tom, you see me."

When the sun set on our day, we at Pritchard's headed for a grogshop. Nearly every city alley had several, but we chose locations for a reason: Stolls Alley near the docks to pump sailors for news, French Alley for bawdy entertainment, Chatmers Alley for socializing with Negroes of all walks, and Line Alley where Philip's friend William Penn Bason served his customers. Good-natured George Wilson orchestrated our laughter by telling jokes and by trying to get the once-happy Tom Russell to crack a smile. But shortly after George Lining's death, a frequent uninvited guest showed up, squelching our laughter and causing George Wilson to leave for home. Our intruder was Denmark Vesey, a free Negro already on white Charleston's "list" of troublemakers.

Denmark was physically imposing: massive hands, broad shoulders, and a towering height of well over six feet. These features aside, it was his menacing face that struck fear into many men, and his unpredictable temper often exploded, making us move softly around him. Even Peter Poyas, Denmark's closest confidant, described their relationship as a "frightful friendship."

Maybe Denmark's personality would have been less aggressive and sinister had he not discovered that "free Negro" imposed new restrictions upon him. Having won a city lottery in 1799, he purchased his freedom, but found his family not for sale. A master's prohibitions that once destroyed George Lining's home life, now assaulted his. Denmark's constant appeals to his wife's master ended in 1820 when a South Carolina law made manumission the state legislature's decision. White Charleston believed that the free Negro issue had been settled. Without a source, they argued, the pond would dry up. Only they overlooked Denmark who sought a different pond: Haiti!

Denmark's bitterness concerned even his closest companions. He could not hide his feelings "under a bushel," and often challenged whites whom he disliked, which meant nearly all whom he met. On one occasion, he lectured a seventeen-year-old white boy about the evils of slavery. Though we agreed with him, we begged his restraint. Somehow he avoided the Workhouse and the bite of the warden's whip.

Our initial conversations were casual, even though I found his constant presence at our group's favorite grogshops a bit odd. I suspected that Gullah Jack had tipped off our locations to Denmark. He told me that he came from St. Thomas, I believe. Before he purchased his freedom, he had been the slave of Captain Joseph

Vesey, a Charleston planter-merchant. He further emphasized his brief enslavement in Saint-Domingue before arriving in Charleston. I asked him the origin of his first name, and he told me proudly that Captain Vesey had named him "Telemaque," after the wandering son of Ulysses in Homer's *Odyssey*. Slaves in Charleston had trouble pronouncing his name and shortened it to "Telmak" which he Anglicized to "Denmark." Thus, his Charleston brothers and sisters gave him his first name, he said smiling.

He kept asking me about the Great Slave Rebellion in Saint-Domingue and the French Negroes in Charleston, whom he believed, wanted to smear themselves again with the white man's blood. His extreme hatreds troubled me, especially questions about why I had spared my boys. I replied that "if you can't stand with the ones you love, you can't stand." He ridiculed my affection for Philip and John with a brutal response: "If you kill the gnats, you can't leave their nits." His thirst for revenge would eventually mark the parting of our ways.

Due to Gullah Jack's constant coaxing, I began attending Denmark's class meetings at Cow Alley AME. On those occasions, he frequently used the Book of Exodus to argue that Charleston and plantation slaves were the new Israelites, and that city whites were the new Egyptians. We must be set free, he exclaimed, for under God's law in Exodus a master could enslave an Israelite for only six years. God's Avenging Angel would enforce this limit with a terrible swift sword. From the twenty-first chapter of Exodus he routinely read God's condemnation of those who bought, sold, or owned a slave. Another favorite of his came from Psalms 58, verse 10: "The righteous shall rejoice when he seeketh the vengeance: he shall wash his feet in the blood of the wicked."

At meetings in Cow Alley's basement, Denmark never suggested himself as a Moses, nor did he advocate open rebellion. Had he done so, certain members of his class might have reported him to city authorities. More important, he avoided a clash with Cow Alley AME conservatives to preserve church unity. Denmark had to tread gently. That is why his classes served as a recruitment center for those whom he invited to secret meetings at his home on Bull Street, or to Monday Gell's harness shop on Meeting Street.

I attended my first meeting at Denmark's home in December, 1821. Getting to and from this meeting presented few problems to participants. We arrived before the deployment of the City Guard who averaged only one patrolman per ward. Then in late evening, we walked back to our quarters. Should we happen upon a foot-sore guard, he would likely be found leaning against a doorway, fast asleep. Even if awake, he only carried a bayonet to enforce his challenge.

Standing before his solemn audience, Denmark's angry face flickered in the lantern light. He began by extolling Haiti as the Promised Land. Reading from Exodus, he rejoiced that God would destroy Pharaoh's people; then he read his favorite verse outside the Book of Exodus: "And they utterly destroyed all that was in the city, both man and woman, young and old, and ox, and sheep, and ass, with the edge of the sword" (Joshua 6:21). Denmark's audience knew that "the city" in the quotation was Charleston. Then he began a singsong chant: "Where is this Land of Milk and Honey?" "Haiti!" shouted his responsive audience. Exclaiming the moment, he slammed his fist so hard against his make-shift pulpit that I expected its boards to crack.

Then he described the glories of Haiti: How black men had dignity there; how hard labor would be rewarded; and how a caring government would nurture the Israelites from Charleston. All would be well, he insisted, when we leave evil Charleston. Accenting his conclusion, he read an inscription on his Bible bookmark by abolitionist Benjamin Lundy: "To Haiti let us go, and then we may enjoy our natural rights; for Negroes there are viewed as men; and there taught as good as white."

So where did this Haitian mania come from? There can be no doubt but from the pen of Prince Saunders, Haitian propagandist first for King Christophe and then for President Boyer. He was a virtual Pied Piper whose tune charmed Richard Allen and Denmark Vesey with false images of Haiti. Both men saw emigration to Haiti as a viable response to racism and slavery in America.

In Philadelphia, Bishop Allen lost hope that free Negroes would ever enjoy equal rights with whites. That is why he devoured Saunders' *Haytian Papers*, a book crediting Haiti with every virtue known to man. Certain that Haiti provided a refuge for free Negroes, Allen invited Saunders to preach his message to Bethel Church. His exhortation fell on willing ears and broken hearts, as Saunders' free Negro congregation felt like Miss Liberty's unwanted children, knowing that they might be expelled from the Union if Charles Cotesworth Pinckney in Congress had his way. Bishop Allen had enough and promoted a trek of Philadelphia free Negroes to Haiti; there, he promised, they would receive President Jean-Pierre Boyer's warm welcome.

Denmark knew Allen's plan, partly through information Reverend Morris Brown supplied him and partly through a copy of Saunders' *Haytian Papers*. But the situation in Philadelphia had essential differences from the one in Charleston. Nothing prevented free black emigration from Philadelphia to Haiti, except means and enthusiasm. White Philadelphia welcomed it.

Charleston's circumstances differed. Had Denmark limited himself to draining Charleston's free Negroes for emigration to Haiti, city whites might have paid their fares, and packed their lunches. But the port city's free Negro issue was tied to slavery. Denmark wanted freedom for his skilled slave friends denied manumission under state law. But we were likely to remain slaves, as South Carolina intended to abolish the free Negro class through exile and prohibition. Men such as Peter Poyas, Monday Gell, Gullah Jack, Mingo Harth, Smart Anderson, Dick Sims, Jacob Glen, Tom Russell, George Wilson, and of course me were faces in a crowd unlikely to ever taste freedom. When I came to Charleston thirty years earlier, I willingly deferred my freedom to raise my boys. Now I feared that I might die a slave. Make no mistake. Should-be-free Negroes drove the developing Denmark Vesey Conspiracy.

After the session, Gullah Jack escorted me into a side room to meet with Denmark and Peter Poyas. Denmark announced that the time had come for my commitment to his plans. He insisted that I sign a ledger, which Poyas held with names of hundreds of enlistees who had already promised to destroy and escape Charleston. He warned that he would kill me if I refused. Again his bullying tactics annoyed and concerned me. I hesitated, but realized that this might be my last chance for freedom. I signed. Poyas smiled, and closed his ledger.

Leaving Denmark's house, I stumbled toward my residence on Elliott Street, wondering had I done the right thing. Neither drifting bay fog, nor flickering street lamps, nor droning harbor sounds, nor even clicking horses' hoofs and grinding carriage wheels could divert my concentration. Did I make a mistake by signing Poyas' ledger?

As I entered my quarters, Gullah Jack stepped from the shadows, grabbed my arm, and told me that Denmark wanted me to lead a company of French Negroes in the coming revolt. "French Negroes!" I was dumbfounded. I laughed, as I told Gullah that our average age was probably over sixty. Then I suggested that Denmark might give us crutches with sharpened tips to rest on between gigging white folks. Gullah was taken aback. I bade him good night, and entered my home.

I went through torture before my final meeting with Denmark. My enthusiasm for rebellion faltered, and Denmark sought to bolster it with wild promises: The British would assist our escape; Haiti would send an army; countrymen were poised to march on Charleston; Haiti would welcome us. Denmark was so prone to fabrication that I did not know when he told the truth. He even told me his strategy for the rebellion: isolate Charleston in a surprise attack, seize its arsenals, rob its banks, loot its stores, rape and kill all its whites, and escape to Haiti. He finished by promising me a second chance to kill you, Philip.

I concluded that Denmark's plan would fail. He schemed opening the gates of Charleston to thousands of pillaging slaves over whom he would have little authority. While they rampaged, his inner-circle would seize ships in the harbor, and evacuate his friends and any countrymen reaching the docks. Then they would set sail for Haiti with their plunder.

A well-trained army might not have executed Denmark's plan. What kind of commander orders his soldiers to loot and murder? Where time would be the essence of victory, too much time would be lost in rampage. Did he even plan on controlling the rebels, or was mayhem his cover for escape? The docks loomed as a disaster as well. A man-of-war could block the channel across the harbor's sand bar, while lobbing shots at the wharves. Evacuation by ship under fire would have tested a veteran army's mettle, much less a mob pushing, shoving, and falling into the water. At best, a thousand slaves and free Negroes might have escaped Charleston for Haiti. You can bet that Denmark and his inner-circle would have been among them.

My concern for the countrymen clinched my decision to leave the conspiracy. Denmark planned to raise them, but not save them. Thousands could have faced slaughter before white armies seeking blood revenge. And what did Denmark think the U. S. Army and state militia would be doing with a slave master in the White House and another serving as secretary of war? The blood of my people would have watered South Carolina's soil, making Old Daddy Andrew cry out from his grave. Then there was you, dear Philip, together we would have escaped Charleston, or died at each other's side.

Nightmares haunted me for weeks. No sooner asleep, a rising blood-tide swept into my dreams. On its swells, sailed a phantom fleet of bad memories, memories of wholesale slaughters, memories of Jeannot's cruelties, and memories of my people's cries. Beside these, bobbed a Satan's navy of the heads of loved ones that slavery and revolution took from my life. No one should go through what

I experienced once; only a fool would do it twice. Had vengeance clouded my judgment? My memory of Zèbre came to mind. Had I avenged Catherine's death, you boys and some of our escort might have been killed. Revenge carried a heavy price then and now. I needed to repair my patience for slavery itself to wear out. Good people must be out there, but O God, send them! I was a weary man.

Now I had to tell Vesey that I quit. The end of January, 1822, marked that moment. Gullah Jack accompanied me on my dangerous meeting with Vesey. Instinctively, Jack must have known that I planned on leaving the conspirators. He reassured me that the rebels would fight their way out of Charleston. Then he confirmed my decision by saying that each countryman would be invincible, because each would have an enchanted crab claw in his mouth. Crab claws? I looked at Jack both amused and stunned. Like the voodoo houngans in Saint-Domingue, he knew how to start a fight, but not how to win it. Neither scattering charms, nor conferring with a rooster under fire could bring victory to the countrymen. The conspirators needed a Papa Toussaint, or at least a Jean-François to lead them. None were available. And so I measured my steps to Denmark's home on Bull Street as perhaps my last.

I timed my meeting with him carefully, about an hour before a secret gathering at his home. What I planned to say might have gotten me killed on the spot, but entering "guests" might stay his hand. Not since my days in Saint-Domingue had I feared for my life like that.

Gullah knocked on Denmark's open door. He bellowed for us to come in and toast to victory over the whites. We raised our glasses. Salute! Then Denmark lifted his glass again in honor of his lieutenants. Salute again! Finally he tipped his glass one more time and shouted: "*Vive la compagnie française*" (Long live the French company)! While Jack and Denmark raised their glasses, mine remained by my side. Denmark had the expression of someone just shot. But soon his face became so contorted that he might have scared the Devil himself. Before he could say anything, I told him that I resigned from the conspiracy.

Denmark unleashed a verbal barrage on me, using the words *nigger* and *coward* like mortar between his brickbats. Gullah grew pale. "Damn your white boy, Saturday!" Denmark shouted, wagging a finger in my face, and saying that I couldn't kill a white man. I was just a house nigger deserving to die.

I stood my ground. Kill me he might, but I refused to yield the righteousness of my position. Maybe it was "my time" to die anyway. I looked into his furious eyes, and told him that saving you, Philip, was not my only consideration. I was standing up for the countrymen, those plantation slaves serving his plans, likely to fall before white armies advancing on Charleston. Their deaths would serve Denmark's escape, not an overthrow of plantation society. By this time, early arrivals calmed him, and he regained his composure. Watching Denmark carefully, I backed to his door, turned, and briskly walked away; but not soon enough to avoid his word-daggers: "Saturday," he roared, "you're dead!"

Walking to my Elliott Street apartment, I imagined assassins in every shadow, competing to give Denmark satisfaction. Once inside, my fears intensified: A turning doorknob, a creaking hinge, a popping board, all concerted to keep me awake by night and nervous by day. I even feared working at Pritchard's. It would have been easy for Gullah Jack or Tom Russell to cause me a fatal accident. That is why I asked you, Philip, for lodging and employment at Tivoli Gardens. You readily agreed, making me suspect that William Penn Bason told you about my meetings with Denmark at his grogshop.

Spring burst upon Charleston in 1822. The lingering fire of azaleas, mingling with early roses, and wisteria and iris in regal purples gave Nature's palette every color and every shade of color known to man, while their fragrances exceeded the finest Parisian perfumes. Mistresses of the home in Charleston and on Low-country plantations leaned over Nature's shoulder, dabbled in her pigments, and painted gardens that bore their signatures, made possible by their slaves. Second only to Race Week, garden tours were *the* social event in springtime Charleston. Outside Charleston, boat excursions with finely attired passengers glided along the rivers of rice country, hoping to see yet another plantation garden.

At night, these same Carolina elite indulged themselves in fireworks displays. Beginning with White Point facing the harbor in early spring, and ending on Sullivan's Island in mid fall, white Charleston enjoyed elaborate pyrotechnical shows. Charlestonians loved lighting up the night sky, and if a falling rocket should start a blaze, they could always blame it on a scheming slave.

Spring in 1822 saw Charleston in an active theater season. Most plays originated in Europe, and most sported romance and cold weather as themes. The hot, humid Charleston air made thoughts of snow and ice pleasant for city audiences. And for a less formal evening, there were the public baths. Charleston had two. The one at the end of Laurens Street could accommodate fifty customers at twenty-five cents per person, and included a serenade for bathers.

Spring in 1822 also found white Charleston in a spirit of self-satisfaction. Charlestonians took heart that the Panic of 1819 had passed, and that their bumper cotton crops rivaled Brazil's. Another crisis passed when the acrimony created by the Missouri Compromise died down. Only a yellow fever epidemic troubled city whites. Some left for Carolina Upcountry, others for the seashore or Europe; most, however, defied the disease by staying in town. All was well in their world. Or was it?

Little things pointed to slave unrest. It wasn't new, but old methods of slave resistance that created tension in Charleston. Arson committed by slaves increased: One white home owner on King Street complained that slaves had torched his property four times in a week. Fugitive slavery increased, peaking when twelve slave carpenters stole a longboat, and were captured rowing home to Africa. Maroonage increased as well. Joe (alias Forest) and his fugitive band lurked in Lowcountry for over three years. Even more revealing was black Charleston's disregard for rules of standard conduct. Not uncommonly two Negro males meeting on a Charleston street might go through elaborate charades, mocking the courtesies a white man required of a Negro. At night, Negroes often disregarded curfews, and frequently disrupted entire white neighborhoods with bar brawls spilling into the streets.

The clearest sign that Charleston had reached dangerous unrest was the wide popularity of a little song: "The dead fear no tyrants, the grave has no chains; on, onto the combat! The heroes that bleed for virtue and mankind are heroes indeed; And, oh, if Freedom from this world be driven, despair not; at least we shall find her in heaven; from life without freedom, oh, who would not fly; for one day of freedom, oh! Who would not die?" When whites sang this melody, they supported Portuguese republicans seeking to topple the House of Braganza; when Negroes hummed the tune, they backed those seeking to topple the House of Buckra.

For a full four months, I stayed as cloistered as a monk at Tivoli. Even so, troubles in Charleston had a way of climbing over Tivoli's walls: Philippe Noisette came to Tivoli to unload more than the beautiful roses bearing his name. Noisette loved Celestine, his slave-mistress, and their seven children who under South Carolina law were slaves first and children second. The South Carolina legislature rejected their manumission, and Noisette was furious. Philip, you hugged your old friend, but Noisette's anger failed to diminish.

Each day might have been my last. Was one of Philip's slaves to be my assassin? I finally began relaxing when in late May Gullah Jack visited me at Tivoli. He told me that "ninety-six" had arrived, and would I reconsider rejoining the conspiracy? "Ninety-six" had special meaning for Denmark and his lieutenants. In January, Monday Gell began sending letters to President Boyer of Haiti, requesting military assistance and sanctuary for Denmark's rebels. Gell found a galley cook on the Haitian schooner *Sally* to deliver his letters on one of its regular runs to Port-au-Prince. If the

Sally carried a reply from Boyer, its captain would raise a pennant bearing "ninety-six" upon entering Charleston Harbor. A "nine" and a "six" meant "I have a reply." Until then, Denmark had been disappointed because the *Sally* flew only the Haitian flag on its returns to Charleston. But now there was a reply, and Gullah anticipated good news.

His joy deflated when he learned that I stood by my decision to leave the conspiracy, but now I knew to brace for the coming storm. Then I hugged the little conjure doctor with all the affection of a close friend. Gullah, I am certain, had kept Denmark from killing me. Besides, Gullah must have known that I would never betray the conspiracy. With his help, Denmark distinguished anger from threat. When Gullah left, I never saw him alive again.

Other conspirators became excited upon sighting the *Sally* with "ninety six" floating from its mast. In one case, it proved fatal for Vesey's plans. William Paul, who served Denmark, stood on Market Wharf, feeling ecstatic over seeing the *Sally* bearing a "ninety-six" signal flag. Turning to Peter Prioleau, another slave, Paul poured out nearly everything that Denmark had shrouded in secrecy. Stunned by what he just heard, Prioleau warned his master, John Prioleau.

Alarmed by his slave's story, Master John rushed Peter to interviews with Intendant James Hamilton and Governor Thomas Bennett. Hamilton listened, but doubted Peter's account; the governor was equally disbelieving, citing his own servants as examples of the loyalty slaves felt for their masters. Ironically, his "loyal" slaves (Rolla, Ned, and Batteau Bennett) stood ready to cut the governor's throat. Skeptical of Peter's allegations, Hamilton arrested William Paul for interrogation. A shaken Paul gave up Peter Poyas and Ming Harth whom Hamilton promptly jailed. Denmark sensed his plot unraveling and moved the attack on Charleston from Sunday, July 14, to Sunday midnight, June 16. Could Denmark outrace the slowly awakening city authorities?

The clinching testimony came from my old friend, George Wilson, who Rolla Bennett warned to "get out of town." George passed this information to John Wilson, his owner. Master John made George recite his story to Hamilton and Governor Bennett, while adding further comments about the conspiracy which Cow Alley congregants had made to his slave. All indications pointed to a rebellion. This was on Friday, June 14, only two days before the planned insurrection.

Fear swept Charleston. Militias were mustered, arsenals secured, and City Guard alerted. Philip ordered his slaves at Tivoli to their quarters, and posted guards at each gate. Inside Tivoli, rested a militia company, ready to sally forth into Meeting Street should fighting grow intense. Time moved slowly, as Sunday night fell, casting shadows of uncertainty across the town. In the streets below Philip's townhouse, marched one company of militia after another. A steady tension gripped the city by nine that evening.

Philip and I pulled his dining table onto his balcony to watch proceedings below. He put down two wine glasses, poured his finest Madeira, and placed a brace of pistols between us. Within an hour, his Madeira was gone; the pistols remained. Should slaves storm Tivoli, the pistols were for our suicides to avoid torture. As the midnight showdown approached, Philip's grandfather clock seemed loud. Years ago, your mother's clocks had unnerved me on the eve of the Great Slave Rebellion. On this occasion, I disabled the Devil's timepiece. Midnight came; all Charleston was awake: Old ladies sipped their tea; fathers cradled their muskets; mothers cradled their children. Nothing happened. One a.m. passed and still nothing. With each stroke of the town clock until dawn, nothing happened. At last, morning came. Squawking sea gulls greeting a rising sun, sleepy soldiers standing down, curious onlookers peeking beyond their doors to see if they still had a town, all proclaimed that Fate had given Charleston another day. The peeling of church bells reminded their faithful that God had spared them. I didn't know about that, but the fresh air of that Monday morning felt to me like the renewal of life.

Arrests followed deliverance. The City Guard apprehended

dozens of conspirators and hauled them to the Workhouse. Denmark fell into their net on June 22, and Gullah Jack followed on July 5. Quickly white Charleston assembled a panel of "judges" for speed, not justice, which condemned thirty-four men to the gallows and sent a near equal number into exile. I held my breath. No door remained closed to City Guards scouring Charleston for Poyas' ledger; should they find it, there would be more arrests and hangings. My name was in that book.

Perhaps the saddest casualty was George Wilson who betrayed his people to keep his master's love. For playing Judas, judges at the Workhouse awarded him his freedom and a stipend for life. But every Negro in Charleston considered him a traitor. George changed his last name to Watkins, and moved to the Carolina Upcountry, but could not escape the Furies of guilt.

Executions followed convictions. Vesey and the Bennetts were hanged on July 2; Gullah Jack followed on July 12. I refused to witness this blood circus and stayed secluded at Tivoli. Gullah's execution hit me hard. He had been a loyal friend, and I grieved his passing. He proved mortal despite his charms, but his invincible memory will always inspire those who would be free.

Tom Russell's execution moved me most. He and twenty other conspirators were sentenced to hang on July 26 at The Lines, north of Boundary Street. Tom and those sharing his fate rode atop wagons up Meeting Street and past Tivoli. From Philip's balcony, I looked down on this morbid parade. There sat Tom on his own coffin, as did the other condemned on theirs. His old happy personality had returned, as he laughed and waved to the crowd. As I stared at Tom's passing wagon, he looked up and our eyes met. He waved at me. Tom was heading home to Africa.

An emotional riptide swept over me. I had been a slave nearly all my life, and now I bore witness again to the tragedy associated with my condition. Would it ever end? Rushing from Philip's balcony, I ran into his parlor, and poured out my pleadings in prayer. I begged for the salvation of Tom's soul and for others so dear in my life that slavery had stolen. Most of all, I wept that God might break the chains that bound me.

At that instant, I felt a hand on my shoulder. It was God touching me through Philip: "Time to go to Cuba, Saturday. Time to set you free."

I'm tired and sad from reliving so many memories. In my next letter, I'll describe my escape from Georgetown and my new life in Cuba. Freedom coming, oh, Lord, freedom coming!
Love to My Boys,
Saturday

When Philip completed Saturday's letter, he saw Susan Elizabeth weeping. "There now, Sweetheart," he said, hardly soothing her feelings.

"I just never knew the injury slavery caused," Susan Elizabeth sobbed. "I never knew until now the treachery to which South Carolina resorted to eliminate free Negroes from its soil."

"Yeah!" Wahl butted in. "I'm not angry, or even sad, just tired. I've been drinking from the same cup as Saturday, and slavery has damn near poisoned my soul. I just want it to end. Free folks have defeats too, but they enjoy mostly good lives: providing for their families, knowing that no massah can take their children away, surrendering to a lover's embrace that only their choice can dissolve, and knowing that their cottages and gardens belong to them. Slaves have none of those things, even those slaves whose masters spare them from the whip."

Philip felt ashamed and lowered his head. "I came into this world the son of a slave master," Philip said softly. "Growing up, slaves were all around me. I thought it a normal way of life. The loss of my mother in the Great Slave Rebellion jolted me, but even then I didn't understand that a whole way of life needed to end. But standing on that balcony, watching a hanging parade go by, hit my soul. Here were men riding on their coffins to meet their executioners, desperate men willing to die for their freedom.

250

When Saturday ran from my balcony after seeing his friend Tom Russell, I felt ashamed, ashamed that I had a hand in squeezing the life out of those souls below my window."

"So why didn't you free your slaves?" Wahl interrupted, displaying her bad temper on subjects which hurt her.

"Would have, if I could have," Philip replied. "I tried years ago, but South Carolina stayed the hand of those with a change of heart. I didn't have the courage of the Grimké sisters from Charleston who denounced slavery, left South Carolina, and became abolitionists. I found life here too comfortable to leave in poverty. Selling my slaves was no option either. They could have ended up with a cruel master. Quietly, I'm trying to do the right thing, but South Carolina's rigid laws against manumission hang over my head like an anvil. Why it is even against the law to take a slave across state lines for manumission."

"Sounds like the Denmark Vesey conspiracy taught South Carolina nothing, except to become more repressive" Wahl interrupted. "That storm missed Charleston, but the next one won't."

"What amazes me, Philip," Susan Elizabeth observed, "is that many of our poor slave-free neighbors would die to defend slavery."

"Doesn't matter if they don't own a slave," Philip answered. "They associate slavery with South Carolina nationalism, and are ready to die to defend it. They don't understand that slavery has shrunk South Carolina economically, socially, and morally. Once a bright star in the Original Thirteen, South Carolina has lost its once-promising future."

"For me," Susan Elizabeth inserted, "South Carolina feels like a small island, growing smaller caused by the erosion of a changing morality."

Then Wahl jumped in. "If Sowth Carleenuh don' duh mo' bettuh sump'n eb'l gonna happ'n fuh sho! Lawd Jedus fo' sutten won' hab pashun fo' dem no mo!"

Philip smiled, acknowledging the truthfulness of her comment, not her poor Gullah.

"I love you, Mr. Philip," Wahl professed, "but I hate what you are."

Philip had nothing to say, as he joined Susan Elizabeth by the kitchen door.

"Aren't you going to tell us about Saturday's escape from Charleston?" Wahl questioned.

"No," Philip retorted, "Saturday will in his next letter. This is after all, his story."

Wahl gave an understanding nod, and Philip promised to return soon. Once in the depot, Philip stopped Susan Elizabeth at the wavy glass window framing the Branch Oak. "Shimmer, shimmer great tree, thou dominates the night" were the only words from his lips.

Philip's praise for the old oak puzzled Susan Elizabeth. There was so much about him that she didn't understand; only she knew that she loved him.

The Tenth Letter

Thunder shook the depot, as Philip and Susan Elizabeth hurried to beat the rain. They reached the kitchen door, when a torrent of water poured from the sky with a gale force wind catching the door from Philip's hand and nearly pulling it off its hinges. With both his hands, he pulled the door away from his invisible opponent, and closed it. Just then a bolt of lightning struck so close that it rattled pots and pans hanging near the fireplace. Two other bolts followed, lighting up the evening like mid-day.

Wahl cowered under her kitchen table, calling for "Sweet Je-sus!" No man could make her cower, but she feared God's business, and wondered if she was prepared to meet her Maker. A trembling Susan Elizabeth joined Wahl, and they rocked and shouted together, like two children too terrified to look under their bed. Then Nature's fury subsided, and the two sisters, now turned brave, stood up, and took chairs near the table.

"Reminds me of the Hurricane of 1822," Philip taunted. "If a little weather like this can make you girls run under a table, I wonder what you would have done back then."

"Shut up! You're embarrassing me," Susan Elizabeth shouted.

But Philip continued. "I just returned to Georgetown from my journey with Saturday to Cuba. My ship docked off the Front Street wharves, the center of Georgetown's commercial district. A simmering heat and humidity met me, as I disembarked. Residents complained, but I considered this normal for a Lowcountry summer. But something was different, as I found breathing hard. To ease

253

my discomfort, I visited several waterfront grogshops. Perhaps too much wine convinced me to stay in Georgetown to recover my 'land legs' and to visit old friends. I drew money from Georgetown's one bank, and found lodging on Highmarket Street. God must have wanted me to stay in Georgetown anyway, because of what happened next."

"Well go on!" interrupted Wahl. "It can't be worse than the storms that I faced in Saint-Domingue and Cuba."

Ignoring Wahl, Philip began again. "God's reminder of our mortality arrived on Friday night, September 27. The weather had been squally all day, but gave no hint of an approaching hurricane, or "gale" as locals called it. That changed at about midnight, as mercuries in Georgetown barometers fell dramatically, announcing the approach of a violent storm. About two hours later, Nature's message made landfall, halfway between Charleston and Georgetown, with her full fury racing across the Santee Delta, drowning over five hundred slaves.

"Like you girls, I panicked but a little table to crawl under wouldn't do," Philip teased. "I left my flimsy lodging to seek sanctuary in Prince George Winyah Episcopal Church. Others escaping the storm were already inside. Windows shook, wind howled with demonic voices, things crashed, part of the church roof flew off, and I crawled under a pew. When the attack subsided, I sat up, and started laughing. There on the back of the pew box were the carvings of an angry British soldier, condemning his sergeant in profane terms. The church had been turned into a British army barracks and stable during the American Revolution.

"When I stepped back into the street, I witnessed spectacular destruction: roofs damaged or missing, live oaks toppled, debris everywhere, the Front Street docks damaged, and flotsam jamming Winyah Bay. Worse still were scenes of human tragedy: scattered clothing, broken furniture, broken bodies, broken hearts. Amid this chaos, Mother Nature made me smile: A squirrel ran back and forth the length of a fallen tree, trying to figure out the top and the bottom of his new horizontal home. I picked my way to my damaged lodgings, and dug out a machete that I brought from Cuba. I wanted to be prepared for swamp creatures likely wandering Georgetown streets. In Georgetown proper, nearly forty people died, but outlying areas suffered more dramatic casualties.

"An earlier storm surge covered North Island at the entrance to Winyah Bay. Over one hundred slaves drowned there. The most pronounced demonstration of Nature's power on the island, however, was that of a vacationing doctor and fifteen members of his extended family. Rushing waves carried the doctor's summer house to sea. Witnesses said that they last saw his house bobbing in the tide with lights still burning, like a ship in distress. House, doctor, and extended family all disappeared without a trace.

"I was stranded in Georgetown. My horse and carriage had been blown away, but travel down the King's Highway to Charleston would have been impossible because fallen trees jammed the roadway, taverns were wrecked, and bloated bodies still floated on flooded land. So I waited until the *Eagle*, a packet ship out of Charleston, dropped anchor off Front Street. With dozens of passengers on board the *Eagle*, I returned to Charleston in late October.

"Charleston had suffered along with Georgetown," Philip continued. "Over forty people died in the city, and hardly a property went unscathed. Nature's premier Charleston performance occurred when wind sailed the roof of the Circular Church on Meeting Street all the way to Queen Street, like the shield of a fallen Greek god.

"The Hurricane of 1822 bore tangible results," Philip added. "On the Santee Delta, planters directed the construction of storm shelters for their slaves, mainly out of monetary considerations. The storm also gave rise to one of Lowcountry's great ghost legends. Before the gale, a young dandy on Pawley's Island raced against his slave attendant to the home of his lover. On the way, he and his horse fell into quicksand and died. His grieving sweetheart wandered Pawley's beaches; on one of her journeys of the heart, she witnessed a shadowy, gray male figure stepping out of a rising mist. As he got closer, she noticed his remarkable resemblance to her lost fiancé. She named him Gray Man, and listened to his pleadings that she flee the island to avoid disaster. Her father heard her story, thought his daughter insane, and took her to Charleston for medical examination before the hurricane struck. Gray Man, a ghost, had saved their lives."

"See," said Wahl, "I've told you that spirits exist on the other side, and can help or hurt the living. Black folks see them all the time."

"I don't know about that," Philip replied, "but the legend makes a good story."

"Story!" Susan Elizabeth broke in. "Let's hear Saturday's tenth letter."

Philip nodded, and began reading.

Labyrinth Plantation
Matanzas
December 10, 1834

Dear Philip and John,

Did Charleston authorities possess Poyas' ledger? If so, City Guards would soon arrest me. This uncertainty gnawed at both Philip and me. But he acted quickly, and hurried to the Charleston docks to arrange our passage to Matanzas, Cuba.

Philip had long prepared for my escape, after learning that I kept company with Denmark in Bason's grogshop. In April, before the revelation of the conspiracy, Philip had travelled to Georgetown, sixty miles up the coast, where he bribed a magistrate to certify U. S. Citizenship for a sick friend. The name Philip chose was George Lining's, unlikely to be in Poyas' book. "Saturday Chartrand" as a legal definition disappeared. Lining's physical description matched mine, and his free status allowed me to leave South Carolina. Philip selected Georgetown because few people knew us there.

Our departure from Georgetown posed a major problem. Few ships departed the little port on the Sampit River for Matanzas, except those from Charleston supplementing short cargos. To solve this uncertainty, Philip scoured ships moored along East Bay Street, making regular runs to Matanzas, Cuba. He found only two. The captain of the *Fame* assured him that his ship would anchor at Georgetown early in August, and stay at least a week. A better bet was the *Mary*, captained by Philip's old friend Benjamin Sutton. Both ships would anchor at Georgetown about the same time. Philip booked our passage on both. Now it only remained for us to get the hell out of Charleston.

The obvious is sometimes the best deception. At sunrise July 28, the gates of Tivoli swung open, and a barouche driven by me with Philip as my passenger clattered into Meeting Street, and headed north. I in my finest livery and Philip in a gentleman's attire made a common sight for our neighbors. Soon we crossed Goose Creek Bridge on the Orangeburg Road, apparently heading toward Philip's property near The Branch. "Apparently," that is, for anyone with spying eyes, because we regularly made this trip for business and social occasions. Only this time, Philip had another destination in mind. At about twenty-five miles north of Charleston, we turned eastward toward Moncks Corner, a tiny distribution center for plantation harvests. Philip planned on reaching the South Santee Road and entering King's Highway about forty miles north of Charleston. He did this to avoid militia patrols likely in angry moods. If they couldn't find a rebel, any Negro might do.

Time was our enemy. Normally, the trip from Charleston to Georgetown took sixty-miles with one overnight at a tavern. Philip's plan required twice that distance and over rougher roads than the King's Highway. We needed almost a week to get to Georgetown. Would the *Fame* and the *Mary* even be there?

We travelled through Moncks Corner and Jamestown, both early French Huguenot settlements. Concern for time must have weighed on Philip because he passed up all four village taverns at

Moncks Corner. At Jamestown, we entered the South Santee Road, and passed some of the great plantations of Carolina Lowcountry. At night, the masters of these estates hosted Philip, while I either slept in slave quarters or in our carriage. I preferred our barouche, as its hood hid me from public view. Mosquitoes interrupted my sleep, but nothing discouraged my cheerfulness that I would soon be free.

On the South Santee Road, I marveled at the beautiful big houses facing the river, even their rears bore a horticulturalist's dream. An occasional deer leapt, or a snake slithered across our roadway. Over the mud-rutted road we flew; and when there were no animals to amuse us, Nature continued her ensemble: strands of Spanish moss gently waving in the breeze, blades of dew-laden grass, smilax and holly in tangled arbors, wild grapes drooping from a tapestry of vines, the morning star twinkling through the crown of an immense yellow pine, and a bog's seemingly harmless attraction so fatal to those answering its sirens' call.

Nature's finale was a young slave woman bathing in the South Santee, framed by two live oaks. In morning's early glow, I saw the silhouette of her supple body and firm breasts. I felt so alive, soaring on the wings of freedom. Past El Dorado Plantation, past Hampton Plantation, we rode until we reached King's Highway, just south of the South Santee. Now our danger became intense. We spent the night at Haliwell's Tavern, just north of the river. I bedded down in our carriage, while Philip lodged in the tavern. He soon returned with my meal, looking worried. A slave patrol heading to Charleston was inside the tavern. He emphasized that I remain out-of-sight, or risk discovery.

That next morning I stood up and stretched before resuming my hiding place. Unfortunately, the slave patrol mounted their horses at the same time! I ducked down, but not soon enough to hide my face. Philip came out laughing, and wondered if they saw his cowardly driver? Didn't they know that niggers turned pale at the sight of white men carrying guns? They all returned Philip's laughter but one, the one who saw me.

When I wheeled our carriage out of Haliwell's, I noticed the patrol heading south toward Charleston, when one of the riders turned back toward Georgetown. I kept my head down, as he galloped by. I told myself that the rider must be from Georgetown, and had nothing to do with my detection. All the possibilities which I invented were wrong.

Just past Six-Mile Tavern, a man on horseback blocked the highway. It was the patrolman from Haliwell's Tavern! He commenced shouting at me, as he rode toward our carriage. Didn't I recognize him, he said? I froze and just sat there. He drew near, demanding that I take a good look at him. He was the guard I often saw with Enus Reeves, Workhouse warden, when I passed their shop of horrors in Charleston. Reeves frequently taunted me by offering me "a little sugar," meaning the taste of his whip. I always parried his sarcasm by saying "Naw suh, I be sweet 'nuff," which always brought their laughter. But now, what could I do? The Workhouse guard made me step down, and placed me under arrest for questioning about my association with Denmark. I knew what "questioning" meant.

Quickly Philip intervened on my behalf. We climbed into our carriage, and continued to Georgetown.

"Intervened?" Wahl snapped. "What in hell does that mean?"

Philip smiled and said "if you can't stand up for the ones you love, you can't stand."

Wahl looked up with an evil look of approval, while Philip continued reading Saturday's letter:

We didn't cross the Sampit River, the threshold to Georgetown, until August 4. Were we too late? I strained to see either the *Fame* or the *Mary* riding their anchors off the Front Street docks. No *Fame*, but there was the *Mary*, ready to receive us as passengers. After Philip boarded his horses and carriage at a livery stable, we greeted *Mary's* captain, and climbed the ship's gangway. My voyage to freedom and to Wahl was about to begin! With the turning tide, the *Mary* entered Winyah Bay the next morning. The smell of salt air, white foam riding our vessel's wake, drifting clouds dotting a blue sky, fish breaking, birds flying, and a sun's gentle rays, all announced that I was leaving slavery behind. As the Carolina coast faded from sight, I thought if only my memories of slavery could fade so easily.

Once the *Mary* reached open sea, I relaxed. With the feeling of infinity which an ocean gives, I reflected on my life and those of my boys. Like most parents, even surrogate ones, I questioned the choices my children made. The part slavery played in their lives concerned me most. John ran off to sea, and became a slave trader and plantation master. By 1810, however, he began delivering coffee cargos from his Cuban plantation to Charleston rather than slaves. Still my disappointment of him lingers even now. Philip made some of John's same mistakes. He bought slaves to provide Tivoli Gardens with cheap labor. By the time that Philip realized his error, South Carolina made it impossible for a master with a change-of-heart to free his slaves.

In personal relationships, however, my boys had successes. John's closest friend was Antoine Barbot who migrated to Charleston from Nantes, France. When Antoine arrived in Charleston, he opened an office as a commercial agent, or factor. In 1815, he married Marie, the sixteen-year-old daughter of Jean Esnard; a child followed quickly, the first of fourteen. I liked Antoine, a dapper fellow and loyal to John. But I saw a problem, because they fed off the other's greed, with slavery at its core.

John's personal life took a fortunate turn when he married Louise Dubois. After losing his first wife in New York, Charles Dubois and daughter Louise moved to Charleston where he remarried, and became a successful merchant-planter. Though some onlookers privately chuckled at Charles' homely appearance, earning him the nickname "Monkey Face," no one could take their eyes off Louise's radiant beauty, or not appreciate her artistic talents. Her voice was soothing, and her soul was kind. She reminded me of Catherine, my boys' mother. When they married in April 1820, I knew that she would soften some of John's harder attitudes. I'm talking about Louise extracting a promise from John to leave the African slave trade before she would marry him. She told him that she refused to become a mariner's widow; but her demand came from the generosity of her soul, not from the selfishness of her heart.

Philip lacked John's social skills, but was intensely loyal to his friends. Undoubtedly, his closest was William Penn Bason. They found common ground in their love for horticulture, as their friendship grew. More important, Bason made Philip consider the immorality of slavery.

While I thought about my boys, I looked at the *Mary's* prow, and saw standing a lonely man staring at the ocean's endless horizon. It was Philip. I looked at him with deep affection. Despite his blemishes, he had protected me with his life. I also felt sad because I would not see him much after I settled in Cuba. An occasional letter and visit would be all that remained of our relationship. I walked over and embraced him. I was proud of Philip then and now. He was, after all, my son.

Two days out of Matanzas, a worried look appeared on our captain's face. For hours, a sail appeared on the distant horizon behind our stern, commenced closing on us, and then fell back, dropping out of sight. Who was it? Was it one of the freebooters infesting the Cuban coast? Raising the captain's fear was the loss of the *Aristide* to pirates the previous November. The *Aristide's* captain had been Sutton's best friend. Then breaking our forward horizon, a ship bore full speed ahead in our direction, pushing cannons through her gun ports as she came. Pirates! We were under attack! We felt like a meal for two sea wolves. That is when our unknown stalker sailed into clear view. She raised her colors, a U.S. Navy sloop-of-war, preparing for combat!

The American ship opened fire. A silent progression of spewing white puffs from our savior's hull, followed by cannon thunder, cast-iron comets of destruction arching over the *Mary* heading for pirate targets, flying splinters from hits, and geysers of sea

261

spray from near misses convinced the pirate captain that his ship faced destruction. With the hunter now the quarry, the pirate vessel turned, and ran for the Cuban coast, seeking a hidden cove for safety. Excitedly, Captain Sutton pointed to the flag fluttering from our enemy's mast. It was a British Union Jack, the trademark of deception used by Diabolito, one of the more feared pirates operating in Cuban waters. Soon the American warship began passing us in full canvas; she was the *Hornet* on assignment to hunt down Caribbean pirates and slave traders. As she glided past us, her captain tipped his hat to Sutton, and he returned the gesture in gratitude. As for myself, I thanked God that some swashbuckler failed to rob my freedom at the point of his sword.

Once the *Mary* made landfall, my thoughts turned to Wahl. What had thirty years done to our once-torrid relationship? Had we built barriers too tall for either one of us to climb, or even want to? I anticipated our meeting with fear and trepidation. For an old man like me, memories become cherished treasures. Should Wahl now love another or, worse still, treat me like a stranger, my dream pillow filled with sweet memories would be lost to me forever. Should I take that chance? I knew that I had to.

Soon we entered Matanzas waters, ending our seven-day voyage out of Georgetown. That was when Captain Sutton walked over to Philip and me, and pointed to where a Spanish treasure fleet had once met its doom nearly 200 years ago. There in 1628, Admiral Juan de Benavides ran his galleons aground desperately attempting to escape Piet Heyn's Dutch ships. The proud Spanish admiral turned cowardly, abandoning his ships to Piet Heyn's sailors, who carried off the king's treasure. A furious Philip IV of Hapsburg Spain made Benavides pay with his head.

Just as Sutton finished his story, we saw a barge with twelve oarsmen dipping the waters in perfect synchronization. Atop their craft, an awning stood in red and yellow Spanish Bourbon colors with pennants gently fluttering. To the barge's starboard, plied a longboat filled with Spanish marines carrying carbines slung on their backs. They escorted the solitary figure standing on the prow of the barge. He wore a white uniform accented with ribbons and brass appointments. Every time the barge ducked into harbor shadows, he disappeared from sight. But when he re-emerged, the sun bore down on him, giving his brass buttons a golden glow. The little man starring in this farce was the customs inspector, subject only to the captain-general, but more powerful than the governor of Matanzas Province himself.

Matanceros (citizens of Matanzas) so esteemed the office of customs inspector that the position enjoyed its own patron saint's day. On St. Joseph's Day, the serving customs inspector would stand beneath the altar at San Carlos Iglesia, while the presiding priest extolled the virtues of this puffed up official. On that day, no cargo moved in Matanzas harbor to avoid committing a sacrilege. The customs inspector was Inspector Ignacio Además, Philip's long-time acquaintance from his travels to Cuba.

When Señor Además boarded the *Mary* with his clerks and soldiers, he found a clean *Mary*, hamper stowed, ropes coiled, carpets laid, sailors in dress whites, and Sutton uniformed in his captain's rank. Even the civilian passengers fell in, forming an imperfect line. Además strutted past this assemblage, stopping at each passenger, demanding his passport, certification of good character, and letter of approval from a Spanish consul. Some he ordered out of formation, because their papers were incomplete, requiring their detention until they gained official clearance. When Además reached us, he saw a valise at our feet that Philip had guarded since Charleston. Además had a clerk peek inside it. The clerk whispered something to Además, who smiled, moved to me, looked at Philip, and said, "*¿Su esclavo, Señor Felipe? No?*" Philip nodded, and Además cleared us for Matanzas after the *Mary* passed health inspection.

As we headed to shore, Philip told me that bribery could replace any missing document a customs inspector demanded. Every time that he landed in Matanzas, he made the same payment to Además:

two bottles of cognac and two of Madeira. So my final barrier to freedom came down to four bottles of alcohol. God certainly has strange ways.

When our lighter docked, Philip and I disembarked with *Mary's* passengers, some Spanish, some Cuban, some tourists, and some foreign residents living in Matanzas. While porters piled our luggage on the dock, a customs sergeant swaggered toward Philip and me like a Prussian drillmaster. He demanded our papers, and on top of them, Philip placed a half-*escudo* (worth about one U.S. silver dollar) for a ninety-day travel visa in Matanzas Province. Underneath, he slipped into the sergeant's hand a second half-escudo; without hesitation the sergeant flipped our papers over, opened his palm, smiled, and said: "*¿Para mí, Señor? Gracias.*" I feared this arrangement until I learned that officialdom in Cuba expected bribes.

A long line of carriage drivers stood by their *volantes* near the customs pier, some to pick up their masters, others to shuttle passengers to public accommodations. A volante is a strange conveyance with only two very large wheels, and a postilion (rider) mounted on one of its horses, serving as a driver. It can carry two people comfortably or three in a crowded condition. I soon realized that the volante symbolized the Cuban upper-class. Women of this station, Spanish or Cuban white, deigned it undignified to walk the streets, a practice they considered fit only for common women, mainly Negresses.

The volante also served their code of conduct in other ways. When riding in her volante, an upper class woman shielded her face from public view with a veil. Protocol further required that a male family member accompany her. Every upper class family owned a volante, and generally housed it in a front room of their townhouse or mansion. Some volantes sported beautiful silver inlays, guided by brilliantly attired postilions; but for many women, the volante was only a gilded cage on wheels.

While riding a volante to John's townhouse, I encountered a

second great symbol of Cuban society: the cigar. Nearly every male passenger departing the customs dock smoked one. Seeing blue puffs of smoke trailing behind a volante, made it seem like it was steam-driven. Even women of all classes enjoyed the ecstasy of a rolled tobacco leaf.

In the streets, I noticed scenes revealing the richness and limitations of city life: head-down Spanish nobles, riding fancy mounts and daydreaming about a Spain of long ago; volantes wheeling privileged women in expensive dresses; free and enslaved Negroes and mulattoes laboring at their daily tasks; Spanish soldiers in white uniforms and straw hats adorned with red cockades, fresh from their continental defeats; *monteros*, the yeomanry of Cuba, seated on horses with straw saddles without stirrups; other monteros leading ox-carts through city byways with a surgeon's dexterity; and finally, came both tourists and immigrants trudging the busy thoroughfares. What Matanzas was, and would become, could be read in that mixed population.

Over the Yumurí River, our volante rolled into the posh Versalles district of Matanzas. Behind grilled windows sat mothers and daughters, like spiritless birds in iron aviaries. Husbands and fathers were their keepers. Loitering on steps and leaning on lampposts were the aimless male offspring of those same fathers. Philip called them *bimbas*, or men about town, enjoying freedoms denied their female family members, and given to gambling and sexual escapades with women of color. They, Philip said, were like overripe oranges, dangling from the stem of their parents. Only in matters of marriage, did their parents rein them in, because white must marry white, and wealth must join wealth.

Not far from the beautiful Paseo de Versalles, we stopped in front of a two-story stone townhouse with an archway bearing the Chartrand coat-of-arms. Philip and I stepped down to the walkway with my heart pounding in my throat. What if Wahl answers the door? How would she react after our thirty-year separation? I felt like a young man on his first romantic adventure, as

Philip knocked on the front door. My excitement soared, as the enormous double doors swung back, and André, major-d´ for the Chartrands, peered out. Philip and I stepped inside. Crossing the Spanish patio, I entered the cook's house, only to be greeted by a plump woman and her pretty daughter. They were Luisa and her babe Frances. So where was Wahl? Luisa told me that she was at the Chartrands' plantation.

Philip sent André dashing to John's Labyrinth Plantation to announce our arrival. Three days later, John walked into his townhouse—older than I remembered, but still vivacious. Though resembling his father, John had more sweetness and a bigger heart. I asked him the whereabouts of Wahl? He became sheepish, but quickly regained his composure. She remained at Labyrinth to attend Louise, their infant John Louis, Désirée, and ailing Uncle Philip. Damn Uncle Philip, I thought, still between Wahl and me after all these years. John shrugged his shoulders, and suggested that we deal with something more important: my freedom! He dodged telling me that Wahl didn't want to come.

John set legal wheels rolling. He engaged an *abogado* (attorney) to transfer Philip's half-ownership of me to him, simplifying the process of setting me free. Then he took me to a *síndico*, an advocate for slaves seeking manumission. The síndico appraised my contract value at twenty *onzas* (three hundred and forty dollars), and added five more onzas (eighty-five dollars) for my skills. Total for one Saturday, or should I say George Lining, was twenty-five onzas (four hundred and twenty-five dollars). My boys wanted to pay my price, but I refused. It was a point of pride with me that I should use my own money to buy my freedom. My boys understood.

Waiting for my freedom papers to pass through the chambers of Spanish justice took patience. Fees had to be paid, and court functionaries bribed, while a judge with his secretary and our síndico sat at a table, one writing long arguments and the other deliberating a decision. No witnesses provided live testimony; only their affidavits reached the court. This was Spanish justice born of Roman law.

266

The delay gave me time with my boys. On Tuesdays and Thursdays, we heard a military band play popular and martial music. But on our first visit, I could not join John and Philip because chairs on the Plaza de Armas were reserved for whites only; instead I joined Negroes and mulattoes standing behind the seated audience. On subsequent evenings, my boys stood with me. At nine at night, the band returned to their quarters, marching to the beat of its drummers.

Sometimes we found amusement walking the streets of Matanzas. Without fail, hawkers accosted us to buy lottery tickets, one of Cuba's great obsessions. This colony-wide venture netted the captain-general and his government huge amounts of revenue. A first winning ticket gained its owner fifty thousand pesos (dollars). We bought chances, never won, never knew anyone who did.

Islander emphasis on strict religious appearance ran deeper than their taste for the lottery. Nearly every street name had a *san* or *santa* (saint) before it. Perhaps Matanceros wanted to impress The Almighty with their addresses. But it did not stop here. Commonly, home interiors had an altar dedicated to Catholic worship, and murals on whitewashed walls, featuring Jesus on The Cross or The Holy Virgin holding The Christ Child. Each day had its patron saint, and there were four major religious celebrations: Epiphany, Carnival, Holy Week, and Corpus Christi. If a dying Matancero needed Last Rites, a procession of priests parading behind the Host required home occupants to join the street crowds in an act of reverence, as the sanctimonious prelates passed. Church and state made these sacred observances obligatory, but substance did not follow appearance.

Sundays belonged to God only for early Mass. After that, shops opened, gambling houses spun the roulette, and card dealers dealt monte, a popular Spanish card game. In the streets, African ethnic groups danced to the joy of being alive, while their drum beats added a sensual air to Matanzas. By noon, crowds gathered for cockfights, Cuba's main gambling sport. Even the governor kept roosters trained for combat. By nightfall, Matanceros turned to dance halls and sponsored balls. Equal to the secularization of Sundays were the festive days and the demoralized priesthood serving them. Some had wives with families.

Immigrants arriving in Cuba had to join the Roman Catholic Church, and pay a tithe tax. Maybe Matanceros became resentful of church and state intrusion into their lives. Maybe this explained a book frequently found in Cuban homes: The Bible. Although on the government's forbidden list (Index), Cubans loved reading the Holy Scriptures and reciting passages from it. Was this Mantancero defiance, or were they searching for something?

On September 18, I celebrated my freedom day! On that day, our síndico personally delivered my approval papers. I was free! Or I thought so at the time. Philip and John were ecstatic. Tears mingled with my sweet and bitter memories. Oh, if those missing from my life had been there. But my boys compensated. Even as I write this letter, I might let my birthday slip, but never my freedom day.

Disappointment followed triumph, as Philip announced his intention to leave for South Carolina. I hugged Philip, and knew that I would miss him terribly, but he never left my heart. As Philip's volante wheeled him away, I rushed to John's balcony to watch him leave. Piano music floated from the *salas* (reception rooms) of Versalles; most were Cuban *contradanza* tunes which rose to join each other in the musical atmosphere above Matanzas. The music served as a recessional for Philip and a processional for John.

Time came for John and me to leave for his plantation. We boarded a skiff on the San Juan River. The day shone bright, the bay calm, as we paralleled the eastern shore of Matanzas Bay. Then I saw those demons of the sea, Baltimore Clippers, disgorging their human cargos. More and more, slavers used those two-mast schooners to outrun British and American warships prowling the ocean to stop "the trade."

When our craft entered the Canímar, I looked at the rocky crags above us, and spied a small fortress atop the south side. It was El Morillo (Little Morro), too ugly for a house and too weak for a fort, though defense was its purpose. Some humorous Spaniard probably named it to mock Havana's big Morro Castle with its many guns trained on the harbor of Cuba's colonial capital. The tropical forest clinging to the high slopes interested me more: fan palms in impressive clusters, regal royal palms, and the *ceiba*, a tree that can reach over 200 feet. When its crown bursts forth with white blossoms in May, even the royal palm must concede that it is queen and the ceiba king.

John had made many journeys up the magical Canímar when he shipped his coffee to Matanzas. But I felt like a child seeing things for the first time. Hanging from limbs were red, white, yellow, and purple orchids; nearer the shore, heavy bamboo patches and mangrove bushes crowded the shallows. Swarms of hummingbirds darted in and out, hovering above Cupid's Tear, a small red flower whose pollen was their addiction. I half-hoped to see a *cuculio*, a Cuban firefly whose eyes, rather than tail, emitted powerful greenish lights. John claimed, probably with some exaggeration, that he had read books from their glow. They must have been short stories. Not seeing an illuminated critter, I contented myself with fiddler crabs. Displaying one big claw for intimidation, while hiding their withered one, they scurried the muddy banks on our approach to predrilled holes to defend their turf, or did they run from the field? Only an occasional coffee barge heading down river interrupted my enchantment.

Despite stifling heat, I regretted our journey's end at El Embarcadero (The Wharf), a shipping point for coffee going to Matanzas. The Wharf had few residents, a main street, three stores, two taverns, two warehouses, a cockpit, no church, and little else. We arrived during slow time, when only a few coffee shipments went out; but at the end of *La Seca* (the dry season) the sugar harvest would pile the docks. Sugar boxes, coffee bags, and barrels of molasses would arrive there by ox-carts, horse trains, and on the backs of groaning slave stevedores. Foremen for this commerce were slave drivers, forever laying a lash across an ebony back. It reminded John of a medieval fair; I thought it more like the Devil's Bazaar.

John hailed a volante to take us to a boarding house nearly a mile from town. The proprietress was Madame LaPorte, a widowed refugee from Saint-Domingue, who provided lodging for John when he stopped at The Wharf. She greeted me like an old friend, and hugged John. She knew much about me, and how I had saved my boys from a slave rebellion. After friendly exchanges, John left, saying that he had unattended business at The Wharf and would return late.

I retired early that evening. The thrill of freedom still rang in my mind, but the yearning for love filled my heart. All the uncertainty that I felt about Wahl on board the *Mary* drifted into my mind again. I remembered our romance and our last sweet moments together in Le Cap. We had been madly in love then, but what about now? A door slammed. My drifting thoughts found anchor. John had returned to Madame LaPorte's. Cards and too many drinks with friends probably slowed his return.

John and I left for Labyrinth around noon the next day. Pretty *cafetals* (coffee plantations) and monotonous sugar cane fields provided most of our scenery. Here and there, tiny montero farms with thatched-roofed huts provided roosts for chickens and doves. At one montero dwelling, a father directed his family's efforts to drag a huge chicken snake (a *maja*) from the palm fronds serving as their roof. The wily reptile had been picking off their fowl, including a favorite hen. Turning the air purple with a profanity that only Cubans can fully appreciate, the angry monteros missed every chance to capture the maja. John and I watched this rustic farce, laughed, and continued our journey to the din of their continuing battle.

When we reached Labyrinth's gates, night had fallen. Only the keeper's lantern, light from big house windows, and a bright moon illuminated our way. Our entry seemed like the portal to heaven: no slaves moaning under a driver's whip and no sad songs. Inside, tall royal palms lining the big house avenue swayed in a gentle breeze, like giant dancers rooted to the ground by an evil sorcerer.

We had arrived late, so early the following morning I raced into the cook's house, not even waiting to surprise Wahl at breakfast. Cecilia, her pretty daughter in her mid-twenties, faced the door as I entered the kitchen, while Wahl had her back to me. "Well, look here!" Or similar stupid words fell from my lips. Wahl turned around, older but still beautiful. I felt passion's gush! My heart raced. I reached to embrace her. She stepped back, surveyed me with a cold expression, and said that it was nice to see me again. Her icy stare told it all. She didn't love me anymore. I was devastated.

That night the Chartrands dined with their friends to celebrate my arrival and freedom. There were the Macombs and Esnards formerly from Charleston now Cuban plantation owners, the Barbots from Charleston, the Mildensteins from Denmark residing in Cuba, and the d'Estaings and Bourgeoises formerly from France who owned cafetals next to the Chartrands. Monsieur d'Estaing served Napoleon before escaping to Cuba, while Monsieur Bourgeoise had served Dessalines in Haiti before fleeing to the Spanish colony. Lovely people! Commonly these close-knit families intermarried, or made "alliances," as such arrangements were known in Charleston.

At the head of the table, John sat at his gregarious best. On his left, his wife Louise radiated her beauty. No one noticed her beginning pregnancy had John not commented that in eight months she would "present him a stranger," his way of describing childbirth. And on John's right, I sat as guest of honor, because on this special night the Chartrands waived the rules of whiteness. But there was a cruel irony: The next day, I returned to the uncertainties of a free Negro.

Soon after arriving at Labyrinth, I surveyed my new surroundings. Like most cafetals, the Chartrand estate had the beauty of a garden. Four avenues approached the big house from opposite directions. Two were lined with orange trees, one with mangos, and the main with royal palms. The big house was less than elegant but comfortable, as most of John's money went to land, slaves, processing equipment, and coffee trees. The one-storied house had a thatched roof and a wrap-around piazza covered with a black tiled roof. Inside was a *sala* (a large main room) for receptions, recitals, dinners, and dances. Around the sala were eight bedrooms, each opening to the piazza. Behind the big house was the *batey*, a sort of square given over to drying tables heaped with coffee cherries, a mill for extracting their beans, a storehouse, a slave kitchen, and a row of well-kept slave huts.

Pleasing to my eye were groves of coffee trees, covered with red, reddish purple, and green cherries, and shaded by fruit trees. Old Uncle Philip also liked that sight, as he often sat on the piazza, admiring what was once his, but now John's. He loved growing coffee, pioneered its introduction into Matanzas Province, and invented a mechanical separator to speed coffee production. As long as Uncle Philip lived, John could not convert Labyrinth into a sugar plantation, else he might lose a hefty inheritance.

Slaves laboring in those pastures of Eden found no paradise. Labor could be grueling. During twice-a-year harvests, slaves commonly worked fifteen hours per day, and frequently the driver snapped his whip on a slave committing a minor offense. I saw Cora spill her basket of cherries three times for which the driver gave her three lashes. This said, life at Labyrinth as a cafetal surpassed that of a sugar plantation. Picking coffee cherries, dropping them into baskets, and sorting them at drying tables benefitted from the female touch. Heavy lifting still required male muscle, resulting in a near balance of male and female slaves. Sexual frustration was less at Labyrinth than on a sugar plantation where labor was harder, females fewer, hours longer, and harvests more frenzied. Finally, my new environment included Limonar, an unimpressive free Negro village, a veritable island of freedom in a sea of slavery, and only a quarter mile from Labyrinth. More and more, I wanted to live there.

I fell into a comfortable routine at Labyrinth. John directed construction of a small two-room cottage for me, where I lived when the Chartrands and their guests occupied the big house. When they left for an extended trip, I moved in to manage household slaves. For this service, John provided me a salary. Sometimes he made me acting manager (*administrador*) in his absence, annoying Patrick O'Leary, the overseer whom I often "crossed swords" over his cruel slave discipline. John further provided me with a small monetary stipend beyond payment for my specific services. He never forgot money that I gave to Philip and him during our economically strapped days in Charleston; so at the end of every week, he handed me three pesos, a sort of love pension. My relationship with John was ambiguous and not unlike Papa's with Bayon de Libertad on Bréda Plantation years ago.

Not everything at Labyrinth suited me. The Chartrands expected me to greet and entertain their special guests with the story about my rescue of my boys. I hated those "monkey moments." I wore my finest white linen suit, carried a fancy snuffbox, and offered its contents to a guest, while making formal bows as might be due royalty. Maybe John intended to show his friends a "Europeanized" Negro, a sort of civilizing of the savage. I found it disgusting. My courtesies to a guest were the most exaggerated that I could concoct, my way of mocking that which the Chartrands expected of me.

My campaign continued unabated to win Wahl back. At the end of my first November at Labyrinth, the Chartrands threw a large party celebrating their successful coffee harvest. Music blared, the sala floor shook, as I entered the piazza seeking relief from my duties, while Wahl stepped onto the piazza from her kitchen. The orchestra struck up a minuet, as couples inside began their "lead out." Then music typically Cuban, the *contradanzas*, poured from open windows, turning the piazza into a romantic balcony. Wahl and I stood transfixed, as voluptuous rhythms tempted our hungry souls. I approached Wahl, touched her hand, and she responded with a dancer's embrace. We whirled and gyrated, keeping time with those dancing inside. Passion filled our veins, and old feelings rose again. We were old friends, once in love, rediscovering the flame that once had melted our hearts together. When the music stopped, so did we. Wahl returned to that indifference that I had come to expect. She dropped her arms, and walked away.

My piazza moment with Wahl inspired me to win her back. I had what I called "anxiety attacks of wanderlust;" that is, I invented every way I could for crossing paths with Wahl, hoping that our next encounter would return the love-light in her eyes. I got only failures and sore feet. I became embittered and angry that I let her indifference control me. I also wanted to ask her who was Cecilia's father, although I knew I wasn't. I dared not inquire because of Wahl's capacity for fury. Besides, she may not know; probably never asked before devouring him after sex. My heart still wouldn't let her go, but my mind demanded that I get on with my life.

My finding a good friend after a romantic shipwreck was like reaching a lifeboat in a tormented sea. That person was Pedro, a slave born on Labyrinth and ten years my younger. A big man with an infectious smile, Pedro had worked his way into John's heart, and held responsible positions on the estate. With hesitation, he became a driver, but his refusal to use his whip forced John to appoint another in his stead. It was Pedro who introduced me to a vibrant African culture rising in Cuba.

From the time that I arrived in Cuba in 1822, Yorubas flooded Cuban slave markets. Their once great Oyo Empire had collapsed due to civil war, Dahoman invasion, and Muslemized Fulanis conducting a jihad. Yorubas became completely dislocated, as western slavers, like birds of prey, carried them across the Atlantic, while eluding the navies of England and the United States. Even more disheartening, Olokún, the Yoruba ocean spirit, failed to block the agonies Yorubas faced in the crossing. Thousands sold at slave marts in Matanzas and in Havana were of a large ethnic nation within the Yorubas, the Lucumís. Some came from villages near where Dahoman slave traders once stole Mother and me. Ironically, I came to Cuba to discard my chains; the Yorubas arrived to wear theirs.

Over two decades, Yorubas rebuilt their shattered society in Cuba. One tool on their cultural anvil was the Roman Catholic Church. Spanish law directed that slaves entering Cuba receive Catholic instruction and baptism. By using religion this way, Cuban colonial government believed that slaves might comply with, and even enjoy, their incarceration like a new wife. It was a marriage designed to oppress the Yorubas spiritually. Instead it was the Yorubas who stole the bride.

Whether masters forced slave attendance at San Carlos Iglesia in Matanzas, or at a small parish church, results were the same. Like slaves in Saint-Domingue, Yorubas appropriated parts of Roman Catholicism to reinforce their beliefs in Olodumare (Almighty God) and the orisha spirits serving Him and humanity. Each orisha they identified with a different saint, hence the term *santería* (Way of the Saints). Believers are called *santeros*.

Santeros see a universal family with Olodumare on His throne, surrounded by His orisha servants, and the living sharing life force with them called *ashe*. When an orisha directs a believer, it is called the "Breath of God." Ancestral worship is equally important. Ancestors inhabiting earth's hidden vale are called "Children of Heaven." Santería further emphasizes divination, magic, animal sacrifice, and that destiny determines human outcome. Santería can also be warlike. Changó is the patron of fire, thunder, and lightning, and is santería's main warrior. Others include the Four Warriors, each with a different combat role, and Ogún who in peace is a blacksmith, but in war a menacing opponent.

Among the orishas with whom I am familiar are Yemayá, associated with the Virgin Mary, the sea, and childbearing; Oshún, the Yoruba Venus, associated with rivers, love-making, and marriage; and Elegguá, the divine messenger and guardian of the gateway to the orishas. Worshippers must pay him his toll before reaching an orisha. Orchestrating orisha liturgy is a high priest, or *babalawo*.

Pedro and I sneaked to santería ceremonies on Sundays when slaves had free time. We risked arrest, since colonial authorities sought their suppression. I never became a santero, but an *aleyo*, a non-believer who respected the cult. My deep Roman Catholic faith held me back. Otherwise, how could I conduct Vespers or Angelus at Labyrinth in good conscience? But santería touched me in a way that Catholicism couldn't. I went to be with my deceased loved ones, those "Children of Heaven."

Santería seeks balance in life. That is why I went to a santería diviner of the highest order, a babalawo, to restore Wahl's love for me. Underneath her toughness, love for me might still burn. I'd have settled for an ember. By shuffling his sixteen cowerie shells (a sacred number) from his left to his right hand, the babalawo arrived at the number five, Oshún's number, Orisha of Beauty and Love. The babalawo referred me to Akanni, a *babalocha* making this particular orisha his specialty. He kept a little shrine near the Río San Juan on the New Town side of Matanzas.

Inside the old man's sanctuary, I knelt and placed a small coin before me for Elegguá. Without his support, Oshún would not have received my pleadings. Akanni collected my offering, a sort of trust arrangement with Elegguá. Then he reached inside a yellow-lidded sopera (jar) containing relics relative to Oshún. Yellow was her color, and small stones inside the sopera held some of her life force. According to santería belief, orishas once lived on earth, but were reduced to a few tiny pebbles cast among the many. Finding these *fundamento*s took a priest who could hear their low voices.

Akanni consulted his divine pebbles, and discerned that Oshún wanted me to perform four specific tasks. After completing my last task, Oshún directed me to buy a tortoise comb *(peineta)* and poem from "Plácido," a famous poet and painter of these small art objects. The peineta was beautiful, even if Plácido's flowery love sonnet went a little far. Symbolizing me as a bee and Wahl as a flower suited my tastes, but my pumping honey down her throat seemed excessive.

After carefully wrapping the peineta and Plácido's poem, I entered Wahl's kitchen at Labyrinth, and handed her my gift. Maybe I should have picked a more romantic moment, but how could Oshún fail me? Wahl took my package, removed its wrappings, saw the comb, read the love sonnet, and rejected my offering. Her face bore no expression, hurting me more. Even hatred beats no emotion at all. If Oshún couldn't win, how could I? My heart finally let go.

When not with Pedro, or at a santería ceremony, I found comfort in the fraternal *cabildo* of the Lucumí nation. This cabildo and others of African nations in Cuba gained the Catholic Church's sanction in the eighteenth century; this way, thought the bishop of Cuba, newly imported slaves (*bozales*) could be taught the True Faith. But cabildos became so much more.

From their Catholic beginnings, cabildos matured into African organizations. Yoruba traditions in danger of extinction found expression in social meetings, dances, and secret santería ceremonies. The Catholic Church, once the shepherd of cabildo members, now became the instrument of its flock. The Church served as treasurer of cabildo funds, money often used to buy a member's freedom. Cabildos even latched upon the liturgical calendar to celebrate their patron saints. Cabildo African Lucumí honored Santa Bárbara, our patron saint, on December 4. On that day, we crowded the streets of Matanzas in our saint's red and white colors, singing and sashaying behind her image. Each month, other cabildos heralded their patron saints as well.

Epiphany (January 6), or Día de Reyes, marked the most important annual event for all cabildos. Tradition in Matanzas has it that on that day Melchior, an African magus, arrived at Baby Jesus's cradle to adore him. At daybreak on the sixth, cabildo drummers in and around Matanzas began beating calls for their members to assemble at the Plaza de Armas. A captain led each cabildo, followed by those decked in full feathers and mirrors, others covered with bells, while the remainder wore red and blue turbans with short jackets and trousers; all were dancing and singing. Whites and mulattoes stayed in their homes. This was our day!

Pedro and I usually spent December and half of January at the Chartrand mansion in Matanzas, while John and family returned to Labyrinth for Christmas season. This way, we enjoyed all of our cabildo's celebrations. During this time, a new female entered my life. She was Luisa, the Chartrand cook, whom I called "Luisita." We both suffered broken hearts. André, doorman and major d,' had deserted his wife and daughter Frances. Luisita didn't begrudge his flight, only that he had left them behind. We shared our stories and our tears. Our developing relationship grew in poisoned soil, because we wished the other was someone else. I confused sex with love. Our liaison began in 1825, and Luisita bore our son and daughter, Victoriano and Ana.

The year 1825 also had dramatic consequences for Partido de Guamacaro, the provincial district where Labyrinth and Limonar were located. Fresh from Africa, the Carabalís raised a rebellion in mid-June, leaving a trail of wrecked sugar plantations, ruined cafetals, and dead whites. John and other planters acted quickly, assembling at Labyrinth mounted monteros and *rancheador* scouts (slave hunters) with their fierce dogs. From the gates of Labyrinth, they sallied forth to join other monteros and Spanish regulars fighting rebels in Guamacaro Valley. I sent God a mixed message, asking Him for John's safety and for the deliverance of my Carabalí brothers. The Carabalís fought hard, but fell to superior numbers and weaponry.

Alarmed by the Carabalí rebellion, Captain-General Vives declared martial law and deepened his tyranny on Cuba through his minions, the provincial governors. Governor Ayllón of Matanzas Province ordered planters to build barracoons to maintain the security of their slaves. Inside, tiny apartments fronted a small square which contained a slave kitchen. By day, drivers let slaves out to tend plantation coffee groves or cane fields; by nightfall, the same drivers forced their return to the barracoons. Vives' security policy had only limited success, as planters resisted compliance, and as serious local violence continued popping up across Matanzas Province.

Recent events troubled John. He resented the governor ordering him to replace his slave huts with a barracoon. Further, he opposed using the foreign slave trade to replenish a dwindling slave population caused by low birthrate and overwork. The specter of another massive slave rebellion like Haiti's wore on John and other planters.

But John looked for new ways to sustain slavery. He and other planters adopted the Virginia system where male-female balance and better physical treatment of slaves led to their population increase, making the foreign slave trade unnecessary. Acting on his instincts, John gave his slaves better food, more free time, and limited severe discipline. Clearly, John was not unduly cruel beyond his breed.

Captain-General Vives extended his new order to include free Negroes whom he believed fomented slave rebellions, and should be kept off the island. White creoles found common ground with the captain-general on this point, because they feared slave rebellions and "Africanization" of Cuban culture. "Orangutan" in reference to slaves and free Negroes often fell from the jaundiced lips of both liberal and conservative white creoles.

But white creoles themselves fell victim to Vives' martial law. Their success against the Carabalís deepened Vives' concern that white creoles might lead Cuba to independence. Determined to hold on to what remained of the Spanish empire, Vives clamped down on them by restricting their rights to travel, bear arms, or hold colonial office. To this list, Vives added his determination to accelerate the slave trade to convince white creoles that they needed the Spanish army to maintain order. Thus, the creole dream of independence would fade.

By 1829, life at Labyrinth and my personal life took dramatic turns. After a four-year absence, André returned to the Chartrand mansion in Matanzas. He claimed that he had been "running" with José Dolores's famous maroon band, operating in the recesses of the Río Escondido in Matanzas Province. But he longed for his family, and returned to be with them. I didn't buy it. André looked too soft to have been splashing through the mud and water of the Escondido, and outrunning the vicious dogs of the rancheadores. I knew André was a scoundrel, and likely had run off to Havana, posed as a free Negro, and propagated a new family. When his nameless lover probably tried his patience, he retreated to Luisita. Probably, too, he found that a free Negro in Cuba didn't fare well. My suspicions didn't matter, as Luisita yearned to take André back. John welcomed his missing servant, but felt the need to punish André for desertion: André could either take twenty-five lashes or face deportation to Labyrinth to "rusticate for a season." André chose the lashes; Luisita chose him; and I had another failed relationship.

In 1829, John finally realized his dream of turning Labyrinth into a sugar plantation, but it was everyone else's nightmare. Uncle Philip died the previous year, and with a hefty inheritance and heavy borrowing, John set his course. He transformed his once-beautiful coffee estate into endless cane fields, while creating a need for more slaves. Even the fruit trees, except those shading Labyrinth's avenues, fell to the axe. Louise wept from her piazza, watching the destruction of her garden paradise. She never quite forgave John for this, and spent less and less time with him at Labyrinth.

The crowning of John's new sugar plantation came with a Catholic-sponsored ceremony, "The Blessing of the Mill." John's new steam engine centered the event. Father Rangel from nearby San Cipriano Iglesia arrived flanked by two acolytes, each bearing sugar cane bundled by a ribbon. Rangel blessed the engine with a benediction, and sprinkled it with holy water, while a third acolyte swung an incense censer. Two young ladies cut the ribbons binding the bundles of cane, and placed them on a conveyor to initiate processing of sugar cane. Afterward, John hosted a fine meal similar to a baptismal celebration.

Like Louise, I was fed up. My body had been free for seven years. Now I needed to free my mind. Not realizing it, I had let plantation life govern my behavior. Labyrinth's transformation into a sugar estate jolted me. I told John that I was moving to Limonar to have free Negroes as my neighbors. I'd continue working for him, frequently visit him and Louise, and greet guests at Labyrinth. But I needed to pull my feet out of the quagmire of slavery and stand on free soil.

John responded angrily, but quickly regained his composure. For him, I was Saturday, his father, not his slave. He even offered to build a cottage for me in Limonar. I thanked him, but declined. I didn't want to live above my new neighbors. But I did ask John for a plantation carpenter to construct a wooden floor for my hut. I was too old to rest my bones on the ground. John sent his best carpenter. Together, we built my wooden floor.

In my next letter, I'll describe my life in Limonar, and the terror that nearly destroyed it.

Love to My Boys,

Saturday

Philip looked up and saw Wahl with her head down. "Why were you so tough on Saturday, Wahl?" Susan Elizabeth asked. "The poor man only wanted your affection."

Wahl growled that "some things are best left alone. Ain't none of your business."

Susan Elizabeth fell silent, fearing that Wahl was about to unleash her fury on her.

Philip rescued Susan Elizabeth, saying "I never knew how much I would miss Saturday until that day when I left him to head back to South Carolina. I didn't see him much after that. His absence left a hole in my life. I never knew my birth father. I didn't want to because he treated my mother badly, and ignored John and me. Saturday was my real father."

Philip's expression of his love for Saturday moved Wahl. She wanted to tell Philip something, but she couldn't shape it into words. All she could say was "when are you and Susan Elizabeth going to return?"

"After I inspect washouts along the railroad right-of-way," he responded. "The Edisto River Bridge may be unsafe until work crews shore it up."

Philip gave Wahl an affectionate nod, took Susan Elizabeth by her hand, and they left the kitchen.

The Eleventh Letter

T wo weeks later, a tired Philip re-entered Wahl's kitchen with Susan Elizabeth. He had just arrived in the engineer's cab on the 5:40 freight bound for Columbia, as no passenger trains yet tested the Edisto River Bridge. In his hand, Philip held Saturday's last letter. His boots and trousers were still mud-splattered from inspecting bridge pilings.

Wahl smiled, and said: "Aren't you a mess! You look like a slave climbing out of a rice paddy, 'cept you're white."

"Might have been easier, "Philip bantered. "I've been knee-deep in the Edisto, avoiding cottonmouths, and falling out of rowboats. Every damn foot of that four hundred-foot bridge, I inspected with a section boss. We even directed replacement of the iron rails with stress fractures caused by a sagging bridge. I'm tired, but I'm here."

"Can't wait to hear Saturday's last letter," Susan Elizabeth added.

"Nor can I," said Wahl, as she sat down by the kitchen table.

With an attentive audience and his own anticipation, Philip drew Saturday's final letter from his coat pocket, and began reading.

Labyrinth Plantation
Limonar
September 15, 1844

Dear Philip and John,
There were two unlikely neighbors in Guamacaro District (*partido*): John's beloved Labyrinth and my beloved Limonar. Slave and

283

free could not be seen in any greater contrast. Slaves dominated the district's population with smaller numbers of whites and even fewer free Negroes. I dedicated myself to this last group.

Limonar was a beacon of hope for those freed from the chains of slavery, and backed up close to the flaming furnaces of John's sugar mill. Those gaining freedom through contract or through a master's outright release, usually because of age, injury, or disease, settled in Limonar. Her light shone well beyond Guamacaro Province. Álvaro saw it in faraway Cárdenas, and traveled to its source. Though born free, he believed tiny Limonar a better place to avoid the captain-general's watchful eye. A small man with an engaging manner, Álvaro established a reputation for hard work and honesty. He quickly became a favorite among villagers and my close friend.

Architecturally, Limonar had little redemptive value. The centerpiece was the church, San Cipriano Iglesia. Box-like with three bells on a wooden platform passing for a belfry, this weathered stucco building reflected the neglect of Catholic values in Cuba. Next to it stood Father Rangel's rectory, the best home in Limonar; then came two side-by-side taverns, each with a bakery, as well as grog for thirsty customers. Past the taverns came the headquarters and residence of the *capitán del partido*, Guamacaro's policeman. Stocks in his front yard advertised his authority. After the captain's house was a small apothecary shop, followed by dome-shaped huts in African style, mine among them. Palm logs for a foundation, palm fronds for a thatched roof, and woven sticks plastered with mud for walls were all that a rustic engineer needed to construct a hut.

The people of Limonar (*Limonceros*), however, made up for its drab appearance. León and Luis, the two tavern keepers, kept us entertained. Both were Catalonians whom other Spaniards accused of being secret Jews. They competed against each other at every level, whether selling *aquardiente* (cheap rum), dealing merchandise, or promoting duels between their fighting roosters. Luis had a

284

slight edge over León because, though a law school dropout, he offered his customers free legal advice. Next came Agustín, the druggist. Thin as a scarecrow, Agustín was honest, but too quick to prescribe drugs in a doctor's absence. García was the town scoundrel who the priest at San Ciprano and the district captain fired for mishandling their funds. García, like Luis, fashioned himself a student of Spanish law; on a sultry afternoon, they often stood on the porch of Luis' tavern in heated litigious argument before an amused audience.

Captain Juan de Flores was the town tyrant, but his few good qualities saved our village. He served as district policeman, a military position reserved only for Spaniards. He had a repulsive appearance: uniform poorly worn, narrow shoulders, protruding belly, eyes squinting through a fat-swollen face, and a head and body seemingly connected without a neck. More disgusting was his social behavior. He suffered shortness of breath, causing him to suck air during a conversation. He made crude flirtations, and believed that every woman whom he ever met loved him. Planters in Guamacaro District invited Flores to their tables to avoid offending this minion of colonial government. His poor manners ruffled his hosts, especially when he passed gas while stuffing himself with the menu. They chose to ignore the captain's contemptuous conduct, but behind his back, planters referred to Flores as *Capitán Ano Gordo* (Captain Fat-Ass).

Plantation owners feared this little round man's insatiable appetite for bribes. A planter resisting payoffs faced the captain's relentless "grinding," a local term for extortion. Infractions were endless: a fine for traveling from one plantation to another without a pass, a fine for carrying a restricted firearm, failure to possess a passport for travel in Guamacaro District, and on and on. Only greasing Flores' palms with gold and silver coins could stop it. John paid the captain a ten-onza annual bribe (about 170 dollars) for protection against petty colonial laws.

For the rest of us in Limonar, Captain Fat-Ass generally left us alone. Why settle for pin feathers when you can have the whole chicken? Maybe, too, the captain felt sorry for those eking out a living. But the potential for trouble was there, explaining why Wahl built good-will with Flores by bringing him pies. I questioned her purpose, but she replied that only fattened pigs give good bacon. As it turned out, Wahl's parade of pies to the captain's door paid off.

This brings me to Limonar's central figure: Father Rudesindo Rangel, parish priest serving San Cipriano Iglesia. Tall, lean, with dark piercing Spanish eyes, Father Rangel made a severe first impression. But he warmed up in conversation, and made a fine table guest at big houses. He did not fit, however, the template of a good priest. He had a large family, owned a small coffee estate with slaves, held Mass haphazardly, and even forgot parts of the Catholic liturgy. He further enjoyed the culinary arts, fine wine, the company of pretty women, and exquisite furniture.

His shortcomings aside, Father Rangel had a big heart. He understood those recently disgorged from the belly of slavery, but blinded by freedom's bright lights. Some limited themselves to fishing the nearest pond and basking in the Cuban sunshine. Rangel, however, demanded more from Limonceros than those things. He encouraged them to learn a trade, hire themselves out, and attend San Cipriano's free school. Rangel and I taught there, and I can tell you that witnessing a child gain literacy was joyous, seeing an adult almost spiritual. Rangel embraced his Negro parishioners, and they loved him for it.

Nothing expressed Rangel's humanity better than the redemption of Pedro. I was at John's sugar mill when Pedro caught his right hand in cane crushers. As Pedro's forearm mashed through the rotating cylinders, a young slave bounded up the ladder, and with one stroke from his machete, took off my friend's arm at his elbow. Pedro's screams echoed through the boiling house, followed by a tomb-like silence. Only hissing steam, gurgling bubbles, and rushing feet hurrying to Pedro could be heard. The hell of the sugar mill had claimed another victim.

Slaves took Pedro to Labyrinth's hospital where Doctor Bonhomme cauterized Pedro's bloody stump to stop profuse bleeding. He declared Pedro's case hopeless. Make him comfortable, and keep him drunk, he advised. But I wouldn't leave my dear friend's bedside. I watched him pouring sweat, while writhing like a snake. By day, the doctor routinely reappeared, repeating his original prognosis; by night, Wahl arrived with medicinal herbs to treat Pedro. Our patient rallied. His fever broke; his infections diminished; his eyes cleared. Pedro was well. Doctor Bonhomme took credit, but it was Wahl who saved the game.

But Pedro's troubles just started. Without a right arm, he became useless to John and to himself. John liked Pedro and made him a gateman. Pedro's spirits sank. For him, Fate mocked him each time that he opened Labyrinth's gates. John offered Pedro his freedom, but Pedro declined, saying he would buy it himself. A síndico set his contract at 200 pesos, money Pedro didn't have, until Father Rangel stepped in. He loaned Pedro his freedom money, and brought him to Limonar.

Pedro remained depressed, couldn't scratch out a living, or pay off his loan. Rangel gave Pedro time to "settle in," and then urged him to "perk-up." Act like a free man, Rangel demanded. Then Rangel offered and Pedro accepted the job of sexton at San Cipriano. That nourished Pedro's soul. He regained his self-respect, could outwork most men with two arms, and paid Rangel every *real* (12.5 cents each) owed on his loan.

After this turn-around, Pedro met Rosita, the woman of his dreams. Her master had released her from Santa Catalina Plantation where she broke her left arm; in recovery, her arm withered, keeping Rosita from her duties. Pedro with one good left arm and Rosita with one good right arm made a sweet couple. With money borrowed from Father Rangel, they settled on a three-acre plot; as before, the priest received full payment on his loan. Father Rangel further performed the couple's church wedding flawlessly.

Truly, Father Rangel was Limonar's guardian angel. In a word, he was one hell of a man. At the Golden Gate, Saint Peter may take away his clerical collar; but he'll get a set of wings in exchange. In a land where the appearance of Catholic religion flooded everyday life, Father Rangel was one of the few who demonstrated its substance.

My life became routine after moving to Limonar: morning teaching at the free school, afternoons tending my garden or at Labyrinth's stables, and paid evenings serving the Chartrands or their plantation neighbors. Except trips to see my children or to celebrate Epiphany, I rarely travelled to the city of Matanzas. More often, my children visited Limonar when Luisita cooked at Labyrinth. They loved "camping out" at my hut. I dearly loved all my children, but Frances and I were especially close. I gave her the attention denied by her father. Victoriano and Ana, my natural children, were considerably younger than Frances and still shedding baby fat. All three children the Chartrands spoiled with candies, clothing, and toys.

Life at Limonar wasn't perfect. Every city, every town, every village had its cockpit. Limonar shared this cruel mania, locating a cockpit at an amphitheater between the two taverns. Nearby stood an aviary to train fighting roosters, which my friend Álvaro tended for a fee from bird owners.

I could hardly ignore this local obsession, when I passed Álvaro's aviary. By the gate, Álvaro would position himself, gamecock in hand, cropping his trainee's plumage, with feathers piled to his knees from earlier clients. Behind Álvaro, every rooster had his place. In the coop, a gamecock was secured to his roost; if in the yard, he was fastened to a post with a strap limiting his mobility. This avoided unpaid combat between two roosters fighting over a kernel of corn.

Álvaro nagged me to attend a cockfight, but it was curiosity that seduced me. On Sunday afternoons, those feathered gladiators fought and died to amuse their human audiences. When I entered the amphitheater housing the cockpit, a gatekeeper collected my fare, and by him was a table piled with swords and machetes. Señor Salvedo, the cockpit's manager, sought a peaceful sanctuary where only roosters died.

Those attending represented a social democracy rarely seen in Cuba: monteros, free Negroes, overseers, drivers, white masters and even a few slaves were thrown together in a spirit of comradeship; all had come to place their bets. A raised finger, a nod, or a blink of an eye was enough to put money down on a gamecock: Money flowed, cigar smoke rose, tempers seldom flared, and defeated bettors never squelched. All had a wonderful time. Only the roosters lost: eyes pecked out, mutilated bodies, torn feathers, deafening crowing by the winners, death to the losers. I vowed never to witness another cockfight. To his credit, John warned me about these cruel events which he never attended. His concern for gamecocks struck me as a bit ironic.

Limonar's main attraction for neighboring plantations was as a dumping ground for unwanted slaves. But a few rays of compassion shone through. John hired laborers from Limonar, but Louise went further. She visited our village regularly, spent time with Pedro and me, and offered the sick use of Labyrinth's hospital; at Christmas, when provision-time rolled around for the Chartrand slaves, she always dispensed extra cloth and shoes to Limonar's children. John grudgingly yielded to Louise's charity. She was waking up to the hardships of slavery; he still slept.

Limonar could always take one more, but I wasn't quite ready for a certain arrival. Late one afternoon as I passed the plantation kitchen, I saw Wahl on its steps, head between her hands, weeping softly. I didn't plan to stop, but wondered what made her cry? So I asked. Looking up through pleading eyes, she told me that she had consulted a síndico who established her freedom price at 500 pesos, an amount far exceeding her lifetime savings. She started sobbing again, stammering the word *slave*, and murmuring that she'd always be a slave, die a slave.

I often walked by Wahl, and never knew that we had passed.

Our once-torrid relationship was like wet gunpowder, never to explode again. Yet her utter defeat touched me. Before I could stop my words, I offered to give her money for her freedom. Gratitude flashed from her still beautiful brown eyes, while emotion silenced her. Imagine that! Wahl couldn't speak. But her old pride soon returned. She accepted my offer only as a loan, promising to pay it back with interest. I doubted her ability to keep her promise, but I kept quiet, knowing that arguing with her was useless. I simply nodded, and moved on to the Chartrand big house.

And so Wahl bought her freedom, and moved to Limonar. We frequently crossed paths, working for neighboring plantations and seeing friends. Our feelings toward each other reached civility, making it possible for us to walk side-by-side and conduct light conversations. Never did I guess that something had changed in Wahl.

As afternoon shadows were falling, I stopped at Wahl's hut, and asked her to hurry. We were late for our duties at Labyrinth. She scurried out, slightly ruffled that someone besides herself gave a command. Regaining her composure, we walked briskly toward the Chartrands' big house. Halfway there or so, Wahl shoved me off the avenue and into some bushes. She was on top of me faster than a lioness on her prey. Lifting her skirt, she unfastened my pants, and mounted me in a fury of passion. All the fluids of nature rose in my body, like bubbling molasses in a sugar mill. My molasses once flowed faster, but at seventy, I had just as much fun.

We struggled to rise, the urge to sleep in each other's arms weighing us down. Standing and facing each other, I suddenly saw stars. Wahl had slapped me with all her might. Staggering back, I thought her after play a bit too rough. But it had nothing to do with sex. Wahl was angry. She shouted at me, wondering why I had saved two future slaveholders in Saint-Domingue, rather than run away with her, even had it ended with a lovers' leap from the walls of Le Cap? Why had I spurned her love?

So the cork was out of the bottle after so many years. I looked into her questioning eyes, and replied that I lacked her depths of emotion and passion, but my feelings of love ran as deep as hers. I did not abandon my little boys because it would have been like plunging a knife into their mother's heart. I told Wahl that love for her filled my soul, but I knew that she would be safe with Uncle Philip and Désirée in Cuba. Choosing between two loves broke my heart.

That night at the Chartrands, everyone sensed that something had changed between Wahl and me. When I walked by Louise, she gave me that knowing smile that only women can give. Or was it the glow of our romance that gave us away? I was confused. Was this an old love resurrected, or the birth of a new one? Forty years had passed, but love found late is more profound, and time more cherished, than youthful romances.

I wish I could say that we lived happily ever after, but life with Wahl was not that way. She could be stubborn, outspoken, and quick to anger. But we always re-centered our different orbits on our love for each other. Her eruptions into sweet ecstasy provided me moments that most men only dream about. Even more, I remember our gentle times together. At night, we often reclined outside our hut, looking at the darkened sky. She called the moon "Heaven's Lantern" and the Cuban fireflies His "Enchanted Spirits." Her imagination inspired a game that we played by naming a star after a person that we had known, and telling that person's story. And at daybreak, Wahl would prepare our coffee by roasting coffee beans in a skillet, sprinkling in a little sugar, pounding the contents after it cooled with a pestle, placing the powdered coffee in a flannel bag, and letting it steep in a pot of simmering water. What aroma! When she finished making coffee, she'd crawl under our blanket, and demand payment for one of her good cups. I willingly paid her price.

Life seemed good. Not only did Wahl and I rediscover our love, but I lived among people who cherished their freedom. On Labyrinth, however, John experienced the anguish of owning slaves. He feared a grand slave uprising led by freshly imported Africans, and deeply resented the colonial government's protection of the trade as a source of its power and wealth. Like other planters in Matanzas Province in the 1830s, John envisioned a Cuba without Spanish rule. Sadly John never extended his criticism to slavery itself.

Increasingly, John spent long periods away from Labyrinth, as he and Louise became world travelers. His absenteeism might have meant harder times for his slaves under a cruel overseer had good fortune not intervened. John's first-born child, John Louis Valentine Chartrand, showed up at Labyrinth near death. Yellow fever had taken its toll, making him look like a scarecrow. But his family's loving care and Labyrinth's salubrious breezes broke Death's grip on the young man, establishing the Chartrands' estate as a place for convalescence.

I liked John Louis, or simply "Louis" as his family called him. Though still gaunt, Louis combined his father's quick wit and energy with his mother's gentleness. Educated in France, well-versed in new age abolitionism, and from a generation younger than John's, Louis was not so cocksure about the virtues of slavery. Despite his reservations about slavery, Louis earned his father's respect for his business skills, and became acting manager at Labyrinth. To assist his son's duties, John bought me a dark bay mare so that I might accompany Louis on his plantation rounds. I named her "Libertad."

My life at Limonar was tranquil, even happy, but the rising swell of unrest among plantation slaves in Guamacaro District prompted my warnings to Limonceros. I pointed out that Governor Oña must know of Limonar's involvement in recent slave insurrections. We needed to be careful about assisting those escaping the slave hunters, or the Spanish cavalry and the points of their lances. Hiding a fugitive in Limonar was, I emphasized, out of the question. Our good Captain Juan de Flores would certainly report such incidences to Oña. If you must help a fugitive, do it away from Limonar. But keep in mind, I cautioned, that Captain-General

Valdés and Governor Oña shared a deep hatred for free Negroes, making Limonar a sure target.

Limonceros ignored my sensible arguments, including Wahl. Sometimes my own emotions swept away my good sense. This happened when a desperate runaway slave dove into our hut, practically landing on Wahl and me. He was Abiola, a Yoruba, recently "liberated" when a British warship intercepted a Portuguese slaver on which he traveled. Brought to Havana, Abiola and his fellow Yorubas stood before a joint court of British and Spanish judges who declared them free, or *emancipados*, as the judges dubbed them.

Each emancipado faced indenture for seven years. His new master could use him directly, or rent him out. Either way, the emancipado got only backbreaking work. Governor Oña purchased Abiola's indenture, including a large lot of Yoruban emancipados to repair public works, drain swamps, and harvest plantation cane fields. Everywhere in Matanzas Province those poor ragged creatures were visible, even at John's. The governor didn't care because straining emancipado muscles made him rich.

Oña rented his emamcipados for sugar harvest on Señor Alfonso´s Triunvirato Plantation. After a grueling day under the Cuban sun, Abiola found an open gate in his compound, escaped, outran plantation guards, and finally reached Limonar with torn flesh and clothing. He apologized for his intrusion, asked for food, and promised to leave afterward. But I foresaw his fate better than he, as Rancheodor López, a feared slave hunter, would soon be on his trail. López had a weapon beyond the usual sword or machete carried by a rancheodor: a double-barreled percussion gun. When one of his fierce mastiffs locked his jaw on a slave's ear, the victim usually went limp and surrendered. Further resistance might bring a blast from López's weapon. Six pesos-worth of fun, he called it, because he lost that amount for a dead slave.

Wahl and I exchanged looks. Before she could lend him her help, I offered to lead Abiola away from Limonar. I didn't tarry, because López would start searching for Abiola at first light. Wahl went to a chest, pulled out two small pouches, and handed them to me: gifts for López's flesh hounds. The first pouch contained ground peppers to spread along our trail to confuse canine scent; this failing, I would scatter bits from the second pouch to poison López's devil dogs. Why had I placed Limonar at such high risk? To impress Wahl? Maybe, but a fellow Yoruba, bloodied and terrified, moved me more.

Off we went along creek beds and dry gullies, backtracking all the way. At times, López's baying hounds made us move faster. Here and there, I spread pepper grains on our path, interspersed with Wahl's poisoned bits. My old maroon skills served me well, as I warned Abriola not to make López's job easy by churning up unnecessary noise. We crawled, climbed, and waded, as we headed for the Rio Escondido where José Dolores, an *apalencado* (a permanent maroon), operated. Every government attempt failed to capture Dolores, or to destroy El Espinal, his hideout on the river's headwaters.

We reached the Escondido, and moved upstream through canebrakes and mangroves. My years and stumbling over surface roots made for slow going. We kept listening for López, when a gang of men stepped from the river tangles, and confronted us. It was Dolores' apalencados, ready to kill us if they thought us decoys for the Spanish. Coal-black, weather-worn, and scarred from head to toe, Dolores looked like an avenging monster that God might have raised from a swamp. He took no chances, as he examined our hearts and weighed our souls. Then he began laughing. So we caused what he had just seen: a slave hunter weeping over his dead dogs. Wahl's poison had worked! Dolores embraced us, and invited us to join his band. Abiola agreed, but I declined. Dolores scowled, but relaxed when I explained my mission to save Abiola.

On my return to Limonar, I did not fear López without his dogs. When I reached home, Wahl congratulated and hugged me for my successful mission, but did it come at too high a price? I swore never again to let emotion overwhelm my good sense, but I didn't keep my well-intentioned vow.

Saint Matthew (24:6) tells us "ye shall hear of wars and rumors of wars" then concludes by telling us "be not troubled." But Saint Matthew didn't live in Matanzas Province, and I *was* troubled. From the time that I arrived at Labyrinth in 1822, slave insurrections became so common that when the bell tolled at John's sugar mill, I wasn't sure whether it was a call to supper or a call to arms. Most were small, like a smoldering compost pile, sending to its surface small patches of fire and smoke from its buried inferno. These plantation upheavals had a human cost: Hundreds of slaves and scores of whites lost their lives. There was one beneficial result: John and other planters elevated their criticism of the foreign slave trade.

Something was different about the year 1843 than previous years. Rumors usually drifted across Guamacaro District prior to a slave uprising. Most were vague: All our brothers and sisters will rise; we're going to kill every overseer and driver; we'll destroy the masters and burn their sugar mills, and so on. And locals mostly spread those rumors. But 1843 saw change.

In that year, unfamiliar Negroes from faraway places came to Limonar to sow seeds of rebellion. One of these, a slave contract worker named José María Mondeja, arrived from the city of Matanzas to clear land for John's expanding cane fields. Slaves and free Negroes were drawn to his ingratiating manner. Once I found him telling several Limonceros that the Day of Judgment had arrived for whites, and that a Haitian army would join our struggle for liberation. He concluded by selling amulets to his audience, claiming that they protected holders from the white man's weapons. His pitch sounded like the build-up in South Carolina before the Denmark Vesey Conspiracy. But desperate people will latch onto absurd promises, anything that gives courage to a noble cause.

In March 1843, a spreading rebellion exploded in Matanzas

Province. It began at Alcanía sugar mill, near Bemba Depot. Slave railroad workers joined those from Alcanía, together burning a swath of destruction across Cimarrones District. In their wake, they left dead whites and several plantations in ashes. Spanish regulars and montero militia under Governor Oña stopped the rebels. Showing no mercy, the governor ordered executions and tortures for hundreds of slaves.

The after-tremors of this human earthquake shook Matanzas Province for months. In July slaves rose at Flor de Cuba sugar estate, but elite Spanish cavalry cut them down. Simultaneously, there came from Captain-General Valdés' furrowed brow vigorous enforcement of existing anti-free Negro laws and a new pile of his own. Under his autocratic hand, free Negroes could not serve as overseers, bear arms, work without a license, travel abroad freely, or enjoy cabildo celebrations except on Sundays and Epiphany (January 6). I felt like South Carolina's cruel free Negro policies had followed me to Cuba.

Something else nagged Valdés: the cloud of disgrace hanging over his head. His critics, including John, called him an *ayacuchero*, a senior Spanish military officer sharing responsibility for losing His Catholic Majesty's Spanish American empire. And damn if it wasn't happening again. This time Valdés imagined a threat from England supported by a free Negro-creole white coalition ready to fly the Union Jack over Cuba. John and other creole planters tried dispelling the captain-general's fears, even supporting Valdés' expulsion of David Turnbull, an abolitionist British consul intent on stirring up Cuba's slaves. Valdés, said John, could feel the last pearl slipping from Spain's once-beautiful imperial necklace. Only the old captain-general's timely departure from Cuba let him dodge his opponents' scorn a second time.

Ambitious and with a history of political intrigue, Leopoldo O'Donnell barely warmed the captain-general's chair before trouble besieged him. In early November 1843, an uprising at Señor Alfonso's Triunvirato sugar estate shocked the young grandee. From

296

Triunvirato, the conflict spread to Ácana Plantation, when Oña-led Spanish Lancers and montero militia showed up, squelching the uprising, and killing and capturing many rebels. Among those the governor executed were two female rebel leaders: Carlotta from Triunvirato and Fermina from Ácana. My concern was that Wahl had worked at Triunvirato just two weeks before the eruption there. Would Oña's investigation of Triunvirato lead him to Limonar?

Across Matanzas Province, massahs met, and massahs talked about rising numbers of imported African slaves and inadequate Spanish military protection of their properties. At Labyrinth, John hosted and I served one of those meetings. Señors Benigno Gener and José Alfonso carried the meek with their arguments for ending the slave trade and for more Spanish troops in the province. Absent from the agenda was their audience's growing desire for Cuban independence.

Armed with a petition of nearly a hundred signatures, Señors Gener and Alfonso headed for the Governor's Palace in Matanzas in late November. Oña treated them rudely, grabbed their petition, perused it, and tore it up, and told the embarrassed duo that he did them a favor. If O'Donnell read it, the captain-general surely would treat them as traitors to Spain. Ending their audience, Oña turned on his heels, and huffed off.

At a second meeting at John's, local planters heard the outraged presenters of their petition to the governor. Gener fumed that Oña couldn't see beyond the bribes of slave traders making him rich. O'Donnell, he argued, was unblemished by corruption, and would receive the petition well. John cautioned prudence. O'Donnell, he said, must be like all other captain-generals, else he wouldn't be a captain-general. He could, he warned, be more belligerent than Oña since he hadn't had his turn to loot the colonial treasury. Gener wouldn't listen, and carried a copy of the petition to O'Donnell in Havana. O'Donnell read it, threatened Gener with arrest, and said that those who signed the document committed treason. A dispirited Gener returned to Matanzas Province; worse still, O'Donnell kept the petition, providing him names of those who might challenge his rule.

The Triunvirato rebellion and planter petition were like swollen creeks, making O'Donnell's river of anxieties rise. But a third event made the captain-general's river jump its banks, flooding Cuba with his bloody purges. It began with a spying mistress, and ended with the murders of thousands of free Negroes and slaves.

Polonia, a concubine-turned-sleuth, claimed to have overheard plans for a massive slave rebellion which she reported to Esteban Santa Cruz de Oviedo, owner of Santísima Trinidad Plantation and keeper of a harem of slave women. Did Polonia actually overhear a conversation? Did she concoct the story to please her master? Did Santa Cruz de Oviedo fabricate the story, and get Polonia to tell it to Oña to win the governor's favor? Did both Oña and Santa Cruz de Oviedo invent the story, justifying an attack on those whom they deemed dangerous to Spanish rule in Cuba? These basic unanswered questions flew around Matanzas Province. Whatever the case, Polonia's story served the purpose of O'Donnell and Oña to launch a war against free Negroes.

O'Donnell ordered his eager governor to dispatch Spanish regulars to Santísima Trinidad Plantation to verify Polonia's allegations. Oña ordered slaves there to stand in line, each awaiting his turn for a soldier to stretch and fasten him face down on a ladder, a technique known as *bocabaja* (face down). A *fiscal* (public prosecutor) then cross-examined a victim, using a whip to ask his questions: Ten, twenty-five, fifty, one hundred lashes loosened a stubborn tongue, while blood and bits of flesh flew. Pain was universal, confessions many. When Oña's regulars left Trinidad, they had put sixteen slaves in their graves, and imprisoned a hundred more. O'Donnell got what he wanted: confirmation of a Cuban-wide slave conspiracy placed at the feet of Great Britain, anti-slave trading creoles, and free Negroes. Oña and Santa Cruz de Oviedo also got what they wanted: protection of their wealth gained from the illegal slave trade.

The shadows of O'Donnell's enemies were cast upon his wall, especially those of free Negroes. From my arrival in Cuba, every captain-general, even milder ones, viewed us as agitators for slave rebellions. They began by restricting our entry into Cuba, but it was O'Donnell's cruel heart that schemed our exodus, trying to tie us to a slave conspiracy that may not have existed.

In late 1843, rumors swept across Guamacaro District of a brewing slave insurrection. If a conspiracy was afoot, I can't say free Negroes were not involved. Why not? Hated by colonial government, feared by creole planters, and scorned by white liberals for "Africanizing" Cuba, free Negroes had but one natural ally—the slaves.

Word was out. The race was on. Trinidad slaves cited Christmas Eve as target date for rebellion in Matanzas Province. Creole planter families crowded the roads to Matanzas, reminiscent of the grand blanc flight to Le Cap fifty years ago. John's family and cooks, my children, Wahl, and I headed for the safety of the Chartrand mansion in the city of Matanzas. When we arrived there, John assembled a small refugee group destined for South Carolina: Louise, their children (Marta, Polly, and Esteban), Luisita, her daughter Frances, and my two children (Ana and Victoriano). John posted a letter to Antoine Barbot in Charleston, asking him to arrange housing for his family and servants on Sullivan's Island. As best she could, Louise disguised their journey as a vacation: time on the beach and time with Philip in Branchville. Marta, known as "Mita" to family, could hardly wait to meet Philip's daughter Harriet with whom she had corresponded. Both girls were twelve years old, and destined to become best friends.

While my family waited for passage to Charleston, Wahl and I avoided the ugly events unfolding in the streets of Matanzas. Free Negroes fell victim to a process hardly legal and certainly not just. Soldiers dragged free Negro "suspects" from their homes and businesses, subjecting them to torture to uncover a slave conspiracy, or plans in league with creole whites to strike for independence.

Jackpot was a victim's confession to both. Many ended up at Numero 80 Calle Medio (Middle Street) where Cuba's most infamous flogger, Ramón González, met them. Some received more than a hundred lashes, causing many to lose control of their bowels. Doctors protected O'Donnell's demon from future litigation, listing "extreme diarrhea" on the death certificates of his victims. At night, guards carted survivors to jails and hospitals in wagons leaking trails of blood.

After our group sailed for Charleston, John, Wahl, and I retreated to Labyrinth and Limonar in early 1844, a year Cubans remember as "The Year of The Lash." John advised Wahl and me to batten down at Limonar to face the coming storm, and he would do the same at Labyrinth. Do not incite Captain Flores, as he could lift the floodgate of O'Donnell's reprisals, engulfing our district. Then in a rare moment of pessimism, he added that we likely would not survive.

The storm John feared hit full force. Governor Oña established a mobile torture bureau to scour Matanzas Province for conspirators and traitors. Santa Cruz de Oviedo and Oña's cousin, nicknamed "Pancho Machete," directed this travelling inquisition. Both inquisitors sent prosecutors to towns, villages, and plantations to gain information through torture. Names such as Ferdinand Percher, Juan Costa, and José de Piso struck fear into the hearts of free Negroes and slaves, a fear shared by anti-slave trading planters. Piso himself reached heights of cruelty that his brothers of the whip could only admire: He provided finales to his tortures by hoisting half-dead victims up a high tree feet-first, then dropping them on their heads. At La Andrea Plantation, Pancho Machete announced to the governor that torture revealed plans for a massive slave rebellion. The rising blood purge surged toward Limonar. We held tight.

At Labyrinth, John witnessed the high price those paid who had signed the petition to end the foreign slave trade. Señor Gener lost his property to government confiscation, and fled to England.

Señors Alfonso, Tanco, Serrano, and Palomeno were arrested and jailed; others avoided incarceration, but suffered state confiscation of their property. John braced himself, daily expecting one of Oña's minions to arrive at Labyrinth for his arrest.

But John decided to extract a high price for his capture. To his son Louis, to his overseer, and to a few trusted slaves, John issued firearms. He loaded a brace of pistols, polished a sword once his uncle's, dug out an old military hat from a trunk, turned his piazza into a command post, and carefully surveyed roads leading to his big house. At Limonar, preparations became frenzied.

What happened at the village of Guiness mirrored Limoncero expectations of our own fate. Soldiers there pulled dozens of free Negroes into the streets, and flogged them before cheering neighbors whom those poor devils once considered their friends. The death toll ran high in Guiness; broken hearts even higher. The tide of government reprisals came closer to Limonar with each passing day.

When Governor Oña fell ill in early February, General Fulgencio Salas temporarily replaced him, and intensified cruelties committed against free Negroes. Meanwhile, Captain-General O'Donnell did with a pen what his new commander did with a whip. He decreed in April that all foreign-born free Negroes must leave Cuba within fifteen days after public notice. For me, compliance was out of the question, but nearly a thousand others left the island. O'Donnell further accused David Turnbull, former British consul to Cuba, of orchestrating the alleged conspiracy, and ordered his trial *in absentia*.

Murder and torture shaped the ghostly Escalera Conspiracy, disguising the real purpose of O'Donnell and Oña to rid Cuba of free Negroes. For the conspiring duo, their alleged plot needed a leader. They found one in Gabriel de la Concepción Valdés, beloved among Cubans as "Plácido." His poems extolling Cuban patriotism and condemning slavery made him an easy target. After torture and his repeated denials of charges against him, Plácido faced execution at the Cristina Barracks, near the Chartrand mansion.

301

The man who painted Wahl's peineta and penned an accompanying verse was dead.

Plácido's death marked high-tide for the Escalera Conspiracy in early summer, 1844, but was Limonar safe? An incident in May probably caught the attention of Oña and Pancho Machete. I had been instructing students at San Cipriano's free school when Wahl rushed up. She shooed my pupils away, and made her plea, while gasping for breath. Follow her, she signaled. We tore through remote pathways to avoid the main road to San Patricio Plantation. Soon, I realized our destination: an abandoned stone cottage bordering San Patricio, once a poet's study, now a way station for anyone escaping Spanish torture and prosecution.

Night had fallen when we reached a crumbling stone building with no roof and a tree inside that pushed up through once carefully laid pavers. Moon beams casting shadowy silhouettes on time-worn walls and Cuban fireflies flashing their little lantern eyes were our only illuminations. There, propped against a wall, was a large man, shackled, and bleeding from iron-worn wounds. He was Ramón Gangá, escapee from a prosecutor's interrogation at Riversol Plantation.

After enduring over a hundred lashes, Ramón had passed out, and a guard chained him to a brick wall to await more torture. Pretending to remain unconscious, Ramón tested his mighty sinews against his chains, bringing down a section of masonry. Before guards could react, Ramón high tailed it into the underbrush, shackles and all, until he reached San Patricio. Now he could go no further, as his chains had sapped his strength. Could we, Ramón begged, break his shackles, and provide him with food and a weapon?

I had repeatedly warned Wahl about the dangers of helping fugitives from the Spanish purge, but it was too late for caution. Besides, I could not abandon Wahl to a rancheador hunting her down, or worse yet, his dogs tearing her apart. I asserted myself with this strong-willed woman, a woman many fugitives called their

"Black Angel." I asked and received Father Rangel's permission to use his plantation forge to free Ramón. A blacksmith's hammer striking a chisel on shackle hinges did the trick. Wahl handed Ramón a sack of food, a knife, and a few coins. He thanked me, hugged Wahl, and rushed to find the pathway to freedom. My Black Angel did it again! Would Ramón make good his get-away, or would he be re-captured and tell the part Wahl and I played in his escape? Would Oña or Pancho Machete find his confession grounds to attack Limonar? I was worried sick, and glared at Wahl, but she avoided eye-contact with me, like an unfaithful wife announcing her affair.

That Limonar had been spared a government attack, may have been the work of Capitán Flores. Not that moral issues drove him, not even Wahl's pies, but greed did. Fleecing the district's wealthy had become an art form for Capitan Fat-Ass, and yielding his power to anyone, Oña included, angered him. When Miguel Ballo de la Rore developed a confidence scheme to blackmail planters, Flores reported him to General Salas who then arrested Ballo de la Rore. No one dared to grind in Guamacaro District but Flores.

Flores worried that too much government scrutiny might bring the governor's cavalry and occupation of Guamacaro District. If Oña or Pancho Machete took over, he would be out. So our clever captain developed patterns of behavior to protect his interests. An old Spanish proverb, "I obey but do not execute" fitted his situation perfectly. He visited Labyrinth, whipped a few slaves, and reported to the governor that John's plantation was properly purged. This routine he repeated with other district plantations.

The soft policies of Flores nearly worked until two events threatened his scheme. One was the re-arrest of Ramón Gangá; the other, the capture of Jacobo Fernández, a Limoncero free Negro bricklayer whom Pancho Machete accused of inciting insurrection across Flores' district. What these two captives might divulge convinced the portly captain that the governor's Lancers might well be on their way to Limonar and Labyrinth. Flores went to John, and warned him that his plantation and the free village would soon feel Oña's wrath.

Wahl and I knew that Limonar would be but a twig tossed into a flame should Oña attack us. Was resistance even possible? We needed advice, so we attended a santería ceremony organized by Angelina, a free Negro priestess living in Limonar. Angelina's orisha was Changó, Yoruba's supreme war spirit; surely, Angelina believed, he would select a Limoncero to lead the fight against the Spanish.

We easily found the gathering in a jungle near Limonar. There, Wahl and I picked up the rhythmic sounds of the *bala* drums, one forming a steady audible base, while the other two "talked" back and forth. Their drummers were calling down Changó. As an initiate into the faith, Wahl wore his colors: red and white dress, five red and white necklaces, a red and white kerchief, and a red sash. My colors were spiritually insignificant, because I was a non-practitioner of the faith, but welcomed at its celebrations. Wahl feared that our late arrival insulted Changó. No one seemed to care, so I supposed neither did Changó.

Amid the frenzied gathering stood Angelina. She, like Wahl, donned red and white colors, and looked just like Santa Barbara, the Catholic saint santeros associated with Changó. Crowd delirium peaked: feet keeping time with drums, thundering voices beckoning the war spirit's appearance, and a large man stumbling into a circle formed by the audience. At first, he staggered like a drunk man, but he wasn't drunk. He was possessed. Dressed like Changó, his early reeling movements turned into rapid twirling in which he exhibited amazing dexterity. His eyes rolled back into his head, his face expressed a mask of pain, drool oozed from his lips. Over his head, he swung two axes: swish to the left, swish to the right, and then he would switch axes in their spinning mid-flights. Changó's words rang from the hollows of his throat, as he circled the inner ring of onlookers, seeking someone to bear his mantel against the Spanish.

He stopped by this person and that, never finding a champion;

that is, until he spied Wahl. He yanked her into the center circle, as the chanting crowd stilled, and the beseeching arm motions of the priestess froze. They waited for Changó to anoint Wahl. Changó spoke slowly, forcefully. He said that Wahl had a warrior's heart. He exalted her, lifted her up, brought her down, and shared his sacrificial meal with her. Then Changó , instructed us to obey her, and follow wherever she might lead. Instantly, the possessed man came off his orisha-high. His weaving steps carried him back into the crowd, while he had no idea of what he had just done.

Wahl found her leadership role troubling. How could she stop Oña's army? The poorly armed Limonceros could barely slow the Spanish tide sure to sweep over their village and John's plantation. Consequently, Wahl sought a *babalawo's* counsel. Only a baba-lawo can invoke the ritual to Orunlá, the supreme orisha oracle in santería belief. After spreading coconut chips and pouring coconut milk (the holy water of santería) the babalawo began. He instructed her to find Osún, and follow his advice. Osún served the orisha war spirits as a scout, and would find the path to save Limonar. But who was Wahl's Osún?

Wahl went from diviner to diviner, piling up so many *registros* (ceremonies) that even the orishas dreaded her coming. She sub-mitted names of those whom she knew wore Osún's green and yellow colors, even boldly suggesting to a babalawo that one-armed Pedro was the anointed one. He wasn't. Finally, Wahl returned to the first babalawo from whom she gained advice. On all her spiritual journeys, I stayed outside of sanctified areas reserved for true believers. This time, Orunlá gave explicit information through his priest, who turned and pointed at me. Me! Had the orisha gone mad? Wahl's jaw dropped. The babalawo explained that every person has an orisha, even non-believers. Osún was mine, and through me he would find a safe path through the fiery wall of Spanish destruction. In a cockeyed way, it made sense. All my life, I had cast unheeded warnings in Haiti, South Carolina, and now Cuba. Would my warnings be ignored again? Would Wahl listen to Osún's voice within me? She never yielded to any man and rarely to an orisha. Osún had his hands full.

By mid-August, tensions tightened at Limonar and Labyrinth. Wahl made what defense she could: She transferred Limonar's children to John's slave compounds for their better protection, and instructed Limonceros to take defensive positions in San Cipriano Iglesia at first sign of trouble. Meanwhile, John's small force served as pickets to spot approaching Spanish forces. We were a ragtag bunch of old and maimed people, but still determined to resist the onslaught of the governor's troops. Even Luis and León, our white Catalonian tavern-keepers, threw in with us. There would be no repetition of Guiness here, no neighbors turning on neighbors. Limonceros stood ready to die, knitted together by freedom.

As Limonar's time grew short, private meetings took place between John, Father Rangel, and Captain Flores. No one knew their content, but we knew a strange sight when we saw one: Father Rangel in a monk's habit with a huge crucifix hanging from a chain, looking more Jesuit than a Jesuit missionary, letter and prayer book in hand, heading for Matanzas. The letter was for Philip in South Carolina, and probably would get through since Spanish soldiers hesitated to search a pious monk.

Back from Matanzas, Rangel resumed talks with John and Flores. Wahl grew suspicious of John, saying how could ex-slaves trust a planter? My suspicions focused on Flores whose loyalty to Limonar lived in his purse. Only Father Rangel, we agreed, could be trusted to defend Limonar. Finally, the negotiators of our fate presented us with their plan that concentrated on Oña's main weakness: his greed. They would leave soon for Matanzas to gain an audience with the governor. But John indicated that should they fail to return, it would mean that Oña had jailed them. In that event, his son Louis would release Labyrinth's slaves to scatter in every direction before the arrival of the governor's troops.

So our unlikely saviors set out the next morning for the Governor's Palace: a planter committed to slavery, a district policeman

306

with a gift for corruption, and a fallen priest. No telling where their negotiations might lead, or how long Captain Fat-Ass might remain on our side. We could only wait. Every day I saddled Libertad, and rode him a mile or two on the road to Matanzas, where false sightings of our trio became so boring that I took more saddle naps than a circuit-riding preacher until John awakened me. He, Flores, and Rangel had ridden up on me. John forced a smile, while his companions remained grim. He said that they needed to discuss results of their conference with Wahl and me.

At Labyrinth, John told us that the governor demanded heavy concessions to keep his troops off our doorsteps. He had been a brutal negotiator and, as John explained, vented much of his spite on Father Rangel. Who, the governor had ranted, permitted the priest to teach "bags of charcoal" to read and write? John said that Father Rangel maintained his composure, but his heavy eyebrows bouncing up and down, betrayed his deep anger. When Oña finished with Rangel, he took the priest's plantation, exiled him, and closed the free school. Then, turning his venomous bite on John, the governor said that he needed an incentive not to confiscate Labyrinth. A huge bribe of six hundred onzas out of John's purse (about ten thousand dollars) satisfied Oña's demand. Still unsatisfied, the governor wrapped his coiling grip around Captain Fat-Ass.

Why had Flores not been more diligent in ferreting out traitors, he asked? In particular, he had interest in a Negress who helped fugitives flee his justice. His victims simply knew her as their "Black Angel." Oña demanded that Flores learn her identity and arrest her. Our captain knew that she must be Wahl, but did not give her up. Perhaps he considered his authority better preserved if he pretended to discover her following a lengthy investigation; perhaps he still savored Wahl's pies; but perhaps the captain had an undiscovered thread of decency.

Then John delivered the clincher: Wahl must escape Cuba before her arrest. Philip had already arrived at Matanzas, ready to escort her to South Carolina. To deceive port authorities, she would travel as his brother's slave. I told Wahl that Osún and I agreed with John's plan to rescue her from the governor.

Wahl's temper exploded, saying that she would rather be in hell than be a slave again! John consoled her, telling her that she would cook for Philip's depot restaurant, and that his brother would treat her as *de facto* free. No! No! No! were words flying from her lips, as she took flight from John's big house, vowing never to leave me or Limonar. I was stunned, for I'd not see Wahl again this side of Heaven. I ran after Wahl, but her long legs and my aged ones held me back. Where had she gone? Was she racing to the mountains of eastern Cuba, or was she nearby? I checked all the logical places for her refuge: our hut, Pedro and Rosita's hut, Father Rangel's rectory, San Cipriano Iglesia, and trees and rocks where we once expressed our love. No Wahl! Then that abandoned cottage at San Patricio crossed my mind. Could the place of our undoing now be her sanctuary?

When I reached the stone ruins on the edge of San Patricio, only an eerie silence shrouded the moonless night. My groping fingers traced the outer walls for an opening to the inside. Then my ears heard what my eyes could not see: Wahl weeping. Between her sobs, she pleaded for my forgiveness, and admitted that helping Ramón Gangá had turned into a disaster. I consoled her, telling her that her good heart would not have allowed less, and that I loved her, will and all. She hugged me, acknowledging her impossible situation. If she stayed, she would face arrest and endanger Limonar; but if she left, our separation would be permanent. I felt, but could not see, her acceptance of my predicament years earlier in Saint-Domingue. We fell silent, finding consolation in each other's arms. We remained at San Patricio, and in the morning headed for Limonar and our last night together.

Shortly before daybreak, Wahl and I roused ourselves at our hut in Limonar. The night before, Venus took me to heavenly heights, but fading darkness brought us back to harsh reality: Our time together had run out. As a mellow glow peeked over the eastern horizon, Wahl and I mounted Libertad, and began a gentle trot to John's plantation. Old Pedro preceded us the day before with Wahl's belongings. From Labyrinth, Philip, John, and Wahl would leave for Matanzas; from there, Philip and Wahl would ship out for Charleston. I was uncontrollably sad and fought back tears.

As dawn broke, Wahl and I reached a low summit, halfway to our destination. I reined Libertad to see where we had been, and where we were going. Ahead, in clear view, were the blazing furnaces of Labyrinth's sugar mill and the suffering slaves attending them; behind me in early light was the free village of Limonar. My life had been a long journey through the bowels of a monster that ate human souls. We sat on Libertad at a time when morning's early light begins melting darkness of night; at a place where the heavy clouds of slavery found lift on the sunshine of freedom.

You may remember the old Yoruba proverb which Mother taught me on our way to Saint-Domingue: "No matter how far a river wanders, it never forgets its source." I've never forgotten mine.

Now you know my story.
Love to My Boys,
Kwambe Ansong
(Born on Saturday, Seventh Born Child)

A reverent silence fell over the depot when Philip finished Saturday's last letter. In a chair near the kitchen door, Susan Elizabeth sat, struggling to speak. "I didn't know much about Saturday when you received his death notice. But now I know Saturday, and his last letter is almost like him dying all over again. This time I'll miss him."

Wahl choked on words sticking in her throat. "I hope that both of you know that I never quit loving Saturday. I was mad at him for a time. Love is like that. I've also come to understand his unwavering love for his boys, since I've gotten to know you, Philip."

"There is one detail in Saturday's letters left unexplained," Susan Elizabeth interrupted.

"What's that?" Philip replied.

"When did John change his plantation's name to Ariadne?"

"Most people," Philip replied, "believe that the survival of his plantation in the great hurricane of '44, prompted it."

"Why Ariadne?" Susan Elizabeth quizzed.

"You know my brother's fondness for Greek mythology. Ariadne was King Minos' daughter who fell in love with Theseus, the Greek hero who came to Crete to kill the Minotaur. She gave Theseus thread to find his way through the maze of halls in the Labyrinth, the structure Minos built for the monster. John's Ariadne may have been Fate who delivered him from the terrible hurricane of '44, but I believe that his Ariadne was something else entirely."

"What do you mean?' Susan Elizabeth puzzled.

"I believe that my closed-mouthed brother celebrated Fate's deliverance of his plantation from the Spanish," Philip theorized.

"Maybe that same Fate saved Limonar," Wahl added. "But it took something stronger than Fate or even Changó. It took God."

Philip began fumbling in his inside coat pocket for a small package. "Here, Wahl, Saturday included this in his letters. I know that he wanted you to have it."

Wahl undid the gift wrapped in old tissue. It was the tortoise comb which Saturday tried to give her years ago along with Plácido's poem. Wahl clutched the comb dearly, pressed it to her heart, and, through tears drenching her cheeks, read Plácido's old love sonnet. "That Plácido sure could be funny," said a grateful Wahl. "Shoot honey down my throat? No sir! Not even on a good day!"

When the three of them quit laughing, Philip hugged and kissed Wahl, and headed for the kitchen door with Susan Elizabeth. They entered the rear entrance of the depot, walked halfway to the dining area, and paused at one of the wavy glass windows facing The Branch Oak.

"Wonderful tree, isn't it, Philip?" Susan Elizabeth noted.

310

"Yes," Philip replied, "but I have seen it so much through uneven glass that I've forgotten what the real tree looks like."

Then Philip raised the window sash, and leaned out. "Damn," he said, "the real thing is so much more impressive than its wavy distortions."

SOURCES OF THE STORY

I. ANNOTATED COMMENTS

The archival sources for Saturday's saga are found at the South Carolina Historical Society (Charleston), Charleston Library Association, South Carolina Archives (Columbia), University of Florida Research Library (Gainesville), Marine Historical Association (Mystic Seaport, Conn.), Maryland Historical Association (Baltimore), Library of Congress (Washington), National Archives (Washington), Bibliothèque Nationale (Paris), and records of Philip Chartrand in the author's possession. My location of Saturday's will in the Chartrand Family Papers at the South Carolina Historical Society provided me with vital information for this story.

Printed first-hand accounts and period newspapers further supplied important facts for the author's consideration. I highly recommend Parham's *My Odyssey*, Moreau de Saint-Mery's *Description*, and Chazotte's *Historical Sketches* as starting points for Saturday's years in Saint-Domingue; for Charleston and South Carolina Lowcountry I recommend the accounts by Charles Fraser, Caroline Gilman, and Ebenezar Thomas; for Cuba perhaps three accounts stand above others for understanding Saturday's life there: John G.F. Wurdemann's *Notes* (1844), Fredrika Bremer's *Homes of the New World* (1853), and Cirilo Villaverde's insights into nineteenth century Cuban society which he expressed in his novel, *Cecilia Valdés* (1882).

Newspapers, especially those published in Charleston, contained a gold mine of information. Commonly ship captains published full-length letters about their experiences in Saint-Domingue, nervous citizens reported slave disturbances, and social customs and Race Week occupied much print space. But most revealing for me were the ad sections which announced ships arriving and leaving Charleston Harbor and rewards for fugitive slaves. Charleston's wealth and denial of humanity to its black population can be seen in those few pages.

Published slave accounts are rare, but two bear upon Saturday's story. Juan Francisco Manzano lived in western Cuba at the same time as did Saturday, and like Saturday he served as a domestic slave. In 1836 he gained his freedom, came under the tutelage of a British abolitionist, and pursued a writing career. His *Poems by a Slave in the Island of Cuba* earned him the unofficial literary title "Poet of the Slaves." More useful to this story was his *Autobiography of a Slave* (1840). The account of Esteban Montejo as told by him to his biographer, Miguel Barnet, better served my efforts to tell Saturday's story. Even though Montejo lived in Cuba two generations later than Saturday, they shared similar experiences: life on a sugar plantation and time spent as a maroon.

II. PRIMARY SOURCES

Manuscripts and Printed Public Documents

Barbot Family Papers. South Carolina Historical Society, Charleston, S.C.

Chartrand Family Papers. South Carolina Historical Society, Charleston, S.C.

Juan Chartrand. Testamento de 16 de marzo de 1820. Archivo de Protocolos del Ministerio de Justicia, Matanzas, Cuba.

Philip Chartrand Papers in the author's possession.

Saturday Chartrand's Will in the Chartrand Family Papers. South Carolina Historical Society, Charleston, S.C.

Cuba, Imprenta de Gobierno de Matanzas. *Reglamento de policía rural de la jurisdicción del Gobierno de Matanzas.* Matanzas, Cuba, 1825.

Jean Pierre Esnard Papers. South Carolina Historical Society, Charleston, S.C.

Edmond Genêt Papers. Library of Congress, Washington, D.C.

Charles Victor E. Leclerc Papers. University of Florida Research Library, Gainesville, Fla.

Manigault Papers. South Carolina Historical Society, Charleston, S.C.

Matbon de la Cour, "Sur la Traite el L'Esclavage des Négros." Library of Congress, Washington, D.C.

Donatien Rochambeau Papers. University of Florida Research Library, Gainesville, Fl.

Santo Domingo Assemblée Genérale. *A Particular Account of the Insurrection of the Negroes in St. Domingo, begun in August, 1791.* London, 1792.

San Domingo File. South Carolina Archives, Columbia, S.C.

Louis Tousard. *Lt. Colonel du Régiment du Cap, à la Convention Nationale.* Paris, 1793.

U.S. Dept. of State Consular Dispatches, Cap-Haitien. Vols. 1-4. National Archives, Washington, D.C.

U.S. District Court, Charleston, S.C. "Aliens Admitted As Citizens." Book A.

U.S. Federal Census. Seventh Census of the United States (1850). National Archives, Washington, D.C.

Vesey Conspiracy Papers. Charleston Library Association, Charleston, S.C.

Newspapers

Boston *Independent Chronicle* , 1789-1804.
Charleston *City Gazette*, 1789-1804.
Charleston *Mercury* for 1850.
Charleston *Southern Patriot*, 1821-1822.
Charleston *Gazette of South Carolina*, 1789-1793.

Charleston *Times*, 1800-1804.
Maryland Journal and Baltimore Advertiser, 1789-1797.
Le Cap François *Gazette Officielle de Saint-Domingue, 1789-1804.*
Newport (Rhode Island) *Mercury*, 1789-1804.
Philadelphia *Aurora*, 1794-1804.
Philadelphia *General Advertiser*, 1790-1794.

Published First-Hand Accounts

Abbot, Abiel. *Letters Written in the Interior of Cuba, Between the Mountains of Arcana, to the East, And of Cusco, to the West, in the Months of February, March, April, and May, 1828.* New York, 1829.

Allston, Robert F.W. *The South Carolina Rice Plantation.* J.H. Easterby, editor. Columbia, S.C., 2004.

An Account of the Late Intended Slave Inurrection among a portion of the Blacks of the City. Charleston, S.C., 1822.

Ashton, Susanna, editor. *I Belong to South Carolina: Slave Narratives.* Columbia, S.C., 2010.

Bremer, Fredrika. *Homes of the New World: Impressions of America.* 2 vols. New York, 1853.

Cantero, Justo Germán. *Los ingenios: Colección de vistas de los principales ingenios de azúcar de la isla de Cuba.* Havana, 1857.

Chazotte, Peter. *Historical Sketches of the Revolution and the Foreign and Civil War in the Island Of St. Domingo, with a Narrative of the Entire Massacre of the White Population of the Island: Eyewitness Report.* New York, 1840.

Clark, Thomas, editor. *South Carolina: The Grand Tour, 1780-1865.* Columbia, S.C., 1973.

Descourtilz, Michel E. *Voyages d'un Naturaliste et Ses Observations.* 3 vols. Paris, 1809.

Discours sur les Troubles de Saint-Domingue. Paris, 1787.

Dana, Richard Henry. *To Cuba and Back.* New York, 1859.

Donnan, Elizabeth, editor. *Documents Illustrative of the Slave Trade to America.* 4 vols. New York, 1965.

Escudero, José Eusebio. *Reflexiones que sobre los palenques de negros cimarrones respecto a la parte oriental de esta Ysla de Cuba*. Santiago de Cuba, 1819.

Estévez, Francisco. *Diario de rancheador*. Cirilo Villaverde, ed. Havana, 1982.

Fraser, Charles. *Reminiscences of Charleston*. Charleston, 1854.

Gilman, Caroline Howard. *Recollections of a Southern Matron*. New York, 1838.

Girod, Justin. *Voyage d'un Suisse*. Paris, 1785.

Goodman, Walter. *The Pearl of the Antilles; or an Artist in Cuba*. London, 1873.

Hassal, Mary. *Secret History of the Horrors of St. Domingo in a Series of Letters Written by a Lady of Cape François to Colonel Burr, Late Vice-President of the United States*. Philadelphia, 1808.

Kennedy, Lionel and Thomas Parker. *An Official Report of the Trials of Sundry Negroes Charged with An Attempt to Raise an Insurrection in the State of South Carolina*. Charleston, 1822.

Lowell, Mary Gardner. *New Year in Cuba, 1831-1832*. Boston, 1832.

Manzano, Juan Francisco. *The Autobiography of a Slave*. London, 1840.

Marryat Code of Signals (for 1826). Mystic, Ct., 1826.

Montejo, Esteban. *The Autobiography of a Runaway Slave*. Miguel Barnet, editor. London, 1966.

Moreau de Saint-Méry, Médéric-Louis-Elie. *A Civilization that Perished: The Last Years of Colonial Rule in Haiti*. Ivor Spencer, editor. Landam, Md., 1958.

Description topographie, physique, civile, politique et historique de la Partie française de l'ïsla de Saint-Domingue. 2 vols. Philadelphia, 1798.

O´Gaven y Guerra, Juan Bernardo. *Observaciones sobre la suerte de los negros del Africa, Considerados en su propia partia y transplanados á las Antillas españolas y reclamación contra El tratado celebrado con los ingleses el año de 1817*. Madrid, 1821.

Parham, Athéa de Puech, editor. *My Odyssey: Experiences of a Young Refugee from Two Revolutions*. Baton Rouge, La., 1959.

Pearson, Edward, editor. *Designs against Charleston: The Trial Records of the Denmark Vesey Slave Conspiracy of 1822*. Chapel Hill, N.C., 1998.

Saunders, Prince. *The Haytian Papers*. Westport, Conn., 1969.

Taylor, Glanville. *The United States and Cuba: Eight Years of Change and Travel*. London, 1851.

Thomas, Ebenezar Smith. *Reminiscences of the Last Sixty-Five Years*. Hartford, Ct., 1840.

Wurdemann, John G.F. *Notes on Cuba*. New York, 1844.

Villaverde, Cirilo. *Cecilia Valdés or El Angel Hill*. New York, 1882.

III. SECONDARY SOURCES

Babb, Winston. "French Refugees from Saint-Domingue to the United States." Unpublished dissertation, 1954.

Bancroft, Frederic. *Slave Trading in the Old South*. New York, 1931.

Barcia, Manuel. *Seeds of Insurrection: Domination and Resistance on Western Cuban Plantations*. Baton Rouge, La., 2008.

Bealer, Alex. The *Art of Blacksmithing*. New York, 1995.

Bell, Madison Smartt. *Toussaint Louverture: A Biography*. New York, 2007.

Bennet, John. *The Doctor of the Dead: Grotesque Legends and Folk Tales of Old Charleston*. Columbia, S.C., 1995.

Breton, Miguel A. *Matanzas: The Cuba Nobody Knows*. Gainesville, Fl., 2010.

Chapman, Charles. *A History of the Cuban Republic*. New York, 1969.

Childs, Matt. *The 1812 Aponte Rebellion in Cuba and the Struggle Against Atlantic Slavery*. Chapel Hill, N.C., 2006.

Cole, Hubert. *Christophe, King of Haiti*. New York, 1967.

Corwin, Arthur. *Spain and the Abolition of Slavery in Cuba, 1817-1886*. Austin, Tex., 1967.

Côté, Richard N. *Theodosia*. Mt. Pleasant, S.C., 2004.

Danzig, Albert van. *Forts and Castles of Ghana*. New York, 1980.

Dayan, Joan. *Haiti, History, and the Gods*. Berkeley, Cal., 1995.

DuBois, Laurent. *Avengers of the New World: The Story of the Haitian Revolution*. Cambridge, Ma., 2004.

Egerton, Douglas R. *Gabriel's Rebellion: The Virginia Slave Conspiracy of 1800 and 1802*. Chapel Hill, N.C., 1993.

He Shall Go Free: The Times of Denmark Vesey. Madison, Wi., 1999.

Ellegot, Carrol A., editor. *Charleston Residents, 1782-1804*. Bowie, Md., 1989.

Fett, Sharla. *Working Cures: Healing, Health, and Power on Southern Plantations*. Chapel Hill, N.C., 2002.

Finch, Alisha. "Insurgency at the Crossroads: Cuban Slaves and the Conspiracy of La Escalera." Unpublished dissertation, 2007.

Foster, Mary Preston. *Charleston: A Historic Walking Tour*. Charleston, S.C., 2005.

Franklin, J. Hope and Loren Schweninger. *Runaway Slaves*. New York, 1999.

Fraser, Walter, Jr. *Charleston! Charleston!: The History of a Southern City*. Columbia, S.C., 1989.

González, Ambrose. *The Black Border: Gullah Stories of the South Carolina Coast*. Columbia, S.C., 1922.

González-Wippler, Migene. *The Santería Experience*. Englewood Cliffs, N.J., 1982.

Hagy, James. *People and Professions of Charleston, 1782-1802*. Columbia, S.C., 2008.

Howard, Philip. *Changing History: Afro-Cuban Cabildos and Societies of Color in the Nineteenth Century*. Baton Rouge, La., 1998.

Hruneni, George. "Palmetto Yankee: The Public Life and Times of Joel Roberts Poinsett." Unpublished dissertation, 1972.

Hunt, Alfred N. *The Haitian Influence on Antebellum America: Slumbering Volcano in the Caribbean*. Baton Rouge, La., 2006.

James, C.L.R. *The Black Jacobins: Toussaint L'Ouverture and the San Domingo Revolution*. New York, 1938.

Johnson, Willis Fletcher. *The History of Cuba.* 5 vols. New York, 1920.

Joyner, Charles. *Down by the Riverside: A South Carolina Slave Community.* Champaign Urbana, Il., 1984.

July, Robert. *A History of the African People.* New York, 1970.

Kean, Virginia, editor. *Noisette Roses.* Charleston, S.C., 2009.

King, Stewart. *Blue Coat or Powdered Wig: Free People of Color in Pre-Revolutionary Saint-Domingue.* Athens, Ga., 2001.

King, Susan, editor. *History and Records of the Charleston Orphan House.* Easley, S.C., 1984.

Knight, Franklin. *Slave Society in Cuba during the Nineteenth Century.* Madison, Wi., 1970.

Leger, J.N. *Haiti: Her History and Her Detractors.* New York, 1907.

Lesesne, Thomas Pettigru. *History of Charleston County, South Carolina.* Charleston, S.C., 1931.

Leyburn, James. *The Haitian People.* New Haven, Ct., 1941.

Lockley, Timothy James, editor. *Maroon Communities in South Carolina.* Columbia, S.C., 2009.

Lofton, John. *Insurrection in South Carolina.* Yellow Springs, Oh., 1964.

Magnan, Abbé D.M.A. *Histoire de la race Française aux Etats-Unis.* Paris, 1912.

McMillan, Susan Hoffer and Selden Baker Hill. *McClellanville and the St. James, Santee Parish.* Charleston, S.C., 2006.

McMillin, James A. *The Final Victims: Foreign Slave Trade to North America, 1783-1810.* Columbia, S.C., 2004.

Miles, Suzannah Smith. *Island of History: Sullivan's Island from 1670 to 1860.* Charleston, S.C., 1994.

Morris, Thomas. *Southern Slavery and the Law.* Chapel Hill, N.C.,1996.

Murdoch, Richard. "Citizen Mangourit and the Projected Attack on East Florida in 1794." *Journal of Southern History,* XIV (November, 1948), 522-540.

Murphy, Joseph. *Santería: An African Religion in America.* Boston, 1988.

Orovio, Helio. *Cuban Music from A to Z*. Durham, N.C., 2004.

Ott, Thomas. *The Haitian Revolution, 1791-1804*. Knoxville, Tenn., 1973.

Paquette, Robert. *Sugar is Made with Blood: The Conspiracy of La Escalera and the Conflict between Empires over Slavery in Cuba*. Middleton, Ct., 1988.

Pérez de la Riva, Francisco. *El Café: Historia de su Cultivo y Explotación en Cuba*. Havana, 1944.

Pringle, Elizabeth Allston. *The Chronicles of Chicora Wood*. New York, 1922.

Ravenal, Mrs. *Charleston, The Place and the People*. New York, 1907.

Reid, Michele B. "Negotiating a Slave Regime: Free People of Color in Cuba, 1844-1866." Unpublished Dissertation, 2004.

Rogers, George C. *Charleston in the Age of the Pinckneys*. Columbia, S.C., 1969.

Rosen, Robert. *A Short History of Charleston*. Columbia, S.C., 1982.

Rubello, Tom. *Hurricane Destruction in South Carolina*. Charleston, S.C., 2006.

Rucker, Walter. *The River Flows On: Black Resistance, Culture, and Identity Formation*. Baton Rouge, La., 2006.

Rutledge, Archibald. *Santee Paradise*. New York, 1956.

Smith, Theophus. *Conjuring Culture: Biblical Formations of Black America*. New York, 1994.

Sullivan-Holleman, Elizabeth and Isabel Hillery Cobb, *The Saint-Domingue Epic*. Bay St. Louis, Ms., 1995.

White, Laura. *Robert Barnwell Rhett: Father of Secession*. Glouster, Ma., 1965.

Wigger, John. *American Saint: Francis Asbury and the Methodists*. New York, 2009.

Zola, Gary Philip. *Isaac Harby of Charleston, 1788-1828*. Tuscaloosa, Al., 1994.

GLOSSARY

Abomey: Capital of Dahomey in West Africa

Amis des Noirs: A French abolitionist society active in Saint-Domingue and Cuba

Aradas: Archenemy of Dahomey; Toussaint Bréda descended from Arada royalty

apalencado: A Cuban term for a permanent runaway (same as a maroon in Saint-Domingue)

babalawo: A high priest in santeria, an Afro-Cuban religion

bacabajo: A victim was placed face-down on a ladder and whipped to gain a confession

barracoon: This is a term for slave compounds in Africa and Cuba

Bréda Plantation: Where Saturday grew up under the guidance of Aunt Carolina & Toussaint

cabildos: They were fraternal organizations representing African nations in Cuba

cuculio: A Cuban firefly that emits a greenish light from its eyes

Crop: A term for sugar harvest in Saint-Domingue from November to May

gens de couleur: A mulatto in Saint-Domingue

grands blancs: Upper-class whites in Saint-Domingue

houngan: A voodoo priest in Saint-Domingue

House of Honnou: The compound in Whydah where Saturday and his mother were sold

Le Cap: Abbreviated name for Le Cap Francois, Saint-Domingue's main northern port

Limonar: Free Negro village near John's Labyrinth Planation

Maréchaussée: Rural police in Saint-Domingue seeking to capture fugitive slaves

maroons: Slaves who have permanently fled plantations and formed into resistance bands

Matanceros: Inhabitants of Matanzas Province, Cuba

Mille Fleurs: Where Saturday served as Grandmother Catherine's attendant

Monteros: the rural folk of Cuba

Orphan House: Center for Charleston orphans training to become indentured servants

petits blancs: Lower-class whites in Saint-Domingue known for severe slave treatment

santeria: Cuban Afro-folk religion

Tivoli Gardens: Philip Chartrand's public garden in Charleston

Whydah: West African port where Saturday and his mother embarked on a slave ship

Workhouse: The building in Charleston where slaves were punished

About the Author

Thomas Ott earned his Ph.D. in Caribbean history from the University of Tennessee. He authored *The Haitian Revolution, 1791-1804* which stands as one of the important books on that subject. His interest in Haiti's great slave rebellion has led him to promote the importance of its leader, Toussaint L'Ouverture, before academic and general audiences.

In 2010 Professor Ott retired from the University of North Alabama to write the story of Saturday, a slave on the French side of the author's ancestors and a participant in the world's greatest slave rebellion.

Also Available From

WORDCRAFTS PRESS

A Purpose True
by Gail Kittleson

End of Summer
by Michael Potts

Odd Man Outlaw
by K.M. Zahrt

Angela's Treasures
by Marian Rizzo

Glory Revealed
by Paula K. Parker

www.WordCrafts.net